British Detective
Mission to India

Attention Authors

'We Convert Fighters into Writers.' That's the motto of Manas Publications since more than four decades. Our message to the world is that India can win the battle not only by the bullet but also by the pen. There is no dearth of intellectuals in our country, but their knowledge is confined to them only. No sincere effort has been made by any other publisher to channelise their knowledge in national interest. That is why the talent of a large number of intellectuals remains latent. An author transforms his knowledge into a manuscript, and it is our job to spread his/her knowledge by converting it into a beautiful book. For over four decades, Manas has been motivating the intellectuals by publishing their manuscripts and would like to publish your manuscript too. So if you or your colleagues have any manuscript ready for publication or are working on it, kindly contact us with detailed synopsis and list of contents. We will transform your work into a valuable publication. If you wish, we can also suggest you the suitable subjects for writing the books related to your area of expertise. Manas is known for its publishing quality and commitments. We take utmost care in production and give wide publicity to the book as well as its author through our national and international distribution network.

British Detective
Mission to India

A Novel by

R A Rodrigues

Manas Publications
(We Convert Fighters into Writers)
New Delhi-110002 (INDIA)

MANAS PUBLICATIONS
(We Convert Fighters into Writers)
(Publishers, Distributors, Importers & Exporters)
4402/5-A, Ansari Road (Opp. HDFC Bank)
Darya Ganj, New Delhi-110 002 (INDIA)
Off. ☎ 23260783, 23265523, Res. ☎ 23842660
Fax: 011-23272766
E-mail: manaspublications@vsnl.com
manaspublications@gmail.com

ISBN 978-81-7049-458-4
₹ 795/-

Designed at
Manas Publications

Printed in India at
HS Offset, Delhi
and published by Mrs Suman Lata for
Manas Publications, 4402/5-A, Ansari Road,
(Opp. HDFC Bank),
Darya Ganj, New Delhi-110 002 (INDIA)

Part 1

Jeet

A Police Potboiler

I

I reached Jeet's house at around eleven, feeling fresh as ever. The long flight from London's Heathrow to Mumbai's Chhatrapati Shivaji International Airport didn't tire me, neither did the long cab drive from the airport. Surprisingly, the cabby had no difficulty in finding the place in the maze of crowded, dusty lanes and by-lanes of the part of Mumbai, I was headed for.

I smiled with relief when I saw the name "Jeet" on a wooden board along with the names of other residents of the apartment building I'd entered. The turbaned Sikh had dropped me off at the right spot which was of great importance, what with me being in a strange city. I didn't want to move in circles in the heat all day.

My spirits were dampened somewhat when I discovered the elevator didn't work. So I heaved my brown Samsonite and trudged up five flights of dimly lit stairs, and halted breathlessly before a polished wooden door with a brass nameplate. "Jeet" it read. Bracing myself, I rang the doorbell.

A tall thin, almost emaciated-looking boy opened the door. Keen dark eyes peered enquiringly at me.

Hesitatingly, I introduced myself, 'Adams from London.'

'Aha I'm Jeet,' he interrupted, grinning. 'Come in David, been expecting you.' He stepped aside and motioned me into the flat.

'Call me Dave,' I insisted and entered. I noted he had a deep throaty voice.

Not handsome, but attractive in a strange sort of way, six-foot-three, dark haired, brown-skinned Jeet somehow didn't appear as though he ate enough. His face looked okay, young and healthy. As for the rest of his body, it could have belonged to an inmate of a concentration camp. Bony arms poked out of the folds of his white tee shirt, and his dark trousers waved about like sails of a yacht on a windy day. I barely discerned his legs buried deep within them.

He plunged onto a black settee, and motioned me to sit opposite him. 'Aha David Adams, nice name, how was the flight?'

'Slept most of the way.'

'Best way to pass time. Would you like to have something, orange juice perhaps?'

I nodded and followed him. He went towards a large refrigerator and took out two tetrapaks of orange juice. He then brought two glasses and poured out the orange-colored liquid and handed me a glass. 'So I'm seeing my distant relation from London finally.'

'Yes,' I took a sip. A Tamilian, Indian Naval officer, while undergoing training in England had a son out of wedlock from an English lady. He returned to India with the son and married an Indian girl. Jeet due to his real mother was a distant cousin of mine. Now both had passed away and Jeet was alone at home.

I watched him gulp his drink and refill his glass. 'Jeet, you could do with some more weight. You look a bit scrawny.'

'Oh no, I'm fit, really fit with no body fat, I'm a runner,' he surprised me, cheeks flushing ever so slightly. 'You and I are the same. You're just fatter.'

'I'm bigger,' I quipped. We were just out of college, in our early twenties. 'We're the same age, and I certainly don't look fat.'

'Fat internally, gets worse, unless sweating regularly.'

I didn't agree with him. But it delayed me asking him whether I could smoke. I'd finished a pack of Dunhills just before leaving the cab earlier. The replacement in my bag would have to remain there.

Cautiously, I offered, 'no point in being fit only to appear like scum to most.'

Jeet burst out in laughter. Pointedly he sniffed the air, wrinkled his nose and proceeded to put me considerably at ease. 'You go ahead, smoke if you wish, only sit away from me.'

***

When I opened my suitcase to reach for my Dunhills, I found Jeet had followed me into the small cozy bedroom. I hesitated.

'What's the matter?' he asked

'You don't like smoking?'

'Oh no, I don't mind others doing what they like.'

But I noticed disappointment in his eyes.

A number of bookcases crammed with books lay flush to the walls.

I turned and regarded the books and changed the subject. 'You like to read?'

He perked up considerably. 'Oh yes, anything in print, and I read it.'

I liked that. I loved to read too. In fact I aimed to become either a journalist or a writer sometime in the near future.

'Any favorite authors, type of books?'

'Yes, I am a military buff. Any books on weapons and military technology, and I read it, if I can lay my hands on it,' he stretched out his hand and removed a few titles. 'I also like matter on police subjects, both non-fiction and fiction.'

'Coincidentally I am a police and military enthusiast too when it comes to reading.'

Sounds of vehicles passing by below assailed my ears although we were right up on the fifth floor. Cars honked, motorcycles spluttered loud enough for us to hear them. I lit up and took a long drag and exhaled slowly, taking care not to let any smoke get near Jeet. He didn't say anything. So I took a couple of books out of the shelf.

'Hmm, like you said,' I checked the titles on the multi-colored jackets. 'Mostly on army, Navy and air force weapons... a few police procedurals... well, well... material here on health and fitness.'

'Another favorite subject, aerobics, matches my body type,' he nodded, pointed to a pair of iron dumbbells and added. 'But learning to handle weights too.'

'Good idea to put on muscles, to look a little decent,' I agreed, took another drag, exhaled, and watched the smoke slowly dissipate. Actually I thought it an absurd idea. Why tamper with what God's given you. Why run? Look like a scarecrow and then lift dumbbells to put on weight which you probably had in the first place.

Jeet lifted a heavy dumbbell and proceeded to make certain movements. I guessed he read of them in books and magazines. He exhorted me, 'lift one, try it.'

I declined to do so. 'You're much stronger than me, although I just look bigger,' I remarked, placing my cigarette between my lips.

'You're like most people around,' he shook his head regretfully as he brushed past me while placing the dumbbells in their original position.

I gave a slight start on sensing something. Jeet had something wrong with him. Fear! When close, he exuded vague feelings of anxiety and apprehensiveness. Odd? Jeet was scared of something despite his open manner of speaking. Of what or whom I couldn't fathom. I decided to hearten him a bit. 'Not like your friends. I presume they're in fitness too?'

I realized instantly I'd made a mistake.

He jerked his head, and glared at me, 'oh no, I have no friends. Currently no one talks to me, and I don't care!'

***

I gazed surreptitiously at Jeet's plate, then carried on eating. He ate like a horse. I hadn't finished my first serving; he had already had two. Heaping his plate with polished white aromatic rice, boiled potatoes, browned veal and fresh salads, he proceeded to gulp it all down with gusto.

The uninhibited way he went about eating riled me enough to perversely needle him. 'You've no friends?'

'Yes, I'm being socially boycotted!'

'Because of your fitness bug?'

'Right,' he responded, swallowed a mouthful and carried on. 'Because I run!'

I continued eating and looked questioningly at him.

'Weird story,' he said.

'Why?'

'Won a few medals in the school sports,' he explained. 'So ordered to report to the track for practice. I didn't go.'

Casually he forked a piece of veal into his mouth and while chewing it, blurted out, 'so the vice-principal of the school called me, fired me, told me to attend the training sessions or else he wouldn't let me sit for my exams!'

'Must've been quite a talent?'

'Then while moving around outside I discovered something.'

'What?'

'Something wrong with me when out of the house! I start getting nervous outside!'

'Oh you'll get over it,' I said, while playing around with the last of the contents of my plate.

'It was like something missing in my genes, and moving about outside was making it up,' he explained. 'The journey to the track was aiding me more than the actual training on the ground.'

'Why are you alone?' I asked. 'You could have just stopped going out.'

He shot me a swift glance. 'No, I was conditioned to listen to authority figures by my now long dead ex-Naval officer dad,' he paused and continued. 'He a BSc Engineering, London, who later held a managerial post in the Mazagon Docks. He specialized in British and Russian Naval weapons; assembly, installation, as well as servicing, repair and maintenance.'

As my late father was a Royal Navy officer from the executive branch, I understood Jeet's dilemma. Slightly gratified, I tried to bolster him a bit. 'You have a rank in your head. When still young, others with different acts will tend to disable you. Maybe they in your vicinity will also provoke fears in you.'

Jeet rewarded me with a smile of genuine approval. 'Orders from the vice-principal were above any pressure from the others. None of whom I really knew; mentally they were a kind of vaguely defined "those people outside from civvy street"!'

He noted the puzzlement on my face and added in a kind of rough yet fluent manner, 'I devised a fitness jogging schedule on the road, beach and track. I also walk about as much as possible outside to get used to it.'

'You didn't leave sports?'

'No I got hooked to the jogging,' he pushed aside his empty plate. 'But others, including the coaches grudged it and have boycotted me. They just don't talk to me!'

I nodded silently. Somehow I felt that Jeet wasn't meant to be a champion athlete. That he regressed into being a fitness jogger seemed highly appropriate.

'Now I'm a misfit. Stopped at a crucial stage of my childhood from properly interacting with others; all because of the orders to run.'

I put my spoon and fork on my plate, finishing my meal. I didn't know what to say. Apparently he or his forebearers had lived some kind of restricted, insulated life. It showed only when Jeet was sent out. Although he appeared sane, he still had some visceral dread inside him. Also, he could really express himself, despite his deep gruff manner. Certainly I felt he'd become better as time passed. Get used to outside or what. Especially with good habits like eating well, exercising and most of all reading a lot.

Books ought to keep his mind above petty worries from around him.

***

Later in the evening I sat on a man-sized wooden box with large steps on the athletic track at Mumbai's University Stadium.

'Timekeeper's stand during the meets,' Jeet had informed me before going out for his regular run on the grassy field with a regulation four hundred-meters athletic track marked in white chalk powder.

I sat there, cigarette in my hand, watching the scene on the ground. I noted the athletes were divided into various groups. One group practised sprints. They'd run fast for a short distance, then after a break would repeat the short sprint. At two points on the track, athletes practised throwing the discus and the shot putt. Others trained on the jumping pits. Coaches watched them respectively and corrected their techniques. One group ran various distances on the track with rest periods; with their coaches timing them. They were the middle-distance and distance runners. Jeet ran on the outer perimeter of the ground. Although he didn't run slowly, his overall pace was slower than the distance running group on the track. Jeet looked like a super-fitness jogger when compared to the trainees under their respective coaches.

Time passed. I shifted my position on the timekeeper's stand, away from the pile of butts lying at my feet.

Somewhere behind, unseen, the sun set slowly, lengthening the shadows. Opposite me, the cerulean haze over the rows of buildings gradually turned gray. Variously colored suburban local trains packed with commuters thundered past. And on the track the sprinters, jumpers and throwers finished their workout. They now jogged slowly up and down, while loosening their arms and legs. They were limbering down.

But the distance running group continued running. On the track their breathing became harder, the yells of the trainers exhorting their charges to run faster became hoarser. Even Jeet who jogged round and round the perimeter of the oval at a steady speed, increased the pace of his laps. A dedicated runner.

Still he somehow seemed an interloper. When he finally stopped running, he came towards me sweating, face flushed with exertion, yet with no sign of exhaustion. I quickly put out my cigarette.

***

Jeet smiled while putting on his black tracksuit and told me. 'Nice run.'

I noted that he whispered to me. As if he was scared of something. He didn't speak normally as he did at home. I watched the expression on his face as I disclosed, 'so you're all alone here; others are in distinctive clubs under their coaches.'

He cast a vaguely flustered eye on me. As though trying to gauge something. God knows what? He proceeded to do a few stretching exercises, and chuckled, 'I can't explain my problem to them.'

'I think you have to follow a training schedule devised by the coaches… join one of the groups?' I said.

'I'm not that bad. I've won a few University titles and races. I've even race walked and set a few records, and represented the State at the national championships!'

'I still don't understand,' I replied in the dim light thrown by a naked bulb hanging from the top of the stands behind us, and hesitated. Then I hazarded, 'If outside or what, what about making it with the opposite sex?'

I immediately knew I'd made a blunder. I sensed a surge of anger or was it nervousness in him. I also vaguely discerned a shiver pass through his body.

After a while Jeet answered, 'no, I'm not ready… tend to get really nervous when thinking of girls!'

I hoped his recovery plan, that is moving around on foot, while jogging on the track, road and beach, and his reading at home succeeded. However I voiced a concern, 'I still think it's peer talk that you need.'

'Can't help the shorting,' Jeet whispered. 'I tend to see ranks. Everyone's higher or lower… so equals or peer's have to be given or arranged.'

'You're rank stuck?'

'You're dead right. I'm too psychologically disabled to be good at anything right now. And with everyone staying clear of me, some other kind of severe limit in me is disappearing!'

I guessed some rank sense deep within his mind enabled him not to get bothered too much at the lack of peer interaction.

A little while later I left the track with Jeet; who constantly kept up a whispered conversation with me. It made me feel remarkably similar to him. Yet he provoked some kind of weird complex in me.

Like that of a co-conspirator accompanying a scared notable or VIP in disguise, whom no one recognized as long as he didn't reveal himself physically, or by his dress or voice. And so he could move about with some kind of freedom and impunity that others of his kind couldn't avail themselves of.

These emotions somehow considerably enhanced the camaraderie between us for the remainder of my holiday in Mumbai, till I returned home to London.

II

Plenty occurred over the next ten years. First, I began to make a living as a freelance writer. I specialized in writing about military, especially Naval technology matters. But I soon discovered I didn't enjoy writing as a full-time career despite it being remunerative enough. It made me feel vaguely unfulfilled, and I decided on taking up a job somewhere.

Then the Pemberton Security Services took me on. I'd answered many advertisements and attended several interviews all over before landing the job. At the fateful last interview at the Londonderry on Park Lane, I met Sam.

He had shinning, aged eyes on his round, weather-beaten face. Like he'd seen too much for any one person to cope with. Thick shoulders and rough hands accentuated the effect he exuded of someone who spent long hours outdoors doing field work. I estimated his age to be around fifty.

He shook my hand warmly. His grandfatherly appearance somehow put me at ease, although I sensed him gauging me. 'Mister Adams, good to see ya, please sit down.'

His slight Glaswegian accent and gruff voice relaxed me even more. I faced him, perched on the edge of my chair, in the suite that clearly had been specifically done up for the meeting, and introduced myself. 'David Adams,' I hesitated slightly. 'I heard there's an opening in your firm?'

He nodded. 'Six feet, brown eyes, dark hair parted in the middle, smooth-shaven, not particularly standing out, ordinary features.' He described me in his rough, gravelly voice with a tinge of a Scots accent, as though speaking to himself. He paused for a few seconds, then in a louder tone confided, 'peculiar job, requires anonymity, the less you're noticed the better you are at it.'

'I presume, sir,' I said. 'I guess I'm about right?'

'Hard work it is, outdoors, rain or shine?'

'Oh that should be no problem.'

Sam's ruddy, red face registered no emotion. 'Difficult for ya to sit still for a long time?'

'No.'

'Like observing, gotta have the knack?'

'I'm willing to put in the effort,' I said. 'Used to observing activity outdoors, then writing stories about it indoors.'

'Kinda same routine with us,' he nodded and rang a bell. An uniformed boy entered immediately. 'Coffee for two,' he ordered and picked up a sheet of paper from the table and read silently from it.

'Hmm... properly qualified with education, still don't act too smart... problem in this line.'

When the coffee came, I sipped the dark brew quietly and regarded him apprehensively. I needed the job and became nervous enough to crave a smoke. But I didn't dare do anything that would jeopardize my chances of being taken on by Pemberton. Not even sneaking a glance at the portion of Hyde Park visible through the open window.

Sam watched me from under his bushy eyebrows. I tried to peer at my wrist watch without being obvious. I couldn't. I sensed he'd notice every move I made. It would go against me. After a few seconds of anxiety, I realized he'd made a decision.

'Right, like to see ya work with us,' he said in a firm voice. 'We're expanding; you'll get plenty of chances to show your mettle.'

***

I began working from day one, solving theft, insurance and divorce cases. It wasn't as I'd imagined it. Dull dreary work most of the time, though not without some lighter moments, and some fulfillment when resolving difficult problems. I put in long hours and learnt a lot. My pay increased considerably as time passed and accordingly my lifestyle.

I left my council house at Chiswick and moved into a comfortable Kensington apartment. And at Pemberton, the management considered me responsible enough to give me my own office, with a secretary.

***

THE PRESENT: This particular morning I arrived at the office in good humor. The reason: not only because I liked my job but because of the effect of an enjoyable previous evening, spent at home watching movies on DVD. I had one of those personal quirks that individuals develop from time to time. I'd become an ardent movie buff and watched them regularly on wide-screen or on DVD. The perfect escape for one as busy as me. I also read as much as before, but wrote only rarely.

As I walked in, Susan Grafton, my secretary, smiled as usual. 'Good morning, Mr Adams.'

'Morning,' I nodded breezily in her direction and entered my office. Barely had I settled down and lit up when the telephone rang.

'What is it?'

Susan's voice came on, 'Michael Collins on the line, the Casserite mining people from Truro, Cornwall.'

'Yes, put him through,' I reached for my in-tray and picked up a blue file. For a fraction of a second my eyes rested on the pile of papers below it. White folders meant requests for help from new customers. Blue meant a regular client. Then I dealt with the call.

Scarcely had I put the receiver down and picked up another file on a messy divorce case, when the intercom buzzed. Susan again. 'James Morgan's called a meeting this evening, you've got to attend.'

'What's up?'

Susan and I got along well. She'd been with me for around four years. I treated her with great consideration. She reciprocated in her own way. That meant revealing bits and pieces of office trivia and gossip, which I'd miss hearing because of my position.

'Employee trouble, rumors all around,' she said.

'Anything specific?'

'No.'

It had to be something pretty important. After all, over the years I'd seen Morgan just thrice. As chairman of Morgan Enterprises, a multimillion-pound group of power stations, he owned a majority share in the Pemberton Security Services. We provided security to his public utilities nationwide. It brought a major share of our business.

I leaned back, took a long drag and sighed. I had a busy day ahead which would end after the meeting and could carry on till late in the evening.

What could be the problem? For a moment I thought I'd call Potter and Devlin, then changed my mind. Finally, I decided to try and extract more information from Susan. Rumors all around, she had said. I rang the buzzer.

***

I arrived in time for the meeting. What with my workload I usually found it difficult to be punctual. Sam, more aged, fully grey now, gave me a mournful look.

'Good to see ya, Dave.'

'And you,' I politely offered while taking my seat, feeling relieved at hearing the familiar voice. I placed my laptop and Black-Berry cell phone on the table by the side of the writing pad and glass of water. We couldn't smoke and drink at the meeting. Morgan's diktat. It would be distracting, he'd said.

Betty Pemberton, a tall, blue-eyed blonde, daughter of the late founder of Pemberton Security Services, came in. She took an active part in the management and her word counted in everything that went on. Usually of a helpful and pleasing disposition, she took her seat without her usual cheerful smile. Nodding quickly at us, she extracted a laptop from its case and put on a pair of steel-rimmed spectacles and waited.

Stephen Potter, head of the detection branch, walked in. He was a square-jawed, taciturn man with slick black hair, originally from a family of fishermen from the Isle of Wight now living in Highbury. He accompanied Roger Devlin, a lean, lanky, hard-working blond Irishman with an expressive face, an ex-army major, now in charge of the missing persons section of Pemberton.

I knew immediately something serious had happened. Except I seemed to be the only one in the dark about the matter. The tension in the room focused on Devlin. He frequently looked at his cell phone on the table as though he wanted to contact someone, but for some reason couldn't. And the expression on his smooth-shaven face reminded me of a convict on death row who'd been told that he'd be hanged soon and couldn't get the impending execution- off his mind.

I arched my eyebrows to the utmost limit and said to no one in particular, 'I'm dying of curiosity. What's the problem?'

Devlin clenched and unclenched his fists and shook his head introspectively as though in deep thought about something.

'Long story, let Morgan bring it up,' he said.

We sat uncomfortably silent for about a minute, till James Morgan walked in. His superbly cut black suit, spotless white shirt and club tie could have come from an exclusive personal tailor on Saville Row, or somewhere equally expensive. People link appearance to manners. Morgan, impeccably dressed, somehow reminded me of Roger Moore in the James Bond movies. He looked like him. Automatically you'd expect a suave and sophisticated manner. But apparently a first generation success, he had to beat and bully others too much en route to his current position. The result was he only looked the part. When he spoke all comparisons ended.

'We have a problem,' he barked in a rough, brutal manner. 'His name is Crawford'. He paused to regard us and spat out, 'Mickey Crawford.'

I placed the sweaty palm of my left hand on my forehead and tried to recall Mickey Crawford. I couldn't. Pemberton's a large organization; still Crawford had to be a newcomer for me to be unaware of him.

Morgan, now comfortably ensconced in his soft leather chair, nodded curtly at Devlin. Besides Morgan, four pairs of eyes gazed expectantly at the boss of the missing persons section.

'I recruited Mickey Crawford just a month ago,' began a considerably agitated Devlin. 'Got a good scholastic record in school, college. He came for an interview in reply to our advertisement.'

He paused for our reactions. None of us showed any. All of us were too experienced in the game.

'You recruited him fresh out of college?' Betty Pemberton queried in her rich high-pitched voice while fingering some data on her laptop.

'Yes,' Devlin spoke slowly, unsteadily. 'Seemed ideal, given the nature of the job, around five eleven, totally anonymous, could blend into the scenery anywhere.'

Devlin had taken a chance in recruiting Crawford. I shivered when I realized I could've made the same mistake.

Sam scratched his snow-white beard morosely. 'Flawed character, couldn't see into his head.'

Morgan tapped his fingers on the table sharply and eyed Devlin pointedly.

The Irishman had employed Crawford. Now with his job on the line, his eyes narrowed with suppressed wrath, and his voice shook slightly. 'Robbed a client on his first case and is absconding.'

Potter, in rolled-up shirtsleeves, had a tight furrow on his brow which indicated his concentration, although he played idly with a folded newspaper and a loose sheet of paper from somewhere. I vaguely sensed he knew something.

Sam scowled and looked quizzically at Devlin. 'Which client?'

Devlin swallowed before replying. He looked at his laptop and pronounced each word with great care, slowly and ponderously. 'The Ferron Iron and Steel people, forge steel plates for shipping.' He gulped some water from his glass and spilled some on the table. 'Managing Director's son ran away. Crawford traced him, brought him back.' He paused, took a deep breath as though it took too much effort to speak, and added. 'Turned out he returned to their residence later, stole some money and a weapon. Hasn't been seen since.'

I shifted uncomfortably in my chair as serious doubts passed through my mind. I turned to Devlin. 'How do we know it's him?'

'Prints all over, the study, safe, gun room. Ferron's a licensed gun collector.'

Morgan, pink-complexioned, fresh as ever, listened grimly and looked around at each one of us in turn. Obviously he could get our attention any time he wanted. He tapped his right fist on the table. Everyone a little strained, centered their attention on him.

'Robert Ferron, the managing director, is a good friend of mine, grandson of the founder of a very respectable firm.' He gazed at Potter for a moment and asked conversationally, 'Stephen you reported something?'

Unmoved, Potter raised his head and his arms with considerable equanimity and rested his elbows on the table. The letter in his right hand filled us with as much suspense as the folded newspaper in his left hand.

'Traced a girlfriend to a Streatham address. Broken-off. Won't see her again and informed her through this letter.'

Sam broke the air of rapt attention that engulfed the room; blushing visibly with enthusiastic fervor as he laughed audibly with relief. 'Ha ha! Greedy tenderfoot slips up.'

Betty, austere and official-looking in her steel-rimmed glasses, nodded understandingly. 'She parted with the letter. Has ended the relationship.'

I sat as still and as restrained as possible. Pemberton wouldn't be stained too much if we caught Crawford quickly.

Potter refrained from actually beaming and waved the letter about. 'Postmarked Colaba post office, Mumbai.'

This came as a shock. The atmosphere quickly returned to one of considerable disquiet. Devlin mopped his brow and glanced exasperatedly at Potter. Possibly because Potter hadn't told him anything before.

Betty looked on, confusion on her face. Sam didn't scowl or frown, but impassively waited for somebody to say something.

Within a second an expressionless Morgan, fully in control, snapped impatiently, 'pass it around, let everyone see it'.

When Sam handed me the letter, I stared at the scrawl on the plain white sheet and tried to apply my by now considerable expertise in the field. But I couldn't decipher anything from it, although it brought back memories. 'Mumbai, new name of the city of Bombay, India, been there once to see a relation.'

Immediately I regretted having spoken, disconcerted with the feeling of everyone's eyes on me, and sighed inaudibly with regret.

Morgan thumped the table again with his fist. 'Been there, got someone in Mumbai?'

Before I could reply, Potter, remarkably calm at the success of his detectives waved his other hand (the one with the newspaper) about.

'Copy of the Mumbai edition of the *Times of India*, three days old, has a report of a murder at Mumbai's Dadar Beach.'

Devlin started and stared at Potter quite aghast. The beads of sweat on his brow trickled down his face onto his checked shirt. What wouldn't he have done for a peg of brandy or something as strong. Or equally maybe a smoke. Anything, like me. Instead he fortified himself with a sip of water. His crestfallen attitude revealed he'd realized his man had gone too far to be recovered.

Betty cocked her head sideways in anticipation. Sam looked appalled, but his eyes rested on me as he wrote something on his notepad. I immediately knew he'd suggest it. Meaning I'd have to make a trip overseas soon, to Mumbai. I adjusted my mental focus towards the forthcoming trip and turned and studied Potter.

He continued, 'point made in the report... killer used a sophisticated weapon not usually seen in that part of the world yet... four point seven caliber slugs, found at the murder site with no empties around.'

'How does that prove anything?' I asked skeptically, in a tone that indicated I knew the gravity of what he'd disclosed.

'Stolen a G-11, Heckler and Koch, fires caseless four point seven into thirty-three millimeter ammunition!' Potter informed us in an icy voice. 'Read, our man is in Mumbai with the stolen weapon and possibly the cash!'

III

So they finally made a decision. I'd go to India. Visit the city of Mumbai for the second time, and trace Mickey Crawford. Somehow Morgan and company felt Jeet would be of great help to me.

I'd kept in touch with him. Only just. He had a computer at home, but wasn't connected to the internet. So I had exchanged cards at Christmas, Easter and on our birthdays. Maybe a letter or two sometimes. He knew I was in Pemberton. He'd written to me about his being employed somewhere. Unfortunately my workload and the distance obviated regular contact till recently. In his last letter he'd informed me of his purchasing a Reliance mobile; and had given me his number. I decided to use my BlackBerry to call him up on his new Reliance.

I settled down in my usual place at home and relaxed on my upholstered mahogany armchair, a whisky and soda within easy reach on a side table to my left. With a Dunhill in my left hand and the BlackBerry in my right, enveloped in the aroma of the finest Virginia tobacco, I punched Jeet's number.

***

'Hello... hello... is that Jeet, David Adams here.'

'Oh Jeet speaking,' a low decibel but clear strong voice responded, somehow sounding jocular. 'Well Dave how are you?'

'I'm fine, what about you?' I replied speaking slowly.

'Oh pulling on.'

He spoke nicely and smoothly. Relieved, I decided to get details, 'Are you alone still?'

'No have a couple of friends… my job helped.'

'Taking orders?'

'Right, and giving orders and had peers.'

'Why had peers?' I got suspicious.

'Left the job now. Exist on an inheritance, savings, and spend time writing; have got a few pieces published.'

This disappointed me. The part that he'd left his job. I tried to ask him a positive question. 'Still read a lot?'

'Oh yes, am able to afford books at will.'

This pleased me no end. Data banks in his mind on various subjects would improve his intelligence. When he refocused on other problems, he'd have the intelligence to solve them.

I adjusted my position slightly to make myself more comfortable and asked, 'do you still run?'

'No. Exercise at home only', he promptly answered. 'But fully… practice shouting, fighting, with specially made up sessions of bad behavior incorporated into the workouts!'

I clenched my teeth to prevent sounds of my chuckle from getting across, then remarked, 'for use in situations outside.'

'No, always keep a straight, right and true face outside. All my training is for my mind only.' He exhaled. 'As louder, stronger and smarter than most, find it easy to stay restrained.'

This relieved me. The Jeet I knew had been skinny and tall. I wondered how he looked now, but decided against asking him. 'No problems otherwise?'

'No. If I look around, feel like on the bridge, at the helm of a fleet, watching a two-sided drama psychologically sitting on the fence… even if participating on either side!'

I puffed on my cigarette and probed deeper. 'I recalled you following a recovery plan which included walking about in the city?'

Jeet guffawed on the other end. 'Now seen too much and the queasy feeling I used to get when outside has stopped.'

'I knew you'd adapt to the new situation.'

'Now I have no rank status to keep up so everything's cheap.'

I shook my head somberly, not knowing what to make out of it. He raised his voice and revealed further.

'After swallowing virtually the whole of Mumbai... been through rich areas, middle-class areas, poorer sections of the city, the shanty towns and the foreigner areas.'

This encouraged me. Jeet had his mind, could think and didn't become a derelict or something. His reading habit reversed the effects of being out, outside or what. Certainly Jeet ought to be of great help in tracing Crawford, especially if he could move around anywhere.

I stared at the wall clock opposite me, fortified myself with some more whisky, and decided to bring up my case.

***

'We have a problem, a detective's run away with some cash and a G-11...'

'Aha! Uses caseless bullets,' he interrupted me.

I felt the sweat on the palm of my right hand and informed him. 'I remember you had gun manuals in your house?'

'Yes the Hecklar and Koch G-11's bullets have the explosive outside and the steel bullet embedded in it. It's caseless and ejects no empties. Carries a fifty round magazine which is over the barrel.'

'For some reason didn't become standard issue of any army and is a gun collector's item,' I added.

Almost immediately I heard a sharp intake of breath. 'At a murder site at Dadar, our police found something wrong with the caliber of the bullet used. Also no empties were found.'

I liked that. All his reading gave him a sharp mind. He had quickly connected up facts. His being outside in a bad world hadn't blunted his thinking.

'Aware of the murder,' I said into the BlackBerry. 'Got a letter from him, name's Mickey Crawford, postmarked Colaba post office.'

From almost two thousand miles away, I could detect the seriousness in his voice as he spoke into his Reliance. 'He's in Mumbai then. Give me details.'

Some more amber-colored liquid burned down my throat before I read out details from a dossier on my lap. I ended my report by adding, 'it says he was a dedicated plodder at work, though a loner.'

I caught the start at the other end. 'Loner, he's alone all the time?'

'From Devlin's report... he's in charge of our missing persons section... it appears so,' I frowned, trying to concentrate. 'I know being alone plays tricks on the mind.'

'Drink, smoke?'

'Never a problem at work.'

Jeet sighed at the other end. 'Placed him. He's on drugs. Needed money to satisfy himself and to get to a place where he'd get drugs cheap.'

'This Colaba area,' I commented, gratified at the interest he took in the case. 'It explains the motive behind the robbery.'

'It's the only explanation.'

I took a long drag and exhaled slowly, and watched the smoke curl lazily upwards and dissipate, then shot a glance at the wall clock opposite me. 'I'm coming down one of these days, but immediately I'll send you details by courier.'

'Fantastic, great news for me, you coming here.' He sounded a trifle elated. 'I'll check Colaba for Mickey Crawford.'

I was glad he'd retained an intelligent thinking mind. I'd definitely need Jeet. After all our quarry on the loose didn't seem to have any qualms about using the deadly weapon in his possession.

I ended the call with, 'let's see if you can locate Crawford from the streets outside, before I arrive and join you.'

IV

Three days later I was in Mumbai.

Seated on the familiar black settee in Jeet's sitting room in his Mumbai flat, I felt as though a ton of bricks had been taken off my head. He had never before climbed more in my estimation than now. I lit a cigarette and sipped some orange juice. 'Sure you saw Crawford?'

Jeet stretched his long legs and made a gesture of dismissal with his head, without looking up. He still continued to examine the weapon I'd given him and said, 'absolutely. Our man all right, according to the photographs you sent me.' He shrugged his shoulders casually. 'Was with a China man. I couldn't make out if he was an Indian or foreigner.'

He'd matured a great deal since I'd last seen him. His face remained almost the same; slightly larger though, but without much of the characteristic sag around the cheeks that heralds the beginning of middle age. With at least ten kilos in all the right places, precious little on his stomach, he looked pretty reasonable, unlike the last time I'd met him.

Another thing, his voice had changed. The last time around he had a deep throaty voice – at least at home, but toned it down to a low whisper whenever I'd spoken to him outside. Now he spoke well and sounded appropriately even. He appeared to have recovered from his earlier days, during which time his talk had been suppressed drastically to almost absurd levels. His new plebian working-class accent had removed some kind of visceral fear which I'd sensed was deep inside him during my earlier visit.

I absently fingered the other gun. 'Both Glock model 18's. Called nine millimeter Glock Selective-Fire Sub-Machine Pistol.'

'Great weapon,' Jeet beamed.

'Yes highly effective in situations.'

Jeet couldn't take his eyes off the Austrian pistol. He slid out the nineteen-round bullet feed box and affixed the thirty-three round magazine. 'Compact little sub-machine gun.'

I nodded in agreement, and got back to Crawford. 'Colaba post office mark helped?'

He gave me the sort of look that professors reserve for younger students who've doubted their answers to a particularly difficult problem. A little more then just reproachful. 'Yes, Colaba's a tourist area, shops, restaurants, can walk the streets there.'

I placed my Glock in its leather waist band holster.

Jeet removed the long magazine from his weapon and carefully fingered the unique safety and trigger-system and disclosed, 'Colaba's full of foreigners on holiday. He had to be hiding among the budget western tourists.'

'Showed his photograph around?'

'Risky, even with two international-class five-star hotels there.' He waved away some smoke from my cigarette, which closed in around him. 'Also catering to the tourists, Europeans, Africans, Arabs are pimps, brothels, foreign exchange touts, drug-dealers... and there are addicts... after money anyhow.'

He glanced at me momentarily; then turned his attention to the Glock's fire selector, clicking it to automatic and semi-automatic modes.

Although his interest in the Glock's pleased me, I wanted to know how he'd solved the case for me.

'Moved around the area and got some roadside characters to cooperate after gaining their confidence, also by paying them.'

When he paused, I widened my eyes interrogatively and enhanced my degree of attention.

'A man who washed parked cars outside the Taj Mahal Hotel, saw Crawford, followed him to the Royal Haven, a cheap hotel full of hippy-type foreigners.'

For a few seconds I ruminated on his disclosures. A sliver of doubt remained. 'You saw him too?'

He replied with utmost certainty, 'spied on the Royal Haven from the street, and saw Crawford.' He raised his voice in emphasis. 'Definitely our man from Pemberton,' he carried on with a grin, speaking normally again. 'He came to his room from somewhere with... with another person.'

Unable to conceal my delight, I smiled and leaned slightly towards him. 'The mystery China man?'

He put his gun to one side. But kept looking at it.

'Came from God alone knows where,' he rejoined, paused as though he needed to think, and reasoned, 'I couldn't go inside or do anything.'

After a few seconds of silence he mumbled something to himself as though beset by some difficult problem.

He noticed the look on my face and said, 'need more than permission from the authorities to carry these guns... and to accost Crawford!'

***

I sat still for a minute, as smoke curled around me. Like the last time, the trip to Mumbai didn't faze me. But this time I had a job to do. Not an easy task, what with me being in a foreign country. But thank God I had Jeet. He took the case very seriously and he proved he could think right.

'Thanks to Pemberton's clout, I was able to temporarily import the two Glock's for personal protection,' I assured him.

On being informed of the case, Mumbai's Police Commissioner had deputed Vivek Murthy, a Deputy Commissioner in the city's Crime Branch, to deal with us. Thanks to Pemberton and direct orders from his higher-ups, we were able to get the guns in.

'Official permission in writing enabled me to get the weapons through at the airport,' I said. 'But got instructions to see Vivek Murthy IPS first thing before doing anything.'

He drew a long breath audibly as though greatly comforted. 'Oh, IPS officer supervising us. Good.'

The relief he exhibited prompted me to ask, 'what's an IPS officer?'

'Indian Police Service, elite cadre of civil servants who've passed a complex nationwide selection procedure. Join police forces directly as Assistant Superintendent's and reach the top slots of Director General of Police,' he clarified, letting his breath out slowly.

I wanted more on the subject. I asked tentatively. 'We operate with this Murthy breathing down our necks?'

'Oh no! Not at all,' he smiled faintly as if amused at my ignorance. 'System does not encourage IPS officers outside too often, while juniors who see everything freely outside, cannot do anything without inside permission... aim of the game, let everything be as it is, act quickly if needed, and get back in and remain still!'

Good news this, I reckoned. 'And Murthy ranks high up, works on information given to him?'

Right. Operates with one hand behind his back; subordinate staff have the other hand tied up, but together, somehow it works,' he went on inexorably exhibiting all the knowledge he'd built up over the years on the subject. 'Play a vital role in keeping the varied multi-lingual ethnic groups divided by caste, religion, politics, and further sub-divided by their business interests, all out to extract as much as possible from each other... in a kind of fragile peace.'

His erudition impressed me immensely and I said with an air of finality, 'ought not to have any problem then?'

He didn't reply. The contemplative expression on his face, furrowed brow and half frown reminded me of a meditating Buddha. I waited till I saw a flicker of inspiration in his eyes, as though he'd resolved some vexatious problem.

'Didn't tell the police about Crawford in the Royal Haven.' His tone implied confusion.

I offered cautiously, 'know of his presence in the city with the cash and the G-11... Pemberton's sent a report.'

'G-11's confirmed here because of the murder at Dadar beach.'

I drummed my feet on the floor and shook my head interrogatively. 'What are you trying to imply?'

'Cops know of his complicity in the murder.'

I finished my cigarette and reflexively checked the time and added, 'not of him being in the Royal Haven.'

'Cannot be. If Murthy's got Crawford's name and description and know of his possession of the weapon... he ought to have nabbed him immediately.'

'Maybe he's registered in the Royal Haven under a false name?' I queried a trifle doubtfully.

'I couldn't check that out. Something more than meets the eye in it!'

I froze momentarily. A chill shot through my body. We were only private investigators. There ought to be no other implication to Crawford, other than he succumbed to temptation.

'Meaning?' I asked.

Jeet flushed. His perplexity became conspicuous all over his visage. 'Can get every single Colaba hotel's guest list; and get the local Colaba police station cops to check every establishment... Murthy ought to be holding Crawford by now!'

***

Jeet and I arrived at the side-gate after a ten-minute drive from home. A khaki-uniformed armed guard looked us over and asked us, 'can I help you?'

Jeet nodded. 'Deputy Commissioner Vivek Murthy, got an appointment.'

'Identification.'

I showed him my passport, a letter from Pemberton, and an *e-mail* from the office of the Police Commissioner of Mumbai which permitted me and Jeet to operate under the supervision of Murthy. Jeet confirmed his identity with his driving licence.

'Wait here,' the constable instructed us; and disappeared into a booth with our papers.

We were in dark trousers and bush shirts, with faded tracksuit tops to cover our Glock's in their waist belt holsters. Nothing on us could attract attention, and we were fairly anonymous amongst the general public out on the streets.

Jeet motioned me to remain silent.

I stood by stiffly and carefully looked around. The Mumbai Police Commissionerate's main building which had a small 1897 etched in white marble above the sealed-off front entrance, was a Victorian brownstone castle. It looked like it had somehow transplanted itself from the rolling English countryside to a congested area right in the middle of Mumbai.

At the apex of two major arterial roads, chock-full of traffic, the compound also enclosed a utilitarian concrete building and barrack-style corrugated iron-roofed huts. Other concrete block-like structures in neat rows, with clothes hanging from lines and ladies peering from balconies, apparently served as residential quarters for the constables.

Outside the compound (where we waited) the footpath had squads of armed constables, seated on wooden benches or in specially made bunkers of sandbags. I noted one Assault Kalashnikov, first manufactured in the year 1947, popularly known as AK-47. Some constables toted the black painted British nine millimeter Sterling submachine gun with their long side magazines, popularly called carbines. Others had the Indian version of the original Belgian Fabrique Nationale Herstal rifle called Fusil Automativ Leger.

Jeet noticed my gaze and said, 'Indian and British army call them seven-point-six-two Self Loading Rifle's or SLR's.'

I nodded in acknowledgement.

'After India's disastrous war with China in 1962, began locally manufacturing them at Ishapore. Now being replaced in the army, and surplus stocks being distributed to state police forces,' Jeet said.

The place was well-guarded in a way as though to put-off suicide bombers with armed squads placed around at strategic points. If the front gates evoked a feeling of aristocratic grandeur (a big put-off to ordinary people), the dusty side entrances seemed designed to frighten away anyone tarrying aimlessly, save those with definite business inside. A blue Swaraj Mazda van with a yellow and red stripe painted on its body lay parked to one side. At intervals on the steel grills covering the truck's windows, were small innocuous-looking apertures to poke weapons through to shoot at criminals or mobs or what, ever a constant reminder of their deadly mission. All this revealed the place was the headquarters of a police organization with extensive responsibilities.

My survey of the place ended when Jeet touched my shoulder lightly.

The uniformed constable returned with an armed man in a white bush shirt and dark trousers. He gripped a black Sterling tightly, it's strap over his shoulder, close to his body.

'He will take you to Murthy sahib.'

***

A medium heighted but well-built moon-faced man in khaki uniform watched us come into the room. 'Mister Adams, Mister Jeet, come in, take a seat,' he said in a pleasant easygoing manner and motioned us towards the chairs in front of his wooden desk.

From between piles of files at both ends of his desk, he regarded us with probing eyes which telegraphed a great big question mark. Two telephones, an ornate pen holder and a covered glass of water stood among his laptop and a thick white file. And within a second he greeted us, sounding polite. 'Welcome to Mumbai.'

'Thank you,' I acknowledged. I hadn't expected someone that young. But as Jeet had said the IPS was an elite selection grade. Murthy had earned his position albeit while being quite young.

'So we're after this Crawford, alleged murder accused?' he leaned forward with his elbows on his table. 'But first let's see the pistols you've brought.'

Both of us simultaneously removed our weapons with the nineteen bullet feed box inside, from our waist holsters, and placed them on the table in front of him. Then we placed the extra thirty-three round magazines.

He picked up the Glock's and took almost a minute to examine the guns. 'Fifty-two rounds each. Before you leave us, I'll need an account of every bullet expended.'

'Sir, everything we do you'll know,' Jeet said.

I nodded in assent.

The slightly balding Murthy brushed his hair back with his left hand and smiled expansively. 'Will you have tea.'

'Yes,' I agreed.

He pressed a buzzer. Someone entered and stood unseen behind us. Murthy gazed over our heads and ordered the three teas.

Despite his youthfulness, Murthy appeared to be an experienced cop. He had the air and manner of someone who reeked of authority. And his eyes were like that of a canny fox.

When the door closed behind us, Jeet asked, 'Crawford's victim at Dadar beach hasn't been identified, sir?'

'Murdered a *hijda*,' Murthy's large face crinkled up with such obvious distaste that I couldn't make out whether it was the murder that upset him or these *hijda*'s, whatever they were.

Curious, I asked, 'what's a *hijda*?'

Jeet answered, speaking with unusual restraint, 'male transvestites, either castrated or normal, who dress in female garb and beg, perform at religious functions, also in the sex trade.'

A constable entered and placed three cups of tea on the table. We took a cup each and sipped the steaming brew.

I sensed that Murthy seemed to be interested in us but was trying not to show it. Also he didn't like these *hijda*'s, and didn't care whether they were murdered.

He glanced to his right for a fraction of a second to another table with a computer; then changed his mind and opened the thick white file in front of him. He also looked into his open laptop. Then abstractedly he muttered as though to himself, yet audible to us. 'Have to get Crawford.'

Jeet smiled and made the understatement of the day, 'I've traced him, sir, to the Royal Haven, a hotel in Colaba, and he's not alone.'

Murthy focused his gaze to somewhere between us and said, 'Oh I see.'

He didn't seem to like this. And the ensuing uncomfortable stillness became tormenting enough as pregnant seconds ticked by, for me to clench my fists till I winced.

'Found out only yesterday,' Jeet said.

Murthy looked into the file. He glanced at a page, then turned it and in this manner he turned page after page.

I offered a little sarcastically, 'your responsibility, he's murdered a man at Dadar beach'.

Murthy's forehead furrowed and his shrewd eyes narrowed. Finally he leaned back in his chair.

Then, Jeet and I placed our empty tea cups on the table.

Murthy once more looked into the file. Something was wrong. I detected the file had something to do with Crawford. Yet it seemed too thick. Murthy must've turned at least fifteen pages of data. About what? And it concerned our man from Pemberton. Murthy seemed to be trying to make a decision from perusing the file.

Then he made up his mind. 'Okay, I'm permitting it. You two go to the Royal Haven and accost Crawford. But I'm allowing you to tell him only of the Pemberton case. Don't mention the Dadar matter or anything else.'

I started getting vague feelings that we were being used as pawns in some larger game. All my experience at Pemberton told me he was trying to hide something from us. What? I couldn't make out. We had to get Crawford somehow to prevent Morgan from being embarrassed by the Ferron people.

Jeet studied Murthy's face briefly and asked sharply, 'what if he resists, sir.'

'Use force up to a limit,' Murthy clicked his tongue, then asked, 'do you two have mobiles?'

'I have a BlackBerry and Jeet has a Reliance.'

'Then punch this number into your memory. It's of Senior Inspector Prashant Nagwekar. If need be, only in an emergency, you contact him, he appraises me and I'll send help.'

***

Before leaving Murthy's office I contacted Sam in London on my BlackBerry. I told him of our locating Crawford, and of us being permitted to go get him.

'Good, I gather you've solved the case,' Sam said.

'I hope so,' I said, still full of doubts due to Murthy's suspicious conduct. I also couldn't tell Sam anything more as the youthful Deputy Commissioner was watching me with perceptive eyes.

'If he's involved in a murder, then it'll be a problem of extraditing him?'

'At least we'll recover the gun… the G-11 and maybe some of the cash.'

'Well best of luck then and be careful, Mickey Crawford has proved he's a murderer.'

V

Less than half-an-hour later I stared at the large, decrepit and sleazy looking villa-style Hotel Royal Haven as we neared it on a quiet tree lined Colaba lane called Henry Road. Although blue paint peeling-off in large flakes revealed patches of bare maroon brickwork, an ornate though neglected arcade disclosed it had seen better days. An ancient, disused elevator shaft visible from outside had a dusty "out of order" board which looked as though it had been there from the medieval ages.

'Cheap dive for foreign tourists,' Jeet informed me, feet crunching on the gravel path leading to the entrance. He then advised, 'and be silent. I'll talk, especially if we've to learn something from the hotel staff.'

I nodded and entered the place, climbing a couple of filthy stairs to an absurdly tiny wooden reception desk tucked behind the rear of the elevator shaft. A small-faced boy, all alone, seated on a stool behind the counter, leaned forward with his weight on his elbows over a red register and a black telephone, and glared suspiciously at us.

'What dya waan?' he spat out, eyes smoldering on his tiny mischievous face. He gave the impression of a volcano about to erupt.

Before Jeet could answer, he peered at me, and waved a spotless white-sleeved arm towards the interior. 'Wanna room?'

Jeet had warned me to remain quiet. I stayed still.

He glanced at me and back to the boy, and put on an act, 'No, don't want a room, men…'

'Can't get dames here, get lost!' the volcano erupted instantly, as powerfully as the one at Pompei that destroyed a Roman town. I got the impression that the "dames here" obsessed him.

Jeet didn't destruct, but I sensed anger welling up inside him for an instant before dissipating. He reached out and touched the boy's chest with a flat right hand and said in a sort of a loud hiss from between his teeth, 'bastard, can just go in and grab and finish them! Not listening to you anywhere, men! Don't want hippy-type dames.'

'Aha,' the boy glanced upwards at me approvingly, as though Jeet didn't want "dames" due to my presence. 'What then?'

Shaken slightly by the fury of the young boy, and the way Jeet quickly adjusted and handled him, I remained motionless and quiet.

When the boy realized I wouldn't answer, he turned to Jeet and sneered, 'then shaddup…'

'Shut down, pull your chuddies up and down!' Jeet calmly replied. He sounded as earnest and dignified as the Poet Laureate would be during a poetry recital for a gathering of Royals and eminent persons.

The boy widened his eyes in shock and stared at Jeet. Vaguely I sensed flickers of recognition pass through his eyes. Then he nodded warily towards Jeet.

'I'm Jeet,' Jeet raised his hands in a placatory manner, then pointed at me. 'This Englishman is Adams.'

My name had an effect. The diminutive boy favored me with a grin. 'Aha… without Eve… ha ha ha!'

Jeet raised his voice a little. 'See two swine's robbed money from him, men.'

'Oh,' the clerk shook his slickly combed dark-haired head. Every move he made accentuated the effect of a tamed brat highly resenting his station. I sensed he was taking great pains to act as un cooperative as possible. 'Can't help, I'm Columbus, not police-ees an'-all-that.'

Suddenly he looked past us at the source of conversation in some kind of European tongue. Two blondes of East European origin approached the counter. In stained, dirty striped pajamas and shabby tee shirts, they weren't members of polite society. One of the girls came to the desk reeking of sweat and stale perfume. She reached out with her hand. The bangles on her arm clanged together as she sneered, 'keys.'

Columbus stared vilely at her. She carefully avoided looking at his face. He turned around, reached for the keys from a small cupboard with a jerk and handed them over while muttering something under his breath. I heard a distinct, 'bloody bitch, I'm a superior bugger also.'

When they left, Jeet changed his manner and confidentially whispered, 'Customer's eehh?'

'Yah, mostly Europeans, poorer classes, hippy-type, wanting drugs and to enjoy.' For a moment he sounded like a billionaire discussing local starving beggars.

Then he glared accusingly at Jeet. 'This is what happens if you don't shout at them.'

'Yes I can do that,' Jeet whispered.

Columbus widened his eyes. He became like a prophet receiving a bolt of inspiration from heaven after years of anguish. A roguish grin on his face, he gleefully suggested, 'go in, men, I'm telling you ah... and shout and beat them.'

He stared at Jeet with so much emotion, that he ignored the gurgling sounds of repressed laughter escaping from my throat.

'Per-haaps...' Jeet half agreed, as though deeply in thought about the matter. 'Dee-pends...' he said slowly as though waiting for the opportune moment, then changed his manner and continued. 'I can shout, but first...?'

Columbus's face lit up instantly like a high-powered bulb receiving a surge of electricity. He looked upwards at Jeet, eagerly searching his face as though he'd bare his soul for him.

'We want to know, men,' Jeet paused, removed Crawford's photograph from his pocket and placed it on the desk. 'This swine we have to catch.'

'Actual type Mickey Crawford, he's with a Chinese bugger,' Columbus immediately revealed.

'Actual?'

'Wearing Adidas shoes,' Columbus said jubilantly, like a detective who'd just resolved an impossible problem. 'Other buggers here always wear fake-eee-das.'

Jeet nodded with great seriousness, and encouraged Columbus to talk.

'Gone out with bags,' he motioned they'd carried their bags on their shoulders on two straps.

So Crawford carried the G-11 wherever he went I deduced.

'Aha,' Jeet nodded in agreement. 'Where have they gone?'

'Heard them say goin' DN Road.'

'Place, like which office or shop or where exactly?'

'Don't know.'

Jeet bolstered him a bit, 'definitely, I'll be shouting at those dames.'

Columbus clicked his tongue with delight. His face unabashedly registered every emotion in the book, and some not in the book. 'Think coming back evening time at nine, and going out again... heard Chinese bugger telling.'

'And the China man's name?' Jeet asked gravely.

Columbus grabbed the register and opened it with an expression on his face of one about to embark on a voyage of discovery. Hastily he ran his finger down a column and barked rapidly and so loudly that I literally jumped in my place.

'Tan-Win-Lee.'

Jeet clicked his fingers. 'We're coming back, then we'll catch them... and shout.'

No sportsperson winning an Olympic gold medal, or academic receiving a Nobel prize, or politician successful in a crucial election could duplicate the triumphant demeanor of Columbus. He seemed convinced Jeet would shout at those "dames". And was cooperating because of it.

He shook his head vigorously and said, 'yah yah and I won't tell them anything, swear men, yah.'

***

Ten minutes later I stared at the books and magazines in front of me. Piles of them lay on the pavement. More books formed disorganized pyramids on small cots. And some more books and magazines on show were held in place by strings on an iron fence of an adjacent building. Customers gazed at them; or perused titles that caught their fancy; and more than some of the browsers brought not a few of the hundreds of new and second-books lying around from shabbily clad boys hovering all over.

For a moment Jeet and I paused at the start of DN Road. Somehow I had a sinking feeling. I hesitated doubtfully. 'Difficult to find Crawford over such a vast area?'

'As a foreigner, he'll stand out and we'll spot him,' Jeet retorted confidently. He thoughtfully looked down the road and advised. 'Must be as invisible as possible. Not look around too much and attract attention.'

We strolled on in silence, crossed a small lane and stepped onto a cramped, enclosed pavement covered by the overhanging arcades of large Victorian-style brownstone buildings.

'Place used to be full of hawker's selling items from kiosks on both sides of the pavement,' Jeet informed me. 'Authorities acted and now the stretch is virtually empty.'

'Crawford couldn't have come here to do shopping outside,' I said.

'Used to be like a large department store controlled by big shot dons,' he launched into an explanation without breaking a step. 'Linked to deadly smuggling and extortion gangs.'

'And Crawford? Murthy was hiding something from us.'

'He could've joined a gang with the stolen money to profit from sex items or drugs.'

I looked around trying to spot Crawford if he was around while trying to keep in step with Jeet. 'And if he's on drugs, his service to the gang will be limited.'

'Crawford is definitely on drugs, and is in some criminal gang, and Murthy knows of it and won't tell us anything,' Jeet spoke slowly as though mentally sifting through various possibilities. The strain of the mental effort of trying to resolve the problem right there on the street among the other pedestrians showed in his frowning eyes. 'But the China man... I can't get it...'

'He's Indian I feel?'

'Right,' he replied quickly, paused and added uneasily. 'But no Indian Chinese gang reported ever. Our China men are mostly respectable restaurateurs, dentists, shoemakers.'

He looked around a few times, this time not at the few displays but at the people around and squeezed his Glock in its holster under his faded tracksuit top. 'We might have a problem if we see them.'

'Why?'

'If we accost them with our weapons, and they resist,' he said cryptically, then still moving ahead, casually turned and grit his teeth and opined. 'Everyone around will mob us, our only hope is that the police come soon'.

I felt my pulse speed up with anxiety. 'Don't fancy being the center of attention of a large mob, even for some time.'

He nodded, crinkling his nose slightly. 'Just alerting you.'

I caught a whiff of a strong perfume. A small crowd around a wooden kiosk inspected a variety of multicolored bottles and sprays. One item sold like hot cakes. Customer after customer brought a little glass bottle and went away with smug expressions of anticipatory delight.

I regarded this most popular item with fascination. A sticker with a semi-naked couple in an erotic posture didn't distract my attention from the writing in thick black print: "Pleasure Prolonging Lotion"!

Jeet said, 'just the kind of thing that sells best here, the "Pleasure Prolonging Lotion".'

***

We neared the end of the block. Ahead, a small lane bisected the pavement. Jeet stopped for a second and patiently surveyed the area around. 'No specific location given; we'll have to check the whole...'

A horrible scream interrupted him! Then a ghastly death rattle and a thud echoed above the street noises. For a fraction of a second the entire street froze and stared in the direction of the sounds. Then pandemonium broke out. Shouts and yells rent the air. Everyone around ran towards a small crowd which had started gathering ahead. I presumed around a body.

And then I saw them. Crawford and Lee! There was no mistaking Crawford with the G-11 in a case slung around his shoulder. Lee tried to hide something between his left hand and his body. I strained my eyes and saw a knife with fresh red blood dripping from it. But both of them also with backpacks as though on a camping expedition in the wild, casually walked past along the intersecting lane, and disappeared out of sight. Surprisingly no one took any notice of them.

Jeet placed his right hand on my shoulder, pushed me gently and ran forward. 'Let's go get them.'

***

I followed the half walking, half jogging Jeet as he dodged past pedestrians and idle passers-by. At the corner, a quick glance to the right before turning left and racing behind Jeet, revealed a small mob obscuring the view of the body. If it was indeed a body that lay there.

Ahead, Crawford and Lee ran into a building and vanished. A few seconds later we entered the small, dark side entrance, weapons drawn.

'Office building, closed for repairs now,' Jeet said.

I nodded, panting. A naked bulb dimly lit an empty dark corridor extending all the way to the other end of the long building. Jeet looked up and down the passage, then motioned towards the wooden stairway.

'They're not upstairs, didn't hear any noise.'

Barely did I make out the various types of locks and padlocks on the shut doors of the rows of offices when I suddenly realized they were only on one side. The single ebony brown wooden door on the other side didn't have a lock.

Still a little out of breath, I looked at Jeet. He nodded and walked towards the door. I stepped towards him and stood by, Glock ready, as he slowly pushed it open, inwards.

Rows of cardboard boxes filled the room, save just near the door. It was as if the long room was being renovated. Now, however, in front of us, a dark, skinny boy sat on a low wooden stool near a small box, an open sack and a bucket of what appeared to be plain water.

Unaware of us, the boy carefully spooned in some indeterminate powder into a tiny bottle. Then with a blue plastic mug, he took water from a bucket and carefully poured in a measure. He held the bottle up frequently to check if he'd got the right volume. Finally he stuck a familiar sticker with the cavorting semi-naked couple on it, and put the bottle to one side, near a row of similar bottles.

I almost choked trying to suppress my guffaw, thus aggravating my already breathless condition. I'd just seen the "Pleasure Prolonging Lotion" being manufactured.

Jeet, lean and lanky but tall when compared to the lean, skinny but short boy in front, walked in, Glock ready. And shouted at the top of his voice. 'Bastard, we're police.'

The boy gave a start. Terrified, about to pour a measure of water into the next bottle, he put it to his lips and drank it instead.

Jeet however had carefully gauged the boy. He smiled suddenly.

'Which way two men went?'

The boy relaxed and cautiously pointed around the cardboard boxes, fingers clenched, index finger straight out, towards the interior. Jeet motioned me to follow him. 'Be as alert as possible.'

***

I felt like a traveller lost in the middle of the Sahara without water as we walked onwards, tense but fully alert, on and on past rows of piled up cardboard boxes. My pulse pounded and my parched mouth cried out for a drink even if just a sip of plain old H2O. The usual occurrence, I noticed, if nervous in an alien environment. Does something to the throat.

I tried to think positively. At least the tube-lights gave us ample luminosity. We ought to see Crawford and Lee clearly. They had to be somewhere around. The boy had indicated it.

Suddenly a short, thickset man in oversized khaki shorts and white sleeveless vest stepped in front of Jeet from among the boxes. Another brown shape hurled into him from the side.

In the microsecond in which I jerked my Glock upwards, an iron bar came crashing down on my gun arm. I yelled in agony. My Glock clattered uselessly onto the floor. But because of my height in relation to the attacker, the downward blow hadn't been with full force. I still had my hands. Reflexively I charged head first into the man, who had been hiding behind the cardboard cartons.

I slammed into him. He staggered back and fell, bringing down a pile of boxes. On top of him, almost overcome with the odor of stale sweat, I grabbed his neck and stood up, lifting him over the contents of the fallen boxes lying all over the floor. Bald, in khaki shorts reaching his knees and in a filthy, stinking sleeveless vest, he struggled stiffly though powerfully. I got the impression he was a dimwit as we moved about, swaying from side to side trying to topple each other. We kicked electrical massagers, deflated life sized nude inflatable dolls and dildoes, all contents of the boxes, all over the floor.

In front, Jeet roared and yelled like a mad man, and elbowed a man in his face who went down with a shriek, collapsing near another. Another pile of boxes fell and DVD's and blue magazines clattered all over. Jeet turned fast. Not fast enough though.

A bearded man in a loose white cotton *dhoti* (loin cloth), and a dirty grey shirt surfaced from somewhere. Coolly and calmly he hit Jeet with an iron rod on the back of his head. Jeet fell onto his knees. Semi-consciously in slow motion Jeet tried to reach for his gun from among the merchandise on the floor.

I tried to kick the man grappling with me and go to Jeet's aid. Before I could do so, someone from behind grabbed me in a half nelson, literally strangulating me. I continued to grip the neck of the dimwit as though my life depended on it. While sweaty and miserable, I struggled helplessly with all my might, trying to shake-off the man on my shoulder.

My mind half registered the bearded man with the iron rod in front. In a surprisingly controlled and restrained manner he hit the half comatose kneeling Jeet again. Jeet moaned and fell face down with a thud, right over the DVD's and magazines strewn all over the floor, and lay unconscious.

I refused to let go the dirty, smelling, bald man I held in front. But on my neck, the vice-like grip from another, tightened. I shouted soundlessly, writhing in pain as blinding tears flowed freely from my eyes. Vaguely I sensed a grey blur with a white *dhoti* – the bearded man. He came towards me with his iron rod. I blinked in agony, heart throbbing as if it could burst anytime, tongue glued to the roof of my mouth, and awaited the inevitable.

It came in the form of a brutal pounding pain on the back of my head which forced me to let go of the dimwit. And then came another blow. Rays of light shot out of my eyes accompanied by excruciating pain. And I blanked out.

***

I winced once or twice sub-consciously. Vague irreverent thoughts passed through my mind, which gradually in imperceptible degrees became fully conscious and aware. I opened my eyes, closed them and opened them again. For a moment I stared in confusion into the sheer darkness engulfing me. Undefined sounds of vehicles passing by added to my confusion. I turned slightly. Shafts of pain shot through my head. And that did it.

Memories of the immediate past came flooding back along with sheer anger and a deepening apprehensiveness at our predicament. I immediately reached for the back of my head. Two tender lumps throbbed with pain. Carefully I felt the bruises and mentally replayed the scenes of the fracas that caused them, over and over again. It took two full minutes for the tidal waves of despondency and the jittery panic flowing through me to ebb and recede; and for me to regain enough of my senses to look around in the pitch darkness for Jeet.

Full of trepidation, I reached out with both hands. After a few seconds of gentle probing I touched someone with my right hand. I almost jumped with joy when Jeet's voice came over in a sharp whisper.

'Expected two, not a mob.'

Half my mind buzzed with intriguing questions, the other half tried to frame satisfactory answers. I spoke out one query from the first half, 'where are they?'

'Gone somewhere. For some time, I've seen no movement around.'

'Must get out of here.' I checked the time on my wrist watch after depressing the light, while secretly being relieved that it hadn't been stolen. '10:30 pm.'

Jeet stood up, checked his watch and his pockets. 'My Reliance mobile's missing.'

'Surprisingly only my BlackBerry's gone.' I felt my cigarette pack, lighter, purse and thirty-three round bullet feed box in place.

'Our guns and our mobile's are gone,' Jeet said, while unsteadily walking forward in the dark.

He led the way back towards where the boy had been earlier, stepping over merchandise strewn all over the floor; and past piles of neatly stacked boxes. I heard a horn blare from the road outside, but it seemed a world away. Where we were, although my eyes had adjusted to the gloom, at times I felt we were moving in a bottle of black ink.

When he stopped all of a sudden I lightly brushed into him.

He directed me, somehow exuding confidence. 'Stay still,' he said.

Breathing in laboriously, I sensed him moving away from me in the darkness. I stood by silently, waiting, head throbbing, throat afire, full of misgivings about our misadventure. Then the lights came on, one by one, along with the clicks as Jeet switched them on.

Everything remained the same in the room. Just like when we'd entered earlier. Save the boy. He had disappeared along with the bottles and stickers of the "Pleasure Prolonging Lotion". Jeet stared at my head for a moment, brow creased. 'No blood, really lucky, you've got only a bruise.'

Not a little comforted, I tried to see his wound as he sidled towards the wooden door. I detected no blood on the crimson lump on his scalp either. 'You the same.'

Jeet ignored me and tried to push open the door we'd entered from. It didn't move. He heaved at it with his shoulder. It didn't budge a millimeter.

He tried to kick it open. Again no result.

Half expecting to be rushed any moment, I nervously advised him, 'maybe another door?'

'Right, let's check the other end.'

The speed at which we would have reached the other end might have done an Olympic sprinter credit, had we not stopped at the spot where we'd got into the scrap earlier. I stared downwards unbelievingly at the brightly lit floor. Right there among all the sex paraphernalia lay our shiny matte black Glocks. Apparently exactly as they had fallen from our hands. They, whoever they were, hadn't bothered to take the pistols away.

Jeet, pale and subdued, appeared deep in thought as he picked up his automatic. I did the same; and like him checked the nineteen round magazine and breech and readied the gun in my hand.

He took a long, deep breath, and stretched out his arms, Glock ready, and looked around carefully. Finally he shrugged his shoulders after a three-hundred-and-sixty degree sweep which gleaned absolutely nothing. 'They appeared dumb, but not that dumb.'

I didn't reply, choosing to remain uncomfortably silent. The illuminated room suddenly became psychologically dark and dangerous. As though some ominous hidden danger lurked somewhere, gathering itself only to surface all of a sudden to wipe us out.

Jeet walked to the door at the other end of the warehouse-like room, about ten meters ahead. With Glock in hand he kicked it forcefully.

He fell down in a heap as it opened outwards too easily. Sheepishly he got up. Perplexedly he screwed up his eyes and turned inwards once more, and searched for some evidence of anything that could affect us.

He muffled his voice. 'Odd, swine have left the door open!' Somehow disoriented by how easily we got out, that too without losing anything except our cell phones, I focused on our next move and stiffly suggested, 'we're late already, let's get to the Royal Haven fast.'

VI

We left the building and walked as briskly as we could in the darkness towards the Hutatma Chowk parking lot. Minutes later, with Jeet at the wheel of his blood-red Maruti Suzuki 800, we eased past the milky white statue of the Goddess Flora of the Frere Fountain, onto the now considerably emptier and quieter main road and sped towards the Royal Haven.

'Coming back at nine, according to Columbus.' Jeet grit his teeth and concentrated on the well-lit road ahead.

'And going out again,' I reminded him and checked the time before gratefully lighting up a cigarette. 'It's "10:45" now.'

We sat in the type of car most commonly found on Mumbai's roads today. The compact box-like Maruti, built in India in collaboration with Suzuki of Japan, was ideally suited for the city's roads where maximum speed and power are superfluous. Its strong points: its maneuverability and easy steering, essential needs on crowded congested streets.

He relaxedly stepped on the gas and evaded the other vehicles moving about, apparently fully recovered from his earlier travails. I heard him half muttering under his breath. 'Pray Crawford and Lee didn't see us.'

I shifted slightly and settled down more comfortably in the front seat. 'That's an optimistic hope, them now in their room unaware of us.' I lifted my right hand and gingerly felt the bruises on my head. 'Also that's if they haven't left the Royal Haven already.'

Jeet accelerated slightly on the well-lit road among the sparse traffic. 'Our only hope is that they entered through one door and left through the other, before we went in.'

Then, Jeet slowed the Maruti down considerably and nodded grimly. 'Too many loose ends.'

He turned left onto the dimly lit Henry Road and cruised on slowly. 'So must be extremely careful when we get to them now.'

I looked closely at a couple of European tourists on the dark sidewalk.

They peered back at us. No Crawford amongst them. And suddenly, involuntarily, I bent over and slammed forward with a jerk onto the dashboard, ears assailed by a momentary screeching of brakes. I winced for a second at the pain radiating from my head. Jeet had braked hard and stopped.

I glanced at him sideways, half in anger.

Without uttering a word he stared intently ahead, hands on the steering wheel.

I quickly looked in front down the narrow lane in anticipation and gasped in shock! I felt my temperature drop by a few degrees.

Far ahead, under the light of a street lamp, Crawford and Lee, with the same bags we'd seen earlier, entered the rear seat of an idling black and yellow taxi. Seated side by side, they haggled with the cabby, who turned and faced them. After a full half a minute, the cabby turned away and adjusted a black meter on his fender. And the taxicab moved away with the duo, gradually picking up speed.

For a moment Jeet stared at the departing vehicle, trying to fathom something. Then he clicked his tongue as though some hypothesis of his had been confirmed. 'Luck, I don't think they know we're after them; let's take the risk and follow them,' he sounded considerably encouraged and released his foot from the brakes.

Their sighting charged me up slightly. But ever the career detective, I drummed my cigarette less right hand on the dashboard. 'Pursue MHA 9109, let's see where they take us!'

***

From the Maruti I peered restlessly at the people strolling about under street lamps on the seaside promenade, opposite the international class Taj Mahal Hotel; and then concentrated on our quarry in front. Jeet carefully evaded detection, driving steadily about fifty to a hundred meters behind them.

He nodded. 'MHA 9109's an Indian version of an old Italian Fiat model.'

I stared at the nondescript yellow-and-black Italian origin designed taxi; then took in the famous Mumbai landmark, the large brownstone Gateway of India monument. My head began to ache. A delayed reaction to the ordeal we'd been through in the building at DN Road. 'Thank God we're alive.'

The cab cruised ahead, around a well-lit junction with a large parking area right in the center.

Without taking his eyes off them Jeet took in a deep breath, as though thinking of the incident pained him. 'Mystifying, they left us untied...'

'Took our cell phones, but left our guns?' I interjected.

'And our personal effects,' he shook his head perplexedly and swung the Maruti left, still following them. He paused till we reached the end of a short, dark lane, and turned towards the right. 'Normally they'd search and rob us, at least empty our wallets.'

I tried to assuage the tension building up within me by gazing out of my side window at a large, dark, tree-lined park and the row of Art deco buildings across it. 'And the door was open purposely?'

'Absolutely confusing all right!' Jeet agreed.

For a moment we stayed silent. I mentally dwelt on the situation we'd faced earlier. Jeet concentrated on the vehicle ahead, now on a broad arterial road, as they swept past a large railway station with colored suburban local trains visible from the thoroughfare. Passengers poured out of the station, even at this hour.

Suddenly I asked about something that had been at the back of my mind all the while. 'Saw a bearded man in a white *dhoti*?'

'No.'

'He hit you from behind, on your head, twice.'

He inclined his head slightly. 'Took me by surprise.'

'Behaved oddly, too controlled, as though he didn't want to hurt us badly, think he hit both of us twice.'

Jeet took a quick look at the Police Commissionerate on the left, before turning away. He followed the taxi to the right along a strangely silent but well-lit road. After another sharp left turn about a hundred meters later, we headed north.

Jeet appeared to make an attempt to focus his mind on what we'd just discussed, and somehow it took too much effort. I barely heard him say above the sounds of the engine, 'cannot take the flyover, we're going through Mohammed Ali Road.' He increased his decibel level, changed his tone and shook his head, an irked sarcastic smile on his lips. 'But the bearded creep succeeded in knocking us out?'

I finished my smoke, threw out the butt and waited till he overtook a red city transport bus, then insisted, 'can't forget his bearded face. Struck as if afraid to hit hard.' I paused and struggled to verbalize the feeling my brief glimpse of him evoked. 'Didn't draw blood, yet knocked us out.'

'Hmm, he could've hit us with full force, and thrown us somewhere,' Jeet assented.

We cruised on the well-illuminated, nearly empty Mohammed Ali Road, below the flyover, through old wooden buildings with clothes strung out to dry on old-fashioned balconies. A continuous row of commercial establishments at street level, closed at this hour, gave the impression of it being a busy business area during the day.

I stretched and sat up. Higher possibilities whirred around my mind. I spoke one out. 'Way to the airport?'

Jeet frowned once or twice as though he knew something and had to dwell on the thought for some time to confirm it. Ahead the cab slowed down and eased left onto an intersecting road. He smiled slightly, and answered my question. 'Not after the last turn; we're in a Muslim area.'

Outside, a crowded, congested feeling pervaded despite everything being closed and empty. Sidewalks, now partly obscured by desolate wooden kiosks, were packed with rows of people sleeping on straw mats or dirty sheets like sardines in a can. Large Arabic-like script on garish green and red banners strung across the road confirmed Jeet's statement.

We were in a Muslim quarter.

I looked at him once or twice, certain he had something up his sleeve.

He stared raptly at MHA 9109 and shook his head. 'Tan Win Lee?'

'What of him?' I quickly tried to encourage him to elaborate.

'Area ahead was like a China Town in the old days,' he began slowly.

'Not officially called a China Town like in Kolkata; but had restaurants for Chinese, private clubs, dentists, shoe makers...'

I noted a dark lonely fenced-off park on one side. When I looked ahead once more, my heart became like the Titanic; cold, freezing and sinking fast. They had disappeared somewhere to the right.

'Walked about this area before,' Jeet, calm and cool, scanned the road casually. 'They've gone into one of the most dangerous areas of Mumbai, Shuklaji Street.'

'Been here before will be of great help, the shabby-looking area disorients me completely.'

My cardiac function felt human again, although I could still distinctly hear my heart beat too loud. He had his eye on them all the while, now he slowed the Maruti to a crawl and turned right. And we sighted them again.

I breathed a little easier when a tall street light revealed a box-like room at the corner. Khaki uniformed policemen seated on a bench were apparently ready for action if needed.

Then came the smell. From a garbage dump and a urinal. Strong enough to bring tears to my eyes. Ahead, the cab slowed down. Jeet reduced speed too, prolonging the olfactory assault, and slowly moved ahead. The odors became negligible only after he edged onwards, till we were between a dirty apartment complex and a white, blue and green mosque with tall minarets, both looming over us on the narrow dark road.

In front, the taxi stopped. Jeet swung the wheel to one side and stopped immediately. About seventy-five meters ahead, Crawford and Lee stepped out onto the dimly lit street with their bags. Crawford stood by unmindful of passers-by as Lee paid the fare. Before the cabby could drive away, they rushed into an adjoining building and disappeared.

'We'll have to go in after them,' I said.

Jeet slowly eased the Maruti forward. 'Too dangerous, we'll park opposite and wait; then go in and grab them.'

VII

Jeet parked the Maruti on the opposite side of the road. We faced a Chinese restaurant, which stood opposite, a little to the right. He backed into a niche in front of the closed gates of a lower middle-class housing colony. Just adjacent to us, a long, ramshackle, single floored hut-like structure with a rusted corrugated-iron roof extending a little onto the road, provided us with a screen. From around it we stared at the restaurant.

'They're in that Chinese restaurant, I've eaten there a couple of times years ago.' Jeet, hands on the steering wheel, gestured with an inclination of his head towards a two-storied brick house with a sloping red-tiled roof. Another floor rose behind the two-storied façade. 'Get authentic Chinese food here.'

'Why don't we go in?' I asked.

'Too dangerous. We'll wait till they come out, or we enter later when the street is empty.'

I saw a white board with something in indecipherable blue Chinese script, over the entrance to the building. Just inside, an enclosed wooden stairway led upwards. A little ahead, over the blue-and-white actual doorway of the restaurant, I read the blood-red English lettering on another white signboard. "Fiery Dragonhead Chinese Restaurant".

Jeet shook his head a little and pointedly stared upwards, above the restaurant, at wide open, blue, wooden-framed glass-paned windows with tightly drawn curtains which obscured the view of the interior. A light in a glass box hanging on an iron rod highlighted the words "Welcome" and the number "420".

'Wooden stairway leads to a brothel upstairs,' Jeet said.

I gazed at the structure, and watched a couple of men enter and climb the stairway. I hesitated, stretched out in the cramped front seat of the Maruti and closed my eyes, feeling unreal and disoriented.

Our experiences at DN Road hadn't left Jeet's mind. He said in a manner that indicated uncertainty about whether he'd deduced a supposition right. 'Don't think there's another exit. So we'll see them leaving.'

Not being sure about our course of action myself, I nodded slowly and reached into my trouser pocket for a cigarette and my lighter. 'What could they be up to?'

'Only smuggling, I think.'

I puffed in silence, not having an answer. My eyes gradually adapting to the street lights, I began to absorb the street scene.

Poverty-stricken people in dirty bush shirts and trousers, or vests and shorts, or *dhoti*'s; and shod in slippers or unshod, passed by scarcely glancing at anyone. Many intoxicated persons staggered past, no one giving them a second glance. A number of men in spotless white and sporting Moorish-style fez caps, with serious expressions on their faces, moved about as if on important business somewhere.

'Ultimate in sin all over for Crawford and company.' Jeet sighed suddenly, getting my attention. He leaned back in his seat. 'Also gang lords controlling smuggling businesses based here.'

I nodded; and both of us quietly surveyed the area in front. A couple of well-dressed gents, eyes down, came out of the brothel "420" stairway and disappeared down the street. Dim street lights illuminated rows of tiny, shuttered shops. Signboards identified the barber shops, watch and radio repair units, tiny convenience stores selling cigarettes, even doctor's dispensaries, and many other kinds of small retail outlets.

Without taking his eyes off the Fiery Dragonhead, he clicked his tongue and said, albeit somewhat doubtfully, 'Murthy was hiding something, probably their link to a drug smuggling gang.'

***

I reflected for a moment. Crawford and Lee had entered a restaurant. Somehow I didn't feel it was only for a meal. But I couldn't infer further.

Jeet gave bored consideration to the customers of the brothels. 'Commercial sex worker territory. Part of the Foras Road, Kamatipura and Grant Road red-light area, reputed largest in the world.'

I shook some ash off my cigarette. 'Has to be more in it. Crawford wouldn't have come all the way from London for girls.'

He glanced at me. For a fraction of a second I glimpsed a row of white teeth when he smiled briefly. 'Street's full of shops selling fake stuff and smuggled goods, plenty of adulterated, spurious country liquor joints, Hong Kong-style opium dens, gambling dens, brothels, homosexual brothels... aha!' He opened his mouth wider as if he'd hit pay dirt. 'These *hijda's* have dens around.'

'Those transvestites, one of whom was murdered by Crawford at Dadar beach?'

'Right. They're a quasi-religious sect.' He cleared his throat audibly and added, '*Hijda* gangs also kidnap boys and girls from remote areas, sell them and themselves from nearby brothels.'

A Dunhill between my teeth, I recalled Murthy making a face every time they were mentioned. 'Not a bunch of saints?'

'No, mostly big, tough, rough, freak buggers, controlling others of their own kind,' he said, looking about the now almost desolate street. 'They're accepted by our poor... majority of the population.'

It explained something. 'Maybe Murthy isn't taking the murder seriously.'

Jeet shook his head and remained silent.

No more of the sporadic vehicles could be seen now passing by on the empty, ominously silent street. A few men staggered past, all in extreme states of inebriation.

Jeet watched them and suddenly opined earnestly, 'Murthy will never not take his job seriously. I'm certain he's up to something more.'

I took a drag and uttered non-committally, *hijdas*, to imagine till now I'd never even heard of them!'

***

Jeet waited as though to gather his thoughts and shifted uneasily.

I chuckled softly. 'Crawford messed up with the murder, these *hijda's*... and Chinese.'

'Here no Chinese ever reported in smuggling gangs or extortion or in anything criminal.'

'Then what?' I asked.

'Don't know; except this area is dangerous with every type of criminal activity and their effects.' He took his eyes off the Fiery Dragonhead and surveyed the area around.

I followed his eyes. At the end of the small block, stinking garbage overflowed from two yellow steel bins and spilled onto the road. Street lights revealed groups of urchins in filthy rags seated nearby, around small fires. Some searched among the rubbish with slow semi-paralyzed movements. Another lot sat in small circles, lit matches under a silver foil and took turns inhaling.

'Taking brown sugar, adulterated heroin,' Jeet disclosed.

'Horrible,' I blurted out, almost throwing up.

'Criminal gangs use cheap labor, slaves, couriers; even pay in drugs and Xerox toner to slowly poison and finish them, then get new workers who get finished in the same way.'

I looked away, wrinkled my nose and discarded my cigarette butt. 'Crawford's doing drugs, and mixed up with a gang.' I tried to shut out the scenes I'd just witnessed and attempted to concentrate on our problem. 'Maybe the murders at Dadar beach and DN Road, are like druggies settling dues?'

'Only solution, he's into drugs,' Jeet agreed nodding, and gestured with both hands towards the Fiery Dragonhead. 'And something to do with the Chinese in there!'

***

Now across the road no activity could be discerned. Street lights cast patches of light onto the pavement less filthy road which was caked with mud. Large black furry rats, looking as though they'd popped out of a science fiction movie, scurried about and disappeared into the filthy alleys and gutters around. Far to our right, a couple of black-and-yellow taxicabs parked for the night, stood out among the scores of black bicycles with their chrome handlebars shining in the dim light.

No one came in or left the Fiery Dragonhead since we'd seen Crawford and Lee enter it. And customers had long since stopped going in or coming out of the brothel "420" above it.

I felt like a schoolboy readying to confront a bigger, stronger bully. I decided on another Dunhill. 'Are they still inside?'

Jeet didn't answer. Instead he stiffened slightly, placed his hands on my lap and inclined his head towards the right.

I quickly removed my hand from my pocket and observed a dark blue Swaraj Mazda van with a yellow and red stripe painted across it, closing in on the now empty street. Reminding me of the old London Dodge Black Maria's, it cruised past slowly.

I detected men in crisp khaki, with SLR's, their brown wooden stocks resting on the floor and black steel barrels glinting in the dim light, grimly looking about. A police Sergeant, yellow chevrons on his sleeve, black Sterling sub-machine gun hanging from a strap around his shoulder, sighted us but didn't do anything. Crackling static from radio handsets broke the eerie silence till the van, engine purring softly, went past.

I felt a surge of emotion. 'Get help to enter, backup?'

'Cannot help us. Different laws apply where illegal activity quietly tolerated for social reasons. Remember how uncooperative Murthy was.'

'And we don't have our cell phones to contact him.'

'More than just that,' Jeet insisted. 'All in some kind of interconnected web, traps people in their slots; area wise, then all try to benefit from each other.'

'What's it got to do with Crawford?'

'Police don't act freely in certain places. Like having one hand tied behind their backs.' He shook his head. 'Act on information on specific issues only. In areas like this, after half a dozen permissions from various authorities who are linked to interests connected to the businesses around.'

'Keep plenty employed, occupied,' I said. 'Providing services, which somehow balances the harm caused, so are tacitly tolerated.'

He turned to me. I sensed his mind working overtime from the expression on his face. 'Right. Act on certain proof. Although I believe Murthy suspects far more.'

Somehow he'd relieved me of the despair gradually overcoming me. I got the hang of what he was trying to say. 'Using us to probe deeper, unearth something to enable him to eliminate not just the bit players, but smash the big fish.'

'Exactly!'

***

Jeet checked his watch, prompting me to do the same. 'Don't think they'll come out tonight.'

'Already two-o-clock, time we did something,' I said, taking my Glock out of my holster and reassuringly feeling the mold checkering on the pistol grip. I didn't exactly relish being used, risking my life, to unearth something bigger, of which I had no idea.

No one had entered or left the Fiery Dragonhead or the brothel "420" for quite some time. The rest of the street, silent and still now, appeared to be sleeping off its exertions, as if having had enough for the day. But the Fiery Dragonhead building somehow vaguely exuded an aura of something very dangerous going on inside.

Jeet drew his pistol and checked the fire selector. 'Semi-automatic mode until problems.' He clicked his tongue. 'Looks like we got to go in.'

'About time,' I agreed.

A sinister light emanating from the open doors of the restaurant lit a small circle on the bleak, deathly still street. Rays of light escaping from between tightly drawn green curtains of brothel "420" upstairs added to the unreal, scary atmosphere. No sound could be heard at all, save the scurrying of large rats. I felt like in the middle of a Stephen King horror movie. Scared, on edge, full of qualms; and now here I imagined the whole red-roofed, blue structure alive, daring us, inviting us in to sure doom.

Jeet shrugged his shoulders, transferred his Glock to his left hand, and opened the car door with his right hand. 'Time we enter the place.'

***

Arms outstretched, guns ready, alert to any eventuality, we paused for a moment before the open blue-and-white wooden doors of the Fiery Dragonhead. Quickly we stepped inside, rapidly moving to the right and left, waving our weapons about to cover every inch of the interior.

We found ourselves amidst a desolating emptiness that aggravated our nervousness. Red-topped tables and stools in the aseptic interior, devoid of the usual accoutrement found on restaurant tables, seemed to be fretting, as if for some custom. Only our labored breathing and Nikes softly echoing on the stone flooring interrupted the pregnant stillness which somehow seemed like a calm before a storm.

'No one,' I whispered, shaking a little.

'Got to be somewhere,' Jeet retorted. Knees bent slightly, he kept moving, gun in both hands outstretched and ready.

A plain wall calendar, a colored painting of the infant Jesus and the Virgin Mary and an ancient white-faced black-handed wall clock on the wall behind the counter somehow lent a homely appearance to the restaurant, in spite of the frightening situation we were in.

On the ebony brown wooden counter I recognized small pictures of Catholic saints which somehow added tension to the grating silence.

Jeet turned to a small, unpainted brick-and-cement-walled room, kicked open a thick, black teakwood door with a thud, but stepped aside.

After a seconds wait, he peeped inside, gun ready and said, 'private room for families.'

I cautiously climbed a few steps by the side of the counter under a "No Admission" sign, across a waist-high enclosure wall, to a slightly higher level. An unmistakable aroma among the metal pots and pans stored in wooden racks, two jet-black stoves and two large cylinders of cooking gas, revealed that a meal had been eaten shortly before.

'Just cooked something here,' I whispered sharply.

Returning from the kitchen, I watched Jeet searching with hawk's eyes, Glock pointing ahead, at an open passageway between a couple of galvanized steel water drums and two brown steel cupboards. A blue checked curtain blocked our view beyond. Gun ready, I moved aside and covered him. I noted a small red fire extinguisher on the wall above.

He inclined his head. 'Got to be a secret…' He sidestepped rapidly, hurting my eyes momentarily as he knelt down and pointed his gun upwards, aiming at the curtained-off passageway.

The curtain had moved a little to one side. A short, stocky China man in a purple robe peered out at us. He was bald, with a thin mustache like a black string on his repulsively large, oily visage. I flushed with pins and needles all over my body for an instant as my eyes locked with his hooded, chinky, inscrutable glare. His eyes lashed with malignant hatred.

My index finger tightened within the Glock's trigger guard. Countless sessions of practice enabled me to sense two of the triple safeties negating. Now on razor's edge, the slightest pressure and I'd fire.

I then focused on his gun. A Chinese version of the Russian AK-47 called Chinese Type 56 Assault Rifle. Commercial versions were semiautomatic and erroneously called AK-56. The Chinese People's Liberation Army (PLA)'s standard issue had among other versions, a folding bayonet under its barrel, and was fully automatic. The gangster in front of us had a folding bayonet on his Type 56, indicating it was a fully automatic, PLA standard issue.

Before we could react, he disappeared behind the curtain.

No half starved worker this, or even Tan Win Lee, but some kind of well-fed prosperous gangster of the type seldom seen outside, at least in Mumbai.

'He's gone!' I whispered hoarsely.

'Identified the Chinese Type 56 from the folding bayonet,' a tense Jeet said. Then in complete contrast to the stocky China man, the lean, lanky Jeet, knees bent, arms outstretched, leapt forward with surprising agility.

He enjoined, 'cover me.'

***

With a bound which could have been the envy of an Olympic gymnast, he reached the open wooden doors of the passage. I followed him with deliberate control and stood opposite him. He pushed the curtain aside and knees bent, Glock ready, quickly stepped in.

'Nothing.' He peered into the two-meters-wide passage over the steel tubs with familiar Pepsi's and Coke's, which provided a contrast to a large washbasin covered by a steel grating full of live crabs.

I contemplated a red door with "Toilet" written in thick black lettering at the end of the passage, about six meters ahead.

'Impossible,' Jeet exclaimed, genuinely foxed.

I solved the mystery. 'Another curtain ahead, left.' I observed, feeling tension rise within me.

Jeet strode there, flattened himself against the wall and pushed aside the thick black canvas curtain. I carefully stepped towards him, ready for action.

About a score dank, black-stone steps of over a foot each, led downwards at a thirty-five degree angle. Jeet went down. I followed him equally alert.

The stairway leveled off into a dark humid passage two meters wide and ten meters long. I strained my eyes staring ahead. A little before the far end, a tiny sliver of light emanated from a seemingly blank side wall, as though from under a shut door or another thick curtain.

We edged forward with frayed nerves, focusing on the light. Any-time Crawford could blast us to kingdom come with that G-11; and the China man would be equally dangerous with his Type 56. We got nearer the light. It came from under a thick, black, canvas curtain.

Claustrophobic and completely disoriented, I watched Jeet lie flat on the cold stone ground. He motioned me to do the same. I did so, feeling the sweat trickling over my brow. Cautiously he raised the thick, black canvas a little. Enough for us to peep in from underneath.

Half a dozen naked bulbs hanging from the ceiling lit up a small cavern. Piles of dirty white sacks filled with cement, I recognized their characteristic odor, lay strewn irregularly about. A brick-walled room on one side somehow gave the impression of enclosing a stairway leading upwards. A possible escape route upstairs and across the brothel "420" and down through the wooden stairway we'd seen outside.

But no sign of anyone about. The absence of Crawford, Lee and the mysterious China man aggravated the haunted house-like atmosphere pervading.

'Ambush situation,' Jeet whispered.

His warning and the fresh wet mud and cement odor compounded the clear danger signals I felt. 'Let's get out.'

That did it. I'd spoken too loud. Blinking, I registered the flash a little before a loud crack zoomed through the hushed quietness. A single pistol shot. The curtain jerked away from Jeet's hands. He reacted instantaneously, grabbing me, and wriggled and squirmed out of the line of fire. When he stood up, he literally pulled me upright too.

A burst of automatic fire smashed into where we'd been a fraction of a second earlier. The cavern exploded with deafening sounds. The canvas curtain disintegrated into thousands of dark pieces, floated momentarily in the air and in a twinkling, showered downwards. The cloud of dust and stinging acrid smoke rapidly enlarged as bullets spattered on the passage wall from fusillade after fusillade. Spent slugs ricocheted frightfully close.

I' d barely recognized the shots coming from Chinese Type 56 Assault Rifles, when Jeet directed me, 'Let's go.'

***

Jeet sprinted out soundlessly. I raced behind him, endlessly or so it seemed, till I breathlessly scuffled up the dank, black-stone steps, turning a few times to see if we were being pursued. We breathed a mite easier. The firing continued at our previous position. They didn't know we'd left. When I pushed open the curtain, Jeet had already gone past the tubs of Pepsi's and Coke's.

He yelled at me, 'shoot and keep them away, exits locked from outside, we're trapped inside.'

My heart fell. I instinctively turned, Glock ready. Rotating the pistol grip in my right palm, I thumbed the magazine catch, releasing it. With a practiced movement, I extricated the nineteen-round feed with my left hand and placed it in my pocket. In a jiffy I slid in the thirty-three-round magazine and clicked the fire selector to automatic. Then I adjusted the slide, savoring like never before the metallic snap that came when the first round chambered.

Shouts, yells and footsteps came from below. They'd caught on to the fact we'd decamped. Thank God for all the compulsory practice at Pemberton's private firing range. Although feeling raw and naked, the training showed. Before anyone showed up from below on the thirty-five degree steps sloping downwards, I pointed the weapon, gripping it firmly with both hands. Then squeezed the trigger slowly, literally feeling the first safety negating, the firing pin lifting, releasing and striking the primer to ignite the first round.

For a fraction of a second I hosed downwards. The dank steps reverberated with Remington's 88-grain jacketed hollow point nine millimeter rounds spraying a deadly impediment to anyone trying to follow us.

An instantaneous burst of agitated howling and expressions of utter amazement indicated the effectiveness of my fire. Then came the reaction.

Volley after volley of Type 56 bursts, like fabric tearing. I ducked and lost my footing slightly, then recovered. The angle of the steps prevented them from directly sighting me. Harmless ricochets swerved and smashed crazily onto the cement walls of the stairs in front of me, kicking up small clouds of white dust.

I pumped in another burst. The firing stopped as though someone had switched off a television set. Intensive argumentation in Chinese carried over from below. I sensed I had the upper hand and felt exhilarated all of a sudden.

Then Jeet exhorted loudly, 'come out of there.'

***

Scarcely seeing anything, I re-entered the main restaurant and stumbled into Jeet. He yanked the fire extinguisher with his left hand and raced to where I'd been. Activating it, he hurled it down the stairs, and charged back. 'To delay them.'

Out of the passage in the main restaurant, he quickly closed the wooden passage door and latched it. 'Push some tables against it.'

I aided him. We pushed two tables upright, flat top flush against the passage door.

Then I turned and glanced in apprehension at the tightly shut blue and white solid wooden doors leading to the street outside. We'd need a battering ram of the type commonly used in the middle ages to enter enemy fortresses, to get out. It also emphasized our predicament and punctured my adrenalin high.

'We're trapped?' I gasped.

He pushed me to one side. 'Away from the line of fire.'

Just in time. A stampede of footsteps and flurry of voices echoed from the other side. Ominous thuds shook the latched and barricaded door.

Then came shots, shaking the table leaning on it. I realized we literally faced an army.

The upright tables leaning against the passage door groaned and rattled furiously. Tremors from the thunderous sounds on the other side almost burst our eardrums. Then a table fell. Wooden splinters began raining outwards from the edges. A shower of wooden chips and dust began to create a frightful haze. A loud crack startled us, then came another, and another.

Jeet, face pale and pinched, spoke urgently. 'The partitioned-off family room.'

Never before did I appreciate the cemented brick construction and the solid teakwood doors of any enclosure more than I did now. We ran inside and Jeet closed and latched the door. I roughly lifted the dining table inside and barricaded the door with it. Then we pushed the chairs against it. Just in time. Another louder crack rent the air from outside, followed by sounds of a large mob shouting uncontrollably and shooting blindly. They had broken the passageway door and were rushing into the restaurant.

Within an appallingly short time a loud knocking sound came from outside the room we were trapped in, curdling my blood.

Jeet who looked white as a sheet, still spoke strongly. 'No way out.'

***

'What do we do?' I asked, breathing in gulps.

A series of thuds muzzled Jeet's reply. The table against the door began to rattle. And the inevitable firing didn't begin, instead I detected the sounds of an axe being used.

Jeet, in a jerky movement, turned and stared at the floor-to-ceiling wallpaper with a poetic scene of a lazy blue stream flowing through a field of daffodils. Not being William Wordsworth, especially here, he reached out without any qualms and roughly tried to tear it off. He didn't succeed too well. Yet he kept trying, searching for something.

Delay the inevitable, I thought, and turned and faced the door. Effective thumps of an axe being used, slamming onto the woodwork resounded into my ear. Still, the thick teakwood of the door ought to hold out for some time, I reasoned.

My mind wandered crazily. Images of my Kensington home kept floating in front of my eyes. And of Morgan of Pemberton. What on earth did I do, that he'd got me into this mess. But a conditioned-in work ethic took over and I made an effort to concentrate on our predicament.

I tried to calculate our chances. The peculiar claustrophobic situation unnerved and paralyzed me. Still I mumbled out aloud, 'Thirty-three rounds at a thousand three hundred a minute, one point five two seconds... no, fired two bursts already, have the other magazine...'

'Aha, a bloody window!' Jeet interrupted exultantly.

I turned so fast that I felt a twinge of muscle strain on my neck. The wall paper had hidden a window.

However, my rapidly escalating mood not only nose-dived like an aircraft stalling into the sea, but vanished completely, as if it had sunk beyond trace in the murky depths. Stout iron bars covered the opening and we were stuck again.

Jeet placed his Glock on the sill, and grabbed the bars and pushed, groaning with acute physical discomfort. Then he tried to pull, screaming aloud with the effort.

The table against the door rattled like in the middle of an earthquake well up on the Richter Scale.

I resigned myself to our fate. To think that after all those years in Pemberton it would end like this. In an eatery right in the middle of a miserable vice area in an alien land.

I lay flat on the ground and faced the shaking door at an angle. Strangely calm and alert, I readied myself for a fight to the finish, awaiting the end.

***

Jeet unbeaten still, commanded me calmly and coolly, despite the gravity of the life-threatening situation, 'Hold that chair over your head, protection from ricochets.'

I grabbed a wooden chair and held it over me.

He opened fire, aiming at the barred window. Unmistakable single shot sounds of a Glock 18 in its semi-automatic mode rent the air.

Between shots he cried, 'screws holding the frame of iron bars.'

I grimly counted seconds as splinters and chips of wood and the haze of gun smoke and dust gradually began to affect our breathing in the enclosed area. I coughed once or twice.

Jeet fired at certain points, upwards at an angle. Iron clanged and hurt the ears; and chunks of wooden window frame cascaded away from the point blank hits. The deafening noise overcame sounds of the racket outside. Luckily, the ricocheting slugs mostly hit the ceiling, safely away from us.

Suddenly sounds of heavy footsteps resounded from above. A couple of men ran heavily across the wooden floor of the brothel "420" above us. And down through the wooden side stairs outside, onto the street. I didn't know what it portended and didn't have time to think about it.

Then Jeet stopped firing and whooped in delight. I turned, and saw him throw a frame with iron bars to one side. With controlled haste he opened the smashed up windows and a rush of fresh air breezed inside and enveloped us.

Smoothly and evenly, like a practicing athlete, he leapt outside and sprinted off like one of our Cruise missiles during an exercise, zooming away from Greenham Common or Molesworth.

I pocketed the nineteen-round magazine and followed him, struggling a little, and got across the street outside without mishap.

Outside, overcome with relief, I jogged up the dirty alley past the yellow steel bins overflowing with stinking rubbish, with the groups of urchins around. They didn't even look up as I passed them and caught up with Jeet.

He was already in the Maruti, engine idling, Glock ready in his hands.

Immediately I got in, he holstered his gun and eased the vehicle forward and turned right.

'They're not following us out,' he said.

I was panting like a greyhound at the finish of an exhausting pursuit and couldn't reply; instead I choked again at the sight in-front of us.

About fifty meters ahead, a small white rectangular box-like car stood under a street light, side door wide open. Someone at the wheel loudly exhorted Crawford and Lee to hurry inside. They got in fast. Before they could slide the side door shut, the car screamed away, kicking up a small cloud of dust.

Jeet urgently told me, 'I'm following them!'

VIII

I shifted uncomfortably about in the cramped front seat of the gradually accelerating Maruti, and muttered hoarsely, 'they'd been inside all the while?'

Jeet shifted gear and roared unsteadily ahead. Surprisingly cool and calm, his voice penetrated my numb mind. 'Footsteps we heard were theirs running from the cavern, to up and across brothel "420" upstairs, and down through the wooden side stairway.'

We raced past the mosque and tried to catch up, jumping and thumping over enough potholes and rough spots to label the road a moonscape.

Still I breathed a little easier. This despite the odiferous stink prevailing.

No one else had come out from the Fiery Dragonhead, and while we were inside no one had tampered with our car.

With some suspense, I glanced over my shoulder once or twice, Glock ready. Nothing but a silent, deserted street met my eyes. No one charged out of the inferno we'd been trapped in a little while earlier.

I stared at the box-like room at the end of Shuklaji Street as we raced past. When we'd first entered the street, earlier, I'd seen armed cops there.

Now its wooden door was shut securely. Within a fraction of a second that I got to gaze at the spot, I registered no policeman or anyone else in sight in the ghostly still, pale circle of light that illuminated the structure and sidewalk in front of it.

Jeet braked hard, tires screeching noisily on the macadam, almost clipping the pavement opposite, as he swung onto the comparatively broader main road, and thundered behind the vehicle carrying our quarry.

I jerked slightly as Jeet decreased speed radically. I regarded him and the vehicle ahead. 'Can't we go faster?'

'Car is erratic at high speeds, lucky so is that one,' he explained, and made no attempt to close in. Instead he cruised on silently, through the archaic-styled wooden buildings on both sides of the empty road, with small signboards advertising commercial services on the railings of wooden balconies. Wooden kiosks completely obscured the pavements. Although empty at this hour, they disclosed that this was an extremely busy area during the day.

'Were on the old Grant Road,' Jeet said.

I leaned wearily back, pistol in hand, trying to enlighten my mental processes while glancing quizzically at him now and then. He accelerated gradually, but they remained about a hundred meters ahead.

'Their vehicle is a Maruti Omni.' He spoke briskly and optimistically with no sign of any adverse effect due to the encounter earlier. 'Have to wear them down.'

'We're stuck without our mobiles?'

'Cops will soon be tracking us. This kind of chase can't go on indefinitely.' I nodded and shivered in my seat, a delayed reaction to the stress of the earlier encounter. 'Some powerful gang, with incredible firepower?'

'Odd, well-equipped China men are foreigners.' He glanced to the left and right of an intersecting road, and cruised on behind them. 'And that cavern...'

He paused, steadied the Maruti and eased it over a bridge. 'Big shock that. Locals would know of it when it was being built, and tell police intelligence, who bound to inform Murthy,' he raptly stared at the Omni in front, which turned left at a junction of a number of roads, and sneered acidly. 'Unless... unless, police intend finding out more.'

'Build up a case?'

'No one interfered, they had to have heard the shooting from outside,' he informed me, then irrelevantly said. 'Nana's Chowk.' And still tailing them as they took a westward road, he urgently commanded. 'Keep your gun out of sight.'

Barely had I switched the magazines and holstered the Glock, when we passed a blue and yellow and red striped Toyota Qualis multi-utility vehicle; parked right in the center of the fully illuminated road. Policemen with Sterling's and SLR's stood around the Qualis and stared at us as we passed them. But they made no move to follow us or do anything else.

***

I stiffened in my cramped seat, mind abuzz with possibilities. Most of them flawed, not explaining all the factors, the puzzling questions I'd inputted into my thoughts.

'Waiting till we lead them somewhere,' Jeet surmised with uncertainty, ignoring the cops and focusing on Crawford and Lee in the white Omni ahead. 'That a mobile police post, essential to maintain peace in certain areas.'

I watched the Omni climb steadily uphill on a relatively straight road, and then roll downhill. Less than a kilometer away from Nana's Chowk, a concrete flyover ahead passed over another junction with a number of intersecting roads.

Jeet gestured to the right with his head and drove on. 'Kemps Corner.'

I looked across him in the right hand drive car. Exceptional lighting illuminated another Toyota Qualis by the side of the flyover. An Inspector in a peaked cap, hand on his brown leather holster, bent forward and peered deliberately at us as we sped past. Armed constables, black steel Sterling's hanging from shoulder straps; or with SLR's, brown wooden butts on the ground, stared on impassively, somehow giving the impression that they could burst into action if given the necessary command.

Seconds later, under the flyover, Jeet braked and with our tires screeching in protest, dragged the Maruti to the left and now tagged our quarry from about fifty meters behind.

Jeet hissed between his teeth, 'wrong way up a one-way street, going to Malabar Hill.'

The congested, crowded and dusty feeling cleared substantially as we rumbled up a fairly steep slope with green foliage on both sides and no other traffic around. Jeet grimly ensured that they remained at the same distance in front. After a while, palatial villas and posh apartment blocks which seemed to be like a planet away from Shuklaji Street, loomed over us on the road, which now gradually sloped downwards.

Cruising steadily about fifty meters behind them, Jeet still didn't try to close the gap.

I could see their figures; I couldn't exactly make out whether it was Crawford or Lee in the rear seat of the Omni. Someone glared at us through the rear windshield. Then the Omni U-turned onto a slightly sharper downward slope

Jeet pressed a little harder on the accelerator, then slowed down and shifted gears.

I gaped at the start of the down slope, at yet another mobile police post. The ubiquitous blue Toyota Qualis again, with Sterling and SLR toting uniformed constables watching us with interest but not reacting.

***

'Walkeshwar.' Jeet tonelessly climbed gears and rolled down a long slope.

I peered out at the old structures on the left which continued along the length of the road, unlike on the right. Here a high compound wall with green-leaved trees and overhanging foliage gave way to an elaborate gate, with a rising barrier and a sentry booth. Armed guards stood at attention clasping SLR's. A couple of khaki-clad cops, some of them armed, milled about a strategically placed blue Tata truck.

Without looking anywhere but ahead, Jeet curtly informed me. 'State Governor's residence.'

I nodded, involuntarily getting faintly amused. In front, past a couple of tall apartment buildings, the right wall now overlooked a broad ocean bay. Sea water glimmered in the moonlight.

I chuckled audibly. 'As guarded as a maximum security cell in Brixton?'

'They've been instructed to leave us alone,' Jeet replied. 'Then no one can aid us unless ordered from above.'

Ahead the Omni turned right along a long sea front road.

***

Scarcely three hundred yards from the posse at the gate of the Governor's residence, street lights lit a small room which heralded the start of a small pavement parallel to a sandy beach. Uniformed cops sat on folding chairs grasping their weapons. Nearby, a Swaraj Mazda van stood as though ready for a prolonged chase. A police Sergeant glared at us from amongst them. He held a radio handset to his ear. I sensed he was itching to roar into action, but was being restrained by some unknown hand.

'Police have spotted us. They're signaling around,' Jeet said.

'What will they do?'

'Blockade the road on our probable route, conduct a naka bandi.'

Jeet followed the Omni, sweeping towards the right onto a long sea front road which curved like the blade of the scimitar of an Indian Sultan. As the unique atmosphere common the public beaches hit us – a sea, sand and rocky feeling, Jeet stepped on the accelerator.

'Chowpatty beach,' he notified me.

The response in front to the increase in sped came instantly. They zoomed ahead with a roar heard even by us about fifty meters behind. And we raced past an assortment of snack stalls, well-lit although closed at this hour.

Jeet held the wheel at arm's length. He kept his eyes glued to the road and continued to floor the accelerator. 'Clear straight road, now we try to close in.'

Our speeding Maruti began to shudder and jerk. The unstable whining sound got worse as the speedometer needle climbed, despite Jeet's rock hard hands on the wheel. But we inched closer and closer.

Tensely I waited, ears shattered by the extra loud engine sounds as we raced under a pedestrian footbridge, and passed yet another Swaraj Mazda van with cops around it.

'Marine Drive now onwards,' Jeet said abruptly, while concentrating at the job at hand.

Three-storied Art Deco style apartment blocks on the left, and on the right the pavemented seaside promenade with its low concrete wall keeping the sea at bay, became a blur. This in spite of the near-perfect visibility offered by a neat row of powerful street lights stationed at regular intervals on the road divider.

Suddenly the Omni veered left, screaming brakes down, and skid into a tunnel-like lobby of a large international-class hotel. Jeet slowed down like a professional rallyist, but still had to swerve frantically to enter the small lane which they'd gone into.

***

'Nariman Point area.' Jeet slowed down considerably, and guided the Maruti behind them. He picked up speed slowly, and zigzagged through the narrow streets with tall broad office blocks which loomed over us.

They twisted and turned, driving moderately fast past the massive buildings. Jeet kept them in constant view; latching onto them like a leech clinging to one's skin in a rain forest, except that he remained some distance behind; till they exited onto a relatively broader main road.

Again we drove on faster, speeding our way past two exceptionally designed concrete buildings. Sterling-toting armed policemen on the driveways and open lobbies of the office complexes ignored us.

'State government offices,' Jeet said, and tried to close in again.

The edges of two dark fenced-off parks and a large nineteenth century Victorian brownstone didn't distract us, as we traversed towards and passed a large well-lit circle with a car park. We'd passed it earlier, when chasing the taxi cab from the Royal Haven. Except they didn't know we'd been after them then.

Two khaki uniformed armed guards sporting a Sterling and a SLR respectively, mounted guard over a walled-off large villa-like brownstone that looked like the residence of an eighteenth century hereditary peer.

They scarcely gave us a glance.

'State Police Headquarters,' Jeet said, and fell in behind the Omni again, on a narrower dustier road. 'In the dock area.'

'How long will it take to get them,' I almost moaned testily. I hadn't come prepared for a situation like this.

'Don't worry,' he reassured me, momentarily looking to the right. 'Indian Naval Dockyard.'

At an elaborate gate of a well-lit securely walled installation, guards in khaki, helmeted with green bulletproof jacket's, stood at ease with their rifle's.

I didn't say anything. I'd seen enough cops to bring to book every criminal locally, many times over.

I shook a little as Jeet braked gradually. Ahead, they braked hard and slowed down in front of a large red-tiled, cream-colored structure which looked like a Town Hall. Long steps led upwards and it reminded me of a Roman senate.

Opposite the Town Hall, they attempted to turn into a narrow lane by the side of a small, dark, tree-filled park and failed. Overshooting it, they brushed a lamppost at the edge of the road, showering sparks all over like a festival firecracker.

We'd neared them, but didn't have time to disembark before they recovered and wrenched away, straight out in the relatively quiet area.

Jeet calmly shifted gear and stepped on the gas. 'Their nerves giving way,' he remarked casually. 'One more mistake and we screw them.'

I remained too tense to reply; waiting for a wirelessly signaled naka bandi on our probable route.

Lighted colonial-style buildings and modern, ugly concrete blocks, on the relatively well-lit clean road, suddenly gave way to filth and hutments on the pavement, with trucks and large cranes parked in rows.

At the point where a number of roads intersected at a junction, the usual yellow and red striped, Toyota Qualis stood by, ready to go. Armed cops, Sterling's and SLR's ready watched us intently. An Inspector in a peaked cap, pistol in a leather holster, spoke rapidly into a handset and moved his head in line with us as we passed by.

'Being tracked through their Motorola's,' Jeet quipped dryly. 'Might have company soon.'

***

We jumped and jerked along the pothole-filled road. Filthy, with patches of oil, the pavements were obscured by trucks parked on both sides of the road. An almost suffocating odor of diesel fumes, spices and chemicals hung in the air.

Jeet slowed down momentarily and then picked up speed. 'Masjid Bunder, docks, trading, wholesale markets, warehouses.'

Suddenly they disappeared into a side lane. Jeet sped up, ploughing through a large oily puddle into a street reeking of engine oil, diesel fumes, spices, chemicals and urine. At the other end four outlets exited in different directions. And they had vanished through one of them.

I strained my eyes searching for them.

'We've lost them,' Jeet cried, sounding a little stressed for the first time.

My stomach convulsing at its pit with a rapidly empty feeling of helpless anxiety, I peered desperately about on the dimly lit street.

Then came another shock. A piercing wail of sirens made us freeze temporarily. Jeet recovered within a fraction of a second. He immediately guided the Maruti to one side, stopped, and removed the key from the ignition.

***

The sirens closed in, becoming deafeningly louder and louder and stopped all of a sudden. Engines growled and revved as they approached. A Swaraj Mazda van full of cops overtook us and stopped a little in front. Uniformed and plainclothes men spilled out with an assortment of pistols, revolvers, Sterlings and SLR's, all trained on us. One man held an AK-47. Instinctively I placed my hands on the dashboard and looked behind. Two jeeploads of officer's and constables' covered us, quashing any spurious hopes of reversing and speeding away.

Static crackled from portable radio's as the cops quickly surrounded our car. Barrels glinted in the lamplight from the weapons pointing at our heads. A burly man in a faded bush shirt aimed a flashlight at our faces and barked in a rough, hard voice, 'who are you?'

Another man bent over and peered into the Maruti, searching about with another torch. 'Identification, papers?'

Jeet calmly replied, 'I'm Jeet, and this is Mister David Adams, a British private detective...'

'*Aaa-chha*... with Murthy sahib's permission,' a louder, rough, throaty voice interrupted him and added. 'Mobile kara... mobile kara.'

I saw a big grey-haired man in uniform with a peaked cap, face large and craggy, with a paunch that extended over his waist belt. Clean shaven and of medium height, three gleaming silver stars on his shoulder epaulets identified him as an Inspector. 'I'm Nagwekar, Senior Inspector, Crime.'

He was the man whose cell phone number had been given to us, to contact Murthy.

Jeet sat still, arms on the wheel and explained, 'Nagwekar sahib, we lost our mobiles in a fight at DN Road.'

Somehow I sensed Nagwekar knew of the encounter at DN Road; but not of our cell phones which were missing.

An abrupt voice asserted, 'no Maruti Omni has left this area'.

Nagwekar, rough, weather-beaten face with specks of grey on his cheeks and eyebrows, leaned forward and looked us over. Satisfied with his spot appraisal he disclosed, 'followed two vehicles from Grant Road.'

I shut my eyes for a second to clear my mind. 'But they've escaped.'

'Aha, Masjid Station.' Jeet turned and stared at Nagwekar. The expression on his face was as if he'd just discovered the key to solving a million-dollar crossword puzzle. 'May have left the Omni and taken a local.'

Nagwekar, with a manner and determination exactly the opposite of what his large body indicated, made a swift appreciation and an immediate decision. He turned to his posse and snapped commandingly. 'Chalo, to Masjid Station.'

***

Less than half-a-minute later, on a small, dusty, smelly, street lined with hovels, at the foot of a silver painted foot bridge crossing over half-a-dozen or so railway tracks, I felt like falling on my knees and thanking God for Jeet's presence. The white Omni lay there, silent and empty, as he'd predicted.

My experience in the field for Pemberton told me something. 'Parked at an odd angle, abandoned in a hurry.'

Jeet acknowledged my observation with a nod and stepped out of the car. I followed him out, towards Nagwekar, who exuded an air of repressed energy.

The Senior Inspector laid a hard eye upon us as though carrying on gauging us. I sensed Jeet got a momentary look of unequivocal approval, before he boomed. 'Gone to the station, my men are checking.' Before we could reply, a shout caught our attention. A plainclothes man walked down the foot bridge. A short, starved-looking, ugly beggar, with raw, pus-filled wounds on stubs where his fingers and toes ought to be, accompanied him.

'Begs on the bridge,' a stocky cop in a cream bush shirt and dark trousers told Nagwekar.

The beggar said something unintelligible to me. In a *dhoti* of an indeterminate muddy color, filthy sandals and nothing else, and with ribs sticking out of his chest, he elicited instant sympathy.

Jeet translated for my benefit. 'Two China men and one European looking man took an early morning local.'

'Can't we go after them?' I enquired, losing hope rapidly.

Nagwekar turned to me and waved his arms towards the tracks. 'Can leave the train at many stations.'

The sun had crept up imperceptibly, its rays gradually lighting up the morning sky, manufacturing a new day. Under the bridge, groups of urchins in dirty black rags with indistinguishable faces, inhaled brown sugar via silver foils over small fires. They ignored the long tram-like colored suburban locals which trundled past with ever increasing frequency.

Nagwekar directed the beggar to return. He barked a series of orders to the uniformed cops near the van. The volume of their

Motorola handsets increased considerably. He motioned towards me. 'Give me descriptions. I'm signaling my main Control Room to direct GRP at all stations to lookout and arrest them.'

Immensely heartened (at least the cops were now cooperating with us), I described Crawford with as much clarity as I could. Then Jeet aided me in detailing a convincing portrait of Tan Win Lee.

When we finished, Nagwekar gazed at us questioningly.

I eyed him apologetically. 'Didn't see the third, the driver.'

Jeet nodded in agreement.

'Know he's Chinese also, from the beggar.' Nagwekar lifted his cap and tousled his grey hair, letting go for a second.

He replaced his cap and supervised his men as they flashed out a call in Marathi, the local language.

Jeet and I stood by. I wanted to be clear about everything, at least as much as could be cleared. 'What's GRP?'

Jeet volunteered at length. 'Big Indian Railways organization has a Railway Protection Force or RPF empowered to shoot and kill anyone stealing railway property. In cities, other crimes committed by commuters in suburban's are handled by another cadre; of city police deputed to a Government Railway Police or GRP, based at stations,' he paused and added. 'Wear red badges on their caps.'

Nagwekar, tirelessly directing his men, established he was listening to us too. 'Watch will be kept, if seen they'll be held.'

Plainclothes men were busy searching for minute clues around the abandoned Omni. Satisfied with the pre forensic processing, Nagwekar checked his watch and turned and beckoned us. 'We'll check the vehicle. You both better come to headquarters to file a report.'

IX

I expected some rancor left over from the last meeting. Instead Vivek Murthy smiled slightly, or at least attempted to indicate a kind of satisfied elation. He welcomed us in and motioned us to our chairs.

'I've to thank you two, very helpful report.'

When we'd returned to the headquarters from Masjid Station in the early morning, we'd made up a report. I also *e-mailed* another report to Sam in London. Then we went home to rest and freshen up. Now, it being about three-o-clock in the afternoon, we were back in the Commissionerate, in a meeting with the Deputy Commissioner, Crime.

Murthy bit his lip and tried to suppress a smile. 'Areas where illegal activities are tolerated, there's a watch system for protection against us, or anyone suspicious threatening their businesses...'

'Noticed our Maruti and laid a trap, sir,' Jeet interrupted him knowingly and turned to me. 'Like neighborhood watch programs in western countries.'

I shook a little. 'We're lucky to have escaped.'

'I commend you for fighting your way out.' Murthy paused, expecting us to say something. We didn't, and he gazed at us beaming in placation. 'We're releasing nine millimeter ammunition from the Police Armory for your Glocks.'

A low hum of agreement came from Jeet.

Murthy continued, 'Additional Commissioner sir, has worked on your report and sent it to Crime sir.'

Jeet quickly informed me, 'highest ranking officer in charge of the Crime Branch is a Joint Commissioner referred to as Crime sir'.

Murthy referred to his laptop and said, 'the *hijda* murdered at Dadar, allegedly by Crawford using the G-11, was one of our informers.'

I gave him a singeing glare. 'So Crawford's in some gang. Informer about what?'

Jeet's voice immediately cut through. 'And the man knifed at DN Road, sir?'

'A gang member. Thought he was spying on them and eliminated him by mistake.'

Jeet, very quick on the uptake in these matters, turned and faced me. 'That bearded man who hit us. You mentioned something wrong... put it in the report?'

This perturbed Murthy slightly. 'Atmaram, another of our informers, they killed a man yesterday mistaking him for Atmaram!'

That explained the way Atmaram attacked us. He'd saved our lives. And somehow left us with our weapons lying about. I exonerated him, 'Left us untied, and a door open.'

Murthy flushed slightly and revealed, 'he's blown. I've pulled him out. And he returned these...' Murthy opened a drawer on his desk and took out my BlackBerry and Jeet's Reliance mobile.

With delight we took our cell phones back.

I, however, suppressed my elation and asked, 'Odd at the Fiery Dragonhead no one helped us. We were in a full scale battle?'

Jeet immediately explained, 'locals and poor around live on distributed profits of smuggling and prostitution, in fear of gang lords, so will remain quiet.'

'Complained of the firing in the morning,' Murthy interjected. 'If they get to us, face a bigger danger when they go back.'

Jeet stared directly at Murthy and bluntly enquired, 'sir, better tell us more, so many China men couldn't have been there without you knowing about it?'

***

Murthy tapped his laptop and disclosed, 'a Chinese Triad from Taiwan called United Bamboo Gang is trying to use Mumbai as a base for heroin smuggling!'

A chill enveloped me for a second.

'A Crime Intelligence Unit formed with members from our anti-narcotics cell and the Narcotics Control Bureau, which comprises of Central Excise and Custom's officers on deputation, has just returned from Taipei. Met Chief Superintendent of Taipei Police Narcotics Cell; and also US Drug Enforcement Administration officials from the local embassy!'

'It's that serious?' I commented.

A Triad or Chinese mafia-like gang meant there were international ramifications. Crawford would be just a small pawn on a worldwide chessboard, controlled by kings, queens, knights and knaves. Besides they could get back at him and us anywhere.

Murthy leaned back on his chair. A half smile on his face, he elaborated, 'knew of them in Mumbai, but not their base. You've given us enough for a search warrant, or even a full scale raid.' He waved his right hand briefly towards us and tried to sound appreciative. 'Although my intelligence network reports two hideouts.'

Used us to discover their hideout. It explained why those mobile police posts didn't help us with the Omni. Thought they'd lead us to another base elsewhere.

Gently yet compellingly, Jeet blithely observed, 'instead of leading us to another base, they escaped.'

'Right,' Murthy asserted. 'Now the Fiery Dragonhead is being watched. No one can leave it without being tailed to wherever they lead us.'

A short silence ensued, broken by Jeet who continued pressing our problem. 'Now the only connection to Crawford, besides the *hijdas*, sir, are the Triad members in the Fiery Dragonhead?'

Murthy raised his slightly balding head. I felt for a moment he'd forgotten our mission entailed capturing Crawford only. Murthy being responsible for the full picture, encompassing every criminal transgression of the Chinese Triad.

'We'll get him soon,' he said quickly.

I recalled a few cases of Chinese criminality at home. 'Had cases in London, mostly of heroin number four, China white.'

'The Fiery Dragonhead is very convenient, can hide among local Chinese; and slit eyed Nepali prostitutes and pimps also provide a cover,' Jeet added.

'Our course of action, now, depends on your men,' I said.

The youthful-looking but cunning-eyed Murthy grinned. 'Additional Commissioners, Crime One and Two are discussing the file with Crime sir, right now.' In crisp and starched khaki, polished badges of rank on his shoulder epaulets gleaming, he suddenly became every inch a police officer. For a moment he glanced at the two telephones on his desk, then changed his mind and stiffly regarded us. 'Expecting to be called anytime, to be given the decision as to our future course of action.'

'And the possible outcome?' I asked anxiously.

'Only hope of getting Crawford is if they approve of my remarks in the file,' Murthy said loudly with a flourish. 'I've recommended borrowing from the Maharashtra Anti-Terrorism Squad it's Quick Response Team or QRT… to assault the bloody Fiery Dragonhead building and its cavern… and finish the damn Triad… *khalass*!'

***

We left the Commissionerate at exactly seven the same evening in a Mahindra Bolero. It was one of the modern day jeep variants of the legendary World War Two American Wilys, which was known as 'General Purpose' or GP. From which came the name jeep. The Bolero in muted blue camouflage had the words 'Combat Mobile Patrol' painted on it.

After a quiet uneventful twenty-minute ride, Sub-Inspector Kadam, a lanky, bespectacled officer with a fair youthful face, rather like a collegian, half-turned and instructed us. 'Weapons ready.' And turned back. He held a crackling Motorola handset to his left ear. Signals came in, and cryptic instructions were received. The uniformed driver next to Kadam eased into Shuklaji Street, then switched on the sirens and roared ahead.

Three groups participated in the raid. Nagwekar's group would seal-off the block. Jeet and I were attached to the second group, led by Kadam, tasked with holding the brothel "420" above, to prevent anybody from escaping through. The third group consisting of two six-man QRT units named 'assault mobile' and 'striking mobile' would attack the main restaurant and the cavern below.

We rumbled over the potholed road, now deathly still – no pedestrians, no vehicles about, and with all shops and establishments shuttered down. An ominous, tense atmosphere pervaded all over.

Ahead, Bolero's, Swaraj Mazda's and Toyota Qualis', all with their sirens wailing, disgorged armed men. The ramshackle one-storied hut adjacent to where we'd parked the previous night crawled with policemen, SLR's and Sterling's incongruously sticking out over boards advertising hairdressing salons and small convenience stores. Armed cops had sealed-off the entire block.

Right in front of the Fiery Dragonhead the QRT squads were readying for action. They wore Level III bullet-proof vests with ceramic inserts, over their muted camouflage suits.

***

The moment our driver stopped, Kadam, radio in his left hand, point three eight revolver in his right, sprang out of the Bolero and strode purposely towards the wooden side stairs which led to the brothel "420".

The men from the jeep and the van following us, as well as Jeet and I, all weapons ready, jogged behind the Sub-Inspector.

A tough-looking Sergeant, dark hair on his head peppered with grey, Sterling ready, led us up the rattling wooden side staircase which wound halfway around once, and ended at a closed and padlocked black sliding steel grill. A green curtain inside the grill blocked the view of the interior.

Kadam impatiently shook the steel bars. A short, plump, chinky-eyed woman in a pink sari thrust aside the curtain, and glared at us. The group of armed, uniformed men had an effect. She quickly unlocked the grill. The Sergeant, using more force than necessary, instantly slid open the grill. The constables rushed in, pushing the woman aside.

Pandemonium ensued in the dowdy, large, rectangular sitting room. Five petite, slit-eyed Nepali girls in colored jeans, trousers, skirts, tee shirts, seated on benches with their backs to the walls, waved their hands about hysterically and wailed and cried in fear.

The policemen ignored them. With trained movements they spread out and entered the three doors leading inwards. The big hefty Sergeant walked slowly about roaring. 'Shut up, *chuup*, sit quietly.'

Kadam, Jeet and I remained in the sitting room as the constables ransacked the other rooms.

Within a minute the cops escorted six more girls, accompanied by two aged-looking women in saris which covered their heads, into the sitting room. The girls sat head down, eyes half shut, shivering involuntarily, oblivious of us. The two old women sat on the floor.

Jeet gave the two old women a perplexed look for a moment, as though trying to recall something. But he didn't succeed.

Kadam, revolver in one hand and handset in the other, received a report from the Sergeant. He turned to us, 'Found the room with the escape from the cavern to upstairs, which you reported.'

***

A waist-high brick-and-cement wall enclosed a space the size of a large bed, flush to the far wall. The walnut-brown wooden board covering the top, and the chairs nearby, gave the impression of a desk. Except for the cast-iron lifting handle, the type you find on suitcases but larger and stronger, which gave it away.

A constable, on being directed, warily raised the hinged board slowly. We peeped in. An iron ladder led downwards to another horizontal board, which blocked further visual access below it. The constable closed the trapdoor.

Jeet made a suggestive recommendation, adroitly toned as though seeking advice from an expert. 'Let's position around, when they try to escape, we finish them.'

Kadam instantly agreed and gave rapid though deliberate instructions to the Sergeant. Thin and wiry, bursting with nervous energy he directed us with controlled urgency. Obeying Kadam, the big grey haired Sergeant, ponderous and rock-like, positioned his constables like a venerable grandfather handling his children.

Jeet, with his Glock-18 in its sub-machinegun mode, and two constables with SLR's – lay flat on the ground a little to the left of the door-less entrance.

The Sergeant with his Sterling and two SLR toting constables lay prone on the ground, a little to the right of the doorway. The Sterling was ideal for the situation, when lying flat as it had its magazine jutting out from the side, unlike the SLR's.

From a room opposite, Kadam and two more men watched the doorless exit from an angle.

I waited in a surprisingly clean and odorless toilet, Glock ready, and peered through the white highlights on the rear and front sights, past a crack in the wooden door into the room with the waist-high escape.

The stewing suspense-filled situation tended to raise sensations akin to panic to boiling point within me, but for a great effort of will. What if Crawford comes out with the Chinese gangsters? They'd have to escape through us. And we'd have to impede them, including our quarry, terminally if necessary.

Kadam signaled on his Motorola in *Marathi* the local lingo.

***

Suddenly sounds of repeated gunfire erupted from way down. The QRT had begun assaulting the restaurant and the cavern below. I discerned seven-point-six-two AK-47 bursts like thick fabric tearing and Chinese Type 56 automatic bursts returning fire, sounding similar.

Silently we waited. Below, the QRT 'assault mobile' and 'striking mobile' had got into a regular gunfight. The furious firing continued for some time. Then it became sporadic. Bursts rent the air with no return fire. It told a tale.

Jeet lost his restrained manner for a moment and warned. 'Ready, they're coming up any moment.'

Kadam added something to his men in *Marathi*.

***

Chinese voices, footsteps and swishing sounds carried clearly over and up towards our ears. Then the walnut-brown wooden board slowly moved upwards. Two cropped Chinese heads, pale and quivering, bobbed out first and scanned the immediate area. The shook and shivered in a state of despondent trepidation. In purple silk robes with black Chinese characters on them, they gingerly stepped out, waving smoking Type 56's menacingly around.

Trembling, they warily scanned the interior of the room, exchanging whispers, and then relaxed considerably but remained immobile. Below, the firing became one-sided. No return fire. They were getting out through the escape here. More footsteps sounded in the deathly pregnant hush before the inevitable showdown. One by one China men, some slightly wounded, with bloodstains on their clothes, stepped out.

Harried and disturbed, many waved their Type 56's about as though apprehending chasers from below.

When no one came out of the escape for some time, I realized neither Crawford nor Lee was amongst them.

I began to relax mentally. We'd trapped the China men completely. Bits and pieces of Chinese trivia floated through my mind as I watched them. But I quickly pulled myself together and tried to concentrate.

***

One group of China men rushed out as recklessly as a certain Chinese alchemist who lived hundreds of years ago. He'd ignited a mixture of saltpeter, sulphur and charcoal in a quest for the "secret of eternal existence".

It exploded in his face. He'd discovered the precursor to explosives that would kill and maim millions in the years to come. The "secret of mass death".

The group of China men made for the door less exit leading into the passage. Right towards us.

A fraction of a micro-second passed interminably. Then the cops opened fire. Suddenly, multiple deafening detonations from zooming lead-jacketed powders, not too different from the discovery of the Chinese alchemist, echoed in the enclosed space. The Chinese "secret of eternal existence" proceeded to establish itself, now from our end, as the "secret of mass death" with terrifying efficiency. The reek of gunpowder filled the air.

High velocity seven-point-six-two bullets punched pieces of flesh, bone and cloth straight through the onrushing human wall. Nine millimeter Sterling bursts added to the cacophony, punctuating the horrible maniacal screams piercing the air. Fresh blood frothed like a red sheet, away from gyrating bodies which jack-knifed and flexed spastically and floated in the air before collapsing in a heap, in the stinging cordite and fallen plaster haze rapidly engulfing the area.

A resounding fusillade of bullets rocketing out of steaming barrels propelled by their countryman's "secret of eternal existence", which turned out to be the "secret of mass death" savagely hurled a China man of the second group onto a wall, pinning him there for a moment. He burst his carotid artery which spewed fresh red blood like a fountain. And in a jiffy an orchestra of coordinated roaring gunshots sliced him into two.

With a defiant shriek one man somehow lunged through the wall of fire, and hurled himself towards me like an enraged wild animal. Strangely calm, I loosed-off a burst of fire. He stopped, his Type 56 clattered to the ground and he crumpled, eerily arching as ear-splitting barrages from the others shred his innards into bits, before he slammed, arms outstretched, onto the floor.

Almost instantly, another, magically surviving, grabbed my legs. He yowled with savage terror and biting agony. I keeled over backwards. Bleeding profusely and with his eyes half shut, the strong gangster went for my throat. I kicked him violently and repeatedly. Simultaneously I drew a bead with a minimum of wriggling about.

Veins bulged on his throat, his eyes turned opaque with abject misery and panic. He was fully conscious of his final moments. And I peppered his head with a spitting cough of automatic projectiles. Endomorphins or whatever, prevented any remorse, but also enabled me to leap upright quickly.

I'd barely noticed him lying on the ground, driblets of blood trickling from various points on his head, when suddenly the firing stopped. A muted orchestra of torturous screams, numbing groans and hysterical moaning replaced the sounds of the gun battle.

Kadam's voice came through, a little excitable, but clearly with full control. '*Chala chala,* let's go.'

***

Kadam, the Sergeant and his constables, in a superbly coordinated movement, rushed the room with the escape.

Jeet and I followed them through the suffocating, smoking cloud, over the bodies and empties lying in pools of bright red, fresh blood, glistening in the light. A distinctive odor from the blood added to the fearsome stressed and unpleasant atmosphere pervading.

Four China men, strips of cloth around their heads, knelt facing the wall, hands above their heads, save one. He held a shattered, bleeding right hand with multiple streams of red blood trickling down in a torrent. I noticed no Crawford among them. I wouldn't have to take a dead body home to Pemberton. I heaved a sigh of relief so audible, that Kadam and Jeet turned to look at me.

'You okay?' Jeet, concern on his face, asked.

'Yes, we didn't kill Crawford by accident.'

Kadam, face wan and pinched, turned away and asked for instructions on the radio.

The Sergeant moving about solidly, eliciting confidence and respect, calmed down and supervised his tense, shaking, trigger-happy constables in handcuffing the prisoners.

A voice crackled on Kadam's Motorola. 'Situation report?'

Kadam reported the encounter, the number killed, captured, wounded and an all clear.

A cryptic voice ordered him. 'Leave the Sergeant and the men, report downstairs to Murthy sahib.'

***

We tagged Kadam down the narrow stairway of the escape hatch, weapons ready, despite the shooting having ended. After a few meters of cautious treading, we stepped into a small brick-walled room. When we exited into the cavern, cops in bullet-proof vests turned quickly, alarmed, and trained their weapons on us. Then recognizing us, they relaxed and continued searching about the room. On one side a couple of men were examining two steel lockers.

Large mobile searchlights brightly lit up the interior. There were no live prisoners in the bloody gun smoke-filled sweaty atmosphere, full of cement dust leaking out of bullet holes in the sacks strewn about. Bodies, clearly dragged from behind the sacks, lay in a neat row. Every head resembled a pincushion, punctured with bullet holes, blood from many still trickling onto the floor.

Jeet carefully looked around. 'Peeped too high, clobbered by direct hits from QRT sharpshooters.'

Just then a youthful but serious-looking Murthy walked in, surrounded by a posse of plainclothes and uniformed policemen. He saw us. 'No Crawford or that Lee chap, but we've almost khalassed, finished the Triad.'

Before we could respond, Kadam stood to attention, stamped his foot on the ground and saluted Murthy.

The medium heighted, well-built Murthy, who somehow seemed like a patriarch now, returned the salute and commended him. 'Shabash, you've done a good job today. I will give you a good report.'

Nagwekar appeared from somewhere. 'Sent the prisoners to headquarters, sir, ambulances have also come,' he paused and added with relish. 'Sir, found ten kilos heroin also!'

Jeet and I stood by silently.

Murthy, who had swallowed the entire scene in the cavern, smiled without parting his lips. 'They've smuggled in the stuff, and have not been able to distribute or smuggle it out... instead have collected the heroin here.'

Murthy turned to us, but before he could say anything, a constable ran up to him, Motorola in his left hand, and stamped his foot on the ground and saluted. 'Sir, Additional Commissioner crime two, sir, on the handset, sir.'

Murthy stiffened considerably. He took the Motorola to receive the call, but before answering, he curtly directed us, 'Adams and Jeet... better return to the Commissionerate and wait.'

X

A few hours later in an interrogation cell of the Commissionerate, Jeet and I peered at the four men strapped securely to their chairs. They breathed in heavily, wheezing in and out with great effort and pain. A specially contrived lamp shade on a bare wooden desk focused light from a powerful bulb of a table lamp, straight onto their faces. Pitch darkness, save for the blinding light on the prisoners, ensured nil visibility in the rest of the room. We couldn't judge the size of the room, the color of its walls or the number of policemen sitting a little in front of us, interrogating the suspects.

Three of the prisoners, heads lowered, gazed downwards, intensely aware of the fourth. The fourth China man, second from the right, sat with his battered head lolling on his chest. Blue bruises on his forehead and puffed weal's on his cheeks and eyebrows had virtually pinched his eyes shut. An overpowering, nauseous stink of vomit on his robe and lap added to the smells of stale sweat and smoke in the room.

The reason for his discomfiture. He'd made the mistake of revealing he spoke English, earlier. Result: the interrogators, consisting of officer's from the Crime Intelligence Unit returned from Taipei, concentrated on him.

An officer spoke gently, with irresistible persuasiveness. 'Come on now, it's all over, you might as well tell us everything.'

One voice came through, loaded with cordial amiability. 'You're determined, but let me tell you it's of no use. We have drugs also. Narco analysis.'

'Now we don't want to go so far. So why not talk for your own good?'

Another officer spoke a little forcefully. 'We know of the United Bamboo Gang of Taiwan. We know you have another base in Mumbai. Tell us where it is and your problems will end.'

A demonic howl of seething rage filled the room for some time from the tortured China man, The officer's waited patiently. The China man suddenly began a delirious ramble as though deranged.

A dark, hairy hand quickly placed a small tape-recorder on the table. The broken man scarcely noticed it, and kept up an incoherent mumble between breathless sobbing moans. Unfortunately no one understood anything he said. And he went on and on, and on and on, in Chinese.

***

When the China man stopped speaking finally, and passed out, we were requested to leave the interrogation room and wait in Murthy's office. Jeet and I were served the usual steaming hot tea and we sipped it in silence for some time. We'd long finished the tea by the time the ebullient Deputy Commissioner, Crime, came in with some papers in his hands, accompanied by Senior Inspector Nagwekar.

Murthy, still starched and crisp-looking despite the hour, heaved himself onto his chair and studied us approvingly. Nagwekar turned a chair in front of a computer on a desk on one side, and sat facing us.

Jeet, for once, appeared to be at a loss for words.

Sorely disappointed, I tried to blink out some of the strain I felt in my eyes. 'After all that effort, we got nothing.'

Murthy nodded grimly at the sheets of paper in his hand. 'Translation into English of the tape-recording in Chinese gives us some facts, though not enough.'

I clenched my lips impatiently. 'Facts?'

Murthy read the ravings of the bashed-up, bruised China man, from the sheets. 'Am only a forty-niner, ordinary gunman. I don't know anything...'

'Nothing else, sir?' Jeet asked in a low key manner.

Murthy stared at the loose sheets, placed his index finger on a line and read slowly, cautiously. 'You killed Shan Chu our leader and White Paper Fan his advisor...' he paused and moved is hands along the lines, then checked the next sheet, his finger stopping about the sixth line. 'Four Two Six our boss is dead. Four Two Six our boss is dead...'

Nagwekar stared on silently. Jeet watched Murthy fascinated. I shifted uncomfortably with a familiar feeling. That of a heavy weight gradually bearing increasing pressure on the pit of my stomach while causing a despairingly empty, vacuum-like discomposure in my upper chest. It came with the realization that we'd reached a dead end.

Murthy pored through the papers intently. He hesitated slightly on the last sheet and made a face. 'In People's Liberation Army, they kick me, beat me, starve me, I fled to Taipei…'

So he was a PLA defector. I shivered slightly as ghastly images of the bloodied, beaten man, writhing and moaning in agony while uncontrollably blurting out something in Chinese, flitted through my mind. But I grit my teeth and tried to shake out any notions of sympathy. I had to repeatedly remind myself that Crawford, and nothing else, ought to concern me.

Murthy grimaced and carried on paying great attention to the translated version of the China man's ramblings. 'Red Pole gives me food. I don't know anything. Red Pole looks after me. I don't know anything. I listen only to Red Pole. I don't know anything. I have no money, no thoughts, nothing, I don't know anything…'

They were only foot soldiers. They actually didn't know anything and only did as told.

Murthy stopped reading and gazed at us with an apologetic look on his face. 'Nothing much. But working on the other's still, with a Chinese translator.'

I squirmed a bit, trying to work out the fatigue, compounded by a terrible disappointment, which crept inexorably over me. I turned to Jeet despondently. 'We're stuck.'

Jeet refused to give up. Fingers drumming on the desk, eyes half closed, he muttered something unabashedly to himself.

Murthy and Nagwekar stared at him, surprise written all over their faces.

Suddenly Jeet took a deep breath as though remembering something, but his expression indicated he was unsure about it. 'Eaten in the Fiery Dragonhead actually, years ago.'

I crossed my fingers and inclined my head in anticipation of hearing something substantial. Murthy and Nagwekar regarded him with interest too.

Jeet hesitantly carried on. 'Two old women served me, sir, you know, placed dishes, refilled the glasses of water, like that… used to sleep upstairs in the brothel "420"…'

'Two old women are in custody from brothel "420",' Nagwekar's loud, rough voice interrupted him.

Jeet looked at Murthy and continued, 'just remembered, sir, they're the same. Maybe served the Triad downstairs at meal times as usual...'

'And heard something incriminating,' I butted in. I recalled Jeet's look of recognition in the brothel "420" when he saw the inmates during the police raid. Still I felt like a drowning man clutching at a last straw.

Murthy clicked his tongue in assent, instantly picked up a black telephone on his desk and barked immediate orders.

***

Within ten minutes an uniformed Sergeant escorted two aged women into Murthy's office. They looked as though crow's-feet had rampaged all over their faces and covered them with a network of wrinkles, so dense and all-encompassing that one couldn't see any individuality in either of them. With their green-and-orange sari's not only wrapped around their bodies, but also covering their heads, they demurely placed themselves with great dignity and pride on the floor, sitting with crossed legs next to each other.

The thin, tall Sergeant saluted Murthy and identified himself.

'Sergeant Patankar, sir.'

Murthy returned the salute and turned to Nagwekar. He appeared too ranked and powerful to be able to speak to the women himself. Crisply he directed Nagwekar. 'Ask about their work?'

Some pecking order became apparent when Nagwekar spoke gruffly in *Marathi*, the local language, to Patankar, without directly looking at the women.

The Sergeant immediately questioned the women in a loud, throaty manner, as if not speaking to either of them in particular.

Both of them shook their wizened heads slowly and replied with a low torrent of words, unintelligible to me.

Jeet apparently understood them and smiled briefly. He leaned towards me and whispered a translation. 'Worked since the restaurant opened. Triad eliminated the original owner's and took over the Fiery Dragonhead.'

'Ask about Crawford, sir, the Triad gangster's had to have spoken in English with him.'

Murthy ever the crafty Machiavelli understood immediately. He gestured to Nagwekar. 'Tend to understand English, but can't speak it. Describe Crawford and Lee, ask about them.'

Nagwekar duly directed Patankar.

The women, eager to please Murthy and Jeet, simultaneously chattered away at express speed.

Jeet's facial expression, though earnest and critical, told me something. I half felt we'd learn something significant. When they finished, they paused and looked at Jeet, as though to check whether their reply satisfied him. He immediately nodded gravelly.

Nagwekar chuckled and eyed Jeet with a trace of awe. 'Crawford and Lee discussed smuggling over dinner. On Dadar beach tomorrow night!'

Murthy gazed somewhere over their heads but remained silent and still.

I allowed myself a broad smile and recalled the aroma of Chinese food that hit us when we'd first entered the Fiery Dragonhead. I touched Jeet's arm. 'When?'

He didn't reply. One of the women shook her bangle-encased hand, making a rattling sound. '*Haa aik vees tareek-la Mahapour Nivas var.*'

Jeet made a great attempt to hide his delight. He acted as though overloaded with urgency and stress. He translated for my benefit between grit teeth. 'Twenty-first night, near the mayor's bungalow.'

The other woman backed her partner. '*Haa... Dadar Chowpatty laa!*'

***

Murthy ordered Nagwekar to get Patankar to escort the women out after he'd satisfied himself that they knew nothing more. He watched them thoughtfully as they left, and turned and asked. 'Nagwekar, which Customs jurisdiction is Dadar beach?'

'Additional Commissioner, Marine and Preventive, sir, sits at Everest House, New Marine Lines.'

I sat quietly, wondering how Murthy would handle the lead.

Jeet shifted uncomfortably in his chair.

Murthy peered at the sheets of paper with the China man's confession, wavered slightly, then pulled himself together. He looked at Nagwekar.

'Get staff to draft a letter addressed to Additional Commissioner, Marine and Preventive Customs, personally requesting him to assist a British national David Adams, a private detective from the Pemberton

Security Services; and an Indian, Jeet, in locating one Mickey Crawford.'

'Yes sir,' Nagwekar assented.

'Then prepare another request, an official one, to the M & P to assist in nabbing the remaining United Bamboo Gang thugs.' He leaned backwards on his chair and exhaled slightly. 'Take care with the facts.' He checked his watch. 'I'll go tonight to our Additional Commissioner, sir's house and get his signature… both letters have to reach M & P office first thing in the morning.'

So we'd have to go through another operation, a Customs one this time, I thought.

Jeet cut in with a request. 'Sir, we may have to accompany the Custom's officers?'

Murthy favored us with a quick inspection. Then returned his gaze to Nagwekar and nodded with noticeable approval. 'Aha, mention that they may go with the Custom's preventive party.'

XI

'Mayor's gone foreign, men,' Francis D'Souza, Superintendent of the Marine and Preventive Customs, glanced lazily and banteringly around.

Seated next to him on bright red plastic chairs inside a crimson-roofed sentry booth of white plastic, Jeet and I acknowledged him with slight nods.

We'd spent the whole afternoon at Everest House, one of the headquarter office's of the M & P. The Additional Commissioner there, a slim dapper highly educated officer, with a string of university degrees, whole-heartedly cooperated with us. Finally, we left the office at around seven, with D'Souza and an armed squad of Customs men.

We were under the direct charge of an Assistant Commissioner. Now, a little in front of us, on the perimeter wall of the bungalow of the mayor of Mumbai, a group of M & P sepoys with two Inspectors lay in wait, ready for the impending operation.

D'Souza, slimly built but of taller than average height, somehow appeared slow and unspectacular; as though he'd witnessed too much too soon and had long since realized the foolishness of too much exertion. Graying at the temples, with a slight moustache on his creased visage, he somehow appeared like an extreme version of middle-class respectability.

I gazed over the sea-facing perimeter wall of the bungalow of the mayor of Mumbai, over a sandy beach about a hundred meters in width. At a sea link about a kilometer ahead, over the sea in front.

Jeet informed me. 'The Rajiv Gandhi Bandra-Worli sea link.'

The two roadways were full of flowing traffic in both directions; over the pearly grey Arabian Sea which stretched out for as far as one could see.

Jeet said of our location, 'cannot look down onto part of the beach, just below us, from up here.'

'Can't help it, men, Singh sahib cleared our position,' D'Souza replied, scanning the scores of people passing by on the north-to-south beach.

Assistant Commissioner Singh, codenamed Red Fox, a well-built, smooth shaven Sikh, sporting blue jeans and a dashing tee shirt, had ensconced himself in a top floor room at the nearby Hotel Shivpark. A technician from the department of telecommunications accompanied him. He manned a sophisticated Very High Frequency or VHF wireless set. Additional trained staff were with the "Indian Customs and Central Excise" officer in the three storied motel, to assist in supervising D'Souza.

The portable radio in D'Souza's hands crackled. 'Cub D'Souza this is Red Fox, are you in position, over.'

D'Souza quickly glanced at the eight constables or sepoys, with SLR's and the two Inspector's with Sterlings. They sat on mats on a paved strip a little behind the outer edge of the sea-facing perimeter wall of the mayor's bungalow. Behind our positions, a group of officers and men manned a couple of powerful searchlights, whose power source was an inverter battery set on a parked vehicle.

'Cub D'Souza reporting, sir, Rabbit Mayekar and Rabbit Srinivasan in satisfactory position with the men, over.'

I extinguished my cigarette, and shook another one out of my pack.

Far past the sea link, at the distant crimson horizon, where the sky merged with the blue sea, the setting sun, a large blob of orange, began its daily disappearing routine as it did from time immemorial.

'Okay Cub D'Souza, remain unseen till they arrive, over.'

***

Darkness came on gradually and imperceptibly and when it did, I first noticed the lamps at intervals on the beach. They threw out a soft yellow light that illuminated the crowds walking past. Couples, groups of boys only or accompanied by girls, single men (but no single girls), all strolled about, many helping themselves to Indian versions of fast foods. At dark corners and niches, below low compound walls of beachfront structures, couples stole a few quiet moments.

People sounds didn't overwhelm the muted roar of the grey sea which all of a sudden became a dark blur. Sharp twangs of ozone nipped into the almost suffocating, humid sea, salt and rocky atmosphere pervading.

Then I noticed something, a single girl, or rather a large woman, structured according to a frame which is usually called gargantuan.

Enveloped in a dark violet sari, she walked about with an exaggerated hip swing, and turned and stared pointedly into the eyes of the single men passing by. Somehow she appeared ridiculous. And the swarms on the beach, which was devoid of any other single women, apparently tolerated her.

Jeet's eye traveled speculatively from me to the woman on the beach.

'That's a *hijda.*'

I stared more intensely at the ludicrous monstrosity in woman's clothing, attempting to stride daintily, like a skinny model on a catwalk, with obviously indecorous and bizarre results. And to think they were a tribe in cahoots with the Triad and Crawford. He'd even murdered one of them.

Jeet stretched his legs out and regarded the *hijda* with a tolerant expression. 'This one's in the prostitution business.'

A couple of badly dressed males, mostly dark and skinny with work ravaged faces, slowly materialized around the *hijda*'s beat. One, dwarfed by at least a foot, brushed past with a deliberate movement. If words were exchanged, we didn't notice. A moment later the *hijda* turned abruptly and walked purposefully away. Waiting for a second, the prospective customer casually looked around, and when satisfied, slunk stealthily away too. He pursued the *hijda* to the dark shadows, in the area around the front hedge of the property adjacent to the mayor's bungalow.

Jeet turned his head, eyes following them till they'd disappeared into the darkness. 'Cannot see what they're up to.'

A couple of seconds later, the customer hurriedly walked away. Breaking into a run, in a state of absolute panic, he left the beach. I drew a long breath through my cigarette, and muttered, 'doesn't look like much occurred there.'

Jeet grinned, 'Do business like this all over.'

Barely had we settled down and I had blown a few cynical smoke rings in the air, when the violet sari-clad *hijda* came out, and continued his weird advertising perambulations on the sand. Within a few seconds he led another customer away and disappeared into the darkness.

I adjusted my position on the chair and gazed from our vantage point at the spot they'd disappeared to, and before I could turn away, I saw the customer run away as fast as he could, as if for dear life, towards the exit of the beach.

D'Souza didn't bother to look, but the crinkles on his visage increased considerably, and his eyes filled with disgust. 'Seeing the bloody *hijda* an'-all-that.'

'Dave here, British, wanted to know about them, because a group is involved with these Chinese gangsters.' Jeet injected a dose of tact into his matter-of-fact sounding voice.

D'Souza reminded me of Murthy. He made a face. 'Dirty buggers these *hijda's*, men, 'omoing away and nobody can do anything.'

Jeet studied him for a moment and nodded self-righteously but didn't say anything.

The *hijda* did roaring business or whatever, on the beach. customer after customer followed him to the dark recesses afforded by the intersection of the two property walls. However, usually in less than half-a-minute the customer's would speed away, most in various states of extreme panic and trepidation. What exactly went on we wouldn't know. But it couldn't have been anything congenial, at least not for the customer.

After a while I'd seen enough and turned and watched the beach.

We sat quietly for some time as I smoked cigarette after cigarette and ruminated on what I'd just seen, and its implication regarding our quest for Crawford.

Jeet broke the silence. He put on a learned and encyclopaedical manner and said, 'controlled by a boss who posts them around the city, supervises them…'

'File says these *hijda* buggers are couriers for the Chinese an'-all-that. One was murdered somewhere here.' D'Souza interrupted, and turned and stared vilely at the busy *hijda* for the first time.

'Crawford murdered one,' Jeet said.

'How do we know?' D'Souza asked.

I answered, 'from the gun used, a G-11, unlikely he'd give the weapon to someone else.'

'Crawford killed a *hijda* who was a police informer in the Triad. This proves he's in the United Bamboo Gang with other *hijda*'s.' Jeet, his brows furrowed, mused in a deeply contemplative manner. He whispered as though to himself. 'Odd! They're a semi-religious cult with strict rules against working outside their traditional occupations.'

***

Time passed and the beach gradually emptied. A few dark figures moved hurriedly past. The low chatter from the squad up front suddenly stopped, and a tense, suspenseful silence ensued instead.

I took one long contemplative drag on my cigarette and extinguished it, discarding it over the wall.

Just in front of us, naked, round glass bulbs on four iron poles were switched off. The electricity to the tangles of wires leading to a multiplicity of bamboo poles with searchlights on them was cut-off too. Our positions, shrouded in an impenetrable darkness, would be invisible to any observer on the beach.

On the beach, tiny bulbs on tall wooden posts threw out tiny patches of light, there being sheer darkness in between. The exception being a large circle illuminated by streetlights at the edge of the intersecting Keluskar

North Lane, which reached right up to the sandy beach.

Well past midnight, even the odd, stray human figures that could be seen passing by in the small patches of light afforded by the beach lampposts, and who temporarily vanished in the pitch darkness in between, disappeared. No sounds could be heard save the muted roar of the sea, its waves swishing into nothingness on the wet sand far ahead. Also, stray dogs barked and howled eerily somewhere in the distance.

A vague, creamy, bleach-like line of froth in constant flux slowly closed in as the incoming tide gradually pushed the sea closer. And, noticeable for the first time, a slight whiff of sewage, which added an unpleasant smell to the ozone tang pervading.

Suddenly a walkie talkie crackled. 'Rabbit Mayekar to Cub D'Souza, sir, a light is flashing in the sea in front. It's coming through the sea link, over.'

D'Souza radioed back. 'Rabbit Mayekar, keep them in sight.' Then, he turned and suggested to us, 'let's go in front and observe.'

***

With the familiar pinching tension, I readied my Glock while lying flat on my stomach with the others. All of us stared intently at the light which flashed at intervals, then closed in slowly and became stronger with every passing second.

D'Souza fidgeted with worry and harassment. 'Srinivasan, locate the return signaler.'

Srinivasan, a tall lean Inspector from the southern part of India, crawled energetically on all fours to the edge of the wall with a couple of sepoys. They peered downwards into the darkness. Other sepoys crept to the side wall and checked below carefully.

We were on top of a wall which dropped downwards in a series of curves, caused by large concrete blocks supporting it. This created plenty of dark recesses and niches to hide in. Especially on the south side.

'Rabbit Srinivasan reporting, sir, can't see return signaler... aborting search as we'll reveal ourselves.'

Nothing could be seen anywhere except for the splashing of waves on the steadily narrowing beach which remained silent and empty.

That is, till the ever alert, dapper Mayekar, of medium height, fair for an Indian and a native of the city, stirred besides me. 'Armed Chinese coming from the south side.'

Two tall China men with close cropped hair, in dark trousers and bush shirts, marched forward with great solicitude. Like prey anticipating an attack any moment, they minutely surveyed the empty beach, PLA standard issue Type-56 assault rifles readied for action. Hard, brutal eyes swept over our positions a number of times, but they didn't notice us.

One more China man, similarly attired but with his hair in a ponytail, tramped on the edge of the advancing sea with his assault rifle strapped over his shoulder. He held a darkish suitcase in his hand. Behind him, two more China men in ponytails followed, alert as ever, weapons ready for action.

D'Souza turned to us. His slight moustache, graying in parts, and his creased visage revealed his age and experience. I sensed that till now he'd doubted the veracity of the report made by the two old women employees of the Fiery Dragonhead. Now convinced, he shook a little as he unholstered a Spanish point three-two Llama Ruby revolver.

'Suitcase got heroin, we get ready to get it,' he said.

Jeet observed, 'trying to smuggle it out.' And chambered a round.

I did the same. On my flanks, bolts clicked, safeties switched off.

The China men paused, looked frequently towards the sea, then clustered together about fifty meters in front of us. Sounds of discordant argumentation reached our ears. Periodically they looked at the flashing light closing in from the sea.

Among us the ensuing tension became so palpable, that we could almost hear the blood coursing through each of our veins and pick up considerable speed, increasing the tight pressure within us.

After an inordinately long time, a tiny wooden fishing ketch came into view through the sea link, with two dark, bare bodied men, lean and sinewy, with the barest of bare loincloths around their waists. One tended the sail, the other the lamp.

The poker-faced M & P men waited silently, SLR's trained ahead. Srinivasan gripped his Sterling and began breathing a little heavily in jerks. Mayekar, similar carbine readied for action, remained stone-still.

D'Souza repeatedly scanned the entire beach, then focused on the China men ahead.

The boatmen jumped into the knee-deep water and looked around nervously, then dragged the wooden boat forward a little. Although handling their vessel with smooth practiced movements, they somehow exuded a feeling of being heavily suppressed and burdened with fear.

One remained near the boat, holding it with both hands. The other hesitatingly splashed little geysers of water as he strolled towards the China men. A mongrel howled somewhere far in the distance. The attack of shakes that shook the fisherman would've done credit to a victim of electrocution.

The ponytailed China man with the suitcase, began an ambulatory hike towards the boatman. The remaining China men warily stood on guard in the ankle-deep water, near the continuously varying chalky white waterline, and glared about contemptuously.

D'Souza, a little detached from the rest, raised himself to his knees like a sprinter ready to burst out. He whispered, 'ready.'

The Inspector's and sepoy's imitated him, adjusting themselves into a set position from which they could run forward and simultaneously open fire. A series of low murmurs and whispers passed among them.

Jeet signaled me. I readied myself, and waited.

Time stood still, or rather moved in slow motion, as D'Souza gave us an once-over, checked his wristwatch and directed, 'searchlights.' Then ordered, 'open fire.'

***

Blinding shafts of luminosity from a plethora of powerful searchlights illuminated the scene in front momentarily, before the roar of rifle and sub machinegun fire cracked through the still night.

One China man dropped backwards, like a heavy rock toppling from a ledge, on the wet sand. The rest froze in shock, then looked about wildly, shrieking and yelling; and quickly recovered and flattened themselves hastily on the sand.

D'Souza stubbornly shouted the famous order, 'charge.'

Shouting raucously, Mayekar and Srinivasan moved purposefully through the lingering gun smoke, Sterling's spewing out little flashes of yellow-orange flame. The men followed them, leaping onto the sand. They fanned out and advanced rapidly onto the China men in a manner that would have done credit to an elite squad of British infantry.

Jeet and I went forward with D'Souza. We faced no danger as no return fire came our way. Also the lights illuminated the scene enough for us to see them clearly. They tried to roll away like eels, but didn't succeed.

Mayekar, unflinching in his bravery, overran the Chinese gangsters slightly, on one flank. Srinivasan and four burly sepoys hit them from the other flank, turned and opened fire amidst them.

The China men, deprived of the use of their weapons, stood up and tried to fight. A nine-millimeter Sterling burst from Mayekar caught one on his throat, piercing his jugular's and ripping open his windpipe. He collapsed with a rasping gurgle as bright red blood gushed upwards like a miniature version of a fountain in an amusement park.

Two sepoys grabbed the unresisting, quaking boatmen, handcuffed them and forced them to kneel.

The charge of the remaining sepoys overwhelmed the rest. They kicked and butted the China men liberally. Unlike the police, they didn't favor using bullets if they could help it. One China man stood up and received a hard chop on his neck. He sagged forward and slithered down as two M & P sepoys wrestled him to the ground, cuffing him on his hands while shouting, '*Pakdo sala ko.*'

Another echoed him. 'catch the bastard.'

Then Jeet and I reached the scene of the encounter with D'Souza, who looked enquiringly at Mayekar and Srinivasan.

Mayekar reported in a clipped, controlled voice. 'One killed, one seriously wounded, three caught, with two fishermen.'

D'Souza glanced at the body, then at the mortally wounded man lying nearby. Thick, dark blood still pumped with a tormenting choking gurgle from a gaping perforation in his throat, and sprayed onto a rapidly expanding crimson pool around him.

He directed, 'pull these buggers inland now, I'll ask Singh sahib to send an ambulance.'

Jeet remained uncharacteristically quiet. I stayed still by his side.

We had failed in our mission. We were still clueless about Crawford's whereabouts. Fretting slightly, both of us watched the M & P staff, all in a buoyant mood, drag the bodies and the prisoner's further inland.

I watched D'Souza bleakly as he scanned the whole beach, as he did ever so often. He lifted his hand to put his walkie talkie to his ear.

I gave a start! His hand stopped halfway. Eyes screwed up on his creased face, he pointedly stared in the direction of where we'd been all evening.

***

Two burly *hijda*'s in salwars, silently padded their way over the loose sand across the front of the mayor's bungalow. They'd arrived while we were in action; and now had turned tail and were fleeing.

I strained my eyes to see them. Their red apparel made sighting difficult in the semi-darkness.

Jeet, Glock in hand, instantly ran towards them. I hesitated for a moment and followed him, panting like a hound within a few seconds at the effort I had to make, to plough through the soft sand.

They saw us and increased their pace, but considerably hamstrung by tight-fitting clothes, they moved only at a fast stride.

D'Souza hollered, suddenly recovering from a momentary bout of inertia. 'Mayekar's squad run, catch them.'

Mayekar, who had already begun jogging towards them, pointed his Sterling straight ahead and increased his pace. 'Come on Bravo squad.'

Four sepoys, SLR's held like infantrymen doing a First World War style bayonet charge, ran towards the *hijda*'s with loud cries. But they weren't fast enough.

Jeet and I kept at it, chasing the two massive shapes in red as they bolted to the head of the Keluskar North Lane. We were about seventy-five meters behind them and closing in gradually.

Suddenly a white Fiat-like car surfaced and braked with a long, grating scream. It slipped erratically down a few inches from the edge of the macadam road onto the beach, and lurched about crazily, kicking up mounds of grainy sand as it executed an about turn.

They were about fifty meters ahead of us. Mayekar and the four man M & P squad were still behind us, but closing in.

Jeet fired a burst and shouted at the top of his voice. 'Crawford's in the car.'

Breathing in wheezing breaths, I stared fascinated at the patch of light afforded by street lamps at the edge of the lane.

Crawford swung open the rear door, lost control and leaned out. He stretched out, grasped the handle and waited. Lee opened the opposite door.

About forty meters more, I thought, stretching my endurance maximally, fighting the pain in my lungs.

The *hijda*'s desperately bundled themselves into the vehicle. Doors slammed shut. The unseen driver stepped on the gas. The vehicle struggled onwards, tires kicking up loose sand, engine revving with a powerful earsplitting resonance; and in slow motion, they inched their way up the short sandy up rise onto the macadam.

Too late for us, I thought, as we struggled to catch up, now about thirty meters behind. Jeet fired intermittent bursts. Exhaustion and a paralyzing oxygen debt prevented me from doing the same.

Like at the start of an automotive race at the Crystal Palace Motorway from the track side, the thundering engine roar suddenly translated itself into an equivalent hurling forward motion on the solid tar road. And off they sped, their shuddering and shaking vehicle shooting up and away through the narrow lane.

***

Jeet dropped to his knees. Gripping his Glock at arm's length with both hands, he plastered their tires as they weaved and swerved, grazed parked cars and accelerated through the tree-lined lane. Within seconds another squealing of brakes assailed our ears as they slid to the left, onto an intersecting well-lit main road and disappeared.

I halted near Jeet, physically tired, a feeling which increased by leaps and bounds and which converted itself into a kind of mental lassitude, especially when I realized we'd been thwarted.

Jeet stood up, eyes screwed, breathing in gulps, and yelled in a hoarse, strained voice. 'White Premier One One Eight NE, number MHA 99017.'

Mayekar stopped near me. D'Souza, panting, neared us and flashed a signal on his walkie talkie. He repeated Jeet's description of the car, gave out the registration number, and added, 'to Red Fox, sir, intercept, intercept, get Kilo Mobile Unit to intercept.'

Assistant Commissioner Singh's flat toneless voice came over. 'I've sent Kilo Mobile Unit after them, and using my authority to activate police patrols.'

D'Souza continued, 'got a suitcase, we can't open it, sir.'

'Back at headquarters, Cub D'Souza, we'll get a locksmith to do the needful.'

'Red Fox, sir, think it's heroin, sir.'

'Am contacting Coastguard authorities to check for a mother vessel. The fishermen were to take the suitcase there, somewhere.'

We stood by silently, psychologically drained and physically exhausted, as D'Souza spoke with his immediate superior.

Singh comforted and encouraged his men over the air. 'Good job D'Souza, now take charge of the prisoners, and tell Adams and Jeet we'll do our best to get their man.'

XII

We'd reached Murthy's office a little after twelve noon, mostly because our exertions with the M & P the previous night, had been exhausting enough to keep us in bed till late in the morning.

Although the efforts of the M & P Customs men had been futile when it came to our nabbing Crawford, news of the Custom's operation had been well received by the police, and we were treated accordingly.

An exultant Murthy finally replaced the receiver, picked a pen from an elaborate pen holder and scribbled some notes on a report from the M & P, in the white file lying in front of him. His laptop lay to one side.

He said, 'We've finished the United Bamboo Gang in Mumbai; but your man got away again.'

'Gone to the other hideout?' I commented interrogatively.

Jeet peered at the report and tried to see what he'd just written on it. Then murmured helpfully, 'we know the *hijda*'s are in it, sir, and Crawford's with them.'

I gloomily ruminated on the big, burly men who escaped us. 'We detected them too late.'

'Found the white Premier One One Eight NE outside Bandra Station, with bullet holes and punctured tires.' Murthy put his pen down and beamed.

'The way Jeet fired,' I offered. 'Ought to be riddled with bullets besides having four flat tires.'

'I fired a couple of shots at them,' Jeet humorlessly observed.

Murthy made a deduction. 'They've caught an early morning local, most probably escaped to the northern suburbs.'

I tried to figure out the implications of his findings. 'Can we be certain?'

'Yes,' Murthy answered. 'I'm keeping the file open, till we detect the other hideout as well as get Crawford and Lee.'

'Feel the United Bamboo Gang is finished, but the Indian's involved will be in the other hideout,' Jeet suggested.

Murthy looked into the file. 'By the way the Omni you chased earlier had fake number plates; the Premier of last night is being checked out.'

Jeet added tautly, 'if a serious manhunt on, then impossible to hide if not an Indian.'

'Have enough for a case against those captured with drugs.' Murthy's grave, dark eyes rested on us momentarily. 'A heroin case means ten years inside; over and above the long time it takes for the case to come up in court.'

I kept focusing on our problem. 'What about Crawford now?'

Murthy's face darkened a little. 'When the Bandra Station investigations are completed, we should get some clues.' He stared right into us, passed his left hand over his slightly balding head and tried to detect or gauge something; what that was, I couldn't make out.

Jeet remained silent, inclined his head slightly and let Murthy observe and extract whatever he wanted to.

***

Murthy's canny eyes lit up slightly. 'You two put up a good performance, found out about the Fiery Dragonhead and about the smuggling.'

I nodded suspiciously, not knowing what to make of the plaudit.

Not Jeet. He lapped it up, a smile of exhilaration on his face. His eyes shone with pleasure. He shook his head as though he absorbed and savored every word, and his overall facial expression encouraged Murthy to go on.

But somehow I detected Jeet was putting it on.

Murthy's face revealed his opinion; he was convinced he had Jeet.

For what I couldn't make out.

The youthful Deputy Commissioner assumed a casual manner and lowered his voice. 'These *hijda*'s first time involved in a crime like this.'

'Yes many sects, groups and frauds also, sir,' Jeet quickly assented, looking at Murthy expectantly as though wanting him to spill something out.

Murthy still beat about the bush. 'Many are big strong men...'

'We scout around for you, sir?' Jeet's comprehension of Murthy's game overcame his patience.

'Yes.' Murthy gave a slight start and his face flushed slightly. 'Thought you did well, so can cope somehow.'

Jeet smiled with confident intrepidity and dashing unconcern. 'No problem, sir, we'll try to learn something.'

'Police can't search them properly, never got permission before as they're considered a social issue.' Murthy's voice revealed he had a conscience and it bothered him. 'My intelligence network also always fails if used against them.'

He wanted us to check them out alone, without backup, I thought a little queasily. I turned to Jeet with my eyebrows raised interrogatively. 'Sure you know about them; not the places but also of the men there?'

'Yes, no problem, live and do business in parts of red-light areas and shanty towns.' An expression of sanguine reassurance spread over his face.

Murthy stared for a moment at the two telephones on his desk. Then he jerked his head away as if he'd suddenly remembered our presence and didn't want us to see him talk to someone. He avoided looking directly at us, clicked his tongue and smiled subtly without parting his lips.

'Keep in touch. You have Nagwekar's mobile number. Before entering any new place, inform us.'

***

From Murthy's office I contacted Sam on my BlackBerry. I appraised him of the case so far and that we'd sighted Crawford with these *hijda*'s.

'Dammit, he escaped again,' Sam rasped through the cell phone.

'Jeet's confident we'll learn something, after we scout around their areas.'

'Why can't you take a constable with you?' Sam asked.

'Problem here, in this situation. They'll clam up and we'll learn nothing,' I said.

'So unofficially investigate about?' he said from a continent away in London.

'Right, we've got backup a cell phone call away.'

'Then be careful, I don't want to lose you too.'

XIII

At around nine the same night, after giving out our location to Murthy via Nagwekar, Jeet and I looked warily across a narrow, well-lit street. Through the scores of men passing by, undeterred by the garbage, slush and the vile odor that hung heavily over the atmosphere. Handcarts, cycles, taxi's, private cars, vans, motorcycles, scooters and busses, all steadily moved, in the two way street, as if like in slow motion.

A little away, to the side as well as opposite us, rows of rooms opened out onto the street. Although curtains blocked a full view of the interiors, we could clearly see the thick iron bars in front, at the entrances to the rooms. They resembled the type commonly utilized in prisons, or to cage animals in zoos.

Girls in varied apparel, ranging from tight-fitting pants to multicolored saris, stood in front of their cages. They yelled hoarsely and waved vigorously, soliciting for customers from among the large numbers of males passing by.

Jeet and I stood on a covered pavement. We were in front of barred and locked steel grill doors of an entrance to a shut-down cinema hall. The arcade over us also encompassed a cigarette shop and a small, dinghy restaurant. Around us, dozens of males gaped at the cages and the commercial sex worker's opposite, trying to work up courage to take the fatal step.

Jeet gazed ahead like them. He somehow very effectively acted like the others, appearing suitably cowed down and scared.

He whispered, 'have to infiltrate in.'

I nodded, and eyed a group of dark sari-clad girls in front of the cage directly opposite, on the other side of the road. Some stood around, while others sat on rattan cots on the filthy pavement. They looked straight at us and waved and shouted raucously. 'Hey fellows, come here, come here.'

Anyone would have been tempted to steal a few moments of luxuriating hedonism; especially with the effect on us of girls calling out like that. Except for the scenes at the adjacent cages.

A couple of dark but pretty girls, you could call them cute, raged and screamed hysterically, and slippered and beat a middle-aged man, and pushed him fiercely out on the street. He hurriedly zipped up his fly and ran away for dear life. Incredibly, no one took any notice of him.

At the cage next door, a skinny man in a torn shirt and *dhoti*, got too close. A couple of girls grabbed him by the collar and arms, and dragged him inside, ignoring his ineffectual protests. Into the dark depths of the unknown he went.

Jeet knew how to deal with their attention. Cool as a cucumber, he deliberately shifted his stance, pointedly turned his face to the left and ogled with his eyes wide open at a group of actively soliciting *hijda*'s.

He licked his lips disgustingly as though indicating his preference. The girls instantly stopped shouting at us and turned their attention to other passers-by.

Jeet gently tapped me. 'Watch those *hijda*'s.'

***

About a dozen *hijda*'s, long-haired, short-haired, in various types of pretty convincing multicolored female garb, clapped their hands repeatedly, or vociferously hollered at passers-by; and grabbed anyone that got too close. They stood in front of a small, dark alley which led inwards between rows of cages and a shuttered-down wine shop. They virtually closed a length of the footpath leading up to a small five-foot-high blue marble shrine to some unknown Hindu God.

'Only one method works,' Jeet mentioned calmly.

I listened in silence, raptly eying the street scene. A thin mustachioed man with sagging shoulders and a face gaunt with the effort of living, got too close. He adjusted his cheap plastic spectacles and leered directly at them. A powerful robust *hijda* in a purple salwar with an expressionless face, aggressively grabbed the man's spectacles.

'Whatever the method, got to be very violent,' I said, sensing normal feelings of respect and decency ebbing slowly out of me; to be replaced by an urge to move in and fight.

The poor man withered like a leaf of a blooming plant in a sweltering drought. He silently folded his hands, murmured something inaudible and pleaded for mercy from the small *hijda* mob. Words were exchanged.

He pulled out a purse, still like a withered leaf, except now he shook about as though buffeted by strong winds too. Quick as lightning, the *hijda* grabbed the purse; emptied it and returned it, while slapping the man resoundingly.

Jeet's eyes reflected a pitiless and implacable attitude. 'Got to be violent at first.'

For a moment I glanced at him away from the minor quarrels, shouting and pushing taking place at various points on the street. Tiny beads of sweat formed on my face.

Jeet explained gravely, 'have to prove complete physical and voice superiority, then only pay them.'

Opposite, a little to the left, a prosperous-looking man in a shining white safari suit stumbled drunkenly out of a cage. He staggered through the curtains of the cage and tripped hard on the pavement. A thick-thighed *hijda* in a short pink mini-skirt and a brown brassiere barely covering his huge pendulous breasts, followed him out, pulled him upright and shoved him away. He railed gruffly. 'Get up bastard, time up, get out.'

The tiny beads of sweat on my face became rivulets and I brushed my hands nervously across my face. 'How do we get in?'

'As customer's.'

Jeet's eyes wandered about the group of *hijda*'s; and finally focused upon a tall, dark, lean *hijda*. He wore a yellow sari. Scars pockmarked his hideously ugly, narrow face, possibly from some earlier attack of smallpox.

The *hijda*'s eyes latched onto Jeet's gaze, and he waved enticingly at us and cried, 'come here darlings, here, here, inside.'

Jeet widened his eyes and licked his lips. He smiled suggestively and shook his head agreeably.

Encouraged, the *hijda* brazenly came across the street towards us.

Just before he came close, Jeet whispered some advice. 'Stick close to me. I'll talk.'

***

The tall, dark *hijda*'s crude make-up only partly hid the tiny pitted scars on his face, which resembled the surface of the moon. Nonchalantly, he led us into the alley and turned into the decrepit three-storied dark brown building that faced the street. His cheap perfume didn't overpower the smells from piles of garbage and pools of dirty water in the filthy, stinking passage. We climbed up a rickety wooden staircase, gingerly stepped over piles of dirt, and turned and entered a room. The *hijda* pushed a filthy, thick curtain aside. We ducked under a lime and a green chili hanging by a string from the top of a blue wooden door frame, and walked in.

The *hijda* swayed and swung his hips in a manner commonly found in buxom maidens. However he exuded an effect, to put it mildly, of gross vulgarity and slovenly repulsiveness. He instructed us, using a woman's voice. 'Sit on the bed.'

We sat on a grimy sheet on the edge of one of the two beds which stood opposite each other. The beds, adjacent to the side walls at two ends of the first half of the room, had large curtains folded over them from networks of string tied to bed posts.

I'd barely got over the sickly smell of incense that enveloped us, when I noticed a whispered conversation taking place in the other half of the room. Jeet and I watched the *hijda* who'd brought us, exchange words with a pink-skinned, moon-faced *hijda* with shoulder-length dark hair, who remained seated on a straw mat on the floor.

His face was like a prettier-than-average girl's, except for the dark stubble on his chin which gave him away, However body-wise, being grossly obese, he looked like a smaller version of a Japanese Sumo wrestler. Lilting music in some strange Indian tongue, from a small radio, somehow added tension to the air, especially when the fat *hijda* gave us an once-over. Black, hard, brutal eyes, like those of a psychopath, searchingly gauged us; for what, I didn't know.

Jeet caught his eyes, then looked carefully around and when satisfied, casually walked to the door, shut it with a bang and latched it. Both *hijda*'s jerked and turned and stared at us, startled and alarmed. A strange anticipatory tension began to build up at supersonic speed.

***

Within seconds every veneer of civilized manners and normal decorum became like paint determinedly rubbed away with emery paper, vanishing completely into dust. The ugly pockmarked *hijda*, acted in a manner one would normally expect from someone of his foul, uncouth appearance to behave in. And the obese one proceeded to establish that he could act with a cold brutal fury; the same emotion that exuded from his eyes.

Roaring like raving maniacs, both charged Jeet with blind wrath. Jeet calmly sidestepped and kicked once, just blocking the fat one who fell like a ton of bricks, though harmlessly, to the floor.

Within a microsecond he launched another forceful kick at a blur of yellow – the *hijda* who brought us up; straight on, with stunning pace and ferocity, right in the face, connecting with a thud. The pockmarked *hijda* groaned, stood still for an instant, then turned to jelly and dropped loosely onto the ground, and lay quite still.

I drew my Glock, nervous and confused.

Lean, lanky Jeet, ever in absolute control, took out his pistol too.

He pointed it at the plump, pink-skinned *hijda* who'd recovered in no time and sat gaping at us. Jeet shouted out aloud, '*sala*, I want to know something or I'll finish you.'

I nearly jumped out of my skin at the decibel level Jeet reached. He had a loud voice all right. I thanked my stars for the first time that, as he'd told me earlier, had actually practiced shouting and fighting and bad behavior.

The pink faced *hijda* pleaded with his eyes. His facial muscles took on an expressive shape that normally indicates desperation, and his voice quaked with fear. 'What do you want?'

Jeet roughly and brutally spat out, 'one man from England and a Chinese man are with you. Where are they?'

The *hijda* breathed hard, and the strange, suppressed noises emanating from his throat revealed his state of mind. 'Don't know, I stay here only.'

I started slightly when a slight moan escaped from the pockmarked *hijda* on the floor. He opened his eyes, blinked, registered me standing over him, and remained still.

Jeet brusquely directed him, waving his Glock towards him. 'Sit near here.'

He did so, slowly and painfully, quaking like a tall building in a California earthquake.

The plump man insisted, sobbing, 'we don't know anything.'

A poker-faced Jeet, unaffected by the emotional display, calculatedly fired a shot. The closed room reverberated with the deafening sound, shaking us all. We remained motionless for some time in the smoky incense-filled atmosphere. In the resultant deathly silence, the gun smoke dissipated, and the small cloud of dust which arose where the slug had penetrated the wall, abated.

Jeet suddenly changed manner. He smiled ingratiatingly and said in a low, confidential voice as though exchanging secrets with a bosom pal.

'Small machinegun... this is a machinegun pistol, yaar, can finish you, police, everyone.'

I sensed he was beginning to pull-off a confidence trick, like he'd done with Columbus of the Royal Haven. This time with a kind of easy, slangy talk.

Their faces became a complex combination of unresolved moods; whether to respond to Jeet's smile, or the machinegun Glock. Ultimately their hate overcame their other emotions and the smoldering look in their eyes revealed it.

I stood still, arms outstretched, Glock pointing at them. I also made an effort to suppress any outward expression of my amazement at Jeet's ability to switch acts so convincingly.

Jeet's geniality and charm suddenly became irresistible enough to put a Hollywood star to shame. 'Want the Englishman, and China man, and can pay money, yaar... or use our guns.'

The effect gradually became apparent. Although their feelings of cooperation increased by leaps and bounds every time they set their eyes on our matte black Glock's, it was money that did it.

The *hijda* that brought us into the room adjusted his yellow sari. 'Our boss in next room, takes money. He knows everything.'

Jeet casually removed a crisp, green high denomination rupee note from the inside of his jacket and handed them over to the pockmarked *hijda*. 'More money for more information.'

The note had an instantaneous effect. Wide-eyed, lips split almost from ear to ear in an inane smile, they obsequiously looked up at us like young schoolboys who'd received great praise from their teacher. They obviously were after money only. For a second I thought Jeet ought to have brought in money earlier. Then recalled the scenes we'd witnessed on the street outside, and realized why we had to show our teeth first.

The pockmarked *hijda* stepped forward and spoke in a flowery sugary voice that sounded ludicrous. 'Going to boss and call him.'

Jeet nodded in assent and quickly handed him another high denomination rupee note. The *hijda* gratefully took the money and left.

***

Jeet and I remained in the room, alert and wary, with the plump, white sari-clad *hijda*.

'I'm Rekha, brothel keeper.' He introduced himself, and tried so much to please us that his voice took on a peculiar, low, hissing intonation that sounded weird.

Jeet smiled with cheerful levity, nodding regularly, and made the appropriate sounds that would flatter and encourage Rekha on. 'You chaps do a lot of work here, yaar.'

Rekha underwent a mood change. With great passion and earnestness insisted. 'We serve our "Master's who're totally superior and can do whatever they like". Take money, so they superior feel.'

I regarded him suspiciously. I'd seen a little of their services on the street outside.

Jeet continued making emboldening noises.

Rekha, head down, waved his hands about with imposing gravity.

Almost like a raving, ranting lunatic, I thought, besides he sounded a trifle psychopathic. As Jeet nodded in silent agreement, I did the same. Till someone entered the first half of the room. Yet another *hijda* led a "Master" to an empty bed.

Jeet holstered his Glock. 'Stay inconspicuous, away from the customer,' he advised me.

I holstered my pistol, made sure that my tracksuit top covered the holster, and waited. What had Crawford got himself into, I wondered, colluding with a bunch of raving lunatics.

The medium-heighted *hijda* extracted money from his customer, who looked like a well fed collegian. Then he went to Rekha, exchanged a few words and handed over some currency notes. Rekha shoved them into his brassiere. The *hijda* returned to the bed and dropped the curtain around it. This ensured complete privacy to him and his "Master" within.

We couldn't see anything on the bed, but less than a minute passed when sharp whispers emanated from the curtain enclosed bed. Rekha casually sauntered to a spot behind the bed and clicked his fingers. Clearly audible clicks came from inside.

Jeet and I stood by quietly. We heard a distinct croon of alluring suggestiveness. 'Kiss me sweetie.'

Whatever went on inside we'd never know. But we could see Rekha reach carefully inside through a gap in the curtain, to the "Master's" clothes, which hung from a strategically placed hook on the rear bedpost. He extracted a purse. Quickly he emptied out the contents, and signaled; another barely audible click.

'Kiss me sweetie,' came another gushing exhortation from within the enclosed bed.

And at the opportune moment, Rekha quickly reached out, deftly replaced the empty purse and calmly walked back towards us as though he'd done his "Master" a monumental favor.

Aghast, I watched him count a small wad of currency notes.

With a crooked grin on his face, he muttered like an immature child. 'Money take always. Make "Master's" feel superior.'

Suddenly a yellow sari walked across, interrupting our thoughts. The pockmarked *hijda* who'd brought us here, came in. Detached and untroubled, he revealed a row of stained teeth with his huge smile. 'In next room boss wants, him coming there.'

***

We waited on one side in the next room, which was identical to the previous one.

After a while a bulky giant who could easily double as a star billing of a World Wrestling Entertainment show, ambled in with a mournful look on his over-large face. A skimpy brassiere barely covered huge breasts and an equally Lilliputian mini-skirt revealed more than it hid.

A smart young man in a colored silk shirt and elegantly cut trousers, tagged him, swaggering into an enclosed curtained-off bed.

'Ah, there you are, I'm Sarita,' a tall aristocratic-looking *hijda* in a black sari diverted our attention and suavely introduced himself. Sharp, intelligent eyes probed at us from under hooded brows on his dark, craggy, square face.

We started slightly as we hadn't noticed him, and took our eyes-off the large *hijda* and his customer. But before Jeet and I could answer Sarita, a sharp, piercing cry of pain made us turn to the occupied bed.

Sarita slanted his eyebrows and clicked his tongue. 'Oh only serving our "Master's" who can do whatever they like and we can't do anything.'

Jeet and I listened, a little dumbfounded at their sense of duty towards their "Master's"! We couldn't even speak properly because of the constant interruptions due to their service.

I looked at Sarita, and shivered slightly on sighting a clearly recognizable tiny cloth picture of the Catholic saint, St Anthony, on a string around his neck.

Came another harrowing scream. A hand grasped the curtain and ripped open a small gap. With horror we saw the seated goliath's large, muscular, hairy left hand gripping his puny "Master" at his crotch. He squeezed periodically, provoking frenzied, agonizing blasts of deeply penetrative auditory insult. The thick fingers of his other hand, palm outstretched, opened and closed demandingly.

'Give me more. Aur dey dow. Give me more,' the gruff growl emanated from somewhere deep within the colossus' throat.

Panic stricken the weeping "Master" hurriedly took a few notes out of his leather purse and placed them in the outstretched palm. The giant quickly shoved them into his brassiere and simply continued to bark, 'Give me more. Aur dey dow. Give me more.'

Sarita stared at us. In spite of him, Jeet and I, shocked, couldn't take our eyes-off the spectacle in the bed ahead.

When the customer's purse was empty, man mountain grumbled and spluttered away, and pushed his "Master" roughly out.

Sarita interrupted our fascinated observations with a flat toneless remark. 'Don't know any man from England or Chinese. They do not come here.'

He appeared to be telling the truth.

Jeet turned and faced Sarita, and somehow still sounded pleasant and amiable. 'Lot's of places here on the street, elsewhere, yaar?'

Sarita insisted with equal urbanity. 'My men checked this area. No Englishman or China man seen, only our customers who're our "Master's"!'

Sarita's eyes flashed a hint of some kind of rambling aberration as he shook his head. He made me really nervous. I sensed a slight trace of derangement in his voice too. The picture of St. Anthony aggravated the scare he provoked. Somehow he reminded me of two other Anthony's at their best – Perkin's in Hitchcock's "Psycho" and Hopkins in the more recent "Silence of the Lambs". He had the same air of hidden menace around him. It took great effort not to turn tail and flee.

'If not here, then where else?' Jeet asked.

Sarita turned and eyed us, an abnormal demented satisfaction on his beaming face. 'Give me money. I want more money.'

Eager to give a convenient and suitable impression, Jeet hastily removed a couple of high denomination currency notes and handed them over to him.

Sarita stared smugly at the notes in his hand and glanced at us smiling expansively. 'We serve for money only.' He blinked once or twice, turned on his heel and pointed towards the door. 'Try Kamatipura, First Lane.'

***

The overpowering dank, fetid, musty odor which merged with smells of sweaty, unwashed linen, surprisingly vanished inside the large airy room in a seedy three-storied wooden building at Kamatipura's First Lane. The piquant tang of spicy curries replaced the malodiferous smells pervading outside.

A dark, thickly built and stocky *hijda* of medium height, hesitatingly searched our faces. But Jeet's eager beaver and endearing manner apparently won him over. Within seconds his lips parted in good humor, revealing a crooked row of stained teeth on his rough bloated visage.

'Come in dears, I'm Mariamma.'

'*Sala*, I'm Jeet, this is Dave,' Jeet introduced us.

Using my peripheral vision I tried to spot a telephone without turning my head. I didn't see one. Probably there was a cell phone somewhere. Clearly Mariamma had been told about us, and he proved my inference right.

Without us mentioning Crawford and Lee, Mariamma cheerily raised his thick, black, bushy eyebrows. 'In all brothels in this building, no Englishman or Chinese coming.'

Jeet's eyes wandered around the room. 'Sure, *yaar*?'

Mariamma flashed his dirty, brown-stained teeth. 'Yes, all rooms checked. Here we keep girls also,' his eyes widened enticingly. 'Give a girl, short time, cheap?'

Jeet meekly folded his hands in condescension and humbly shook his head with great self-effacement. Then he quickly reached into his pocket and handed over a high denomination rupee note.

Mariamma's eyes lit up like an exceptionally bright firecracker. But I suspected he viewed Jeet and me as fools, to be taken advantage of by extracting as much money from us as possible. He dispatched another beaming, brown-stained dental broadside, but sounded absurd when he spoke, trying to mimic a woman's voice. 'Take inside darlings, see all here for yourselves.'

***

Three rooms lay in a row with a corridor linking them. Mariamma took us from the room we were in to the room in the center. We peered uselessly at two empty beds with the usual curtains folded on strings above them. But when we left the empty room and turned for the next room, we brushed past a tough *hijda* in a sari who led a badly dressed customer onto one of the beds.

Mariamma made a painfully imitative similitude of Sarita as we entered the next room. 'Always we serve our "Master's who're totally superior and can do whatever they like"!'

A familiar icy feeling began to overcome me. I grit my teeth and forced myself to bear it.

In the next room, a row of beds with wooden partitions between them faced us. A couple of doll-like girls in varied colored costumes preened themselves and gossiped away. Minors, I thought, till I noticed streaks of grey in the hair of some.

'Our girls, specially thought to please our "Master's"!' The self-satisfied look and glowing smile on Mariamma's face could have rivaled the expression used, by headmaster's of noted institutions like Eton, when showing-off particularly gifted pupils.

They stopped chattering, combing their hair, patting powder onto their heavily made-up faces or applying blood-red lipstick on their lips, and stared impassively at us.

Suddenly a piercing wail came from the middle room we'd left earlier. 'I've given you money already, bastard.'

'*Aur dey dow*, give me more,' came a blazing growl.

'Robber, swine,' the customer whined and sobbed. 'I'm superior to you servants, leave me.' Sounds of a violent struggle assailed our ears.

The sound of something falling to the floor diverted our attention. A small bottle rolled along the floor and stopped near our feet. I gasped with mirth. I recognized the sticker of the semi-naked cavorting couple on it. I'd last seen the item on DN Road. A bottle of the "Pleasure Prolonging Lotion" had interrupted us!

I felt partly like throwing up, partly like laughing my head off, with the ultimate effect of staying as I was.

Clearly the *hijda*'s strongly resented their customers, and did their utmost to loot and cheat them.

Jeet turned to leave. I followed him.

Mariamma, unaffected by the scorching exacerbation caused by his services, calmly led us away to the exit, a narrow wooden staircase that led downwards. Our search for Crawford had so far come to a naught.

XIV

'We're near Bandra Station, east, and we've to walk a bit from here,' Jeet said, as he gently eased the Maruti between two parked taxicabs amongst a row of private cars, vans and two wheelers.

We'd been driving for quite some time on Mumbai's crowded roads, before Jeet had stopped. He didn't tell me anything en route and I didn't ask. Mainly because it had taken me quite a while to mentally recover from the scenes we'd encountered in the *hijda* dens.

Before leaving the parked car, he said, 'let's contact Nagwekar.' He punched the appropriate buttons on his Reliance and got through.

'No success so far,' Jeet informed the Senior Inspector. 'Although seen scenes no police officer able to see.'

'Yes they stop everything when we arrive, even if in mufti.'

'Plainclothes cop's identified by them and they close down,' Jeet added.

'Cop's have to be in it,' I muttered inadvertently.

Jeet ignored me. 'It's like social corrections taking place.'

'Where are you now?' asked Nagwekar.

'Bandra Station, east,' replied Jeet.

'Not a *hijda* area.'

'Do business here, nearby. We'll try to learn something from them.'

'I'll note your location.' Nagwekar crisply encouraged Jeet. 'Take care, and report to me when go elsewhere. I'll inform Murthy, sir.'

Jeet placed his Reliance back into his pocket. He hadn't been affected at all by what we'd been through. His moving around outside on foot, while fitness jogging and reading a lot at home, had righted him; at least for street level field work.

I hadn't become like him. Areas, so distinct from each other, peopled by types of human beings involved in some kind of unique service unparalleled anywhere, tended to confuse and disorient me into a kind of slow apathetic paralysis.

I reassuringly felt my Glock in my holster as I strolled on behind Jeet.

***

I followed Jeet as he turned left onto a dark, muddy lane parallel to a large pipeline. My mind, full of conflicting emotions, buzzed as if under the influence of some drug.

'What now?' I asked.

Jeet carefully climbed a rusted iron stairway onto the top of the black painted pipeline. 'These *hijda*'s have a boss who leads them.'

'They have one?' I had to concentrate on walking behind Jeet, step by step in the dark, on the seemingly endless pipeline.

Jeet waited till a train clattered noisily past on tracks which were beyond a small swamp and another pipeline, similar to the one we were on. 'Yes the system needs a boss, absolutely powerful, who posts and transfers and directs them.'

'Jeet get to him. Money appears to work with them.'

He slowed his already cramped gait and advised me in a different tone. 'Careful till we come out of the tunnel.'

Silently, inching ahead, we entered a dark tunnel. For two full minutes we shuffled onwards and finally exited at the other end.

On the other side Jeet minutely scanned the dark, rough ground under the dim starlight and moonlight. 'Got to convince their buggers we'll not harm their businesses; and only need Crawford.'

I watched a long suburban local clatter with a god-awful racket over an iron bridge a little ahead, to the right. 'Odd place to find a *hijda* don.'

'Don't know the boss, so we're here! Find out about him.'

This confused me like hell. How was he to find out about the don in this godforsaken place. The sinking feeling gradually overcoming me in the dark, dreary atmosphere became more acute, leaving me with a sore sensation in my mind. Numbly I jumped behind Jeet from the pipe onto a narrow strip of rough ground, beyond which lay a stinking creek. 'Who is he? How do we get to him from here?'

He didn't reply immediately, and about turned.

Gingerly he picked his way over rocks, past small bushes, now moving in the opposite direction. 'Rumors of a shadowy leader, controller of all *hijda* operations.'

I noted we were beyond the pipeline. The creek lay a little to our right. The steep hillside sloped upwards on our left up to, presumably, (it remained unseen from below) a well-lit arterial road. Clear sounds of vehicular traffic passing by on top, assailed our ears.

'What of this shadowy leader?' I asked gloomily.

Jeet made his way to a low stone wall extending from the top of the slope to the bottom, probably built to reinforce the slope. 'Supposed to be in Bhandup area, a suburb, in a shanty town called Sonapur.'

'Here?' I queried, feeling a little nauseous, although the putrid stink abated slightly.

'No,' he shook his head with mild regret. 'Police once sealed-off Sonapur and searched for him. Checked all hutments, hovels, tin shed brothel's... but he escaped... if he was there at all.'

I came next to him at the bottom of the stone wall in a mood of muddled lamentation. 'Here we comb the metropolis for Crawford, who's amongst a unique group who'd stand out anywhere. Yet we're lost.'

Standing near me, Jeet confidently touched my shoulder, turned and cast a heartened eye on me and whispered with optimism, right here in the lonely, sickening, infernal spot. 'They do business here, this place is isolated, ideal for my plan.'

A dog howled eerily from the vast, dark, dense mangrove swamp across the creek which extended as far as our eyes could see. Nearer, where we stood still, the stink of garbage enveloped us. And aggravating our discomfort further were large mosquitoes which buzzed around with a disconcertingly loud humming sound.

Jeet peered upwards, over the stone wall. 'Got to force one of them to take us to his big shot boss!'

***

The bushy rocky hillside sloped upwards to a waist-high, black concrete wall. It extended from one end of the top of the hill to the other, beyond which lay a main road. A distinct shape in a familiar salwar sat on the wall, soliciting for customers from among the passers-by on the well-lit road.

Soon the tall, willowy, handsome *hijda* straddled the wall and made his way downwards. A fresh-faced man attired smartly in an expensive tee shirt and corduroys, hesitatingly followed him. He picked his way slowly down slope to the *hijda*, who stood immobile, waiting. They were about fifteen meters in front of us.

For a moment I thought I'd seen some movement in a man-sized clump of bushes lower down the slope. Maybe a peeping Tom. I stared hard. A train noisily thundered past, behind us. Strays barked incessantly and howled harrowingly from the dark, shadowy mangroves on the other side of the creek. But my determined survey didn't reveal anything behind the dark bush. So I turned and concentrated on the scene ahead.

The frenzied bargaining in whispers between the customer and the *hijda* took less than a minute. Money changed hands. The well-built *hijda* lifted his loose shirt above his waist and knotted it. Then made to loosen the strings that held up his tight *salwar* lower.

He adjusted his position slightly and nodded encouragingly at his semi-scared customer, and forced the man to face him at an angle. All the while he urgently waved his right hand up and down, enticing the customer to drop his trousers.

Jeet touched me, placed his fingers on his lips and inclined his head. I turned and inhaled deeply with astonishment. My suspicions had been well in order earlier. A furtive voyeur had been hiding behind the bush all the while. A vague blurry, white figure slowly became apparent, advancing tenaciously from behind the offending bush.

A big-made man, dirty, white long-sleeved shirt hanging loose over his *khaki* trousers, wearing brown regulation shoes, silently crept towards the back of the customer and the *hijda* facing him. Not a hidden snooper but a stalking policeman in plainclothes.

Meanwhile the customer, shaking a little, unzipped his corduroys and slowly lowered them.

Like a wild animal at the climax of a chase, the cop bounded up to the man and grabbed him brutally by the collar, nabbing him literally with his pants down.

He wilted, and hurriedly pulled up his corduroys. Shivering with fright, he abjectly pleaded for mercy with folded hands. From our position, we couldn't exactly hear what they said.

Jeet tightly whispered. 'Famous racket. *Hijda*'s and cops join up against nut-cases who think they can actually do anything they like... screw them up like this!'

'Slightly different way of serving their "Masters"!' I nodded, dazed with bewilderment.

In front, words were exchanged and some kind of compromise reached. The *hijda* stood by watching, head down. The customer extracted a few notes from a leather purse, and handed the money to the cop, who snatched and pocketed it. Then, he slapped the customer on his back and forced him to stumble away.

Thoroughly spent and chastised, the man increased his pace and barely in control, lurched up the slope and disappeared over the wall.

The cop counted a small wad of currency notes before pocketing them; and returned to a safe and invisible concealment behind the large bush. The *hijda* went away, climbing back atop the concrete wall to await more customers.

Scarcely half a minute passed when a different person straddled the wall, following the *hijda*.

Vehicles whizzed past on the road above. Far-off in front, on the same slope, occupants of a Stone Age-like hutment colony sat around small fires gossiping, unconcerned, feeding the small flames with twigs and pieces of waste paper. Way behind us, trains noisily clattered past. Across the shimmering waters of the foul smelling creek, strays howled and yelped from somewhere within the dark, silent and forbidding mangroves.

And just in front of us the routine went on and on and on. Foolhardy customer after impetuous customer rashly came down with the *hijda*. Money would change hands. The *hijda* ensured the customer was positioned appropriately. The customer droped his pants; and the physically robust cop struck like lightning, roughly grabbing him. Again some more cash was forfeited. And the sheepish customer hurriedly escaped, minus a sizable amount. Some customer's were manhandled and slapped about in the process.

The constant action in front of this latest scheme of *hijda* enterprise to serve their "Masters" enabled time to pass fairly quickly and entertainingly. Gradually the gap between the "loot the customer" routine, lengthened as the hours passed, till no one came over for some time. Then, the *hijda* climbed down the slope to the impassive cop who waited in the open for him.

When they met, they behaved like two overworked Old Broad Street stockbroker's who'd made a killing at the London Stock Exchange.

Whispers were exchanged and currency notes changed hands both ways, like accounts being settled and squared-off at the close of trading. And after quite a bit of jocular bantering, the cop finally turned, climbed the slope and disappeared, all the while patting a large bulge in his trouser pocket.

The *hijda* stayed in place and casually surveyed the whole area around. He remained for some time after the cop had left, then jauntily swaggered away, heading towards the road on top.

Jeet tapped me and leapt over the low stone wall. 'Let's go get him!'

***

Jeet, Glock in his right hand, rushed the narrow-faced but thick chested pink salwar-clad *hijda* and rapidly locked his left arm around his neck. I ran around them and pointed my Glock straight into the *hijda*'s face, and watched it slowly turn crimson as Jeet squeezed hard, throttling him. Suddenly Jeet sat down heavily and brought the *hijda* down; both landed with a loud thump, falling hard on their buttocks on the rough, stony ground.

The *hijda* cursed viciously, ignored me, and desperately lashed out with short arm elbow jabs, which thudded like sledgehammers that threatened to crack Jeet's ribs. Jeet didn't let go his grip. Heavy rasping breaths struggled to enter and leave the *hijda*'s lungs, while his steadily weakening blows interrupted his convulsive twisting and frenzied turning as he squirmed with all his might to extricate himself.

Jeet increased the pressure of his left arm and barked a warning as I made fake preparations to shoot. 'Don't shoot the joker yet,' he said.

The tremendously strong and active *hijda* understood and suddenly went limp. Throbbing jugulars laboring to explode on his neck indicated his pain, and the fact that Jeet hadn't loosened his grip one bit.

Jeet forced the barrel of his Glock against his teeth and interrupted the momentary silence with a threat. 'Keep quiet, or I'll fire a bullet.'

A low moan interspersed with a variety of other sounds of indefinable quality answered him.

Jeet forcibly pushed him flat on the ground, turned him over onto his stomach, and pressed the muzzle of his pistol into his neck. He hissed to me, 'reach into my pocket, take a handkerchief, large one, and tie his legs; use your handkerchief to tie his hands behind his back.'

It took me two minutes to do this. When I did, Jeet sat on the prone man's back and began to play-up. His hard, tough voice sounded extremely realistic. With great show he chambered a round. 'After we shoot him, what do we do?'

I caught onto Jeet's game. 'Throw the damned fool into the swamp.'

The *hijda* quivered agitatedly with raw, naked fear. Although his large hips, too narrow waist and extra large chest gave him the body of a girl, I sensed his inner strength. But this was of no use now, facing two Glocks.

'Who's your leader?' Jeet rudely and nastily snapped.

He remained mum, but writhed and trembled and struggled against his bonds. I could almost see his palpitating heart speed raging, scalding blood throughout his inflamed body. Jeet squeezed his Glock harder into his neck and he gave up his silence with a spasmodic cry of pain.

It upset me no end. I hated dealing like this with anyone, even if they'd revealed themselves to be psychotic scum. Not Jeet. He knew what he did, and carefully watched the *hijda* as though waiting for an opportune moment to change his tactics.

And it came soon. Jeet reached into the *hijda*'s salwar pocket and extracted the fat wad of rupee notes he'd taken from his customer's earlier; and held it in front of the *hijda*'s eyes.

'We'll not hurt your business, *yaar,*' Jeet said in a strong, hard yet friendly manner. He added a high currency note from his pocket to the wad and returned the bundle to the salwar pocket.

Jeet's changed manner didn't have an immediate effect, for the *hijda* took a few seconds to relent. Then he spoke for the first time in a quavering voice. 'Let me sit.'

Jeet turned him over and lifted his back up, enabling him to sit with his legs stretched out, and said as amiably and genially as possible to soften him, 'we want to meet your leader, *sala*, we mean well, *yaar*, and can pay.'

I stepped to one side to get a better angle to aim my Glock into the *hijda*'s face.

Sheer isolation and the resultant corroding sickening fear showed in his eyes. Jeet, ramming home his absolute superiority with his unconventional approach, forced him to take the easy way out.

'Our leader is Mata Radhika Amma.'

Jeet immediately took out a high currency note and shoved it into his pocket. He reciprocated with a forced, bitter smile, pregnant with muted recrimination.

Jeet apparently had cracked the secret of highly skilled and extremely successful negotiators. Give the *hijda* tons of undue respect, but only after having ensured, with almost inhuman ferocity and brutal savagery, that they didn't dare cheat him.

Now, charm oozed from his voice. 'We can pay more sala, just take us to your leader.'

Reassured and gaining confidence with every second that passed, the *hijda* gazed at us with dark, vacant but still troubled, almost malevolent eyes, and shrugged his shoulders. 'If lot money pay, I Usha taking you to Mata Radhika Amma in Bhandup Sonapur.'

XV

After driving for about fifty minutes from Bandra, Jeet stopped, and parked the Maruti near the main Lal Bahadur Shastri or LBS Road. From there, Jeet and I casually strolled onwards, as unobtrusively as possible, a little behind Usha. The *hijda* walked on surely and deliberately, and somehow even more inconspicuously, into Bhandup's Sonapur area.

While walking, Jeet informed Nagwekar on his Reliance. 'Following *hijda,* Usha to meet Radhika Amma in Bhandup Sonapur.'

'Through Murthy, sir, I'll inform Deputy Commissioner Zone Five about your movements. He'll flash the information to all concerned.'

'I'll get back to you later,' Jeet said.

'Right, and be careful.'

The Sonapur shanty town, constructed like a maze of the type you see in amusement parks, forced us to twist and turn through a veritable warren of alleys and passageways. Shabbily clad men, boys and women passed by or gossiped under dim streetlights, in the small tea and cigarette shops housed in tin-roofed mud huts on raised mud plinths.

After about a minute of walking, a little confused, I turned to Jeet.

He walked on steadily without looking to the left or right, following Usha, with no expression on his face.

I took the cue and ignored the tough-looking, khaki-clad uniformed policemen around a stationary Mahindra Bolero jeep. They didn't notice us or care about us, being engrossed in chatting amongst themselves. They'd probably receive instructions about us, later.

Well past them on the narrow, dusty mud lane, Jeet came close and whispered. 'Won't interfere till we discover something, or are signaled by higher-ups.'

I nodded in acknowledgement.

Ahead, Usha stopped to enable us to catch up at the end of a short lane which turned to the left, right into a small square. The two-storied wooden board houses around could've stepped out of a wild west movie, except for the scores of girls in *saris*, jeans, *salwars*, all exhaustedly gazing at us in the early hours of the morning. They made no movement or sound.

Usha carried on, strolling slowly and casually. Somehow it didn't seem right. I'd expected him to stride briskly to wherever he was headed. Then I heard a sound. Maybe it explained his amble. A faintly audible click came over, then another and another. I felt my hair beginning to stand on end.

As with Rekha in the *hijda* den earlier, he or someone else had signaled something, about what, I couldn't decipher.

Jeet didn't show any reaction, but unobtrusively glanced at a couple of *hijda*'s seated among the groups of girls standing around.

I followed his eyes, but couldn't exactly make out anything. Once or twice I thought I saw the *hijda*'s around signaling to Usha with their fingers, their arms straight down by their sides.

Usha led us into a long barrack-style single-storied hut. We stepped onto the white stone floor of a long corridor running through the hut. On one side, blue wooden doors led to small rooms in front of which, on small raised cement platforms, *hijda*'s and girls lounged about relaxedly on cots or on the floor. On the opposite side, girls washed clothes under running water from taps placed at intervals over a long drain, like a communal bath.

Finally, we entered a filthy four-meter wide alley between windowless walls of two-storied cement buildings. Stepping nervously over the stinking garbage, eyes sore, especially at the sight of large hairy rats scurrying about, we reached a solid two-storied concrete block-like structure.

Usha pushed aside a thick black curtain, stepped into a dimly-lit room and directed us. 'Wait here.'

***

A crushing emptiness and a biting silence enveloped us as we stood on the cream-colored tiled floor, and faced the door that led inwards.

Then I sensed rather than heard someone coming up from behind me, silently and with increasing velocity. Instinctively I turned as swiftly as I could, and reached for my Glock. Too late. A pair of strong hands grabbed me, powerfully crushing me around the waist, like a misjudged rugby tackle, higher up than usual. I couldn't reach for my gun.

Jeet, similarly pinned down, exploded into a thundering roar, and struggling desperately, crashed onto the tiled floor with two *hijda*'s holding on for dear life. His arms and legs splayed and kicked outwards like pistons. To no avail.

Six more big, tough-looking *hijda*'s, dark and ugly enough to be called "monsters" rushed in and grabbed us. Our resistance ceased immediately.

Quickly they handcuffed us, hands behind our backs, and tied our legs too for good measure. One jet black, superbly muscled man searched us in turns, relieving us of our Glock's, spare magazines, cell phones, purses, everything save our clothes. Another blindfolded Jeet. Then he came to me and did the same, and everything disappeared into an all-pervading blackness.

A little later I was carried into the bowels of the building. I felt myself being moved around for some time, before being unceremoniously dropped onto the floor. I groaned in agony. I'd landed on iron bars. I heard another thump. They'd brought Jeet here too. I heard the clang of iron striking iron and a bolt being slid, followed by a final click of a key turning. We were locked in somewhere.

'Led into a trap prepared by Usha's signals,' Jeet muttered angrily. 'We're in some kind of a cage.'

***

Before I could reply, the cage vibrated with sounds of drumming and chanting and clapping. Then someone removed our blindfolds.

A blinding luminosity emanating from all around forced us to close our eyes tightly. Loud sounds deafened us temporarily. And the sweet, smoky odor of incense aggravatingly assailed our olfactory sensibilities.

When our eyes accustomed to the light, we found we were in a cage in a largish hall. In front of us were dozens of variedly dressed *hijda*'s with complexions ranging from ebony, black to brown to fair-skinned. Seated on the floor in rows, they clapped vigorously, chanted lustily, banged away on drums with great intensity, and energetically clashed large bronze cymbals together. The resultant din seemed calculated to turn anyone prematurely stone deaf.

A tall, dark, well-built man sat on a raised dais, on a splendidly upholstered couch of woven silks and exotic fabrics. Although he held a cell phone in his left hand, he lucidly contemplated us with an air of serene detachment. He tossed his long, well-oiled, loose, dark hair like an Indian version of Samson. His face radiated vitality and great intelligence.

I detected a trace of humor flashing through large, sharp black eyes. I presumed he was Radhika Amma, the *hijda* don.

Two baby-faced young boys in green-and-red saris, long dark hair in plaits, massaged his feet.

Overall, the multicolored costumes and exaggerated and exotic features of the *hijda*'s, everything in the startling scene evoked bizarre, outlandish feelings. I felt like a caged animal being given a bird's-eye view of a set from a stagy, spectacular Steven Spielberg movie. Everything was a hyperbolized exaggeration, yet exuding a precise authenticity with scrupulous exactitude. If any special effects occurred suddenly, they wouldn't be too much out of place.

'Stay silent, we'll play it by the ear,' Jeet whispered.

***

Prone and passive in a blood-red sari, a youngish *hijda*, lay on a bed of ashes, pinned down by his spread-eagled arms and legs by four burly *hijda*'s. Each held a limb firmly on the ground. He offered no resistance but his eyes rolled as though under the influence of some drug.

Nearby, an old-grey-haired *hijda* tended an orange-colored bronze pot resting on a steel frame over a live fire.

Two more black sari-clad *hijda*'s stood near the prone man. One held a foot-long bamboo rod; the other had something indeterminable in his right hand.

The frenzied chanting, drumming and cymbal-clanging and clapping beat to a faster and faster rhythm, gradually rising to a crescendo. Radhika Amma raised his right hand, and the two *hijda*'s clad in black, the usual color of executioners apparel from time immemorial, closed in.

The one with the bamboo rod bent over and lifted the blood red sari slowly, deliberately to above waist level, revealing a pair of well-shaped brown, hairy legs and a long, large though limp male organ, on a clean shaven crotch. He split the bamboo rod, widening a pre-cut slit like a pair of scissors, and with it he held up the entire male organ, including the testicles, of the prone man.

The other black-clad *hijda* moved in and raised his right hand. In spite of myself I trembled on recognizing the object gripped between his thumb and forefinger. An ordinary, silvery, safety razor blade.

Radhika Amma, somehow regally disassociated from the rest, yet controlling the show, dropped his thick, dark, hairy hand.

The *hijda* in black with the razor blade, swung his upraised hand downwards in a powerful but smooth swooping arc behind the bamboo rod. He severed the organs from near the pubis completely, leaving a gaping, bloody wound.

Benumbed, I watched the bamboo rod pull away the loose bloody male organ, which fell onto the ashes.

The castrated man frantically rolled and thrashed about strenuously with scalding agony. But the foursome held him down firmly. He screamed soundlessly, his neck bulged, his veins and other blood vessels threatened to burst. His facial muscles contracted repeatedly with agonizing torment.

However deafening sounds from the rest drowned out all audible signs of his helpless anguish.

The aged grey-haired *hijda* tending the bronze pot, extracted a wooden ladle full of boiling oil, bubbling, sizzling and spluttering, and calmly poured it onto the wound. A piercing, harrowing scream momentarily rose above the other sounds, and the writhing ceased. The castrated man passed out.

Bright red blood pulsing out of the crotch suddenly transformed into a blackish brown scab. Then someone placed a white cotton rag on the wound. No surgery, antiseptics, antibiotics, nothing.

Radhika Amma leisurely looked about and raised both his hands. The acute hush filling the hall became deathly silent, enough to actually pain our over-insulted auditory mechanisms inside our eardrums.

The foursome who'd pinned down the now castrated man earlier, lifted the unconscious body by the arms and legs, and walked out.

Then the *hijda* chieftain, Radhika Amma, calmly raised his head and stared pointedly at us. All eyes from among the crowd, loathing, detesting, insolent eyes, were suddenly riveted onto us. The rabid mob bayed for blood; waiting for a signal to grind us mercilessly into miniscule pieces.

***

Tall, well-proportioned Radhika Amma pointed at us, a crafty look on his eyes, and grandly announced to the congregation of *hijda*'s, 'they enriched us, but learnt too much.'

A creepy, corroding feeling began to crawl up my spine as murmurs of assent rippled around the group.

Radhika Amma tightened his attractive aquiline face, but still appeared to assess us. 'If they go to the police, they'll finish us. *Khataam*!' He paused with mockery in his eyes and curled his lips derisively. 'Can we trust them?'

Loud, gruff negative sounds came from all over, like the repressed Roman citizenry giving a thumbs-down signal at the behest of some despot. Vile psychotic eyes revealed they avidly yearned to tear us to pieces.

A corroding, creepy, crushing sensation now took over my entire body, like thousands of stinging fire-ants crawling about me at random.

Radhika Amma's eyes showed his satisfaction at having proved to us his hold over the *hijda*'s who'd do his bidding. Now we'd be appropriately scared of him. 'You wanted to learn about us from us, ha, ha, ha... as if we'd let down any of our friends... ha, ha, ha!'

Jeet emoted a cynical remoteness, yet cried firmly and full throatily, 'We need only Crawford, no one else, *yaar*.'

Radhika Amma's brows rose with mild amusement, his sharp eyes drifted over us searchingly and he spoke almost languidly. 'So you two were involved, almost finished us due to our new business.'

A spasm of petrifying dread almost choked me as a howling clamor arose from the *hijda*'s, like hyenas waiting for a meal.

'We're not Police or Customs, nor do we know your business, sala.' Jeet insistently shook his head, but with an imperturbable, nonchalant expression on his face.

A faint expression of surprise flitted over Radhika Amma's face. Then he laughed heartily. 'Sometimes we make mistakes. Got involved in the wrong line. I even had to get my British friend to finish one of my traitor men. But I'll cover him, like my men.'

That accounted for the murdered *hijda* at Dadar Beach; and the fact that Crawford still remained in league with them.

Jeet switched his manner. He shrugged his shoulders diffidently and smiled with complete friendliness. 'You lose nothing by telling us where to find Crawford, yaar.'

He overdid it. The friendly part. This time it didn't work.

Radhika Amma's eyes flashed a warning, his nose crinkled, and his facial muscles adjusted to telegraph a disdainful disconcertment. 'I lose, all will have no faith in my power to protect them.'

Jeet caught on quickly. He applied a layer of meek submissive self effacement onto his visage.

It had an effect on the oily-haired Radhika Amma. He waved his right arm about with a flourish and bragged with superlative satisfaction. 'Our friends Mickey and Tan-Win are in Goa. Among western tourists same like them, they'll be safe.'

Jeet, ever the sleuth and mindful of our predicament, queried, although in a servile, obsequious manner. 'Where exactly in Goa?'

Radhika Amma didn't like Jeet speaking at all. His face took on a cocktail of expressions, a somewhat undecided mixture of humor, fear and mortification. 'I'm a fool, with all these people.' The cocktail resolved itself into a rum punch, the predominant rum being a forceful punching query. 'Who are you to talk to me? What do you know of us and the United Bamboo Gang?'

Jeet bit his lip, and mutely shook his head negatively.

I eyed Radhika Amma with a blank, vacuous expression of ignorance; while in the innermost recesses of my mind thanked Murthy for not telling us too much.

Radhika Amma elevated a mildly disparaging brow, and stared at us with scornful uncertainty. As if he'd read our minds and the results didn't agree with him. 'Really, you don't know much.'

Restive sounds came from the *hijda*'s all around. As though raring to finish us. Radhika Amma, ever alert to their feelings smiled briefly at them and signaled abruptly to a thin, stick-like *hijda* in a loose salwar. Whispers were exchanged. And the stick-like man disappeared ominously, only to return within a few seconds with Usha.

Usha held a thermos flask of the type that keeps the coffee warm. He glared frequently at us with cold contemptuous savagery. Memories of Jeet's treatment of him on the Bandra Station hill slope clearly hadn't been completely erased.

The thin man motioned others to join him. They opened the cage. Big strong men roughly held me as Usha unscrewed the cap of the thermos flask, thrust the neck between my lips and tipped it over. The flow of the liquid, hindered by my tightly grit teeth, spilled over my lips onto my body, wetting my clothes.

Strong hands gripped my throat. Helpless because of my bound arms and legs, I sat still. Someone shouted into my ear, 'drink, or we'll kill you.'

They kept forcing the flask into my mouth till I involuntarily gulped down some tasteless liquid, like plain water. I choked and swallowed again. Then they left me.

Slowly my arms and legs grew unwieldy and cumbrous, as if they'd become blocks of lead. I tried to speak and couldn't. A somnolent drowsy stupor gradually became a creeping paralysis. I tried to turn my head from side to side, and desperately fought my drooping eyelids, but finally gave up the struggle.

However, I caught a fleeting glimpse of them forcing the liquid down Jeet's throat, before consciousness mercifully left me.

XVI

I stirred slightly, the first consciousness being a curious feeling of warmth. Then the degree of darkness in the void enveloping me began to vary from a sooty black to a mosaic of leaden ash colors. Finally, I blinked. Somebody shook my shoulders gently but persistently.

I opened my eyes, and before my blurred vision could focus, I shut them almost immediately. A blinding spectrum from a large, circular ochre us glare bored intensely into my eyeballs. So close, I almost felt I could reach out and hold it. It took me almost a minute to register the sun, and to feel Jeet's hands. He repeatedly prod me on my shoulders, which enhanced my wakefulness by leaps and bounds.

'Dave, get up, Dave,' I felt his warm breath on my face, and gradually his muffled voice became clearer.

'Where am I?' I mumbled with uncertain bewilderment, half-blinded by the sun, and further nonplussed by the clearly visible steep, green, forested hillside sloping downwards, for about a hundred meters in front of me.

'I don't know?' Jeet appeared a little out of breath. I noticed him equally confusedly trying to decipher something out of a large tank further down the slope. Its aqua-blue pool-like water shimmered in the sun, below a squarish, pump-house type of structure, painted white.

I turned and looked backwards. The rough, rocky slope rose about ten meters above a low, dark tunnel. Just before the entrance to the small tunnel, three tough-looking *hijda*'s lay flat on the rough rocky ground, bound together in a strange irregular manner. Their hands and legs were splayed over each other as if they'd attempted to display some kind of feat of exotic contortionism, and then suddenly fallen asleep. Jeet said by way of explanation, 'four handcuff's only, to use on three pairs of hands and legs.'

He lightly kicked three wicked and deadly-looking knives, instruments of their vicious intent onto a patch of dried grass. They lay there with their black shafts standing out, and their curving blades shone repellently in the early morning sun.

It reminded me of something. I rubbed the dark red weal's on my wrists and asked groggily, 'How did we get here?'

Although he appeared to be trying to resolve something in his mind, Jeet grinned with self-satisfaction. 'From Bhandup Sonapur by truck, after they'd knocked us out.'

Memories came flooding back. I suddenly remembered the tasteless liquid from the flask and the consequent blackout. Involuntarily my right hand made a movement which I'd be aversely disinclined to make; especially with anyone watching me, even Jeet. I felt my crotch! Not without a great degree of relief and disburdenment did I feel everything in place.

***

Jeet laughed out aloud, and quickly controlled himself.

That helped the cobwebs disappear almost completely from my mind.

'How did we get away?'

He cast a victorious eye on me and spoke in a low keyed manner with masterful understatement. 'I acted unconscious before drinking the liquid.

They forced too little into me.'

He paused and turned and regarded the motionless *hijda*'s and continued, 'didn't get fully knocked out and recovered soon, and kept up the act till they unbound us here... then suddenly shocked them by getting up and pasting them.'

I froze in place. For a moment he sounded like a bigger version of Columbus of the Royal Haven.

He turned and faced me and grinned. 'Really tanned the bloody bastards, ah!'

Despite my nervousness, if I were the Regent, I'd bestow a George Cross upon him. Unfortunately I wasn't anyone, and would have to wait till my final report to Pemberton for any reward to be forthcoming.

'Have to get out of here?' I said weakly.

He nodded and went towards the small tunnel, and became more normal. His facial muscles tensed and his eyes crinkled slightly, as if he was vigorously exercising his mental processes while walking. 'They brought us here by truck and… I'm certain… a boat?'

I rose a little shakily and readied myself to move. 'Brought us here to kill us?'

He turned, pointed at the knives, and his eyes fastened fractionally upon mine. 'Yes, those Rampuri's used mainly to murder people.'

***

I suffered a brief moment of intense depression. We were naked without our weapons or any of the contents of our pockets. We had no means to defend ourselves, or communicate, or to buy our way through.

'We leave those knives alone, let's go,' Jeet said.

'How do we get out?' I asked, nervous and trembling a little, although Jeet somehow seemed confident.

'Brought us up this way,' he said, deep in thought, pointing into the tunnel. 'Struggled to lower us down narrow steps; so we escape the same way.'

He injected a calculated dose of reassurance and encouragement into his voice, which inspired me with hopeful optimism. He wended his way through the low tunnel, knees bent and hunched over, and stopped at a slightly larger cavern where he slowly and measurably turned left. A sliver of light dimly lit a small patch in front of musty stone steps which led upwards.

'We're in the ruins of an old fortification,' Jeet informed me.

Vigilant, heedful of anyone against us surfacing silently, we gingerly climbed and exited into an open-air well-like shallow pit. Iron steps enabled us to get onto a thick, circular iron sheet around ten meters in diameter, but rusted badly and in an irreparable state of disuse.

A long black iron cannon resting on iron mountings, a relic from the previous century, indicated the place faced danger sometime in the past. The rotatable mechanisms, now rusted, ruined and disintegrated, were stuck for all time, never to be used again.

I thought of our Glock's and muttered inadvertently, 'Lost our Glock's?'

Jeet, relentlessly focusing on trying to get away, spoke with some remoteness. 'And everything else in our pockets, but just don't think of it.'

I didn't reply. His attitude wouldn't help us, but at least we'd feel better.

He walked to the edge of the long west-to-east hill and stared ahead eastwards; over the verdant grass and a large stretch of open sea, at some kind of port. Tall, yellow cranes unloaded containers from ocean-going vessels berthed there and stacked them amongst hundreds placed in long rows.

'Jawaharlal Nehru Port Trust or JNPT port at Nhava Sheva,' he informed me.

Perplexed, he shook his head and turned abruptly, and surveyed the hill facing westwards. Finally, he nodded to himself and marched determinedly forward. 'No way down the east-side, we follow the trail westwards.'

Dried grass crackled under our feet on the dusty ground as we made our way around short trees, remnants of brick-and-mortar fortifications, rough stones and wild unchecked shrubbery.

'There's Mumbai. We're on an island.' Jeet raised his right hand and gestured westwards.

Ahead, over a few kilometers of open sea, the long high-rise skyline vaguely visible through a misty haze reminded me of London city if seen from afar, while cruising up the Thames, early on a spring morning.

I asked a little relieved at sighting the city, 'where are we?'

'Elephanta Caves Island. I've been here before a long time back.' Jeet shrugged his shoulders as we passed another cannon on the western edge of the hill.

Carefully we picked our way on the now wider muddy stony pathway as it curved downwards, till it branched-off into a narrow trail knifing through the thickly forested hillside. Merging with the twittering of hundreds of awakening birds were the strange, eerie swishing sounds from gusts of wind blowing in from across the sea. It sounded almost ghostly on the lonely, silent trail. Small, brown, furry monkeys frolicked all over, ignoring us as we marched onwards and turned left.

The flat terrain now enabled us to stride briskly forward. Then I noticed a hint of a smile passing over Jeet's face as he glanced to the left. A large monolithic cave stood silent and lonely, full of debris, with piles of rubble in front of its entrance.

Then came another cave, empty, isolated, emitting time-worn feelings. And came one more cave. This time the large magnificent stone carvings dedicated to Hindu God's, which were part of a larger cave temple complex, inspired breathless awe and dazzlement despite chunks of missing sculpture.

Jeet turned to me. 'Confirmed, we're on the Elephanta Caves Island.'

***

Silent and deserted at this early hour of the morning, the caves evoked a strange apprehensiveness. It provoked us into hurrying onwards as fast as our feet could take us, without actually breaking into a jog.

Jeet shook his head and reminisced. 'We just saw the ancient caves of Gharapuri island now called Elephanta island,' he paused to take a breath, and added in a serious manner. 'Means police would've taken a long time to find our bodies.'

Panting slightly, I gazed questioningly at him.

'Tourists come to see the caves, not the old fortifications.'

We stepped onto an uncomfortably designed stone stairway; and bounded ahead past a few small restaurants and shops, all shut securely, doors locked, shutters down, with no one about. We moved endlessly downwards under the shade of tall, green, overhanging trees, watched only by curious monkeys chattering away amongst themselves, till we reached the bottom of the hill.

'Crawford's in Goa. At least we know that?' I'd recovered enough for my mental processes to begin functioning. Now thoughts other than just those of self-preservation became endurable.

Jeet advised me with amiable deprecation. 'First we get home and to Murthy.'

He stopped at the start of a long, open jetty which curved to the right and regarded a small kiosk-like room as though trying to jog long-forgotten memories.

Closer, I read a white sign on the locked doors. 'Elephanta Island Police.'

'No use, duty hours are later. They'll come from Mumbai by boat,' Jeet said, solemn and still as he gazed thoughtfully at a couple of rusted hulks and rotting wooden boats stuck in the marshy silt surrounding this part of the island.

I twitched my nostrils at the dank, sea salty odor, raised my hands above my head, and stretched out and shuddered involuntarily. 'Got to be someone around?'

Jeet, unemotional as a rock mused. 'Should be a fishing village somewhere… convince them to take us to Mumbai.'

***

We retraced our steps and walked through the rough foliage skirting the outer edge of the island. A minute later I sighted something.

'See huts ahead.'

Jeet tersely suggested, without breaking stride, 'great, we go there.'

Soon we strolled cautiously onto a small, sandy beach towards a cluster of straw and palm leaf huts. We relaxed considerably at the scene confronting us.

Everyone was outside, hard at work. A group of young girls stood in a small queue, one by one they filled burnished bronze canisters with water from the village well. A little apart, large, buxom women tended yards of long, blue, nylon string nets strung from bamboo poles. Another lot of sari-clad women took dried fish from wicker baskets which smelt to high heavens, although not with a rotten smell, and carefully placed them on straw mats on the sand. Lithe, dark, bare bodied men in string-like loincloths, attended to a row of canoe-like wooden boats.

Jeet genially eyed a big-made grey-haired individual, in vest and shorts, with strong shoulders and a large paunch. The dark patriarch-like man turned to us. His eyes widened and his smooth-shaven pudgy face broke into a quizzical smile as we neared him.

Jeet shook his head with regret. His face took on an expression of self chastisement and he spoke as though reprimanding himself of some great iniquity. 'We want to go to Mumbai.'

The man's eyes widened. But I sensed he saw through Jeet's act and didn't like it. 'Spent the whole night here?'

Jeet, head down, twisted the palms of his half-outstretched hands, and continued using a pretty self-denunciatory tone. 'Too much beer... got up in the morning and no money... robbed!'

'Aha,' the aged fisherman nodded understandingly. He smiled with such fraternal camaraderie that I got the notion the same occurred frequently with him too. I mean the over-drinking beer part.

With an ear-to-ear grin he patted his large paunch. 'Got a house?'

Jeet blinked admiringly at his stomach and said with cordial intimacy, 'in Mumbai got a house.'

'We can come back and pay for the trip,' I butted in.

He peered at me for an instant and shook his head vigorously and jovially. 'No, no, nonsense. I'm going to Sewri,' he pointed to a wooden canoe. 'Take you two anytime. Going in ten minutes.'

Before we could thank him, he turned to an oldish-looking woman who was placing dried fish from a basket onto the mat, and snapped gruffly. 'Get tea, hot tea, ah, these two coming with me.'

The woman left the basket immediately and ambled away.

The big fisherman chuckled affably. 'Have tea, good for morning head,' he half turned as if to leave and continued. 'I've to meet someone, then coming back.'

And he marched heavily away on the loose sand.

***

After he disappeared, Jeet vocalized a warning. 'Got to check it with a boss somewhere.'

'With whom?'

'Don't know exactly,' he explained. '*Hijda*'s brought us here by boat. At this hour only these fishermen have boats plying!'

'They're in league with those *hijda*'s?'

'Have to be,' Jeet revealed. 'So we'd better be careful of them.'

Then someone nudged me. The old woman, reeking of dried fish, brought us two steaming cups of brew. We accepted the proffered tea and sipped it in silence.

When we finished, a dark, well-muscled young man came towards us. The only addition to his loincloth was a string tied around his waist.

He said in perfectly accented English, 'my uncle has other work, I'll take you across.'

We returned the empty teacups and followed the square-faced fisherman to a boat. I noticed he consciously avoided our eyes.

This gave rise to some degree of suspicion. Somehow I became acutely conscious of something amiss. I sensed Jeet did too. A vague sense of disquiet began to spread out over my body. Not only we'd lost Crawford and all our personal effects, but were struggling to get away safely.

But Jeet didn't do anything. Instead he quietly helped out in pushing the narrow canoe-like boat with a long bamboo mast, into the knee-deep water.

Then one after another we clambered onboard, before the fisherman finally jumped in. Silently, he paddled onwards for about five minutes before unfurling a dirty, white canvas sail. And at last we sailed the few kilometers westwards, to the city of Mumbai.

XVII

I sat slightly crushed with my arms on my lap, by Jeet's side. We were a little behind the prow of the small boat which slid lightly onwards, towards the hazy Mumbai skyline. Despondent and subdued, but appreciating the respite, I watched in the early morning light, a group of snowy-white seagulls screeching shrilly and incessantly while lazily diving up and down with graceful waving wings.

Behind us the fisherman deftly handled the sails and the tiller, gently persuading the boat into keeping course. All the while he remained silent, ignoring us, concentrating on the job at hand.

Jeet casually bowed low and leaning close to me, divulged under his breath, 'something wrong. They've stopped the other man from taking us.'

'What should we do?' I murmured and shrugged my shoulders slightly. When he didn't reply immediately, I focused my eyes on the towering Mumbai skyline closing in as the small craft rose and plunged through a momentary rough patch, before smoothing its way in the otherwise not too choppy sea.

Jeet finally suggested in a low undertone, 'act as if enjoying the view innocently.'

I viewed the construction activity on the sea. Spans of some kind of large bridge were being built.

'Building the Nhava Sheva to Sewri trans-harbor highway,' Jeet said.

'Big contrast to these backward-looking fishermen, the development around.'

For a moment we shook a little as the boat curved sharply. The fisherman expertly evaded another small boat, and realigned the dirty canvas sails to adjust course. He skirted past an island with pipelines extending along concrete jetties, like the arms of an octopus. Jeet pointedly scanned the oil tankers moored at the end of lengthy jetties, which loomed over our craft. He announced grandly, like a guide of a conducted tour for retired couples who were slightly hard of hearing.

'Butcher Island Oil Terminal.

Then he disclosed under his breath, 'brought the *hijda*'s with us to Elephanta, expected to take them back, not us.'

Suddenly a thought crossed my mind. 'The M & P operation at Dadar beach. The two fishermen caught there are identical to the man here.'

'Yes could be in the pay of the United Bamboo Gang Triad.'

I nodded, head down, and licked salt water from my lips, not really seeing anything properly other than the grey sea water flowing past, spraying unceasingly onto my face. My mind remained fixated on the crux of our immediate predicament. What would occur when we left the boat?

The skyline ahead now defined itself into individual structures as we, in the open sea, crossed the Mumbai harbor inner anchorage. We slipped through large hulking merchant ships and a variety of specialized vessels, all anchored at intervals as though in a long queue.

The fisherman adeptly maneuvered the vessel and sharply evaded a small hovercraft, which sped past with a light blinking on its small mast. Without uttering a word he centered towards the southern side of a large bay.

Jeet proclaimed loudly, more for the man's benefit that for any other reason. 'Sewri. Going to a fishing village there.'

The fisherman ignored us and silently guided the boat onwards, cruising past the headland jutting out at the southern edge of the bay.

Factory chimney's belched out smoke and piles of sea cargo containers were visible in stacks from over long compound walls. However, no humans were in sight on the long swathe of land. Slowly and steadily we advanced towards a large, dense forest of tall, green mangroves.

Suddenly the fisherman stopped the boat, and rolled up the sail. For a second he looked around, then punted the boat forward with a long bamboo pole, towards a rod with a red flag sticking out from the depths of the now murky, muddy water. Inexorably he neared the marker.

'What will we do?' I asked Jeet.

Jeet tapped me on my lap and muttered under his breath, 'we've to sprint full speed away.'

Tensing my cramped muscles, I silently readied myself to do so.

The man punted the canoe expertly into a narrow channel, cutting through a sticky, muddy, silt bank. He zigzagged onwards towards dry land, which lay unseen beyond a thick, dark, forbidding wall of mangroves.

A few shallow twists and turns later the channel straightened out, knifing through the forest of mangroves, and dead-ended about a hundred meters in front. Beyond lay a narrow macadam road, under the shadow of rust-red containers piled a few stories high, visible over a long wall which extended for as far as our eyes could see.

The briny sea smell tinge pervading in the air increased considerably and merged with a putrid stench coming from the swampy land. This added to the abrasive, shadowy atmosphere which turned increasingly somber, overpowering us with a mystifying subtle and imperceptible, yet menacing premonition of concealed danger.

Then we saw them.

Far ahead on both banks of the muddy channel, dirt-poor fishermen in wretched clothes stood in front of a couple of wooden boats with their heads lowered. Some of them couldn't help raising their heads to peer at us.

That gave them away. There was no mistaking the diabolical, fiendish glint in their shinning eyes which let out their murderous intent. Vicious-looking meat chopper-like knives and large wooden paddles in their muscular arms accentuated the demonical and primeval effect the reception committee exuded. They looked like representations of Stone Age aboriginals from some picture book suddenly come to life. Now they confronted us, clearly with a deadly malicious and homicidal intent.

Jeet whispered, 'mobiled them from Elephanta to prepare a mob to attack us!'

***

Jeet stood up with a jerk and yanked me upwards and yelled. 'Follow me.'

He hopped-off the moving boat, plunged into the slimy silt bank which inclined slightly upwards and ploughed through the mud, struggling briskly to move ahead.

With an energetic alacrity catalyzed by fear, I instinctively leapt out behind him onto the glutinous muck, and labored onwards with great effort and exertion. Thighs burning, sucking sounds coming from the gluey treacle below every time I planted and lifted my feet, my toil paid- off, and I moved onwards more and more easily. Just in time. A vicious swipe with the punting pole swished past my ears and missed me by millimeters.

The fisherman from our boat consequently lost balance and splashed into the cloudy tan waters of the narrow channel.

Upstream, a rowdy clamorous tumult broke out from the mob waiting for us. I didn't dare look back, instead ran on and on towards the comforting wall of mangroves.

I slid forward erratically on the ground which seemed to rock from side to side, slipping onto all fours at times, struggling and straining, with my strength gradually leaching out of my muscles. Resolutely, obsessively, with a one-track mind locked like that of some primordial creature tenaciously questing for self-preservation, I grabbed a tree stump and dragged myself onto comparably harder land. Soon I breathed easier under the cover of darkness afforded by the dense grove of mangroves.

The ground enabled me to tread on a little bit faster. But knotty tangles of soaking wet underbrush and networks of webbed branches with needle-like thorns, bedeviled further advance at any conventional speed. I struggled to sight Jeet. And recoiled with unnerving panic when an arm reached out and grabbed me, and pulled me onto what was a concrete slab.

'Not following us. Still just keep close to me.' Jeet's comforting voice heartened and bolstered me considerably.

I felt like the ancient Israelites must have felt in the wilderness when provided solace and succor with manna from heaven. But when I opened my mouth, no sound came save a continuous gasping and wheezing for breath.

Jeet held my hand and strode briskly towards the shore. We were on some kind of long trail of concrete that extended from the sea all the way to the shore, right through the middle of the mangrove swamp.

Wearily, thoroughly winded and stinking of sediment and sludge, I tagged him up till a narrow pebble-strewn macadam road. There he left my hand.

Cautiously, wary of anyone trying to surprise us, we hiked past a dread-stimulating signpost. A large, gleaming skull bone of a cow, with extra long horns pointing straight up, stared hauntingly at us from atop a wooden stake on one side of the road.

At the end of the road we still weren't being followed.

Jeet turned and said with an element of a mild sneer in his voice. 'Can't get close to civilization in their loincloths.'

I scanned the road with Jeet as a prelude to crossing it. And literally rattled out of my stunned anatomy with astonished amazement. A deep voice with acoustics as though audioed through some kind of machinelike contrivance, came over the air.

'Adams and Jeet, remain there.'

Flabbergasted, Jeet jerked to the right and quickly raised both hands and waved. A dark blue Swaraj Mazda van closed in. A loudspeaker on its roof flashed the presumptuous order from between an orange and a red light.

An Inspector in a crisply starched uniform swiftly stepped out of the cab even before the van pulled up, and jogged to us. 'Adams and Jeet?'

'Yes that's us,' Jeet answered.

The Inspector didn't express surprise at our ruined clothes, or waste time or mince words. Instead he handed a Motorola handset to Jeet. 'Murthy sir, will talk to you.'

***

I stood by wearily, jaded and worn-out, and rested my hands on the open rear doors of the van, near half a dozen grilled steel shields hanging to one side.

From outside the van, Jeet spoke into the Motorola to Murthy. 'Jeet speaking, sir.'

I heard Murthy clearly. The familiar-sounding voice enquired, 'Adams and Jeet... how are you two?'

'Jeet on the line. We're safe, sir.'

'Thank God you're safe.' Murthy sounded concerned. He added. 'Broken down some *hijda*'s and got information that you were to be murdered and disposed-off at Elephanta.'

'Sir, I've cuffed three of them there.'

'Am sending a police party there to take charge and investigate an attempted murder case also.'

Although I felt inanimate and lifeless, like a corpse, I still tingled as if thousands of tiny barbs had suddenly come alive all over my body.

'Did you see our Maruti parked for too long, sir?' Jeet queried.

'Yes. It's now in the Bhandup police station,' he said, paused and continued. 'Our men spotted you entering Sonapur.'

The constables in the van looked on impassively, but I detected some of them fidgeting restively. Similar men had been around a Mahindra Bolero jeep at the entrance to Bhandup Sonapur. Except they didn't seem to notice us. Maybe they did, and didn't give it away. A pity they couldn't accompany us inside for whatever reason. As Jeet had said, they had one hand tied behind their backs.

'And saw us leaving, sir?' Jeet probed.

'No didn't see you leave for too long,' Murthy said tightly.

'They took us out by truck, sir.'

'Anyway I convinced my Additional Commissioner sir, to request East Region sir, to order Deputy Commissioner, Zone Five, based at Tilak Nagar, to conduct a raid.'

Jeet turned to me, I was listening in too, and explained, 'Additional Commissioner in charge of the East Region, is East Region sir.'

My exhausted, dead and spiritless disposition began to vanish and I felt like thawing ice, flushing with a slow warmth and an enervating lifting of the mood.

'Sir, what about Radhika Amma?' Jeet continued.

'He escaped.'

I detected a trace of relief in Murthy's voice. I reckoned other factors came in the way or what, I couldn't make out. Or probably he really escaped.

Murthy proceeded, 'nabbed a big group of these men, mostly castrated. Held on a number of charges. We also think Sonapur was the second hideout of the United Bamboo Gang in Mumbai.'

'Got evidence for the Triad case, sir?'

'Can pin down the heroin case as we know of them on Dadar beach. We're holding them for questioning for as long as statutorily possible. Then we'll charge them,' he paused and added with genuine ruefulness and regret. 'No help regarding Crawford.'

Jeet looked momentarily at me and got back to the handset. 'Radhika Amma bragged they're in Goa, sir.'

Murthy made a loud sound of satisfied achievement. '*Shabash*! Better go there then, try to find out something.'

Murthy and his Mumbai cops had come out with flying colors in their case, finishing the United Bamboo Gang Triad and its cohorts.

But although they'd cleverly used us, we hadn't got Crawford yet. Luckily we had a clue.

Jeet glanced at me, nodded and looked downwards and spoke a trifle hesitantly, 'we will... ?'

Murthy interrupted him. He established his policemen's efficiency when his hands linked with that of his subordinates; both hands joined up and acted in concert.

'First wait at your residence. I'll get a constable to drive your Maruti to your house, with your Glock's, mobile's and other personal effects... recovered them and everything else from Radhika Amma's hideout!'

XVIII

I rubbed my eyes and peered about in the semi-darkness outside. I was in a tastefully paneled and furnished chestnut-brown lounge of a small wayside inn situated in a town named Kudal. The early morning sun filtered through a line of dark willowy trees and revealed our Maruti parked amongst a row of vehicles. Birds awakening, though still invisible, twittered all over as the new day unhurriedly dawned in imperceptible increments.

We must have driven for over four hundred kilometers since we'd left Mumbai the previous afternoon. Luckily Jeet had hired a driver and while we dozed-off in the back seat, he'd driven us this far.

Jeet, as fresh as ever, returned from the washroom. He loosened his tracksuit top by unzipping it till his sternum and lowered his lean but strong frame onto the couch besides me.

He expelled a deep breath and sighed with relaxation. 'Sent the driver back to Mumbai.'

A blue uniformed waiter came towards us.

Jeet ordered another round of tea for us. And the waiter walked away to get the brew.

Our forthcoming hunt in Goa occupied my thoughts. I couldn't work out any viable solution to our problem. I remarked with genuine disenchanted bafflement. 'Where do we start searching from, in Goa?'

'Among the western tourists there is what Radhika Amma had said... think we check out the beaches?'

I detected a trace of interrogativeness in his reply, as if he wasn't sure about something.

'Beaches, means more than one beach,' I asked with my mouth full of smoke.

The waiter brought our tea's.

Jeet sipped casually. 'From Arambol in the north to Polem in the south is about a hundred kilometers!'

I took in a deep breath of utter dismay. 'Rather long stretch to search?'

'Yes,' Jeet agreed, paused and injected an optimistic note into his voice. 'Not to worry, we'll manage because I think there's a drug angle.'

'If he's doing drugs, easier to find him?'

'Yes.'

I puffed in silence, watching the miniature white clouds of exhaled smoke dissipating into the cool early morning air; and in between tried to finish the steaming, sweet tea.

Jeet finished his brew and confided, 'Murthy has sent a message to the Goa police...'

Then his Reliance jingled a Christmas tune. Someone was calling him.

***

Jeet punched appropriately and spoke into his cell phone.

'Jeet here.'

Someone spoke at length from the other end.

I waited with suspenseful expectation. For the inevitable news, unhurried and unhasty, motionless, like a marble statue.

'Ha Nagwekar sahib, so another murder. This time at Arambol beach?'

Nagwekar continued talking for some time.

They had to be grateful. After all we'd helped in destroying a branch of the Triad in Mumbai. And led the police to a number of suspected *hijda*'s.

'So the mortally wounded man let out their location before dying,' Jeet said.

Nagwekar continued on the line. I couldn't hear him.

Finally, after a prolonged period of time psychologically and emotionally, but chronologically only a few seconds, Jeet ended the call. He turned to me, eyes twinkling with a type of elated fulfillment that comes from solving a complicated problem.

'Crawford's up to his stunts again. Committed another murder, similar to the killing on Dadar beach.'

'Got his probable location?'

Outside, sounds of heavy vehicles passing by on the nearby highway assailed our ears. Somewhere in the vicinity a cock crowed lustily and provoked a series of barks from stray dogs.

'Forensic processing revealed a G-11 caliber four-point-seven millimeter bullets,' Jeet explained.

'Then it's Crawford all right.'

'He breathed deeply in, and steadily exhaled. 'The victim, before dying, let out that Crawford and Lee were in the Vagator Beach area!'

***

A few hours later, Jeet and I stood on the sunny, sandy Vagator Beach. Barely a minute earlier we'd parked the Maruti safely near a bar-cum-restaurant named Carneiro's.

Jeet looked to the left and right; and finally began strolling northwards on the slightly curving beach. 'We'll walk up and down and check if Crawford and Lee are anywhere around.'

'Unlikely,' I vented my feelings and trailed Jeet. 'If he's committed a crime, he'll hide inside. More so if he's an addict.'

Jeet didn't reply. Instead he determinedly ploughed his way onwards, past rows of tall coconut palms, and across a wide band of hot grainy sand, towards the wetter but firmer sand near the shimmering ashen grayish yet faintly azure sea.

A peaceful laid-back holiday atmosphere pervaded on the wide beach. I recognized many Britons enjoying themselves, away from good old Blighty's winter cold. All over, groups of tanned Europeans in swimming trunks sunned themselves, lying on plain straw mats or brightly colored mats. Topless blondes and brunettes along with dark haired Europeans lay singly or in pairs or in groups on mats. Everyone took advantage of the effectively warm yet pleasant Goa winter sun, rays of which poured down and reflected radiantly-off the light brown sand.

'Jeet, it's like in a European country.'

'That's Goa in winter. Plenty of Europeans come,' he said and surreptitiously scanned the sunbathers for any sign of our man, while continuing to casually stroll ahead. 'Easy for Crawford to hide anonymously, although Lee will stand out.'

'So that's what Radhika Amma meant 'among others westerner's there', they're safe?'

'Right,' Jeet agreed, and climbed onto a narrow strip of coal-black and peppery grey rocks which ran out to the sea from the base of a short hill.

I followed him, jumping down on the other side, onto another beach far shorter than the previous one. A couple of big-made British sunbather's relaxed, whiling away their holiday in the sun. Others, again mostly Briton's on easy chairs under sun-shades, gossiped amongst themselves.

At the end of the sandy strip, under lazily waving verdant leaves of tall palm trees, more European tourists sipped their drinks and stared at the beach and sea from a couple of beach shack restaurants made up of coconut fronds.

Also on display were a lot of substantial, superb bronzed fitness muscles on European males, mostly hovering about their generally cute, doll-like girlfriends.

I surveyed their faces furtively. 'No Crawford. Maybe he's somewhere in the interior?'

'Not worth checking ourselves,' Jeet grit his teeth and shook his head, and passed embarrassingly close to a grey-haired European couple sunbathing on straw mats. They appeared to be on a single post-retirement jaunt to mysterious Goa before returning home with memories to keep till the end.

Jeet finally stopped a few meters ahead, at the foot of a hill with a fortress atop it. At sea level, powerful waves hit the rough, jagged rocks with tremendous force and energy; and converted into a swelling, frothy foam before flowing back into the vast mass of the heavy sea.

A powerful ozone tang became stronger here, fusing with the all prevalent salty-sea odor and the mild vinegarish scent of wet mosses and foliage clinging to the rocks.

Jeet pointed upwards at the dark brown walls of a ruined fortress that enclosed the top of the hillock. 'Chapora fort. Across the hill is the Chapora river; and across it is another set of beaches.'

'But Crawford's here in Vagator?'

'Right.'

'What do we do now?' I asked, feeling a bit spirited and buoyant due to the fresh, invigorating, open-airy atmosphere.

'Maybe we'll see Crawford if we walk back, southwards... see the rest of the Vagator beaches.'

***

We retraced our way over the narrow, rocky outcrop, and hiked briskly southwards across the longer beach. And up to another broader band of charcoal-black and ashen-grey sun-baked rocks that cut across the sand, beyond which lay yet another beach.

'Let's go across to the next Vagator beach,' Jeet suggested.

I trudged onwards determinedly onto the broad band of rocks; past a small block of concrete with a somber-looking cross atop it. Dark skinned fishermen in loincloths and little else gossiped amongst themselves near a couple of wooden boats, and scarcely gave us a second glance as we stepped down onto the next Vagator beach.

We walked on and on, past more Britons, Russians, Italians, Germans and French tourists, all engrossed with each other. Frequently we stepped on rough rocky outcrops devoid of tourists, hotter than the sands around.

Clandestinely, I regarded the rust-brown to cherry rouged complexions on the well-tanned bottoms, breasts, and hairy chests and muscled pectorals on the large, well-built Europeans. But there was no sign of Crawford amongst them.

Uptight at the uneasy distress beginning to overcome me as we sauntered onwards without seeing Crawford anywhere, I queried, 'what if we don't see him outside?'

Jeet didn't take his eyes-off the chlorophyll-green hillside beyond the sands, with rows of gloomy thatched huts that somehow evoked a dismal melancholy mood.

He said with deep thoughtfulness and solemnity, 'plenty of hotels, restaurants with rooms, even local villagers and fishermen give parts of their huts to the tourists.'

'Got to check them all?' I inquired, daunted and disturbed at the thought of checking every local home.

We passed a group of male and female Europeans, attired in loose pajamas and colorful sleeveless vests, with headbands around their heads. Their glazed eyes and skinny appearance, besides frequent twitching and runny noses, gave them away as drug addicts of some sort.

Two watery-eyed men banged away on small drums. One pathetic faced, haggard and wearied blond man, with shinning eyes depressed under bony beetle brows, played haunting notes on a flute which provoked an aching nostalgic pang.

I recalled last hearing similar music once in a Robin Hood film seen on DVD in my Kensington flat. It sounded like music played by

Englishmen in the Sherwood forests of England in the fifteenth century.

However their attention mostly focused on a small wooden pipe which they passed around amongst themselves. Each man and woman took a long continuous pull, held in the smoke for some time, and exhaled slowly, before passing the pipe to the next person.

Jeet leaned close to my ear and divulged, 'druggies... Vagator was the original Goa beach where hippies came in the sixties.'

I nodded. A few seconds later I felt vaguely relieved at having passed them.

Ahead, more normal tourists lay on mats in a long row till the end of the beach. There a lush green hillock surged upwards out of the sands, blocking further advance.

Within the shadow of the short hill, English and Russian children frolicked with their mother's in the shallow aquamarine-blue pools, created by the peculiar configuration of the rugged, craggy, raven black rocks. Some kids, squealing and yelling hoarsely swam or raced each other up and down the wet sand. Slightly older boys threw pebbles at an upturned bucket. Their sister's collected seashells nearby. A few bare-bodied men kicked a soccer ball about. Couples in skimpy string bikinis and nothing else, strolled hand in hand along the edge of the breaking surf, displaying magnificently tanned bodies.

Jeet stopped and pointed to the rocks at sea level and mused thoughtfully. 'Can walk across to the Anjuna beaches. But don't feel he'll be there.'

At the base of the hill, a rocky ledge a few meters above the sea led to the Anjuna beaches on the other side. At the start of the rocky outcrop were inexplicable stone carvings of a large face with two small skulls.

I faced Jeet, feeling indecisive and skeptical. 'What do we do now?'

Jeet half turned to walk back. His face had an expression, which indicated he was struggling mentally with a comprehensive scrutiny over all possible modus to nab our quarry. 'Searching all huts, rooms impossible...' He hesitated and clinically suggested another operandi. 'Or go to the police?'

'I don't want to get into Mumbai-type escapades again,' I confided.

Jeet grinned. He closed his right palm and shook it in a deliberate gesture of terminally conclusive finality. 'Like at the Royal Haven... get to a local tout... get him to help us.'

***

Carneiro's Bar and Restaurant, a shimmering white box-like concrete hut right next to the pathway leading down to the sands below, stood atop a low hillock facing the beach. Inside, European tourists – men, women, couples, many with toddlers – sat on cheap, red plastic chairs exchanging whispers, or loud mouthedly argued about something while partaking of meals or sipping their drinks. Most were working-class Britons and East Europeans recuperating from hard work in their colder climes. They just gazed idly at the lazy scene ahead. We could have been in the South of France or Spain or Portugal or even Greece, given the fully European atmosphere pervading.

We squeezed around a rectangular table. Then Jeet leaned back and casually gave the other patrons a once-over. I did the same, eyes roving among the rest, and when I finished a trifle disappointed at not sighting Crawford, I lit a cigarette.

'Welcome to Goa. Nice beach to enjoy here today, ah,' the waiter greeted us and added. 'Beer ah?'

I nodded and puffed on my cigarette.

Jeet sighed and reached for his wallet to pay in advance for the drinks, surprising me. 'Two beers, men, and bring the menu. We're hungry.'

When he left, Jeet placidly placed an elbow on the table and pillowed his chin on the palm of his hand. 'Playing the part, Goa is like heaven for drinkers... pubs, taverns, wine shops all over.'

'Ideal scene for me. Crawford ought to have come here in the first place,' I quipped.

The waiter returned with two large mugs and two bottles of ice cold beer. He fastidiously wiped the table clean before setting them down. He also left a menu card. Jeet almost instantly ordered a meal, barely needing to peruse the menu card. When the waiter left, we poured ourselves our beer, filling our mugs till the foam-like heads reached their brims.

Jeet held an ice cold mug to his cheek as if to cool himself, and surveyed the restaurant. 'Now to get to a local tout.'

And he finally saw someone. He stared hard for a few moments to catch his eye. Then he raised his hand and motioned across.

***

A diminutive roly-poly dark-haired man in a creased short-sleeved cotton tee shirt that had possibly been white sometime in the past and in an oversized pair of black patched-up shorts, waddled over to us.

Jeet introduced me directly. 'This is Dave from London. I'm Jeet, men. We've come to Goa to find someone.'

The pudgy-faced local furrowed his brow and crinkled his eyes as though Jeet's oratory was too much for him to comprehend. He shrugged his shoulders as if to express his helplessness.

Jeet invited him to join us. 'Sit men, drink, ah?'

'Yah beer,' he replied hesitantly in a hoarse, full-mouthed growl.

I slid a cigarette an inch out of my pack and offered it to him. He declined, angling an outstretched palm of his right hand in a negative gesture. I pocketed the pack, blew out some smoke and remained engrossed in motionless reflection.

Jeet ordered another beer and turned to him. 'What's your name?'

'Socrates,' he announced grandly.

Jeet arched his eyebrows and said, 'we want to find a chap who has robbed money from us. He's also murdered people.'

Socrates shrugged his shoulders with irksome unconcern, and his eyes strayed away from us. The waiter returned and placed a mug and a bottle of beer in front of him. He quickly poured himself some beer, but sipped it as though imbibing poisoned hemlock.

Jeet took a long swig from his mug and persisted in a mildly assertive tone. 'Think one of our buggers murdered in Arambol by him?'

Moon faced Socrates visibly blanched with shocked stupefaction. Flabbergasted, he peered at us through wrinkled eyes, then shrugged his shoulders. 'Oh Henriques... yah he was murdered at Arambol, men.'

Jeet glanced at him and remarked, 'very bad. Henriques got killed. Why, I don't understand.'

Socrates' disassociation suddenly disappeared. He almost broke down with passion and shrugged his shoulders and emoted in a crude rasping voice. 'Don't know who shot him, men. Some mad man.'

I lifted my mug and gulped down the last of my beer and gazed indolently at the entrance of Carneiro's. A peculiar Goa effect began to overcome me when a bolt of astonished amazement raced through my body, jerking me stiffly upright and almost choking me!

I stared intently. No mistake. Columbus! In a fresh white tee shirt and stiff khaki shorts, he casually stepped into Carneiro's. Yes, Columbus of the Royal Haven of Henry Road, Colaba, Mumbai. The raging inferno, if I recalled right, looked around with vague familiarity and faltered hesitatingly when his eyes rested on Jeet and me. He wavered and vacillated on the spot.

Jeet broke the inertia hindering Columbus and revealed that he recognized him by breaking into a wide grin. He waved to him and motioned him to join us.

***

Jeet greeted Columbus with great sincerity, like meeting a long-lost bosom pal. 'Aarrey Columbus you bugger, what are you doing in Vagator Beach, men?'

'Live here, men,' Columbus replied a little wanly though in an even voice. The old fire had fizzled out of him.

Socrates' ears cocked up like a pups, curious at Jeet's ease and familiarity with Columbus.

Columbus grabbed an empty chair from a nearby table and seated himself.

The waiter added to the confusion by bringing the meal Jeet had ordered earlier. Jeet made amends by ordering a few more dishes to accommodate Socrates and Columbus. 'Bring full speed, men. Our food becoming cold otherwise.'

Then he turned to Columbus. His visage indicated sublime delight. 'You're just the chap we need.'

The waiter performed some kind of culinary feat, given the crowds at the other tables, bringing the newly ordered dishes within a couple of minutes.

Jeet served himself some rice and poured a little fish curry over it with a spoon.

I lit another cigarette and served myself.

Socrates and Columbus joined in, helping themselves.

Columbus speared a piece of fried pomfret and savored it, trembling slightly, a wry look on his face. 'Left Royal Haven. Trying for a ship job.'

Jeet kept spooning in his rice with small pieces of fish, and nodded, gravely circumspect all the while. Then, controlling himself impeccably, he raised the decibel level of his voice, yet sounded affable. 'Anyway you two better help us, men, about our problem!'

'Need help?' Columbus gazed at him enthusiastically.

Jeet jogged his memory. 'Same chap, men, Mickey Crawford and a China man...'

'Who took money?' Desperate movements on Columbus' dark eyes and facial muscles indicated a valiant attempt to recall events at the Royal Haven.

Jeet pumped in some more information. 'Except now think he murdered Henriques.'

Socrates, who'd finished his meal first, now sounded more confident while speaking. 'Our police didn't catch him.'

I finished my meal, placed the spoon and fork on the plate and pushed it away, and added, 'think Crawford's doing drugs.'

Jeet calmly reassured them, 'We're here to get them. Only need help, men.'

I took out a photograph of Crawford and gave it to them. 'He's with a China man named Tan Win Lee.'

Columbus, eager as a beaver in the last stages of building a dam, flaunted an ability folks like him usually have. 'Can find out anything in Goa, men.'

Jeet slanted his eyebrows interrogatively. But his eyes indicated an absolute certitude and a faithful confidence in Columbus' boast. 'Find out where they are. Police already know of them. But haven't caught him yet.'

My right thumb froze on my lighter just before depressing it to light another smoke. 'How can they help?' I asked.

Jeet replied quickly, shaking his head and widening his eyes in a manner calculated to boost their morale and self-esteem. 'They're all over. Drivers, cooks, canteen boys, waiters, peons, touts... can find out anything.'

XIX

Later in the evening I had my drink quietly, seated comfortably on a wooden chair, and in between sips puffed contentedly away. I stared vacantly out over the dark beach and the shimmering sea, at the crimson ring of fire going down on the far western horizon.

Jeet, next to me on a rocking chair, gazed silently at the ceiling, his hand on his orange juice on the side table.

Carneiro's Bar and restaurant had three rooms to rent out. And because a German couple vacationing there had left the same morning, they had one room to let. We moved in after Jeet had successfully haggled with the owner about the rent. Our Maruti remained safely in a small, enclosed compound nearby.

The single room had a floor of creaky wooden beams, the bathroom had no hot water and the entire place reeked of stale perfume and sweat.

But a steady, cooling sea breeze and a magnificent view of the beach below and the sea beyond, somewhat made up for any shortfall within.

I decided to call up Sam on my BlackBerry.

'We're in Goa, in a place called Vagator,' I informed him.

'He's somewhere around?' Sam enquired.

'Yes, he's here somewhere around.' I detailed facts of the case to him, and about our difficulty in finding him amongst the tourists here.

'When caught he'll be charged in Mumbai and Goa?'

'Yes, will have a drug case against him; and a couple of murder cases.'

'Difficult to extradite him when caught then,' Sam remarked.

'We'll get him first, at least it'll satisfy the Ferron people.'

'Right, and the G-11 will be used as evidence. So it'll take time to get it back,' Sam hypothesized.

'We're waiting for information from some local boys. Chances he's an addict and they'll locate him because of it.'

Sam wished us the best of luck and advised, 'keep in touch. Inform me of any new development.'

***

Gradually, as the clock ticked on, the Goa holiday mood caught up with us. Jeet rocked slowly on the wooden chair with his eyes closed. I passed time lazily doing nothing, gazing out of the windows which momentarily blazed with the setting sun; watching the twilight descend as a prelude to the coming darkness. The temperature of the breeze coming in from the sea lowered by a few degrees, which somehow aided me in forgetting the Crawford case and the worry and tension it had caused us.

That is, till a series of knocks resounded on our rickety wooden door. Several hushed whispers outside portended we had more than one visitor.

'Columbus and Socrates with what they've found out,' Jeet said, and got up. He pushed aside the rusted latch and swung the creaking door inwards.

Columbus entered with another boy, followed by Socrates who carried an ancient-looking long barreled revolver. If weapons were ever recovered from galleons wrecked under the sea for hundreds of years, or someplace similar, they'd probably wouldn't look much worse than the weapon in Socrates' hand.

Jeet didn't show any surprise at the additional guest. Instead hospitably offered, 'orange juice?'

A chorus of muted "ayes" rent the air.

Jeet poured three glasses and passed them around to the trio who sat on the edge of the bed.

Columbus sipped some juice and revealed, 'this bugger is Hitler. He's a waiter.'

I regarded the short boy, under five feet tall with a narrow, almost emaciated body and a too large face, with large dark active eyes. In dark shorts, he appeared to have wiped his hands regularly on his food-stained tee shirt.

Socrates pointed at Hitler. 'He's working near the police station.'

Jeet held his glass in his hand just below his chin and gave a dignified nod. 'Found out anything?'

'Police also had photo. The fellow who murdered Henriques wasn't outside yesterday,' Hitler said.

Columbus between sips smugly revealed, 'police sent plainclothes men to all restaurants, bars and beaches. Didn't find him and the China man.'

Jeet kept up a kind of act, vaguely ringing cinematic bells. Like Spencer Tracy in the film classic "Boy's Town". He had their confidence, yet kept them at a safe distance, and could get them to do as he pleased.

'Where is he then?' Jeet queried.

A sudden gust of wind rattled the open window and shook the tall coconut palm trees outside, rustling their leaves with a swaying, swishing sound.

'Don't know,' Columbus answered.

'Haven't searched the inside of the rooms available?' I asked.

'No,' Socrates said. 'Think the robber bugger is somewhere inside.'

Outside, various tropical hues alternated on the beach and sea, each growing a shade darker and duskier as the sun indiscernibly lowered on its daily disappearing motions. Jeet stood up, walked to a switchboard and turned on the lights; and returned to his chair in the somber yellow glow that bathed the room with the light from two naked electric bulbs.

'Police say he's still in Vagator,' Hitler added.

I turned to Jeet. 'What are we going to do now?'

'If local cops couldn't find them; might have to contact Murthy to give us a Goa police contact.'

Columbus, who exuded a hint of intelligence, waved his right hand southwards. 'Big party at Vagator, men, everyone coming. The robber bugger with the gun may come also.'

'Aha, the party, fantastic, men.' Jeet whole-heartedly agreed with him. 'If on drugs he'll come there definitely.'

I looked at Jeet interrogatively.

'Like a big rave party. Everyone'll come. In fact if anyone from around doesn't come, they'll get to know.'

'So we have one last chance to get Crawford, before we go to the police?'

'We'll find out at the party,' Columbus said.

As the evening wore on, vague sounds of suppressed talk from the restaurant below became louder and louder. Crowds of tourists returned to the Carneiro's Bar and Restaurant for drinks and dinner. A distinct aroma of cooking victuals, vegetables, chicken and fish seeped upwards into our room, activating our gastric juices. I became ravenously hungry.

I lifted my glass for a final sip, not knowing what exactly Jeet had implied regarding Crawford being there at the party. But he sounded fairly confident.

***

Around midnight, Jeet and I strolled a few meters from Carneiro's towards a small hillock adjacent to it. As we tramped on, I watched scores of tourists on foot and in vehicles disappear down the other side of the short hill.

'You know where we're going?'

'Yes,' Jeet replied. 'Hold the party here sometimes.'

We reached the other edge of the hill and made our way down to a small plateau of flattened mud. It jutted over a small narrow east-to-west valley which was bound by a forested hill on the south side and bare hillside on the north. Scores of motorcycles, cars and vans were parked side by side on the dusty ground. Long cables extended downwards from a noisy generator truck to a collection of searchlights and naked bulbs. These were affixed to the top of long bamboo poles at certain points in the valley.

The lighting in the small, cozy valley illuminated hundreds of tourists from every European country, especially Britain. They were all dressed in multi-colored clothes – pajamas, shorts, vests and many had headbands. They sat on plenty of straw mats lying about at random, around portable lanterns, and drank tea or partook of the fruit and biscuits available, while gossiping amongst themselves. Many were barefoot. Some of the single girls had backpacks, like those used when undertaking a camping expedition in the jungle.

Grey haired women, with a couple of boys to help out, sat on each mat. They tended small kerosene stoves with boiling pots of tea and a paraphernalia of pots, pans, cups, glasses as well as bowls with bananas, oranges, apples and grapes. Extremely busy, they constantly handed out fruit and tea to the tourists lounging around.

Further eastwards lay a large circle of flattened rust-brown earth. A dance floor. A lot of lighting focused on it. Red, blue and green streamers hung around the floor at points. On the north slope adjacent to it, a big long-haired, bare-bodied blond tinkered with an expensive sound system on a wooden table. Large amplifiers stood ready to blare out dance music on the tables flanking the music system.

Near us, every few seconds, roars of arriving motorbikes, cars, vans rent the air, and additional groups of western tourists would join the throngs on the mats, adding to the cacophony around. Right up here at the parking space, despite the noise of the generator and vehicles, I identified British-accented English, various cockney slangs, Irish brogues, Russian, German, French, Italian and a variety of East European dialects. A virtual cacophonous Tower of Babel.

Two swarthy tourists stepped out of a jeep and exchanged a few words in some exotic tongue, near us. Then they moved away and joined the others on the mats.

I confusedly tried to recognize the language.

Jeet leaned close to me. 'Israeli's on holiday, speaking Hebrew.'

I nodded, gradually becoming ecstatic. Crawford would surely feel safe enough to merge with the crowds around. 'What do we do?'

'Sit on the hillside and watch. They'll certainly come here.'

***

The long-haired blond at the table tested the music system. Hard Rock came on through the large amplifiers at various volumes. He selected the volume and started the music. The mildly grating sound went on and on with near perfect acoustics despite the open-air venue. Maybe the low hills on the north and south helped.

One by one the girls got onto the floor and danced; their blonde, brown and dark hair flowing in the air as they shook about in abandon. Some of the girls discoed away with backpacks on. Then, the men one by one trickled in after them. Within twenty minutes, plenty were on the mud floor, discoing away to the continuous synthetic-sounding beat. Most of the men danced in a stupor, eyes up in the air, vigorously moving about seeing nothing.

A pall of dust gradually rose over the floor. The ozone tang in the air merged with the odor of sweat and stale perfume.

Jeet, motionless on a small rock, minimally shifted his head and scanned the place with continuous movements of his eyes. He warned me. 'Many on drugs. Don't stare too much at any one person.'

I shook my head and added an estimation. 'Crawford will find it difficult to keep out.'

Jeet nodded in agreement and remained silent.

The individual at the table constantly adjusted the volume of the music, as crowds kept dancing and hundreds more sat on the mats. Dozens of local boys were about. They danced away or moved among the tourists on the mats.

I sighted Columbus, Socrates and Hitler at widely separated points. They constantly moved about, and continuously looked at everyone. Sometimes they exchanged whispers with the tourists, trying to find some clue as to Crawford's whereabouts. I noticed Socrates wasn't carrying his revolver. I suppose he kept it somewhere for safekeeping.

Jeet's eyes continually swept the floor, the mats and the hill slopes. I did the same while going through cigarette after cigarette.

Groups of men and women, sweaty from their exertions on the dance floor, would return to the mats to refresh themselves with tea and fruit.

Other groups would go onto the floor, keeping the prancing, swaying population there stable.

Couples sometimes disappeared behind a small, abandoned concrete blockhouse on one side, with weeds and vegetation poking out through the entrance and exit. Maybe to steal a few quiet moments.

On the southern hill slope behind the blockhouse, the moonlight revealed groves of tall trees. A few strong and powerful-looking men waited near the perimeter and watched the show. Further into the distance, vague dark shapes of small huts could be faintly discerned far on the gloomy, shadowy slopes.

Almost imperceptibly, the music reached a deafening crescendo. Dense crowds on the jam-packed floor matched those on the mats and the near slopes. Most of the men were under the influence of drugs. Many sneaked-off with their mates to the nearby beach. Possibly there was no space around the ruined blockhouse. Wild unabashed enjoyment was the order of the day, or rather of the night; or better still, of the early morning.

Instead, a sudden explosion of sound almost burst our eardrums and I got back to reality. The volume of the sound system was turned up. Revelers' all around responded with a renewed burst of energy.

On the mats, groups of drowsy, intoxicated men passed pipes amongst each other.

Then I saw them. For the first time they made an appearance here.

***

Indian girls, over a dozen of them, like twins of Columbus, Socrates and Hitler, suddenly materialized all over. In tight-fitting clothes, they mostly stood at the edge of the dance area watching the show.

Jeet shook his head thoughtfully and informed me, 'they help in looking after the tourists.'

I took my time lighting another smoke, and watched Columbus, Socrates and Hitler casually make their way towards a couple of their girls. They exchanged whispers and moved away to other girls, they kept at it, moving from girl to girl. Then they reached a duo of two particularly strong-looking females.

I watched them for a few minutes and soon sensed something was up. They shared confidences for a rather prolonged period of time. Minutes passed. I glanced at Jeet near me. He nodded and acknowledged that he'd noticed Columbus, Socrates and Hitler with the two dark, short – under five feet, yet powerful-looking girls.

They had thick thighs, thick wrists, fully developed forearms and upper arms and strong-looking upper bodies. Frequently the five-some interrupted their frenzied whispering and stared pointedly southwards, through the groves of tall trees at the huts far in the distance.

Then Columbus looked north, upwards in our direction, and scanned the bare slopes till his eyes rested upon us. He turned to Socrates and Hitler and muttered something. The three of them gazed at us for some time before turning away.

The two thickset girls, like mini-madams, stood still with their hands on their broad hips. They didn't have muscles as such of the type that comes from gym work, but exuded a strong look which somehow develops from undertaking day-to-day household chores, and eating and drinking well, right from the first day.

I shook with a kind of nervous excitement, and felt my Glock in the holster under my tracksuit top. I also made a slight motion to get up and go to them.

Jeet put a restraining arm on my lap and observed compellingly, 'we stay here till they come to us. They've found out something from those girls.'

XX

Columbus' facial muscles adjusted appropriately to indicate he felt he'd attained a phenomenally superlative exploit of extraordinary accomplishment. The modified countenance included a grin that would have done tremendous justice to a prize-winning advertisement for any noted brand of toothpaste.

'Found them, men, got the robbers,' he said.

Jeet arched his eyebrows and widened his eyes. 'Where?'

Socrates quivered with electric excitement and pointed a pudgy hand towards the dark huts faintly visible between trees on the hill slope opposite. 'In those huts over there.'

Jeet turned away from the noisy, tumultuous party and, eyes down, pointed at the two girls. 'These two dames told you?'

'Our dames, men, seen them inside and told us,' Hitler proudly revealed.

Columbus gazed delightedly at us and gestured towards one of the girls. 'Purification.'

Her thick lips and cheeks, like the jowls of a bulldog, altered fractionally into a slight smile. Her almond-shaped dark eyes lit up momentarily. She brushed her shoulder length hair with her right hand and spoke endearingly in a sugary sweet voice.

'Didn't know they shot Henriques, no, thought they were ordinary tourists, no.'

The other girl had short, cropped hair, the narrow aquiline face of a Roman aristocrat and dark, sharp intelligent eyes. She added, 'doing drugs. They haven't come to the party.'

She spoke in a high pitched voice as if she'd just stepped out of a church choir.

The expression on Columbus' face revealed his mental state. Although rooted to the spot, he psychologically strutted about like a peacock in its pride, and smiled glowingly. 'She's Cleopatra.'

Jeet, deeply in thought, clarified. 'Sure they're inside.'

Socrates answered, 'our dames didn't see the photo...'

'But he's with the Chinese bugger,' interrupted Columbus. 'That's how we know it's your bugger.'

Purification, in a tight black tee shirt, stated, 'we can call them... no?'

Jeet shook his head. 'We'll have to go there. They're dangerous.'

I felt my Glock inside my tracksuit top, nervy and fidgety with apprehension. The loud sounds of the music, the dancing and the chattering on the mats added to the tension. At last we've got Crawford, I thought. We'd just have to go with them to him.

Columbus, Socrates and Hitler regarded Jeet as if for further instructions.

Jeet stood up and made a final decision. He spoke commandingly to the boys. 'We'll take Purification and Cleopatra, men... you call more chaps, tell them to come to tan the murderers.'

He turned slightly, faced the chubby Socrates and added, 'and bring that revolver of yours.'

***

Jeet and I strolled casually behind Purification and Cleopatra, skirting past the crowded mats, and threaded our way through groups of European men, women, boys, girls and even a few children here and there. It took us a full three minutes to go past the dense crowds and reach the south slope; where we scrambled upwards into the thick grove of tall coconut trees.

The atmosphere cooled considerably as we picked our way through the rough stony ground in the light of the full moon. Gradually sounds of the revelry grew distant. But every step we took onwards activated some kind of nocturnal turmoil, revealing signs of lower life around us.

Awakened birds twittered and cawed every now and then and suddenly became silent. Insects chirped continually in the darkness and not a few mosquitoes buzzed irritatingly close.

I huffed and puffed on, sweating slightly, more with nervousness than anything else, but kept up with the girls and Jeet. I noted the angry roar of the sea coming from somewhere to the right, adding to the whispering undertone emanating from the woods.

Purification and Cleopatra weren't too fazed. Apparently they were used to walking boldly in the dead of the night. Onwards they led us, heads high in the air, marching with spring and confidence to our quarry's lair. They were utterly unprepared disposition-wise and would be defenseless if any eventuality arose. They'd be a liability to us if a shootout ensued.

Jeet, lanky and lithe, kept low and ambled along with his knees slightly bent, fully alert, ready for anything untoward. He cautioned the girls with a note of admonishment. 'Take care they're murderers, can kill us all!'

Purification blinked, rubbed her large doe-like eyes and exhaled wearily. 'Playing talking games only, no, those jokers, no.'

Cleopatra giggled quietly.

But both heeded Jeet's advice, and moved onwards deliberately with more cognizance and regard for the possible dangerous reaction we could invite from Crawford and Lee.

We neared the rows of huts. They were dimly illuminated by shafts of moonlight piercing through the dense green cover afforded by the leafy fronds of tall coconut palms. The air grew vaguely malodorous with nauseous whiffs of dried vomit adding to the smells of stale sweat and perfume.

Jeet silently motioned Purification and Cleopatra with his left hand to slow down.

***

We'd reached the first of the huts constructed with dried coconut fronds. They were dark and desolate, vacant, devoid of any occupants. I surmised they were probably at the party.

Jeet leaned towards the two girls and whispered, 'which hut?'

'Other side, men,' Cleopatra replied in her high pitched voice. I felt like a priest conducting a mass, who'd signaled the choir to begin, and it had.

Jeet put his finger on his lips. 'Shhh quiet. They mustn't know we're coming.'

Purification and Cleopatra tried in vain to appear serious, instead their faces took on a faintly amused expression. Both of them stared at a small hut about a hundred meters away which emitted a dim luminosity; and which unlike the other huts clustered together, stood all alone and a little apart.

Jeet didn't share their mirth. With an earnest and serious manner he raised his hands, signaling us to stop. The girls stood still. I stood by.

Jeet affixed the long thirty-three round magazine to his Glock. I thankfully did the same and readied myself for action.

Jeet advised, 'first we observe them from behind an empty hut here, men.'

***

We took cover, and peered at the hut with the light. No voices or any signs of life appeared from inside.

My mind filled with conflicting emotions. We were nearing the end of a long chase. I made an effort to steel myself, and suggested, 'got to go in and surprise them?'

Jeet agreed. 'Right,' he said, and turned to the two girls and directed. 'Go back and bring Columbus, Socrates, Hitler and the others, here.'

I peered in the moonlight at Jeet, then transferred my gaze at the two retreating girls.

When they were out of sight, Jeet sharpened his voice considerably and clarified, 'must overpower them with a mob to offset their weapons.'

He slowly stepped to one side, weapon ready. I did so too, quickly moving away from him. Suddenly he lurched and slowed.

I froze as I detected a vague hiss! My head whirled to the source of the sound.

A pebble dislodged somewhere. A muzzled pattering of paws came, and loud barks pierced the night sky. An angry crazed mongrel appeared in front of Jeet, snarling menacingly. It crouched, preparatory to pouncing upon him.

In one movement, Jeet checked the fire selector, and loosed a single round right between the shinning eyes of the dark animal. After the initial flash, the pistol-shot sound echoed for a microsecond and the stray dog moaned and lay quite still. A trickle of blood oozed out of its punctured forehead.

Jeet stood still and dropped onto one knee, smoking Glock pointing ahead. I stood motionless, stunned, breathing aloud, and turned my attention back to our target, the lone hut.

Too late. The sudden explosion of sound brought two dark shapes out of the hut. They sighted us and quickly re-entered their abode.

Within a few seconds they exited again, and raced down slope towards the beach.

Heart pounding, I recognized Mickey Crawford with the G-11 as he surged through a patch lit by shafts of moonlight trickling through the canopy of trees. Tan Win Lee tagged him, pistol in hand. He had some trouble from the uneven undergrowth, then regained his balance and scrambled away, disappearing behind Crawford.

A surge of adrenaline galvanized me swiftly into action. Unmindful of any personal danger, I charged forward headlong behind Jeet, who determinedly chased the fleeing duo.

***

Rays of invisible sunlight reflecting-off the beaming full moon radiated onto the shining, burnished sea and glistening sands. This resulted, despite the early hour of the morning, in a kind of a dim somber visibility, eminently favorable to us.

I clearly made out the two dark outlines of Crawford and Lee rushing northwards on the deserted sands of the beach, weapons plainly visible in their hands. At the band of rocks that divided the beach, they hastily clambered over, lost their footing now and then, and faded into the gloom.

Ahead of me, Jeet tried to side-slip towards the firmer sand nearer the sea while steadily gaining on them that is till he reached the rocky outcrop. There he bounded up and over and raced ahead, momentarily disappearing.

I huffed and puffed on at a jog-trot, Glock ready. A few seconds later I painfully negotiated the large, flat-slab boulders of the rocky outcrop and leapt onto the next beach.

Running desperately away, Crawford and Lee turned sideways and looked backwards at us, checking on our progress. A shaft of nervous alarm jerked me into raising my Glock, my trigger finger tightening for about five millimeters, nullifying the first safety. They were too far ahead for effective shooting. Then they turned and continued running across the length of the beach towards the next band of rocks.

The duo crossed the next rocky band without turning back. Jeet, only about sixty meters away from them, still kept his gun hand low.

Eyes raptly focused on the advancing shapes, I watched them near the end of the beach. Ever vigilant, I slowed down and in anticipation raised my Glock. Apprehensively squeezing the trigger slightly, I negated the first safety. Any moment I expected them to turn and loose-off automatic bursts.

Jeet's heedless, hot pursuit frightened me although so far he remained safe.

But they didn't stop and shoot back. At the northern edge of the Vagator beach at the base of the Chapora fort hill, they didn't bother to even turn back and look. Instead they simply scrambled upwards and disappeared into the dark thickset bushes and rough foliage on the upwardly-slanting slope.

***

I reached the approximate spot where Jeet had vanished behind them. Thighs burning, breathing in short gasps, I hesitated. I looked around desperately, lost in the dark, in a despondent and disheartened mood. After a few deep, steady breaths to recover and gather my wits, I steeled myself and cautiously climbed a rocky goat path, towards the dark walls of the medieval fortification on the summit of the mount.

From somewhere unseen below came the thunderous roar of the powerful sea striking jagged rocks at the base of the hill. It aggravated my stress; which became unbearable when a dark shape materialized ahead. Delicately balancing myself on the slope, I readied my Glock for the third time, holding it straight, pointing ahead with both hands. The slow movement of the figure forced me to waver and vacillate.

Jeet's voice came over in a low whisper, as calm and cool as ever. 'They're hiding inside the fort.'

How can he be so unruffled, I thought, but felt better almost immediately.

'What do we do?' My tone delivered my emotions – a mixture of breathless exhaustion and helpless frustration.

'Follow me, we'll walk around the fort and block them from the other side.' Jeet turned and briskly hiked upwards into the low foliage.

He didn't give me a chance to reply. I wearily trudged on behind him, trying to keep my bursting heart as steady as possible. The myriad of insects, especially the loud crickets chirping shrilly at sudden intervals, didn't exactly aid me in this.

The muddy pathway we negotiated shelved upwards and downwards. But we moved as swiftly as we could, given the constraints of the terrain, over loose stones and uncut dried grass which crackled under our feet. We hugged the unbroken perimeter wall of the fortress on our right, brushing past weeds and intertwining roots of short trees on the thin, narrow trail.

To our left, a couple of feet away, a sharp rocky down slope led all the way to the placid Chapora river.

Every now and then I peered upwards to the top of the wall, Glock ready. The rough bricks of the bastion provided a form of cover on one side. Yet I half expected the Portuguese guerreiro's on guard atop the wall, to peer downwards and challenge us. And every now and then a vague, apprehensive suspicion that instead of Portuguese warriors of the old, Crawford and Lee would lean out from above and cut us down, filled my every step with fearsome hallucinations and suspenseful anxiety.

The moonlight filtering through the battlements and crenels threw vague, strange and unnerving shadows onto our path. A decaying, timeworn, musty odor and the ancient feelings permeating the atmosphere, evoked spooky delusions. All these factors combined to provoke a sweat intense enough to drench my clothes, despite the dry Goa air.

Jeet suddenly stopped and turned to me. 'Better we climb the wall.'

***

He hoisted himself upwards onto the low, rough, red laterite brick wall, disjointed with age, and peered carefully through the ruined crenels. He saw nothing and scrambled over, into the fort.

I joined him within seconds and stood near him, weapon ready.

No structures, save in the center of the enclosed hilltop, were around. At the midpoint of the fort was a pile of rubble with wild bushes growing out of its bricks. Bizarre teasing and dancing shadows evoked delusive specters of droves of ghostly apparitions if we stared continuously at any one spot, as we had to do to spot Crawford and Lee.

Suddenly, a petrifying patter of invisible footsteps somewhere in the wild grass and irregular scraggy underbrush interrupted us. It came from the north-western side of the fort walls.

Aroused and appalled with horror and dread, being almost as blind as a bat, due to the darkness, I froze. Wild uninhibited maniacal laughter filled the air, along with a couple of piercing shrieks. A short, hushed silence followed, aggravating the confusing and scary situation. Then came another round of maddening, grating howls and screams, somehow defiant and challenging, although unintelligible.

I shivered as if I were in the freezer compartment of a particularly efficient refrigerator, except that it was sheer terror that caused my blood to run cold. Trembling with fright, eyes riveted to the source of the noise, I pointed my Glock, near some wild rugged bushes at the north-western side of the fort.

'We take cover first,' Jeet suggested, and instantly ducked behind a pile of rubble at the center of the fort. In a kind of a defensive shelter. He hid behind the loose bricks and stones with wild foliage around it.

I rapidly stepped in behind him and scanned in front.

'There's a kind of a trench behind some bushes. They're hiding there.' Jeet pointed at the spot he deduced they were in.

I'd barely knelt down behind the protective cover, when I noticed the faint flicker of a flame, followed by a loud report. The shot whizzed past frightfully close. I involuntarily leaned on Jeet.

'Pinpointed their hiding place,' he said.

I peered over the rough stones. This time I registered a prolonged flash which glimmered a split-second too long. I ducked instinctively.

A sharp piercing crack resounded from the wall behind us. The sheer velocity and disorienting power of the impact shell-shocked and deafened us to a degree. Fragments of ancient laterite bricks and mortar showered onto us, traumatizing us further. It also caused a minor cut or abrasion on my scalp.

Eyes screwed almost shut, I shook my throbbing head and said, 'looks like they've fired some kind of a high velocity bullet.'

XXI

Jeet, flat on his stomach on the parapet but acutely alert and primed to react, quickly laid a reassuring left hand on my right shoulder. 'They're using the G-11's three-round burst mode.'

Despite our situation, I recalled reading manuals on the weapon back home in London which was now a world away. 'Two thousand rounds a minute rate of fire, means three bullets hit almost simultaneously.'

Another three rounds of Hecklar and Koch's four-point-seven into thirty-three millimeter case less, with a louder than average whiplash crack, slammed into the aged bastion rubble in front of us.

Prone, propped up on my elbows, I trembled a little. 'Maybe they're about a hundred meters away, facing us, from somewhere in that bush ahead.'

'There's a shallow trench there, just in front of the fort wall,' Jeet said.

He, unflinching and rock steady, pointed his Glock in the direction of the sound and let loose one round. It was ineffectual, almost absurd. The nine-millimeter bullet had comparatively far less striking power than their G-11 in its three round burst mode.

Immediately a volley of single pistol shots whizzed harmlessly over us. Lee doing his bit, probably. Scarcely had the sounds died out, when Crawford hosed us with a prolonged burst of supersonic G-11 projectiles.

The pain in my head vanished and I concentrated on the task at hand.

I straightened both arms, rested them on a pile of bricks and squinted through the white-lined rear and front of my Glock. One was an open U shape, and the other a tiny hole in a small black steel pyramid at the end of the barrel. Unfortunately I couldn't sight anything in particular.

Still I exhaled slightly, and squeezed the trigger for a fraction of a second.

The thousand-three-hundred rounds a minute Glock-18's rate of fire, considerably slower than the G-11, didn't induce any reaction. The slugs, spinning clockwise once every two-point-five centimeters, lanced through the greenery, lost velocity and veered right ways and struck the far wall of the fort. Muffled pops of nine millimeter lead ending their murderous journey futilely, came from slightly away, a little to the right of where I'd pointed.

No cries, shouts or sounds emanated from the waist-high grass, dark thicket bushes and a swaying short tree. I felt helpless and impotent.

Jeet tried to reassure me. 'Not to worry, all we have to do is not let them escape.'

Another G-11 burst rent the air, impacting behind us with the effect of a higher velocity bullet; followed by single pistol shots, presumably from Lee.

'Need a higher caliber weapon,' I whispered. 'Like those seven-point-six-two SLR's.'

Jeet nodded, and eyes still raptly focused on the dark bush ahead, advised, 'don't waste our bullets, ensure they finish their bullets first.'

'We go slow in expending our ammunition.' I recollected some of the lectures organized by Pemberton for us, on what to do in such situations. 'In the battle of attrition, unsettle them constantly till they run out of ammo?'

Jeet assented and waited calmly for a while. Then, head hunched behind cover, arms angled above and ahead, he emotionlessly fired a single shot.

I peered over, and quickly stooped downwards. The image of spurts of flame spearing towards us like horizontal bolts of lightning remained in my consciousness momentarily. And raking fire swept across us, and peppered the wall behind.

I sighed with relief. 'Can't angle their shots upwards; aren't getting the right trajectory to be able to hit us.'

'We have the same problem,' Jeet said, taut with tension, and advised caution. 'Still be careful'. He paused and scanned the fallen stones and bricks ahead carefully and added, 'it's who finishes their bullets first.'

'The G-11 holds fifty rounds. Can't gauge how many rounds have been expended by Crawford?'

Jeet discharged another round. When the pistol blast subsided, asked, 'might have extra clips?'

'We're lucky. The report states categorically he's got only what's in the magazine... but there's Lee's pistol.'

Just then a swathe of chalky-white, cumulus clouds enveloped the moon. The resultant charcoal-black darkness remained for what seemed an interminably long time. Suddenly a loud, rough, howling curse disturbed the tense atmosphere. The subsequent pregnant silence in the sooty pitch darkness, accentuated the eerie creaking and swishing sea breezes sifting and straining through the rough foliage.

Jeet eased into firing position and zeroed another single shot towards them, again with no audible outcome from the other side.

Within a second Jeet signaled me. 'Got to get them to fire at us...'

A scurrying, scuffing sound of someone stealthily trying to sneak-off somewhere interrupted him.

I peeped forward feeling helpless and ineffectual, but shot in the direction of the sound.

Jeet almost simultaneously fired a small burst of warning. The sounds stopped, and the moonlight returned and bathed the locale with a gloomy murky light.

Jeet gazed intently ahead and estimated. 'Don't think they can escape now. We'll see them if they move.'

I peered at the spot where they presumably remained hidden. We were higher up and well-concealed; they couldn't approach us without being sighted. A clear, flat area lay between us and the bushes and tree from where they'd been shooting at us. The fort wall lay just behind them.

'Can't advance or withdraw from that clump of foliage,' I said, as the darkness gradually eased with the coming of a new day. 'The flat ground surrounding them is most convenient to us.'

I sensed Jeet's smirk as he exhaled slowly and agreed. 'Fantastic. They're stuck there, especially now.'

The first rays of the vaguely orange early morning rising sun crept upwards from behind us.

I shook my head. 'But they're still invisible; just as we're hidden from them.'

Jeet screwed his eyes as if straining his brain while peering ahead and mused. 'Too dangerous to crawl away and charge them from both sides.' He paused and added an afterthought. 'Because can't make out their ammunition position.'

Prone and uncomfortable, I shifted the sweaty Glock in my hand slightly. 'Yes, it's too risky. I vote we wait here. We're in an advantageous position.'

***

We reoriented ourselves to a different kind of wait. Although prone and motionless, my elevated pulse rate kept me fully alert. A mild feeling of expectation gradually became outright euphoria. I'd finally got him. They couldn't elude us now. Retreat and we sight them and react; advance and we clobber them too.

Near me Jeet fidgeted uncomfortably.

'Keep our eyes fixed on them,' I advised.

He adjusted his position, and remained still after ensuring he was comfortable.

The sun rose higher on the eastern horizon behind us, gradually rendering the moon and stars invisible, and imperceptibly changed the hue of the sky and the clouds. Night sounds of chirping insects suddenly became inaudible, and the twitter of awakening birds took over. Sparrows fluttered about the short trees and stunted bushes in front. Crows cawed from somewhere on the unseen slopes. But no movement or sound came from the thicket in the general direction of where Crawford and Lee hid.

Jeet checked his wrist watch, turned to me and faced them again and mocked, albeit a little above a whisper. 'How long? How long?'

I checked my watch but remained still, reconciled to waiting patiently for as long we needed to.

Jeet inclined his head slightly towards me. 'They and us are safe only if we stay still...' He turned back and froze mid-sentence! Then he leaned forward, screwed his eyes and stared intently ahead.

I steadied my Glock and peered attentively in the general direction of where his eyes were riveted.

A thick, dark forearm appeared over the far wall right opposite us, groped about and disappeared. Someone had tried to haul himself into the fort. Then the arm reappeared at another spot. And yet another dark hand could be seen a few meters away.

XXII

Within a few seconds, Purification, still in her black mini-skirt and tee shirt, stood atop the laterite wall. She paused, looked around, and jumped down into the interior of the fort. She scanned the foliage on one side, and finally focused her gaze at a particular spot.

Her bull-dog face and jowl-like cheeks stretched out with delight and her thick black lips widened into a broad smile. She bulldozed her way forward like a mini Challenger tank and spoke loudly at the top of her voice. 'My God, no? What are you two buggers doing here, no?'

Before a reply could come, Cleopatra, in tight blue jeans and tee shirt surfaced suddenly from behind and muscled her way forward. 'Yah everyone's enjoying over there at the party ah.'

'Shhhhhh...' Sounds of the desperate entreaty reached our ears from somewhere deep within the clump of rough foliage, a bush and a short tree.

Both girls stood by, hands on their hips, and glared downwards.

The fervent appeals of the two men had no effect on them. Apparently Purification and Cleopatra didn't have time for a prolonged firefight like the one we'd been in earlier. Instead they had the personality and confidence to actually overpower Crawford and Lee.

Jeet and I tensely watched the drama unfolding ahead.

Purification's thick head turned upwards and she pouted with reproach. 'What, no... no one is there, no. We come from there only, no.'

No reaction could be discerned from Crawford and Lee, presumably hiding somewhere within the rough foliage, about a hundred meters from us.

'Yah... only you two blinking joker's are here, ah.' If Luciano Pavrotti ever needed a substitute, Cleopatra could be one right here in the middle of the ruined and abandoned Chapora fort. The tenor of her admonishment could have put a trained choir to shame.

But no sound or movement emanated from Crawford and Lee. The two girls adjusted their positions slightly and faced a clump of bushes near a short tree. It enabled us to precisely pinpoint our quarry's hiding place.

Purification applied an as impure a shroud as she could over her bulldog-like visage. Her large, expressive eyes lit up wickedly, her face expanded exaggeratedly and she chortled with glee. 'Ha, ha, ha... missing the party, no. All enjoying with their dames, no, charas, no... all being free, no.'

Still no response came from Crawford and Lee.

'Come on out, got a present for you also, men,' enticed Cleopatra.

'Blow up your mind with a kick, men.'

She held out something in her closed fist. The palm of her hand and her fingers covered the object completely, and I couldn't exactly see what she held.

The entire thicket bush they'd spoken into behaved like the one that confronted Moses during the Biblical times. It shook agitatedly, desperately with such spirited vigor as though burning furiously, almost enough to provoke divine feelings. Not only could one sense their hesitation, but it looked as if the green, leafy bush would actually burst into flames at any moment. Crawford and Lee wavered for some time in their hiding place.

'Think it's some drug,' Jeet whispered.

And proof that the bush wasn't hiding God came when the temptation to 'blow up your mind with a kick' won out.

Crawford, in ill-fitting clothes, weapon in hand, stood up cautiously. He looked extremely shabby and scruffy, with a few days growth on his cheeks. He was clearly on substance abuse. His tired and exhausted eyes peered in the direction he presumed us to be in, instead of at Purification and Cleopatra. His eyes groped around the spot where we were, with malevolent concentration. The G-11's thick barrel with its peculiarly placed magazine, flat over the barrel, pointed ominously in our direction.

Then Lee stood up slowly besides him, pistol in hand.

We stayed silent and still, controlling our breathing, Glock's ready. For some time I desperately had to subdue an immediate urge to pick them-off right there.

Crawford waited a few seconds before being wrongly satisfied that we'd gone away. Then he stepped towards Cleopatra, reached out and violently snatched and pocketed the gift.

Cleopatra smiled with great self-satisfaction. She casually sidled towards a slightly bemused Lee.

In an easy, rapid but unobtrusive movement, Purification calmly stretched out her thick hands and snatched the G-11 from Crawford. She shook her shoulder-length dark hair and took a hasty step backwards with the weapon, saying, 'my it's so hot, hot, no.'

Crawford stood stiffly by, haggard and weary.

Lee was quite nonplussed at Crawford not reacting to his weapon being taken away, but didn't do anything. However, he stared raptly at Purification, who rapidly distanced herself from them.

Right at that moment, aristocratic-faced Cleopatra roughly grabbed the unsuspecting Lee's pistol, and cried out in a stretched octave ranging from below middle C to the A above it. 'Got... the... jokers!'

Scarcely had the high-pitched musical yell died down, when a thunderous blast assailed our ears. Stunned, we remained motionless.

Ahead the foursome froze into a temporarily paralyzing stillness.

***

We could have been watching a battle scene from the celluloid extravaganza "Braveheart". A chorus of yells, squeals and shrieks that would do justice to an ancient English or Scot's raiding party of another era and another place, came from over the walls of the fort. Except that the warriors were led by Columbus, Socrates and Hitler. Socrates furiously waved a smoking Colt 45 in the air and charged forward. About a score of local boys with hockey sticks and an assortment of bamboo poles and what appeared to be wooden boat paddles, followed him.

They swarmed over the walls and rushed in, running forward at top sprint speed. Before anyone could regain their composure, they swamped the helpless Crawford and Lee.

Two boys gripped Crawford's hands. The veins on his neck stood out, bulging with coursing blood that simmered and seethed. His eyes raged with a brutal venomous fire.

Some boys held Lee firmly by his hands. The China man, face wan and utterly desolate, looked down at his feet.

Jeet watched the show without any comment or movement.

I began to feel the effects of our long, exhausting day. The action ahead began to pass by in front of my eyes like a film playing on a visual fast-forward mode.

Purification and Cleopatra ambled victoriously past Crawford and Lee. They triumphantly waved the weapons in their hands.

The smoldering blaze visible in Crawford's pupils ignited into a flaring inferno of wrathful infuriation over his helplessness caused by them.

The China man, Lee, remained unemotional, and stared stoically downwards.

I sighted Columbus prancing away, up and down, swinging his arms and rising high up on his toes. His fevered countenance seemed in danger of exploding with uncontrollable exhilaration.

A voice bellowed from somewhere within the mob. 'Call the police.'

Columbus, who behaved as if he'd just discovered America, could barely manage to speak, and somehow hollered, 'aha, Hitler has already phoned them.'

Hitler exuded hate in his rough throaty voice, and acted as if he'd directed the head of the Gestapo. 'Told police to torture them, men, for killing Henriques.'

Jeet finally stood up and jumped down onto the ground. He suggested, 'let's go there.'

***

I forgot my cramped, aching muscles and followed Jeet, elated; left hand reaching out for my BlackBerry to contact Sam. Casually we strolled onwards towards the group ahead.

They sighted us and greeted us with loud yells of recognition, waiting for us to stroll the hundred meters or so to get them. Socrates waved his Colt 45 about and babbled like his illustrious Greek namesake might've done thousands of years ago in the Athenian squares.

Jeet calmly took it all in. I walked by his side, Glock in one hand, BlackBerry in the other.

The local boys kept up the cheering. The Chapora fort became like Wembley Stadium on Cup Final Day. As if we'd just scored the winning goal in the terminal match to decide who gets the years FA Cup. While the acoustics were like at Wembley; energy-wise it was as if our nuclear power station at Calder Hall had suddenly started up after a shutdown. As though massive bolts of intensely concentrated energy had swiftly electrified the local gang. They nodded, shook their bodies and jumped about, shivering with uncontrollable excitement. The high wattage generated by them, targeted, but bounced-off Jeet and I.

Crawford stared at us as we reached them. He was in a temper. But I could detect some degree of mirth gradually beginning to overcome him. With an impulsive burst of insane energy, he suddenly wrenched his right hand from the boy clinging to it.

Jeet lifted his Glock instantly.

I, a trifle slower, side-stepped and did the same, although I had my BlackBerry in my left hand. I stared through the sights at Crawford's temple. For a micro-second I registered the tiny wrinkles on his forehead.

Crawford reached furiously into his pocket and extracted a tiny bottle. He hurled it downwards with exasperated indignation, but amazingly he also tried to break into paroxysms of frenzied laughter. With the result that he inhaled and exhaled noisily. Like out-of-breath wheezing, as if he'd just finished the London Marathon with a sprint over the last quarter mile.

Jeet unwound immediately, and lowered his Glock.

I relaxed instantly too.

After the long chase through DN Road, the Fiery Dragonhead and the Chinese United Bamboo Gang Triad, the Customs operation at Dadar Beach, and those *hijda*'s, it had finally come to this tiny bottle. It had enticed Crawford out and into our clutches.

I gasped with steadily intensifying familiarity and gleeful amazement as the bottle rolled to a stop a little in front of us.

Near me Jeet burst into peals of laughter.

On the small bottle, the clearly visible thick, black print on the sticker with the semi-naked couple cavorting on it read, "Pleasure Prolonging Lotion"!

Because of it Jeet had finally proved himself outside and we'd easily nabbed Crawford.

Part 2

A Nautical Prelude

A Maritime Drama

I

I pondered introspectively over Jeet's remark. I didn't reply immediately. Instead I deliberately shook some ash-off my cigarette onto a conveniently placed ashtray near my deck chair. Then I lazily scanned the busy dockside. Gradually my consciousness began to absorb the hectic activity around.

The scene in front of me consisted mostly of workers operating with a kind of a casual effortless efficiency. They used automated winches and shipboard derricks to load and unload mostly rust-red containers-off the rows of merchant ships moored nearby. Semi-balding and gray-haired men looked upwards as hooked cables lowered from the jibs of tall cranes.

They barked orders and gave directions to the other workers. Younger men sprang into action. They attached massive cast iron hooks onto the large crates. Boisterous yells interspersed with foul mouthed curses and the metallic cacophony of whirring motors rent the air, as the cargo rose and swung onto waiting trucks. On one side, containers were placed gingerly onto large trailer trucks by specialized cranes. On the other side, brown colored sack-cloth bales of some indeterminate commodity were unloaded, and carried into a covered warehouse. The large Mumbai harbor was an extremely busy place indeed.

I lowered my gaze and glanced through the gleaming white painted deck railings; at the couples walking up the accommodation ladder of our vessel. One by one they disappeared below, into the interior of the ship we were on.

We were seated on deck chairs on a deck, virtually open on three sides, under the navigation pilothouse. The sea breezes wafting by, over the polished white, meter high guard rail, somehow stirred gustily and whipped about cool drafts of air which created a refreshingly cozy atmosphere.

The tall lanky Jeet appeared to be fast asleep on his deckchair. Yet in spite of his languorous stillness, a kind of liveliness surged through his motionless body.

Finally, I took a deep pull, flicked some ash onto the ashtray and got back to Jeet. 'Not a very common name?'

Jeet shifted slightly on the deckchair near me, while his eyes roved speculatively amongst the passengers boarding our vessel. He didn't turn and face me, but chuckled softly. 'True the name Jesus isn't common, but it's not too much out of place.'

For a moment I formed a mental picture of the tall patriarchal Jesus Antonio D'Costa, Captain of the Malabar Star. The over six feet tall Skipper had impressed me all right. He exuded an air of relaxed laid back efficiency, of the kind that encouraged blind trust. We'd be in safe hands for the duration of the trip.

***

Outside, the last of the passengers had boarded the vessel. I guessed that from the conduct of an uniformed crewman who strolled down the accommodation ladder with a note pad in one hand and a pen in the other. He had a satisfied look on his face, of the kind that usually indicates the thankful completion of a tedious job. Probably he'd been ticking-off names of the passengers as they entered the ship. A Customs officer in a resplendent white uniform, shoulder epaulets gleaming in the sun, followed him. They stopped at the foot of the accommodation ladder and exchanged words for some time. Finally, the Customs officer turned and suspiciously looked over the ship, which included giving us a long searching stare. Then he turned on his heel and abruptly marched-off.

I tapped my feet on the steel deck plates of the floor, and grit my cigarette between my teeth. 'First time I'm looking forward to a holiday like this.'

Jeet didn't remove his gaze from the colonial brownstone buildings near the perimeter wall of the docks. But there was no mistaking his highly pleased feelings as he nodded. 'Luckily Pemberton decided to reward us after the success of the Mickey Crawford case, with this trip on the Malabar Star.' He paused and adjusted the tone of his voice. 'Nothing like cruising down the enchanting Kerala coast for a holiday.'

I turned right ways and observed the weather stained freighters; tugs with their characteristic black color; and the orange painted oil exploratory and specialized ancillary vessels to oil rigs elsewhere.

After a few seconds I confided, 'holiday needs that develop. It's only now that I feel like a holiday outside. Maybe our travails during the last case created the need.'

'Good effect that,' Jeet turned to me and smiled. He purposefully took out a leaflet from the hip pocket of his blue jeans and read from it. 'We have short stops for sightseeing at Cannanore, Mahe, Calicut, Kochi, Allepy, Thiruvananthapuram. At Kanyakumari we turn back for Mumbai.'

I nodded in agreement and remained silent.

***

The pecuniary condition of the other passengers, while not veering towards indigence or pauperism, wasn't quite enough to actually afford a large passenger liner. But there really wasn't a bigger ship running along the Kerala coast these days. Besides, most normal working-class people couldn't cope with the artificial scenery or participate in the various activities available on the big sophisticated liners. Our companions on the lower deck were a kind of travelling class; a type of working class tourist set found worldwide at a certain economic level these days.

I snuffed out my umpteenth cigarette. 'Seems to be a popular cruise for retired working-class Britons and Americans, given the number I've seen boarding the vessel.'

Jeet fidgeted uneasily as though troubled with vague restive doubts. 'I think I saw a couple of West Asian types with their veiled women too.'

***

Earlier, we'd left our luggage in a simple but attractive cabin. Later, we came to the deck beneath the pilothouse, on which we were presently seated.

The Malabar Star wasn't a cruise ship of the type usually seen in advertisements for sunny cruises in the Mediterranean or the Caribbean. The bantam sized passenger vessel of intermediate dimensions; displaced approximately two thousand tons; was ninety meters long; and had a beam of about twenty meters. Her diesel engines propelled a single screw into thrusting the ship forward, to a maximum speed of about fifteen knots.

At her water line, her long and narrow wing-like stabilizers lay inert and still, not needed in the calm waters of the dock. A few meters above them ran a long series of portholes. I tried to visualize the maze of machinery that ought to be inside; the diesel engines, its valves, ball bearings, cables as well as the oil, grease and dirt; and gave up after a while.

Above came two decks. The accommodation ladder led right into the main deck, the lower of the two decks, into a lounge situated in a large rectangular elongated box-like structure. This structure began from a few meters behind the forecastle, and stretched to almost all the way up to the stern. When Jeet and I had first entered the ship, we'd been told that along with the lower lounge, this structure had twenty tourist class cabins which housed most of the passengers.

The cabin class accommodation at the next higher deck included four larger passenger cabins. Jeet and I occupied one of these cabins. We'd left our belongings there. The rest of this area encompassed shipboard offices and the accommodation for the Captain and his officers. I presumed the crew stayed somewhere in the lower deck down below.

The deck on which we were presently seated, comfortably savoring our impending holiday, was right in front of this higher deck. We got a birds-eye view of everything around. A clear field of vision lay straight ahead over the forecastle and prow, and on the starboard and port sides.

The navigation bridge or pilothouse or wheelhouse of the Malabar Star perplexed me. When we'd entered the ship, I'd had a good look at the pilothouse and mainmast behind it. It appeared unlike most pilothouses on civil vessels. As if the Naval architect began by designing a passenger ship. Then three-fourth's of the way through, forgot himself and thought he was designing the bridge of a destroyer or battle-cruiser. And the yard that built her apprehended some danger to the pilothouse, and armored it. Somehow it reminded me of a turret of a Challenger tank, minus the cannon.

Impenetrable-looking thick boxy plates of iron covered the pilothouse. A kind of a thick pelmet held the inclined plexiglas, as though having to shield it from unforeseen projectiles at some future date. The citadel-like pilothouse appeared incongruous on the Malabar Star, given the peaceful nature of its mission.

A twenty meter tall mast, with the usual radar antenna and radio aerials, stood with its base flush to the center of the rear of the pilothouse. On one side of this mast structure, a thick iron door accessed the pilothouse.

This thick iron door accessed out onto an open sun-deck-like area, which extended for about fifty meters; till a large white funnel, with a black strip of paint about a meter below its top. Just behind the single funnel, on both the starboard and port sides, were two large lifeboats. Although now glued securely to their davits, they still seemed ever ready to provide succor in case of an emergency. About halfway to the funnel, on both starboard and port sides, an open companionway led downwards to the deck below.

From outside, the ship appeared squat and spare. But it's gleaming white hull and burnished topside, even the radar antenna and radio aerials appeared to fit into the general scheme of things, and was inviting enough. The Malabar Star exuded a stately air, yet was earthy enough to attract the right kind of customer.

According to literature made available to us, the vessel had been tropicalized. This consisted mainly of tinted glass at the portholes, which could be opened or sealed shut. And, a specialized air conditioning plant that drew in air, chilled it appropriately and vented it into the cabins. The resultant atmosphere in our cabin became more than bearable due to this.

As for the deck we sat on, it was fully ventilated by the sea breezes blowing through. This created a cool, pleasant and cozy environment.

The travel brochure emphasized that the Malabar Star offered a simple cruise, with a chance to enjoy a tour of places steeped in deep history. Ancient Portuguese mariners first landed in India on the Malabar coast. Everything that I'd heard or read about the trip so far, reeked of mystery and romance; like sailing to an obscure destination with the promise of exciting discoveries.

II

I casually glanced towards the entrance of the dock, more for want of something to do, than for any particular reason. Within moments, I spotted a gray Ford. The vehicle entered through the gate, and stopped a little inside the dock. Two white uniformed Customs officer's, accompanied by a khaki clad Sterling sub-machinegun toting police constable, emerged from the office under the gate. One of the officer's bent low and exchanged a few words with the passengers of the car.

Jeet recognized the yellow colored diplomatic licence plates with the CC before the numbers. He turned to me and frowned slightly. 'Consular Corps. Think it's US Consulate staff taking a cruise with us?'

I shrugged my shoulders, made to reach for my cigarette pack, then thought the better of it and continued observing the gray Ford.

The two Customs officer's and the police guard stepped away from the Ford with expressions of satisfaction on their faces. Almost immediately the vehicle started and cruised slowly into the dock. Slowly it crawled along the quay. Then halted suddenly.

I held my breath.

The Ford had come to a stop near a rundown freighter in a dry dock. A couple of workers doing minor repairs on the hull of the freighter, interrupted their hammering and welding. They turned and stared at the stationary vehicle.

Jeet clicked his tongue. 'Funny, not bringing them right up to our ship?'

I nodded slightly. 'If they're headed for our ship?'

The rear door of the Ford opened. A single, slight, spare man appearing in his late thirties, in an expensive tee shirt and blue jeans, stepped out. His left side had a carry bag slung over his shoulders. With the palm of his right hand he brushed back his sparse blond hair, and sauntered towards the rear of the car. The uniformed driver, a short, dark, swarthy Indian, followed the American out. He inserted a key into the boot, opened it and took out a suitcase and briefcase, and handed it over to the American.

'Only one person has come out from among those in the car,' Jeet observed.

'Right,' I assented, and ever the career detective I added. 'Something wrong with that briefcase and suitcase, oddly sized.'

'What?'

'I can't exactly make out. Just my gut sense telling me something,' I said. 'The suitcase isn't shaped right. Like it's carrying some electronic item.'

Ahead, the mystery man raised his head and looked around. His gaze fell upon the Malabar Star. He remained still and stared at the vessel for a few moments. Then he shrugged his shoulders and purposefully began to trek towards the ship.

The driver got back into the Ford, reversed a little, and turned round and drove away.

'Walking all the way here, when the car could come right up to the ship?' Jeet half muttered to himself.

I shook my head as I watched the new passenger stroll the hundred meters or so to our ship. He stopped for a while at the foot of the accommodation ladder and looked up at the ship. Then he stepped forward and briskly strode into the Malabar Star.

***

I lit a cigarette and turned to Jeet. And froze into a stillness, but not without a slight feeling of relief. A couple of voices came over through the half closed door. We'd spent quite some time alone waiting for the vessel to cast-off. Now any company would be welcome.

A rough man articulated distinctly. 'Refueling operation terminated.'

Then Captain Jesus Antonio D'Costa's voice came over clearly. 'Ballast okay and fuel tanks full... have a good margin till we reach Kochi at least.'

I turned slightly and watched the door swing inwards. D'Costa in a spotless white uniform and peaked cap stepped into the deck. His brow was deeply furrowed and his eyes had a kind of a busy, concerned look, that is usually found in highly responsible people who're fully occupied in organizing and running difficult charges.

Two uniformed officers were with him. Another lean, lanky man also in uniform followed them. The raged expression on his face gave me the impression that it was his rough, gruff voice that we'd heard earlier.

D'Costa adjusted his visage so as to enliven us and this included a slight smile. 'Leaving in a few minutes time, everyone on the manifest is onboard.'

Jeet raised himself slightly on his chair and nodded.

I blew out some smoke. 'We're looking forward to the trip.'

D'Costa turned slightly and introduced his officers. He pointed to the stocky, thickset and powerful-looking man, 'Gonzalo Tavares, my First Mate.'

The other officer, medium heighted, with looks of a film star announced himself. 'Sean Mendes the Second Mate.'

I favored them with a slight shake of my head and drew a long breath through my Dunhill.

Jeet gazed searchingly at the third officer as though trying to recognize him.

He had a perpetual scowl on his dark, sunburned and slightly mustachioed face. His eyes shone brightly as though he raged on inside about something. And right now he focused his eyes upon D'Costa.

D'Costa smiled. He exuded an air of someone who'd come down from somewhere miles upstairs, to take charge of us down below. 'This is Napoleon Fernandes our Chief Engineer. One of our chaps who made it by actually studying. We call him just Napoleon only.'

Napoleon blinked. Some kind of grudge from somewhere deep within him seemed to vent out from under his breath. 'Bastards made me come up straight...'

'Aha, but you've become a better class now.' D'Costa grinned amiably.

Just then someone entered. With a shock I recognized him! But before Jeet and I could say anything, D'Costa revealed. 'Columbus, steward for the upper deck passengers.'

Columbus's smile of recognition and relief revealed a spotless row of gleaming white teeth 'Great,' he said. 'Will be serving you all whom I know beforehand.'

***

D'Costa took a half step towards us. He had a serious expression on his face. 'The reason why I've come here is about the two Glock pistols which you've declared.'

'We've handed them over to you on instructions from the police.' I tapped out some ash, then looked up from the dockside in front of me and widened my questioning eyes slightly.

'Yes. Both pistols and spare magazines are in a locker in the pilothouse.' D'Costa shook his head imperceptibly, as though waiting for us to absorb his statement. 'When this trip ends we'll return them to you.'

Columbus, in spite of his senior's presence, flashed a wide grin. 'Other passengers get scared, men... if see pistols.'

D'Costa frowned slightly. He lifted his cap with his right hand and brushed his graying semi-bald pate backwards with his left palm. Then replaced his cap.

Napoleon winced as though struck by a high velocity bullet and glowered at Columbus.

Tavares and Mendes stood by quietly, a little away from us.

I nodded quietly. Not quite knowing how to react, I rested my eyes on a freighter moored at a dock nearby.

Jeet however looked up at Columbus enthusiastically. 'Passengers that get scared are downstairs.'

From somewhere far away, sounds of a bell ringing reached our ears. The chimes clearly heralded a change of a work shift.

D'Costa glanced at his chronograph with an air of finality. 'Right, we've got to go.'

I decided to elicit some information before they left. 'I noticed an American, official-type?'

D'Costa disclosed as he walked away, 'American national, booked through a travel agency... Peter Perez.'

***

Scarcely had they left, when a loud gruff cry assailed our ears, over the rattling of winches and the other noises that filled the air. With a continuous low toned straining screeches and squeaks, the accommodation ladder eased up, and disappeared into the ship. The Malabar Star heaved and fell ever so slightly. Then the idling engines powered considerably. Gradually the mild vibrating hum of the ships propulsion system enhanced in decibel level. Moderate tremors began to shake the vessel almost imperceptibly.

The mooring ropes were singled up and hauled away. Suddenly a loud, long wail of a shipboard siren rent the air. The Malabar Star jerked slowly as if readying to move. Then began easing out of its berth. The space between the dock and the port side of the vessel began to enhance in small increments. Fresh vibrations of the engine increased, a little by little, the speed of the vessel's movement away from the pier.

The Mumbai dockside began to slowly recede. Far ahead, the workers disappeared like the pile of crates that had been there a few minutes earlier. From high above, the sun shone savagely onto the rows of electric and diesel cranes, all clumped together at odd angles. They suddenly appeared remote and distant. Even the moored cargo ships and small tankers around, now seemed a world away.

Then a deep resounding hooter horn blasted away once, then twice. And the ship now sufficiently away from the pier, turned, then jerked slightly and began to move forward. At last the Malabar Star commenced upon her voyage.

III

A varied maritime scenery passed before our eyes. The sights were in common with those usually found at harbors of immense portside metropolis. Varied types of boats ranging from wooden fishing vessels to packed passenger ferry's to specialized tugs, all passed to and fro on unknown but seemingly urgent missions. Across the sea, the long, low hills of mainland India filled the eastern horizon.

Columbus returned, carrying a tray with two glasses, a small bottle of whisky, a tiny icebox and some orange juice in a tetrapack.

Jeet's eyes strayed nonchalantly towards Columbus. But he spoke eagerly. 'Good, another juice for me.'

I pursued my lips. 'And a chhota peg.'

Columbus dexterously poured some orange juice into a glass and handed it over to Jeet. Then like an expert bartender at a West End pub, he decanted a measure of whisky into another glass, and gingerly picked and dropped some ice cubes into the amber colored liquid. When he finished, I reached out and took the glass from him.

After he left, we sipped our drinks in silence as the Malabar Star cleared the Mumbai harbor, and reached a patch of open sea. Gradually the engine sounds powered and deepened, and the vessel slewed around and curved towards a row of freighters and small tankers, all anchored in a line, under a virtually cloudless and sunny sky.

'Inner anchorage.' Jeet inclined his head towards the merchant vessels. 'Awaiting their turn to berth at the docks.'

The Malabar Star steamed eastwards and cut through the line of anchored vessels. Then trembling slightly as the engines revved up, it executed a long ninety degree turn. As the single screw thrust the ship forward, the sea bubbled and churned into a phosphorescent white wake. A long, thin, white plume of smoke hissed backwards from the single funnel. Then the Malabar Star emitted a low rumble as its engines settled down, while it bored inexorably southwards, through an invisible commercial sea channel, which ran parallel to India's west coast.

To the west, the city of Mumbai lay under streaks of gray cumulus spread over the early afternoon sky. Large patches of sunshine shone through the fleecy clouds. Quays, docks, warehouses, all slipped past smoothly; like the hills on the Indian mainland on the eastern side opposite, as though someone drew backwards, a rope attached to them.

I sipped some whisky and let it burn slowly down my throat and checked my steadily shortening cigarette. When I looked up, I noticed the door to the deck opening slowly.

The American Peter Perez stepped onto the deck. He regarded us with a curious expression of enquiry in his eyes. And he said in a smooth even voice, 'good afternoon gentlemen, may I join you.'

***

I turned my head partially and gazed at Perez. The medium heighted American, with a slim and spare physique looked around for a chair. Despite his soma type he wasn't a man with a weak body. His lean and mean figure exuded a vitality that indicated extreme physical fitness from an active lifestyle. His creased forehead and gray hair, as well as his aged but lively deep blue eyes, distinguished him as a senior officer somewhere. Clearly he held some kind of major position of vital responsibility elsewhere.

Jeet who had an expectant air about him as if waiting for the climax of some box office hit; braced ever so slightly. 'Of course, pull up a chair.'

Perez reached out and grasped a chair and placed it opposite us and sat down. He introduced himself, 'I'm Peter Perez.'

I noticed his faint look of distaste at my cigarette, which had diminished almost to extinction. So I stubbed it out on the ashtray and discarded it. 'Captain D'Costa told us your name.'

Ahead the nature of the waterfront changed. There were distinctly separate harbors. The walled-off commercial port ended, and a stringently guarded Naval port began.

Jeet's eyes remained raptly focused on the Naval dockyard, while remarking, 'saw you come in an US Consulate car?' he then queried casually. 'We'll have to call for another drink?'

Perez smiled. 'No drink for me now.' Then he drew in a deep breath. 'You know I'm from the US Consulate... but I don't know you two?'

'I'm David Adams, British.' I tried to sound as nonchalant as possible. 'This is Jeet, a distant relation of mine.' I inclined my head towards Jeet. 'We're private detectives.'

'Private detectives, good to hear that.' Perez's eyes lit up. But ever so slightly that had we not been facing him, we wouldn't have noticed it.

Odd, I thought to myself. Why good to hear we're private detectives. I began to get mildly suspicious. All my years of experience as a detective warned me about something not jiving. He raised an alarm in my mind that he was far more than met the eye.

Jeet meanwhile concentrated on looking at the Naval shipyard. The near perfect visibility enabled us to take in the entire Naval base area. Dockyard workers, uniformed sailors and officers were all hard at work. The wet and dry docks had sleek-looking vessels in battleship gray. Gun turrets, sophisticated radar arrays and lethal missile canisters let out the deadly mission of the warships.

Perez, seated facing us, let out in a matter-of-fact voice. 'Was Third Secretary in the US Embassy at New Delhi for two years. Now have been posted to the Mumbai Consulate.'

'As Third Secretary?' Jeet, attention directed on the submarine conning towers visible at a submarine pen, asked informally.

'No, I'm now an Officer on Special Duty.' Perez screwed up his eyes slightly, then relaxed and continued. 'Using up some leave before taking up my new posting in Mumbai.'

Means he's not yet an Officer on Special Duty. For a moment I thought of asking him about his family, then gave up the idea. He didn't seem the type one could freely talk to, leave aside ask personal questions. This despite his attempts to act friendly.

Jeet looked at a white painted island-like concrete structure surrounded by the sea. Gleaming black anti-aircraft guns pointing skywards at various points, revealed it a Naval installation.

Jeet continued to stare at the guarded island as if loath to miss any part of the Naval scenery in front of him and disclosed. 'Middle Ground Coastal Battery, also an ammunition dump.'

Perez turned and briefly glanced at the installation.

I broke the ensuing short silence. 'Nice way to relax, go for a cruise.'

'Yes,' Perez agreed. 'This is an old ship, but well-maintained.'

Then a helicopter clattered past.

Jeet like an over enthused school kid regarded the chopper. '*Chetak*, Indian version of the French Aerospatiale Aloutte III.'

The three of us watched the helicopter hover over a part of south Mumbai. Then it began to descend.

'Landing at a Naval heli-base... Indian Navy Ship or INS Shikra,' Jeet said.

Perez seemed to be evaluating us. Somehow, now, I sensed we'd been semi-cleared in some way in his mind.

I gazed vacantly out at the open Arabian Sea. A vast semi-circle of anchored merchant vessels and medium oil-tankers stretched around the southern part of the island city of Mumbai. This was the Mumbai harbor's outer anchorage. Without taking my eyes-off the waiting ships, I remarked, 'type of passengers and their paying ability decides economy and state of the vessel...'

'Type of passenger all right,' Perez interrupted me.

'Besides Britons and Americans, they're some West Asians too,' I said inadvertently.

Perez shifted slightly. I also caught the almost imperceptible adjustment in his aged, yet sharp blue eyes. He alternatively regarded Jeet and me in a probing, investigative manner.

Then he said, 'I've checked out the Malabar Star from friends in the insurance business. It's an interesting story.'

IV

Both of us looked expectantly at him.

Perez began conversationally. 'This ship was built by Vickers Shipbuilders, Barrow in Furness in the late nineteen seventies, for some vague company registered in Panama... and operated as the Arafura Star.'

'Odd name,' I said. 'Wonder what it means or signifies?'

'Name of a sea like the Arabian Sea, North Sea, like that,' Perez calmly explained.

'Cruised there probably, in the Arafura Sea?' Jeet added. He somehow sounded as if he was used to hearing the name.

'Right, operated in the Arafura Sea, Timor Sea, Celebes Sea, Java Sea, Bali Sea, South China Sea... in that area.'

Perez's geographical memory stunned me. But both Jeet and I remained silent. We kept mild interrogative expressions on our visages.

Perez continued the explanation. 'Kind of ferry for locals between various small islands of Indonesia, the Philippines and New Guinea.' He grit his teeth and waited for some reaction from us.

'Oh that part of the world.' I shook my head slightly and tried to appear deeply interested.

'Area even now...' Jeet gazed at the open sea in front of him. 'Has a pirate problem.'

'Right, so this vessel has adaptations.' The blond haired Perez looked at Jeet appreciatively. 'The pilothouse is armored with steel plates.'

That explained something to me. 'I noticed that when we'd entered the ship.'

Perez glanced at me. 'Some kind of stronghold in case attacked by armed pirates, who're commonly found in the area around those islands.'

The Malabar Star pitched and rolled slightly and steadied itself. Momentarily I felt droplets of spray on my face as I commented, 'good to know the Malabar Star was the Arafura Star with an armored pilothouse, which is of no use now.'

Perez licked his lips in one rapid movement, and continued, 'ownership changed hands a few years ago. A group of Indian businessmen brought the ship and renamed it. Use it for the Malabar coast run a couple of times a year.' He paused and intensified his gaze upon us. 'Also charter it out for periods of time.'

I nodded sagely. But could detect Perez expected us to know something, especially of the other charters. As I didn't know anything of the Malabar Star's other runs or cruises, I remarked, 'quite a story.'

Jeet shifted easily on his chair. But remained silent and viewed the open sea as the Malabar Star cruised onwards.

Perez seemed deeply in thought. A bit too deeply I reckoned. He moistened his lips. 'Vessel didn't start out from Mumbai.'

I glanced at Jeet. 'We boarded at the starting point of the cruise, Mumbai.' I tried to scrutinize Perez's face. He seemed to be playing some kind of game with us.

Perez remained expressionless. His eyes searched deeply within us for any reaction to whatever he'd told us. 'The Malabar Star was serviced and repaired at Mumbai's Mazagon Docks after the last Malabar run. Then on a charter went to Karachi, to Aden, to Djibouti… and back to Aden, and then directly to Mumbai.'

'For this year's Malabar run?' I shifted on my chair to view a mechanized fishing boat that we passed. A flock of screeching and cawing gulls from over the stationary boat came towards the Malabar Star, then flew back as we moved past.

'Yes.' Perez half turned to see the source of the bird sounds, then leaned back on his chair. 'Thanks to my friends, I could access the information.'

Jeet acted as casual as can be. But I detected that like me he suspected something more than meets the eye about Perez. This in spite of him having come onboard from a US Consulate car. I remembered that the vehicle had stopped quite a distance away from the ship. Also, Perez released information while watching us too carefully, as if to catch any reaction or response.

Jeet looked at the blue sky over Perez's head and remarked, 'you learned of this ship from friends.' He exhaled wearily as though trying to ward-off boredom and asked diffidently, 'wonder how they knew so much?'

Perez didn't bat an eyelid. 'Oh they're from Lloyds of London.' The reply came rather too quickly as though prepared beforehand. 'Were insurers... had to complete some kind of survey... because I knew them, they told me a lot.'

Jeet shook his head slightly to indicate that he was satisfied with the answer.

I sat motionless, in perfect repose on my chair.

Perez shook his head too. But I sensed him a trifle nervous. After a few seconds silence, I heard a distinct mutter under his breath. 'Karachi, Aden, Djibouti... Aden then Mumbai.'

I acted as if I didn't hear him and said, 'some of that crowd downstairs could've embarked at the other ports?'

'You're dead right,' Perez replied slowly.

'If along with stores and luggage,' Jeet added. 'We can be in danger. There's a lot of terrorist activity these days.'

Perez shifted uneasily and stared a bit too hard at Jeet, as though waiting for him to say something more. Then he said after a while, 'the US and UK have let out a travel advisory, to be careful, of a possible terrorist strike somewhere in India.'

Jeet hesitated for a second, then tried to change the subject. 'Anyway, upstairs we're safe together.'

Perez shook his head. He disagreed with Jeet. 'When I passed one of the upstairs cabins, I heard plenty of men discussing something or arguing out aloud.' Perez attempted to sound as certain as he could. 'And they didn't speak English!'

***

For quite some time, may be a few hours, we just sat still and stared at the swiftly passing azure-gray sea and the darkening sky. Our conversation became desultory. Eastwards, the green hills of the Indian mainland gradually became invisible as darkness fell.

After a while visions of Captain D'Costa and his officers on the armored pilot-house, operating the ship, ran through my mind. And after some time I couldn't help commenting, 'Anyway, we're lucky we've got a level-headed Captain and crew running this ship.'

'I met Captain Jesus Antonio D'Costa when I entered the ship.' Perez stretched his lips ever so slightly in a kind of a quarter smile; while gazing from somewhere between us two, eastwards.

I attempted to inject some humor into the situation. 'We ought to have a peaceful trip… what with a Jesus in charge!'

Both Jeet and Perez opened their mouths to say something; and froze suddenly. A loud yell interrupted them. Then another indecipherable blast came in over the chugging sounds of the Malabar Star moving through the Arabian Sea. Finally came a rough, hoarse shout. 'Murder!'

***

Onboard lights illuminated the sea around the Malabar Star. The waters rushing by, suddenly appeared a bleak and dreary gray, as the vessel's southwards pointing prow cut through it. Little waves and rollers which passed by, scarcely denting the passenger vessel, appeared drab and monotonous. Luckily the sea was comparatively calm. The ship pitched and rolled too inconsiderably to affect us, as it ploughed its way relentlessly towards its destination.

Perez, Jeet and I stayed hushed and immobile for some time as the import of the shout penetrated into our minds.

Secretly, I hoped that some mistake had been made. Like a bored young steward crying wolf as part of some harmless prank. I disbelievingly set my eyes upon the iron door which led to our deck. I half expected someone to enter and apologize to us, for needlessly worrying us.

Perez leaned back on his chair. He inclined his head slightly towards the door; as if to catch any faint sounds that would give him a clue as to what exactly had occurred in there.

Jeet looked at Perez, then at me and finally made a decision and stood up. 'Let's go and check.'

Perez and I got up too.

The door of one of the cabins was ajar. A frowning D'Costa stood outside. His jaw was set hard, his mouth was compressed and his cheeks quivered with apprehension. The distress and anxiety in his eyes indicated his worry and disquietude.

He directed someone inside the cabin. 'Send a signal to head office. Then wireless the Mumbai Police… also we carry on sailing to Cannanore, unless the police direct us to return to Mumbai.'

A soft, low voice, too clipped and restrained to indicate any adverse emotion, responded from inside the cabin. 'Sir, should I contact the Port Zone Deputy Commissioner, who has his office in the Mumbai Port Trust Railway building... or the officer who sits at the Yellow Gate police station?'

D'Costa looked up and crisply ordered, 'contact the Yellow Gate police station, Indira Docks... and let's go immediately to the wheelhouse.'

He turned and saw us. Immediately he changed his manner and attempted to express a kind of vexed regret, although his face remained a dismal, murky gray. 'Sorry gentlemen, a passenger from the lower deck, a Kamran Yazziz, came up and got killed on the stairs.'

We came closer and saw the body on the steps leading upwards.

'West Asian?' Perez asked, sounding sincerely grieved.

D'Costa nodded. 'From Dubai.' Then turned to leave. A uniformed Gonzalo Tavares came out of the cabin and followed him. Both of them briskly walked away and disappeared down the passageway.

***

Jeet regarded Perez and me, he hesitated a bit, then unemotionally suggested, 'let's go close.'

I took a step forward towards the body. An aseptic atmosphere like that of a hospital ward greeted my eyes. Like the area around had been scrubbed clean for the event of the day. On the stairs leading from down below, heavily diffused light from hidden tube lights, illuminated a corpse. The light played ghoulish tricks on the contorted legs of the man. His arms were stretched out with their palms outstretched, like he'd attempted to push someone or something away as life ebbed out of him.

The short but well-built, semi-balding individual lay on his back. His smooth shaven face had a macabre scowl. A trickle of blood oozed from a neat round bullet hole right in the center of his temple. A dark ring of powder around the bloody aperture indicated that he'd been shot at point blank range. Possibly even with the barrel of the offending weapon touching his forehead. Somehow the scene resembled a set of some particularly scary horror movie. Even the atmosphere around was extraordinarily quiet and subdued.

Perez stared impassively at the lifeless body. I sensed him deeply in thought about something. Like he was aware of far more than he'd revealed.

Jeet looked around, moving his head slowly. From point to point his eyes roved, striving to elicit any hint or clue that would help solve the mystery of the ghastly murder.

'The victim must have been with his killers when I last passed the cabins to come to the open forward deck,' Perez gloomily said.

I shook my head sadly as I recollected Perez telling us about the discussion or argument he'd heard earlier. But I continued making a preliminary survey of the scene. However I couldn't infer much from the body. 'Death must've been instantaneous after the shot.'

Jeet opened his mouth to say something; and stopped abruptly and peered down the passageway.

***

D'Costa briskly walked towards us along with Tavares his First Mate and Chief Engineer Napoleon. They grimly halted near the body and surveyed the scene.

Tavares, rock hard and steady, and as cool as a cucumber just removed from a refrigerator, calmly glanced at us and executed a deprecatory shrug of his shoulders. 'Passenger from downstairs comes up alone and gets murdered.'

D'Costa, arms folded across his chest, fastened his eyes onto us. 'A preliminary search of some cabins has been made. No weapons have been found.'

I rested my eyes for a second on the white marble-like face of Kamran Yazziz, then glanced at D'Costa. 'As everyone is enclosed in the vessel, just have to keep them like that till the police get to us at the nearest port.'

Perez who somehow still appeared to be hiding facts from us, disappointedly asked, 'back to Mumbai?'

D'Costa gravely faced us. 'We've been instructed to return to Mumbai.' He paused, took a deep breath and raised his voice. 'In the mean time gentlemen, I request you to stay in your respective cabins.'

V

Jeet lay flat on the wide double bed in our cabin and stared steadily at the ceiling. 'I can't believe it, the whole trip has been spoilt.'

I stretched my legs out on the settee facing him and turned and glanced out of the open porthole. I focused my gaze upon an illuminated, visible patch of the azure-gray sea, which steadily moved past. 'Don't know what to make of it. Don't think we're going to be in it?'

Jeet followed my actions. He turned his head slightly, and peered outside through the porthole. 'Perez will have to tell D'Costa about the discussion or argument he'd heard earlier.'

'And tell the cops when they arrive.' I blinked when sounds of a hooter reached us. Outside, through the porthole, I saw a medium sized oil tanker speed past us and disappear.

Jeet shifted uneasily. Then propped himself up on a pillow. 'According to novels on similar situations.' He paused and injected a dose of levity into his voice. 'The Captain will come to each cabin and interview us in turn.'

I laughed out aloud. 'Yes, but with us accompanying him. We're the detectives not him!'

'But we'll be suspects too.' The lean, lanky Jeet looked straight into my eye. I noted humor, albeit of a cautious and circumspect variety, on his face. 'He'll probably move around with the police.'

'Absurd,' I retorted immediately. 'He'd be daft to suspect us.' I took in a deep contemplative breath as I suddenly realized something with a shock. If I were D'Costa, I'd suspect us too. Yes Jeet and I would definitely be suspects in the Master's eyes.

Jeet widened his eyes slightly and shook his head slowly with concern. 'D'Costa will suspect us till Perez tells him of the argument or discussion he overheard.'

I shivered involuntarily. 'I'd say Perez heard an argument, not a discussion… because it ended with a murder.'

'Can't be sure.' Jeet, brow furrowed with the effort of deep thinking, resumed staring out of the porthole. 'In languages other than English, even mild discussions can sometimes sound like arguments!'

'But it ended in a murder, so they fought each other.'

Jeet shrugged his shoulders imperceptibly. 'If he told us the truth?' He infused a note of skepticism into his manner. 'Everything about Perez seems doubtful.'

***

'Perez?' I pronounced the name slowly, somehow wishing Jeet wasn't right.

'He's supposed to be a US Foreign Service officer?' Jeet tried to encourage me to say something.

I disagreed with Jeet's doubts about Perez. 'When he came to us on the deck outside, he was too calm and composed. I don't think he'd have recovered so soon after committing a dastardly act like killing someone.'

'Still there's something wrong,' Jeet insisted. 'Like his car didn't drop him near the ship.'

I didn't like this at all. Jeet was right. At least about Perez's manner, something just didn't jive about it. 'Knew a lot about the Malabar Star's previous stops. Too much really. Also was as if trying to elicit some kind of response from us.'

Jeet conjectured. 'Maybe he's a CIA agent?'

'Then even more unlikely about him murdering someone carelessly.'

'Lots of terrorist activity going on around the world.' Jeet spoke very slowly and carefully as if to ensure I got the full import of his statement. 'The CIA even has an assassination list.'

'Kamran Yazziz could be one on such a list and Perez somehow killed him?'

'There's something going on, on this ship. He may be on the Malabar Star on duty,' Jeet hypothesized. 'I think his behavior from the car to now and the murder, are all connected somehow.'

I tried to make an effort to work it out, especially of Perez's posting in Mumbai. He said he hadn't started working yet as an Officer on Special Duty. Maybe it was a lie. He was on special duty already, onboard the Malabar Star. Which meant the murder had far greater implications than a simple argument which turned into a crime. Jeet was very convincing about there being something fishy going on, on the vessel. But I remained silent on the issue, not having something specific to say.

Jeet broke the short silence by clicking his tongue pessimistically. 'Earlier on it would have something to do with smuggling or gang wars... these days it's terrorism.' He paused and took in a sharp breath as though he'd hit upon something positive to us. 'Good thing our guns are in the pilothouse.'

We couldn't be suspected on that score. Our Glock-18's being safely locked away in the pilothouse. But we had another problem. 'If there's a terrorist attack, we'll have to go get our guns!'

'Yes,' Jeet said. 'But now D'Costa will order a search of our cabins, to find the murder weapon.'

Just then a series of sharp knocks on our cabin door interrupted us.

***

I got up and opened the door. Columbus in dark trousers and a white tee shirt faced me.

Jeet still on the double bed, lay propped up on the pillows. He calmly waved his hand towards the door. 'Columbus you bugger, come in.'

I moved aside. Columbus stepped into the cabin and stood at the foot of the big double bed. A pleased look slowly spread over his face.

Jeet composedly surveyed him and proceeded. 'Great we know someone on this ship from beforehand.'

'Yes.' He favored us with an ear to ear grin. 'I like serving those whom I know.'

I leaned back on the settee and reached for my Dunhills. With a slow deliberate movement I lit a cigarette.

'What happened, men, someone got murdered?' Jeet took a deep pensive breath and cast a solemn eye upon him.

'Kanran Yazziz,' Columbus replied. 'Has business in Bahrain and Dubai. And no one knows why he got murdered.'

'But we're going back to Mumbai.' Jeet glanced at Columbus and me.

'Police buggers signaled it on the radio,' Columbus disclosed.

Jeet shifted himself on the bed and remarked to me in a deadly serious manner, 'we'll reach Mumbai sometime in the morning.'

Columbus shifted weight from one foot to another and added, 'and no one can leave, till they check the whole ship.'

Then a hooter sounded rather close. All of us looked out of the porthole. In the starlit night, we saw the lights and silhouette of a ship speeding past.

And I noticed the cabin door swing inwards. My right hand remained frozen in mid-air, cigarette a few inches from my lips, as Chief Engineer Napoleon Fernandes ambled in, only to call Columbus away.

VI

I woke up with a start, all so suddenly with an abrupt jerk. It was early next morning. But it was a bit too early in the morning for any decent awakening. Something had made me open my eyes when not yet fully awake. Now I continued to lie still in bed, but with heavy eyelids. I peered about the darkened cabin. A clear premonition of some unknown ominous threat hung in the air. It evoked a kind of strange racking discomfort which

I couldn't exactly place. And this disagreeable feeling seeped excruciatingly into my awakening consciousness. Quietly I made an effort to gather my wits about me. And gradually my senses began to register everything around.

Earlier I'd been troubled by a bad dream. Maybe it was the feeling of drowning in hot water that had awakened me prematurely. I squirmed uneasily. Amazingly I was wet all over. My pajamas were drenched as if I'd been through a torrential downpour. Then all of a sudden I got it.

Sweat! Yes I was perspiring profusely. Besides my clothes, the part of the bed I lay on was wet too. Then I woke up enough to note the temperature of the cabin had somehow risen to an uncomfortable level.

I inclined my head slightly in the semi-darkness, till I sighted the white painted switch box of the cabin. I tried to make out the small night-light on the board. Now no illumination emanated from the small bulb of the night-light. This meant that the electricity had been shut-off. Maybe because of some generator fault. Information on the company brochure about the ship being tropicalized passed through my still half sleepy mind. Unfortunately the literature didn't disclose solutions to a situation like this. A pity I thought. Power failure had cut short my sleep, and had spoiled the forthcoming morning.

Sleepiness still half overcame me. I lay still because of it. But as time passed in little increments, I began to find it easier to remain awake. I blinked now and then. My ears caught the hushed death-like silence.

The more I thought of it, the more spooky I felt. The faint vibrations and the constant low hum of the Malabar Star's engines had disappeared completely. Besides the regular beat of the engines, the whispering of the sea breezes and the muted swishing of sea water rushing by, as usually can be felt when a ship ploughs forward, all had stopped. A minor breakdown of a generator wasn't much of a problem. They should have a standby generator. But the entire ship at a standstill, meant we were burdened with a far more complex and difficult situation.

Cobwebs cleared rapidly from my mind. I recalled the murder last night. That was another thing that went wrong. I tried to remember the activities the previous evening. Napoleon and Columbus had left our cabin. Almost immediately afterwards Columbus returned with our dinner. We partook of a simple meal. Then Columbus cleared the dishes. And a little while later Jeet and I retired to bed.

Had we reached Mumbai now? But that didn't explain the cessation of all the ships systems. I checked my watch. The light button revealed the time as five-thirty.

Finally, I turned and directed my eyes towards the other side of the bed. A shockwave of fright literally made my hair stand on end. Jeet wasn't in his place. With a pained and sinking feeling, I looked towards the small bathroom-cum-toilet. The sight of his slippers outside the shut bathroom door caused me a great deal of easement; and a relative disburdenment of my rapidly enhancing previous fears. I made my first sounds of the new morning. An audible sigh of relief.

The moonlight filtered through the open porthole, and rendered the outside visible. I squinted and peered through the open porthole. And gasped!

***

Outside, a grim forbidding black stone wall, like that of an impregnable fortress, rose from the sea. Sinister crenellations shaped like burning tongues of flames, menacing black ramparts and the bleak malevolent watch towers; all deserted and ghostly, somehow provoked haunting fears of the unknown. I could barely make out a hillock inside the fortification, which loomed over the ominous black stone walls.

An over-bright luminous spot, the rising sun, rose from somewhere high in the cloudless sky, far beyond the dread-provoking fortress. Then something struck me.

Yesterday I'd seen the setting sun through the only porthole in our cabin. It faced westwards as the Malabar Star sailed towards the south. This meant that unless the sun had on an impulsive whim, decided to rise for a change from the west, which was highly unlikely, our ship now faced north. And the porthole now opened out towards the east. I tried to rack my brain cells, attempting to remember if there was any fortress at Mumbai.

Somehow I felt too lazy to get up. Dark, disquieting thoughts about the murder the previous day; the mysterious sounds during the night; about the now silent and still ship; and the fortress outside, passed through my mind.

Then I heard the flush operating in the toilet.

Jeet in blue jeans and a tee shirt, breathlessly rushed out of the bathroom. He hurriedly glanced at me as he hastily went towards his Nike's. 'Good thing you're awake.'

'Yes something's wrong? The electricity has been shut-off. The ship's stopped moving.' I tossed my damp head towards the porthole. 'I've no idea where we are.'

'Better get ready, dress up,' he advised, uncharacteristically scuttling almost sideways to the settee, where he sat down heavily. He seemed not a little apprehensive. His tense manner indicated his alarm. He grabbed a pair of socks lying nearby and quickly proceeded to put them on. 'I think the Malabar Star's been hijacked!'

***

Stunned, I remained rooted to the spot for a moment. Plenty had taken place on the Malabar Star earlier; enough to give rise to suspicions that all was not well onboard. Still I wouldn't have believed it just yesterday, that the vessel would actually get hijacked.

A worried Jeet anxiously glanced up at me. I sensed dismay and foreboding in his mind from the concerned expression in his eyes. 'Better get ready fast. Somehow they've missed us and can come here anytime.'

I nodded and literally leapt towards the bathroom.

As he laced on his Nike's he warned me, 'I've locked the door, but they have automatic weapons.'

I shut the toilet door behind me. Ten minutes later, after rushing through my morning ablutions, I re-entered the cabin and proceeded to rapidly put on my clothes. All the while a jumble of questions and answers buzzed around the four corners of my mind. Unfortunately every solution I worked out to our predicament, created even more dreadfully troubling and insolvable problems.

'Where exactly are we?' I voiced one query.

'The Janjira fortress... that's the Janjira fortress, on an island outside.'

I completed tying up my shoe-laces and stood up and regarded him. 'We might have to go out and investigate. Our Glocks are in the pilothouse?'

'At least we've got our cell phones.'

I gratefully took out my BlackBerry and punched Sam's number in London.

***

'Hello Sam,' I said.

'Well what is it now?' Sam came in on the line. 'How are you enjoying your cruise?'

'The vessel's been hijacked. They, the hijacker's, haven't got to us yet.'

'Have to inform the Indian authorities,' a deadly serious Sam advised.

Jeet interrupted, 'tell him of our location near the Janjira fortress... inform the Indian authorities from his end.'

I did so.

'I get to them and tell them about the ship,' Sam told me. 'You be careful don't do anything rash that would provoke them.'

I signed-off feeling much better. We'd have to wait and see what we'd got into.

***

'Big problem our Glocks.' A restless Jeet adroitly swept towards the porthole. He cautiously peered out taking care not to be spotted by any unseen watcher outside. 'I saw some Arab dhow-like boats alongside which were definitely mechanized.' He minutely surveyed the sea between the Malabar Star and the medieval island fortress of

Janjira. 'A dhow is alongside the prow. There's another at the stern. Means the others are on the other side, the port side.'

An overwhelming feeling of despondency gradually filled my entire body. I shook a little with despair. 'The hijackers must have been on the Malabar Star itself. Their accomplices from the dhow's must have come in later.'

'They've taken over this ship.' Jeet had a grim thoughtful expression on his face. But he also exuded a quiet and confident air. 'I saw at least five dhows earlier, circling the ship.'

An empty vacuum-like ache of hopelessness began at my sternum. We were in a tight spot all right. Five dhows meant we faced an army of them. If outnumbered too heavily, we'd have no chance at all against them.

I voiced my doubts. 'They must have got D'Costa, Tavares, Mendes, Napoleon, Columbus and the rest of the passengers and crew in bondage...'

'And that Perez,' Jeet interrupted.

***

The realization of the Malabar Star's hijacking had inflicted a severely rattling blow to my mind. So much so that I'd clean forgotten about Perez. Now I recalled the lean US Foreign Service officer with a sense of great relief.

'He's just next door.' Beams of a kind of favorable and anticipatory expectation flashed through my unnerved mind, and expressed itself outwardly in my slight smile of self assurance. 'Let's go to him.'

'That's how I got to know we were hijacked.' Jeet proceeded to inspire further fear. He appalled me with his explanation. 'Heard sounds and woke up. Opened the cabin door and peeped out. Armed men were taking him away. I quickly closed and locked our cabin door. But then had to go to the toilet. Luckily they didn't come back for us!'

So Perez was a prisoner. I shot an apprehensive glance at the securely closed door. I turned and faced Jeet. 'What type of men?'

'Blue track suited armed West Asians!'

Suddenly a loud scream of extreme torment, from somewhere down below, rent the air and interrupted him. We tensely waited as a pin drop silence, pregnant with imminent sinister implications, ensued. The muted hush aggravated our misgivings. It also established that the Malabar Star was taken over by a hostile group.

I promptly moved towards the shut door and pressed my ears against it, and waited silently. No more sounds came over. I said, 'if somehow they missed us at first, they're bound to see a passenger manifest or some such document soon?'

'Then will come here.' Jeet calmly regarded me. He shrugged his shoulders as though we had no other option but to do the inevitable.

'We've got to hide somewhere. Or take them on after finding out how many of them are there.'

'If you saw five dhows, there should be plenty of them.' I somehow hoped he'd gone wrong when assessing the number of dhows. I reached out for a cigarette, then thought the better of it. 'So they've solved the murder of that Arab yesterday. Probably had some differences with the rest so they simply eliminated him.'

Jeet shook his head slightly in acknowledgement. 'Better we go out now. If careful, nothing should happen to us. At the most they'll capture us like the others.' He suitably toned his suggestion in a manner that immeasurably bolstered my confidence. 'We just try to find out more and get to our guns.'

Just before he applied some pressure and twisted the door handle, I said under my breath, almost to myself.

'As bound to search for us, we should be on some passenger register or the other, we might as well go out and risk it.'

VII

Jeet slowly nudged open the cast iron cabin door.

Warily I stepped outside and looked carefully to the left and right. The dark passageway was silent, empty and forbidding. No sound could be heard. No movement could be discerned from anywhere around, above or below.

Jeet cautiously closed our cabin door, and froze into a stillness. Startled by something, he glanced apprehensively towards the direction of the open deck.

The sounds of a series of hushed whispers and of frenzied murmuring came from the direction of the open deck.

A vague curtain of extreme vexation beclouded Jeet's dark eyes for a moment. 'They're somewhere around.'

'As we're unarmed we've no choice,' I grimly advised as an acute burn of an over-awareness of our predicament began to trouble my mind. 'We'd better check out in the other direction.'

Jeet turned cautiously and tread lightly towards the stern. I ever watchful and wary, waited for a few seconds, then moved quickly towards him.

'We've to get to the pilothouse somehow,' Jeet suggested in a barely audible whisper, as we passed a couple of doors leading to cabins that were empty.

I unequivocally agreed with him. 'We'd have better chances with our Glocks.'

Suddenly three armed bearded men in dark blue tracksuits charged out of a seemingly empty cabin.

Stunned to the core, and frozen into a semi-dazed stillness, I just stood on the spot focusing on the weapons in their hands. They held AK-74's. Lighter-looking than the more common AK-47's; and slightly longer in length. I also noticed portable radio's clipped to their waist belts.

Fearful and edgy I swallowed spit queasily and coughed. My mouth had dried up completely.

One armed man rapidly scuttled sideways, promptly going to one side. All the while the black barrel of his AK-74 pointed malevolently at us.

One of the bearded, tracksuited men, remained right in front of us. He snarled threateningly. He also waved his rifle from Jeet to me and back.

The third man raced to somewhere behind me.

I shuddered with trepidation. I sensed they were scared and extremely paranoid. And fully aware and alert because of it. Like they feared we could retaliate. So they had to be absolutely on guard to thwart us.

The wild eyed man in front of us shouted threateningly in a guttural, throaty voice. 'Hands up. Don't move or we shoot.'

With my spirits sinking, I raised my hands.

The terrorists were tense and nervous. The black barrels of their AK-74's pointing at us, shook slightly because of it.

Jeet with a blank look on his face, lifted his arms slowly and deliberately.

***

For some time we stood still. The early morning sun had just made its appearance. Opposite across a swathe of the sea, the medieval black stone fortress of Janjira rose out of the waters like a fortified island. Observable around the edge of the fortress and across another body of water, was the shoreline. From amongst clumps of foliage and tall coconut trees, I could discern the roofs of white painted houses.

Choppy waves hit the shoreline, and creamed into a bleached white froth before disappearing into nothingness on the rocky shore. A part of a line of rocks appeared like the start of a rocky mole. However the large stones stretched out only a few meters from the shore. As though some ancient conqueror had attempted to capture the Janjira fortress by building a mole; then gave up for some reason.

Hugging the sides of the Malabar Star were wooden dhows. I noticed the forepeak of a dhow at the stern rising and falling gently in the shallow swells. But I couldn't see any crew on the boats.

'Come with us,' directed one of the terrorists. He led the way towards, I presumed, the pilothouse.

We followed him with two armed terrorists walking behind us. While tramping onwards I noticed two dark shapes wallowing in the waters between the fortress and the Malabar Star. They floated eerily in the sea, moving imperceptibly towards the shore. A paralyzing chill of intense dread and extreme consternation ran up my spine.

Trembling slightly I pointed with my head at the two dark shapes visible in the grayish sea and whispered, 'looks like two bodies?'

Jeet, while striding forwards, peered keenly at the floating shapes. 'Killed them and thrown them overboard. Means these bastards are killers.'

VIII

Jeet and I entered the spacious pilothouse. We were motioned towards one side. The three men that had captured us joined two terrorists that were already in the pilothouse. They'd kept a watch on D'Costa, Perez and Napoleon who were standing by.

One of the men made us stand a little away from each other. And began to frisk us one by one. He extracted my BlackBerry from my pocket. He took away Jeet's Reliance. D'Costa's Sony Ericcson and Napoleon's Nokia were also taken away. Perez didn't have anything on him. Then the three terrorists that brought us went away with our cell phones. Just two armed men stood on guard against us. One of them spoke into his portable radio, not in English. I gathered he spoke in Arabic.

D'Costa was pale and strained.

Perez peered a bit too deeply at us. He tried to gauge something. Then he wearily looked away as though he'd felt the inevitable had occurred. Napoleon's internal fury was the same as before. Now he stood by silently, frequently looking down at his shoes.

D'Costa apologetically regarded us and wailed. 'These terrorists have hijacked my ship. Won't leave us till some prisoners are released.'

No one replied. Instead we focused on the two guards watching over us. The armed men didn't appear to understand English. They didn't try to stop us from talking.

A harried-looking D'Costa threw up his hands in a helpless gesture of extreme disbelief and severe shock. 'They've killed my First and Second Mate.'

So Gonzalo Tavares and Sean Mendes had been murdered. It confirmed that we'd seen two bodies floating in the sea earlier.

We continued staring at the four men guarding us. The small dark exit holes of their AK-74's pointed squarely at us. But they let D'Costa talk.

'Authorities will send the Navy and Coastguard and finished. We'll all be finished.'

'They've one leader and two main buggers,' Napoleon added.

'Who?' Jeet asked, eyes lowered.

Napoleon let out in a low growl. 'Buggers called Zohran and Wassif are led by a Zwankwid al-Jahiz!'

***

Just then two burly men in tracksuits entered. They carried portable radios clipped to their waist belts under their tracksuit tops. One of them had a suitcase sized Very High Frequency or VHF set in his hands.

D'Costa regarded them frustrated and shook his head with impotent anxiety. 'We'll be finished... finished.' He raised his voice. 'We all will be finished. Navy and Coastguard buggers will blast us all to hell.'

One of the two men shrugged his broad shoulders and looked at D'Costa. Large maniac eyes peered out from swollen cheeks, which were covered by a large beard peppered with gray. In a deep profound voice he intoned. ' So be it. I Zohran would have made the ultimate sacrifice for our goals.'

The other man, a smooth shaven Wassif, placed the VHF set carefully down and proceeded to point a radio aerial northwards, towards the city of Mumbai.

Then a thin, very tall, lean lanky man with a serious expression on his lightly bearded face came in. A great degree of intelligence exuded from his dark eyes which rested on his work ravaged, wearied yet child-like facial features. I recognized the arch-terrorist from newspaper photographs that I'd seen before. It was my first view of the dreaded terrorist Zwankwid al-Jahiz.

I tried to recall whatever I'd read about him. He was the scion of a fabulously wealthy West Asian family. They had reputedly billion dollar interests in the construction line. Roads, highways, airports, seaports – all had been constructed in the Middle-East by the al-Jahiz conglomerate.

Now I watched the man who'd been the focus of plenty of newspaper articles and magazine features. Television had carried endless debates about his character and psychology. He was the perpetrator of feats of terror in the western world.

***

Zohran turned to Zwankwid and said gruffly in English. 'We'd like to eliminate these swines. But have to keep them as part of our plan'.

In a low guttural voice, not in character with his looks, Zwankwid answered, 'if the US and Indian's release our colleagues, we'll leave them.'

They were speaking in English, I presumed, to frighten us.

Wassif added without looking up from his radio. 'Right. It takes me a great deal of effort not to blast them to pieces.'

The low menacing tone he used caused slivers of intense nervousness to flash through our bodies.

D'Costa, Perez and Napoleon impassively stared at them. Jeet and I remained silent.

Zwankwid spoke as though lecturing to us. 'Finally we take revenge for the crimes against us committed by the American dogs. And for the repression of these accursed Indians against our brothers here in India.'

'Amazing, men, this is actually happening to us,' Napoleon remarked.

Zohran gave him a vile look. 'Our brother Amjad Mubarak has been captured illegally in Afghanistan.' He paused and felt his gray beard with his left hand and continued in a rough, nasty voice. 'He has to be released, as also ten of our brothers held in Indian jails.'

'What if they don't leave them?' D'Costa's voice exhibited the fatigue and strain he felt.

'We'll kill you all. Everyone on this ship!' Zohran's large, flaming eyes shone with a kind of ferocious fanatical glint. He proceeded as though he enjoyed committing his radically extremist thoughts into words. 'You all here and the rest from down below will be torn to pieces!'

Zwankwid nodded slowly and ominously in agreement. 'By the will of God a just and fair end!'

IX

Suddenly loud sounds of crackling static from the large radio filled the air. All of us turned towards the direction of the radio. Wassif twiddled a knob and lowered the volume. He adjusted the direction of the aerial to get optimal reception. The air filled with crackling sounds of free electrostatic charges being received by the set. Then he carefully tuned the set onto a specific frequency. Every few seconds, whenever he picked up something, he'd stop and carefully listen.

Clear cut orders to someone were being transmitted across the particular radio frequency he was tuned onto. Satisfied, Wassif turned to Zwankwid and said something in their tongue.

Zwankwid took out a paper from his pocket, and began calling out into a microphone.

'This is the Al Jahiz Tiger Force... the Al Jahiz Tiger Force...' Zwankwid scarcely glanced at the sheet of paper in his hands. 'This is the Al Jahiz Tiger Force...'

'Western Naval Command Communications Center.' A terse no nonsense voice came in on the air. 'You are on a restricted Naval channel. You are broadcasting on a banned to civilians frequency.'

'The Al Jahiz Tiger Force has an urgent message for the Indian government.'

Someone on the other end passed an aside which we distinctly heard. 'Some college boy Ham Station, yaar...'

But quickly the hard, strong and terse voice continued, 'Detectors will be activated to pinpoint your location. The penalty when caught is imprisonment.'

An imperturbable Zwankwid unflappably carried on, 'the Al Jahiz Tiger Force has an urgent message for the Indian authorities.'

'Clearance from Vice Admiral Konda Venu Rao, Flag Officer Commanding in Chief, Western Naval Command, is required to use this radio channel.'

'We have taken control of the Malabar Star... repeat we have taken control of the Malabar Star... the vessel is in the control of the Al Jahiz Tiger Force... we have already executed one passenger and two of the crew.'

'Aachha.' A gasp of astonished amazement and accentuated comprehension came across the air. The terse Indian accented voice became dramatically more laconic and curt. 'We can relay your demands to the authorities... what is your message... repeat what is your message.'

I sensed that my signal to Sam about us being trapped inside the Malabar star hadn't reached the authorities. Only now they would be aware of the hijack.

Zwankwid read out from a note in his hand. 'In the name of the Al Jahiz Tiger Force, I the supreme leader Zwankwid al-Jahiz has taken over the Malabar Star. There are thirty-nine lower deck passengers... sixteen US nationals and twenty-three British nationals. Three upper deck passengers... one US national, one British citizen and one Indian are also hostage. Fifteen of the remaining crew are held also, till our demands are met.'

Zwankwid took a deep breath. He added like a seasoned BBC newscaster reading out headlines on television. 'We regret to announce that in taking over the Malabar Star, one passenger Kamran Yazziz, who tried to defy and obstruct the plans of the Al Jahiz Tiger Force, had to be executed. Also two merchant marine officers, Gonzalo Tavares and Sean Mendes were shot dead for resisting the will of the Al Jahiz Tiger Force.'

The radio crackled on. There was deep profound urgency in the accented voice on the other side. 'Where is the Malabar Star located... repeat, repeat, what is your course, heading, bearing, or where is your location... where is the Malabar Star now?'

A short silence of a few seconds ensued.

After a slight pause the duty officer at the Western Naval Command Communications Center announced, 'passing on your message to the Maharashtra State Police Wireless Receiving Station, Malabar Hill, Ridge Road. They will inform the Chief Minister at Mantralaya, Home Minister, Police, Navy, Coastguard and all others concerned.'

Zwankwid proceeded to read from the paper in his hand. 'In protest against American high handedness in Afghanistan and Iraq; and the repression of the Indian authorities against our brothers, the Al Jahiz Tiger Force has decided to act, with brutal force if necessary.'

He waited till he inhaled and exhaled deeply, and added, 'we demand the release of Amjad Mubarak who is in the custody of the American devils. We also demand the release of ten members of the Al Jahiz Commando Force and the Al Jahiz Killer Army who are in Indian jails. They have to be flown to Maqdisho, Somalia, and left there.'

Zwankwid gave out the ten names. And then warned. 'Failure to release them will result in all the hostages being killed one by one. This ship will also be blown up.'

The crisp, urgent voice on the line replied. 'We will pass on your message... keep this line open, you can communicate with us on this radio channel... I repeat a query... where are you located? What is the course, bearing, heading of the Malabar Star... are you anchored at a fixed point?'

D'Costa, Perez, Napoleon, Jeet and I grimly stood by watching.

Zohran and Wassif waited patiently.

The two bearded guards implacably kept their AK-74's trained on us.

Zwankwid spoke firmly into the microphone. 'Over... my message is over... repeat, my message is over... I am coming back onto the air, same channel in two hours time... that is ten-thirty Indian Standard Time.'

Scarcely had he put the microphone away, that an overloud shout of warning came from somewhere from the deck below.

***

Zwankwid, Zohran and Wassif immediately looked at the sea around. Then Zwankwid pointed southwards and the rest began looking in that direction.

The five of us strained our eyes too and soon discerned a white painted fishing boat-like mechanized vessel coming towards us.

'Didn't expect company so soon,' Zwankwid said.

Jeet calmly leaned towards me and divulged in an aghast and exceedingly distressed undertone. 'It's a JSP or Joint Sea Patrol of the Marine and Preventive Customs and the Maharashtra Police conducted in these coastal areas. Operates under the jurisdiction of the Assistant Commissioner, Marine and Preventive Customs, Alibag.'

He had answered my unasked question. D'Costa, Perez and Napoleon, standing by, also were interested in the matter.

Jeet continued, 'think it's an overnight patrol ending. I'm certain they've not been informed about the state of the Malabar Star. And are coming here, under armed, to check out this vessel.'

From the south-south-west side the largish boat steadily advanced towards us. The white painted boat looked like a wooden fishing boat minus the sails. The addition of a diesel engine had converted it into a JSP patrol boat. A chalky white, foamy wake became distinctly discernible on the grayish-blue sea behind the vessel. It revealed the boat had taken a large curving detour, so as to approach us at an angle.

D'Costa wiped sweat from his brow with the palm of a sweatier hand.

Perez and Napoleon were a little restless and uneasy.

Jeet's gaze was raptly focused upon the approaching Customs boat. He muttered to us, 'three distinct parties onboard. The tandel or Master and crew. Two police constables with a Sterling and a SLR. A Customs sepoy with a SLR and a Customs officer with or without a revolver.'

I realized that if a firefight ensued, the armed terrorists in the lower deck would have a big advantage with their AK-74's.

A concerned Zwankwid directed, 'we have to destroy them.'

X

D'Costa, Perez, Napoleon, Jeet and I stared at the boat as if hypnotized into a helpless stillness. Our two guards aggravated the situation by suddenly crouching on one knee each; and kept a closer and more intimidating watch on us. We were over aware that the M & P Customs men and police constables weren't informed of the deadly terrorists they were about to confront.

When the JSP vessel was around a hundred meters away Jeet suddenly trembled with nervous tension; but quickly subdued himself. He muttered. 'Well within AK-74's effective range of three hundred to four hundred meters.'

The boat closed in. It was about seventy-five meters away. I identified a khaki uniformed M & P sepoy with a SLR. He stood near a dark big made man in a sleeveless white vest who held the wheel. Two police constables on the prow were armed. One carried the familiar nine millimeter Sterling submachine carbine; the other held a SLR.

A slim dark haired man in regulation khaki with three stars on his shoulder epaulets, came out of the wheelhouse. He wore photo chrome spectacles and held a revolver in his right hand.

Jeet whispered to me, 'they've had it now.'

***

Zwankwid gave tense instructions into his radio.

A shout came from the deck below. And a volley of five-point-four-five rounds, surprisingly without raising too much of a din, slammed towards the incoming patrol boat at six-hundred and fifty rounds a minute.

The sepoy's face burst instantaneously into a number of ragged raw, red fragments of flesh. His headless body twisted and turned and rolled over the guard rail of the boat and fell with a splash into the sea. A large, dark, crimson patch enlarged in the waters, as blood poured out of a large gaping, bloody orifice created where his head and neck had formerly been.

They'd killed the sepoy; but the boatman or tandel at the wheel was apparently unharmed. He threw the boat into reverse gear.

Within seconds a volley of return shots slammed into the Malabar Star. The return fire was comparatively pathetic, although far louder. The SLR single shots whizzed towards us, and struck the Malabar Star's steel hull plates with sharp twangs.

In the pilot-house the mild odor of bullet primer and powder charge seeping upwards aggravated the waves of jittery nervousness flowing through all of us.

Zohran directed another fusillade through his portable.

The terrorists from below, fired a sustained burst.

The shuddering patrol boat, all the glass of its wheelhouse smashed to smithereens, suddenly stopped reversing. And the engines got cutoff. The tandel had been hit because the boat appeared out of control. Now it inched forward, loitering its way nearer and nearer the Malabar Star, while twisting around in a slow corkscrew motion.

Wassif ordered another round of fire through his radio.

The next volley of automatic AK-74 bursts at nine hundred meters a second smashed into the JSP boat for the third time. Desperate shouts and pained screams indicated that some of the rounds had found their mark. An oil leak sprung from somewhere. Within moments a large patch of pitch-dark oil covered the water around the now wallowing boat; which continued to gently drift towards the Malabar Star. But the boat party, or whatever was left of them still fired back. One round at a time.

Along with the single revolver shots, came a flurry of automatic bursts from somewhere within the wheelhouse cabin of the luckless JSP boat.

'Inspector and a constable with the Sterling still around,' Jeet whispered to me.

A motionless Zwankwid unflappably advised something into his portable radio. I caught the English words 'RPG-7'.

***

Two terrorist came up from down below. One held a green tube-like weapon. The Russian Rocket Propelled Grenade or RPG-7. The other had a couple of rockets in his hands. I knew about the RPG-7's and was aware it couldn't be fired from a confined space due to its excessive back blast. Now the duo stood on the open sundeck behind the pilothouse and began arming the weapon.

D'Costa, Perez, Napoleon, Jeet and I remained inert; but interestedly watched the ghastly finale to the encounter that was forthcoming.

One terrorist screwed a cylinder containing rocket propellant into the warhead. Then loaded the complete round into the muzzle of the tube-like launcher. The other man uncovered the nose cap of the warhead which struck out of its launcher barrel, and removed a safety device.

The terrorist with the RPG-7 on his shoulder aimed it towards the boat and squeezed the trigger. An explosive back-blast was followed simultaneously by a trail of smoke which rushed towards the wheel-house of the oncoming boat.

The RPG penetrated the cabin and the resultant explosion destroyed it. The vessel pitched and lurched under the impact. The brown wooden sides of the wheel-house cabin sagged inwards like the side of a deflating balloon, as fragments of debris burst upwards and fell down. Pieces of lifeless human being spattered back onto the boat, smudging it with bright red sauce-like stains of bloody flesh, which looked like tomato ketchup.

Two men, khaki uniform in shreds, bleeding profusely, stumbled over the twisted rail stanchions and fell howling and shrieking into the sea. One man sunk without a trace. The other clearly visible under a white pall of drifting smoke, tried to swim. He retched violently, wailing in agony as he frenziedly threw his arms about. Within seconds he began to weaken and foundered helplessly. And sank slowly out of sight, while screaming his lungs out.

In front the JSP patrol boat, now clearly out of control, slowly drifted closer. A couple of single revolver shots smacked into the Malabar Star uselessly. Incredibly someone from somewhere within the doomed boat still bravely put on a futile resistance.

'Inspector in charge is still alive,' Jeet said.

D'Costa, Perez, Napoleon and I remained severely daunted, watching the gruesome scene.

Zwankwid gave further instructions to Zohran.

Zohran relayed orders through his radio.

The terrorists on the sundeck had armed and extracted the safety pin of a reload RPG-7. And aimed and hit the boat for the second time.

The boat literally exploded into pieces of wood with an eardrum bursting detonation. A scream emanated from within the charnel house-like atmosphere within. But when the smoke abated the boat still floated, with a severe list. Now it was like floating scrap consisting of wooden beams, iron pipes, cables – all a twisted charred flaming mass of junk.

The lightly bearded Zwankwid stood watching the scene like a rock. Somehow he was like the epitome of an elite kid that had got mixed up with scum. He ordered another round of RPG-7 fire.

The next RPG-7 struck the fuel tank. A searing orange-white glare of immense magnitude flared for a fraction of an instant. It was as if a mini sun had been temporarily created too close to us. For a moment it blinded us completely. The graphic, vivid glare disturbed our vision for some time. Long enough to slightly affect our view of the explosion that the flash metamorphosed into. Then the layer of oil floating in the sea around the boat ignited.

Dense black smoke materialized. It ascended via a long, dark, hazy drifting pillar towards the blue sky. The boat shuddered. Her bow rose upwards, trembling and quivering, then dropped abruptly. The angle of her list enhanced enough for sea water to rush in and inundate her. A low crackling hiss of steam came over as the sea water ran over red hot parts of the burning mass.

With a clearly audible low decibel roar, the sea water deluge shook and strained the boat, forcing it to sink lower and lower. Within a few seconds it disappeared with a foaming, bubbling gurgle along with what remained of the brave Customs and policemen.

Nervously the five of us stared at the smoky haze enveloping the debris of bits and pieces of charred driftwood, floating about in the Arabian Sea.

The sudden silence that ensued hurt our auditory sensibilities almost as much as the explosions had done earlier.

Zwankwid broke the inertia that usually comes at the aftermath of extreme nervous effort. An apathy that usually tends to hinder further action. He regarded us and said to Zohran and Wassif in English. 'We'll leave them here with two men. And we will clear out of this place and remain in the interior of this ship, to be near our dhows.'

D'Costa made a slight choking sound. He grit his teeth and swallowed once or twice. As if to prevent himself from throwing up. Then he muttered in a low voice of acute, somber torment. 'You won't get away with this. Using my ship to murder those poor Customs and Police buggers!'

XI

An exhilarated Zohran and Wassif turned to D'Costa. Zwankwid too stopped and regarded the Captain of the Malabar Star.

A distracted D'Costa mumbled something indecipherable to himself. He was visibly distressed. More than overwhelmingly outraged at the needless loss of lives.

Perez made no movement in any direction.

Napoleon was unusually aware and consciously alive to the situation and stood by well in control of himself.

As for Jeet and I, we waited for the inevitable. The destruction of the patrol boat and the loss of lives was a grave matter. Clearly the Customs men and armed police constables hadn't been informed that the Malabar Star had been taken over by armed terrorists. Now the situation was serious enough for the Indian authorities to react drastically, with terminal force if necessary. They might attack us anytime. Launch a commando operation which could result in severe casualties.

Perez's eyes roved quietly over everyone. Suddenly he spoke for the first time. He rasped in a low unthreatening manner. 'What do you want with us?'

'Nothing much,' sneered Wassif looking at D'Costa. 'Except as we have listed in our demands.'

D'Costa aware of the gravity of the situation nodded with his head bowed down. He'd realized his inadvertent impetuosity could provoke them. Jeopardize the safety of his passengers and crew.

Jeet infinitely concerned about our situation, said, while regarding Zwankwid, 'area will be teeming with hostile security forces, including the Navy and Coastguard.'

Zwankwid suddenly appeared haggard and weary in his eyes. He retorted, 'we'll be deep inside the ship with the hostages. Near our modified dhows. You all will be locked in an upper cabin. If they try to hit us with their big Naval guns you will suffer the most upstairs.'

He then signaled Zohran and Wassif. And started moving out of the pilothouse.

Zohran snapped orders to the two men guarding us, and followed his leader out. Wassif took the VHF set with him. The two terrorists with their AK-74's pointing at us nodded at them and continued guarding us. And the five of us were left alone with the two armed guards.

***

Wearied by the constant standing up, my eyes roved the pilothouse for the first time. I took in the wheel of the ship. The navigation consoles, radar screens and dials and displays on the control panel by the side of the steering wheel were smashed up. However to one side a largish looking ship radio appeared intact. The main communication set had been untouched by the terrorists. If only we could use it to get to the authorities. Two menacing AK-74's prevented us from doing the needful.

Napoleon's eyes wandered furtively from the radio to his shoes. He too was thinking of communicating with the authorities through the now out of bounds radio.

To one side I noted a wall locker with a shelf underneath it. It was where D'Costa had probably kept our two Glock pistols for safekeeping for the duration of the trip. Now we needed them and couldn't get to them.

The waist high shelf under the locker had two bags. I recognized them. They had been brought onboard by Perez. One was a briefcase. The other was a smaller than average suitcase. The odd size was as if it contained some electronic item. What were they doing in the pilot-house. If weapons carried by passenger's were kept in the pilot-house, the two bags would have to be emptied out and its contents stored in the locker. Why were the two bags here? I inadvertently glanced at Perez who stood near the briefcase and noticed something. He was surreptitiously adjusting the position of the briefcase on the shelf. As if to point it at one of the terrorists.

He was doing so in a slow, imperceptible, unnoticeable manner.

I looked away. I didn't want to give him away to the two watching terrorists. I thought of the keys to the locker. We'd been searched and only our cell phones had been taken away. I tried to recall if any key, like that of the locker, was found and taken away. If my memory served me right, no key had been found. The mystery of the missing key dwelt in my mind when a sudden sharp knocking sound came from outside the open door of the pilothouse.

The two armed men guarding us changed their focus of attention towards the door.

Perez in a sudden, rapid movement placed his right hand on the briefcase handle, lifted it slightly to point at one of the armed terrorist's – and opened fire!!

***

A small circular hole with a blue, black colored circumference formed on the terrorist's temple. Before it could turn red with welling blood, the man dropped like a ton of bricks to the ground. His AK-74 clattered to the floor.

Instantaneously Perez pointed the killer briefcase at the other terrorist who seemed paralyzed with shock. The man lurched sideways. His scream got cut-off halfway through. Bullets lanced through his throat and splashed blood outwards in a wavy manner. Irregular patterned bullet punctures shred to indiscernible fragments the bearded terrorists lower jaw, fleshy upper throat, windpipe, gullet, carotid arteries, jugular's and the top of his spinal column. Within a minutely microscopic fraction of a sudden flash, time-wise, he convulsively jerked, before crumpling onto the floor with a deeply resounding thud. And lay inert and lifeless over his rifle.

As an uneasy, nervy Columbus entered with a tray with five tiffin boxes on it, Jeet and Napoleon rushed to the bodies and stripped them of their AK-74's, spare magazines and portable radio's. They then dragged the two bodies out of the arc of the door onto the sundeck. Then shut the door and securely bolted the three thick steel bolts from inside.

When they returned, Napoleon quickly took out his left shoe and extracted a key from it. He'd hidden the key to the locker in his shoe all the while. He went to the wall locker, opened it and took out our two holstered Glock's with the spare thirty-three round magazines. He contemplated them for a moment, then with a nervous motion he handed the pistol's to Jeet and me.

The sight of my trustworthy Glock which had extracted me from a number of tight situations before, more than considerably buoyed me up.

I buckled my waist belt holster; while half-watching a more than visibly bolstered-up Jeet do the same.

Perez opened the briefcase and extracted a gun from inside. 'Hecklar and Koch MP-5 KA4. Can be installed in a briefcase.' He held the gun while examining the spare magazines that were with it.

D'Costa checked the armored door was latched securely from the inside and said, 'we're trapped inside, but we've got the radio, weapons and some food.'

XII

'I have to confess gentlemen,' Perez leveled a shrewd calculating eye on us. 'We were expecting this kind of situation!'

While Napoleon and Columbus took the fallen terrorists AK-74's; and Jeet and I held our Glock's ready; Perez held the MP-5 KA5 and said, 'I work for the US Central Intelligence Agency. Yes I'm a CIA agent.'

All attention from the five of us instantaneously centered onto Perez with a swift alacrity that almost could have competed with the rays of light racing from a just switched on bulb, to around the room.

In my mind certain points regarding Perez fell into place quickly. Like the Consulate car not coming up to the ship's boarding ramp. Also the American's keen interest in anything regarding the Malabar Star rang bells of alarm. Moreover he exuded an air commonly found in those undertaking undercover work. And this manner was detectable only by a trained detective.

The space between Perez's eyebrows narrowed as he crinkled his eyes ever so slightly in an effort to gauge our reactions. 'I'm on the Malabar Star because of certain information that we had!'

'Amazing,' I said as my eyes semi-disbelievingly roved over his aged, creased visage.

A flabbergasted D'Costa pensively stared at Perez.

Napoleon and Columbus with the AK-74's peered out of the small aperture in the shut and bolted armored door, at the open sundeck outside. Waiting for the terrorists to arrive. But they also had their ears tuned to Perez.

Jeet silently watched Perez, scarcely batting an eyelid.

'Two crates of AK-74's with spare magazines went missing. They were stolen-off a larger consignment from a warehouse in Karachi harbor, Pakistan.' Perez seemed significantly relieved at letting the intelligence out to us. 'The weapons were being imported for use by the Afghan police and para-military forces. They were destined for Kabul.'

'And the same weapons are being used by these terrorists?' Jeet probed lightly.

'How did the Al Jahiz Tiger Force or AJTF get them?' I couldn't help asking.

'We got to know because of Amjad Mubarak.'

'One of the buggers they wanted released?' D'Costa enquired. The dazed amazement on his face had abated somewhat.

'Same man,' Perez concurred. 'When captured in Helmand, Afghanistan, they found documents and CD's with information about planned terrorist strikes.'

Perez paused, took a deep breath and continued, 'one of the CD's was damaged. The only intelligence readable on it was the name of this ship. And two eight digit numbers.'

He then went to his small suitcase and opened it. Inside was an extremely sophisticated-looking portable radio with a complex set of dials and knobs, which included an intricate frequency tuner.

'Name of my ship?' A noticeably tired D'Costa asked with not a little astonishment gradually taking over his facial features.

'Yes the name of the Malabar Star was mentioned on the CD. We knew this ship had something to do with terrorists,' Perez nodded, hands on his radio.

'And of the two, eight digit numbers?' I queried gravely.

'The numbers were on the two crates that went missing from the warehouse in Karachi.' Perez made a snappy, curt, responsive movement with his head. 'Incidentally they got the RPG-7 and reloads from elsewhere.'

His revelations assuaged me like hell. It meant that US intelligence was keeping tabs on the Malabar Star. Assistance would be on hand soon. 'So the missing crates with the Afghan police bound AK-74's and spare ammunition and this ship were linked?'

'That's where we made a mistake.' Perez bit his lip. 'The concerned CD was damaged. CIA experts using sophisticated computers couldn't extract more information.'

'What mistake?' Jeet homed in specifically to the point.

'Thought they were using the Malabar Star only to transport the stolen consignment to somewhere,' Perez replied.

That explained his knowledge about the ship's halts before this year's Malabar run, I thought.

'We watched the vessel,' said Perez, 'A little after it had left the repair yard in the Mazagon Docks. And at Karachi, Aden, Djibouti and the return stop at Aden... at Mumbai I boarded the vessel.' A chill of uneasiness overcame his creased face. As if faulty interpretation of a CIA intelligence report was his personal fault. 'No weapons were loaded onto this vessel.'

A nervous D'Costa sighed. 'Have to report all this to the Police.'

Napoleon, peeping out through the aperture at the sundeck, uttered a warning. 'They're gathering near the funnel and lifeboats.'

He shifted slightly, as he was listening to us too, and disclosed, 'they captured us with pistols forcibly... shot Gonzalo and Sean and stopped the ship here.' He noisily exhaled some highly raged, overheated breath and continued. 'Extra buggers in tracksuits ghussaoed in... charged in from those dhows with rifles.'

An electrified D'Costa instantly whispered some highly confidential advice to Napoleon. 'You can't use those words. You've become a higher, better class now.'

Unfortunately everyone heard him and suppressed various degrees of giggles.

The CIA agent ignored the interruption. 'The US Embassy informed the Indian Research and Analysis Wing. We knew Zohran and Wassif were onboard!'

'I can't believe it,' Jeet said. 'Authorities could've nabbed them easily?'

'Think a US Navy Task Force along with the Indian Navy was to intercept this ship later on,' revealed Perez, 'They misjudged the interception because those modified dhows enabled the hijackers to come in too soon!'

Napoleon suddenly dropped like a sack of potatoes onto the floor, and shouted in alarm. 'Duck they're...'

XIII

A sudden volley of shots slammed the thick steel plating on the door with a resounding clang. The shots were coming from somewhere behind the funnel. They were being careful. They'd seen the bodies of the two slain terrorists and knew we could kill if the need be.

A couple of bullets smashed through the narrow rectangular peephole on the single door. They hit the front glass screen of the pilothouse. The glass shattered into smithereens with a sharp crackling sound.

Scarcely had the mellifluous tinkle of broken glass impacting on the forecastle deck below died down, when Napoleon returned fire. The sheer intense fury of his prolonged burst momentarily stopped their firing.

A fierce second barrage spattered against the armor plated steel.

The resulting clamor reverberated throughout the pilothouse. Again they stopped shooting. But the consequent lull only served to add an intense nervousness to our tense restless selves.

'We've to conserve ammunition. They'll wait and then charge into us,' Jeet instructed.

I showed Napoleon and Columbus the combined safety and fire selector of the AK-74's. 'The lever on the left side above, is to be moved all the way down to fire single shots.'

Both Napoleon and Columbus selected the single shot mode on their AK-74's. They knelt down and poked the barrel's of their rifles through the aperture, above their heads, and blind fired a series of single shots. They struck the funnel futilely and ricocheted-off harmlessly.

Perez then fired a three round burst from his MP-5 KA5. The disturbing clackety-clack of the lightning fast action of German gun-metal slamming three nine millimeter slugs made a stunningly noisy report.

Then the terrorists outside, fifty meters away, opened fire again. A tempest of rifle ordnance clanged incessantly on the armored steel outside like a deadly orchestra. But only stray bullets sometimes whizzed through the narrow aperture, and exited harmlessly.

A sudden cessation of the firing took place. It caused a frightful, portentous, hush-like atmosphere. It somehow presaged a lethal escalation, intensity-wise, of the imminent continuation of the encounter.

Zohran's voice came over from somewhere outside. 'Come out. Surrender and you live. Otherwise we'll get you and kill you all.'

Napoleon abruptly altered his manner. He roared at the top of his voice. 'No you bloody bastards. Come out in the open so we can bloody blast you all to hell.'

The terrorists responded immediately. A savage ear-splitting drumming of a ferocious volley of shots struck the armored steel door outside. Then the firing stopped.

***

Jeet solemnly aimed and fired a round from his Glock. Then lowered himself. He turned gravely to us. 'We're in serious trouble if they use the RPG-7 to blast open the door.'

'Then they'll charge inside,' Napoleon gruffly added.

Outside a number of flashes emanated from around the funnel and lifeboats on their davits. A stabbing single shot whizzed past, miraculously speeding through the narrow opening. The remainder shots struck the steel plating outside.

'If they launch a mass assault or infantry-style charge,' Jeet said, kneeling way down the aperture. 'All rush forward and blind fire into them.'

'They'll use the RPG-7 first,' I let out.

Jeet thoughtfully retorted, 'think they don't have enough rockets otherwise they'd use the RPG-7's by now?'

Perez smiled for the first time. 'So don't have reloads and have to fire to get to us.'

Columbus turned and looked upwards suddenly. He put his right hand to his right ear and said, 'planes are coming. I can hear aeroplanes.'

The rest of us strained our ears; and D'Costa agreed. 'Yes I can hear aircraft also.'

***

An agonizing lull and a consequent hushed, silence that actually hurt our ear drums for some time ensued. The menacing interlude, pregnant with the threat of an impending escalation of the firefight aggravated our qualms and fears. This despite our only hope; the aircraft sounds might materialize into being our saviors. Currently we were fully protected inside the pilothouse. We were almost impregnable to gunfire. The thick steel shield on the door window facing the sundeck had aided us immeasurably. The twelve inch long by four inch wide aperture on the door had been too small a gap for a sufficient volume of their bullets to effectively penetrate into the pilothouse.

Outside orders and commands rent the air. The terrorists were regrouping for a renewed assault.

Jeet risked a peep out towards the open fifty meter sundeck. And cried, 'had it. I can see them arming a RPG-7.'

I raised myself and looked outside. I could detect the tube-like weapon on a man's shoulder behind the port lifeboat.

Gradually the aircraft sounds became louder and louder.

Jeet peered out rapidly and lowered himself and said, 'whatever is arriving must come soon.'

A continuous, noisy din at a unique frequency and at a decibel level totally different from the sounds heard so far interrupted the combat.

In front the terrorists disappeared from view. This included the man with the RPG-7.

The aircraft noise, as it got closer, clarified into a steady clattering of easily recognizable helicopter rotors. Two choppers made a shallow pass. They veered steeply away. We got a clear view of the undersides of the two blue colored aircraft from the pane less side windows of the pilothouse.

Jeet focused a highly gratified eye on the cause of our reprieve. 'Coastguard Chetaks.'

D'Costa made the sign of the cross and mumbled a few words of thankful prayer at our deliverance.

Napoleon and Columbus couldn't pull their gaze-off the whirlybirds as they executed a long turn and began to fly back towards us.

Perez went to his radio.

D'Costa motioned to Napoleon. The chief engineer bounded to the ships main radio and switched it on.

Outside the sharp continuous clatter of another helicopter, with a different type of acoustics, became louder and louder. The chopper slowed down and hovered over the stern area of the Malabar Star.

'The terrorists are hiding from an eye in the sky. They've disappeared into the ship,' Jeet informed.

The rotor sounds emanating from the oddly designed helicopter enhanced. With a clangorous roar it ascended rapidly. Banking sharply, it veered-off eastwards.

The mood in D'Costa, Perez, Napoleon and Columbus lifted considerably.

Jeet watched the compact airborne chopper. It looked totally different from the previous two. It had two main rotors one on top of the other, rotating in opposite directions. It operated without a tail rotor. He couldn't hide the elation in his voice. 'Indian Navy's Russian Kamov or KA-28. It has contra-rotating rotors.'

I'd heard of the helicopter. 'Called Helix by us in England.'

Then the Malabar Star's main radio crackled to life.

Napoleon and Columbus whooped with delight.

The rest of us heartened considerably, heard the call being given out by the authorities.

'Western Naval Command Communications Center... Western Naval Command Communications Center... to the Malabar Star... to the Malabar Star... do you read me over... !'

XIV

D'Costa hurriedly picked up the largish mouthpiece with an electrifying alacrity that shocked us, given his usual bearing and manner. He spoke.'This is the Malabar Star... this is the Master of the Malabar Star, over.'

'Confirm identity of speaker... we're checking the channel... we're due to talk to the Al Jahiz Tiger Force in an hour's time,' revealed a crisp authoritative voice.

'I'm Jesus Antonio D'Costa, the Captain. I along with two crew and three passengers have escaped them. We're stuck in the pilothouse surrounded by these terrorists. The rest of the passengers and crew are hostage below.'

The sounds of the sharp exhalation that came over the radio was of the type that indicated an extreme case of astonished amazement.

'Our helicopter pilots reported gunfire?'

'On seeing them they hid. They had a RPG-7 also and have taken it away somewhere,' revealed D'Costa. 'We also have guns but will run out of bullets.'

Outside the three helicopters flew patterns over the Malabar Star, criscrossing over each other like angry dragonflies. However they circled and swept over at a safe distance, out of range of the terrorist's weapons.

There was no sign of the terrorists who'd been shooting at us on the sundeck. Clearly they'd readjusted their combative, hostile focus and concentrated on the new airborne threats that had materialized.

'I'm Commodore Kuldeep Singh Kohli,' a cryptic voice disclosed. 'I'm speaking on behalf of Vice Admiral Konda Venu Rao the Flag

Officer Commanding in Chief Western Naval Command who has been selected by the government to handle the situation.'

Perez left his radio, an ardent persistence detectable in his tired eyes, and leaned close to D'Costa and said, 'this is an open line. They can overhear us?'

'Aha... is that Peter Perez?' The American voice that came over the air conveyed a combination of surprised wonderment and an elevated sense of superlative relief. 'I'm Tony Preston from the US Consulate. Hostage negotiator representing the US and the UK from the Western Naval Command Communication Center.'

Perez equally comforted smiled slightly. 'How do you do Tony.' He paused. The clamorous whirr of high RPM rotor blades of the helicopters above became too loud momentarily. This prevented normal conversation for a second or so.

From the WNCCC Kohli agreed. 'Yes they can overhear our conversation. We'll be conducting negotiations with the AJTF on this channel. You can eavesdrop on the cross talk on your ship's main radio.'

Preston came in on the line from the WNCCC. His voice sounded hard and official-like. 'Use the CIA satellite radio with Perez. It frequency hops between a range of frequencies, so that talk can be received only by those having the same radio sets.'

Kohli directed. 'Switch-off the main set and communicate further now on Perez's radio. We have a similar set here with us.'

***

Perez activated his radio and tuned it slightly. Soon we continued talking to Kohli and Preston in the WNCCC.

Kohli reported on the "secure against eavesdropping" line. 'Received a message from a Sam of the Pemberton Security Services, London. Pinpointed your location. And due to operational readiness of the Indian Navy ship's Godavari, Ranvijay and Vindhyagiri, they were selected for the hostage rescue mission. Two Coastguard offshore patrol vessels the Sangram and the Vajra will accompany them.'

'Five ships coming,' D'Costa clarified.

'Right,' Kohli's laconic voice cut in. 'Rear Admiral Darius Hormusjee Contractor, Flag Officer Commanding Western Fleet, using the Godavari as his flagship, will be the Indian Naval tactical commander.'

Scarcely had he finished when Preston proceeded to remove a lot of our suspense. 'A US Navy Sea Air Land or SEAL team didn't arrive in time. So an US Marine Corps amphibious unit with a Royal Navy frigate left Diego Garcia a few days ago without them. Has sailed from a prepositioned force based there into the Arabian Sea.'

Preston paused and continued, 'intended to intercept the Malabar Star on its route, with Indian permission, to nab Zohran and Wassif who were known to be on the vessel.'

A wave of exultation passed through us. The mood on the beleaguered pilothouse became considerably lighter.

'Misjudged the case,' Jeet nodded in comprehension. 'Never expected they'd hijack us that close to Mumbai.'

'They'll arrive possibly in the early hours of the morning.'

'That soon?' asked Perez a trifle suspiciously.

'CIA interrogators broke down Amjad Mubarak at an undisclosed safe house.' Preston tersely explained in an official voice. 'Let out the AJTF intended hijacking the Malabar Star as it carried mainly western tourists.'

'I didn't receive a warning?' A significantly perturbed Perez injected a hefty dose of reproach into his question.

'Got to know just yesterday,' Preston's imperturbable voice explained composedly. 'Couldn't get to you in time. But the US and UK task group was informed. Immediately changed their heading so as to get here.'

***

I spoke for the first time to the duo in the WNCCC. 'Any details of the US Marine Corps amphibious unit arriving as also of the UK warship?'

'Rear Admiral Daniel Alexander will be the overall Naval Commander Amphibious Task Group or CATG from the United States Ship or USS Saipan which is an assault landing ship that also carries plenty of helicopters and vertical short takeoff landing Sea Harriers'. Preston said at length. 'Colonel William Williamson will be the Marine Amphibious Unit commander.'

Preston took a respite, then added, 'the guided missile destroyer the USS Arleigh Burke will escort the Saipan. Also the Royal Navy frigate the Her Majesty's Ship or HMS Cornwall, commanded by Captain Rodney Le Harrington will come with the US force. An elite Special Air Service or SAS Boat Troop squad is onboard the Cornwall. And Le Harrington will nominally be operating under Alexander's orders.'

This meant a virtual fleet of eight surface combatants would be surrounding the Malabar Star soon. How they'd fare in trying to rescue us and the rest would be interesting for us. We were relatively safe where we were, especially now.

'The Coastguard helicopters have gone.' Napoleon jerked us back to the situation around us currently.

I noted the Kamov 28 or Helix still there overhead. Then it was joined by two other helicopters. These were heavier-looking than the Chetaks. I recognized the choppers.

'Westland Sea Kings,' I said. 'Can see heavy machineguns installed on them.'

'Mark 42 C,' revealed Jeet immediately. 'Coastguard markings on the commando version of the Sea King. Carrying a contingent of Marine Commando Force or MCF. Also has a twenty-five millimeter Aden Cannon on it.'

Preston announced. 'Contractor on the Godavari, Alexander on the Saipan, Le Harrington on the Cornwall as well as us two at the WNCCC have the same type of radio sets that you have. Means we have a "secure against eavesdropping" tactical radio net consisting of five groups.'

Kohli further directed, 'now switch on the ship's main radio at ten thirty Indian Standard Time to overhear our negotiations with the AJTF.'

'We'll try to buy time till the US and UK Task Group arrives,' Preston disclosed. 'Also will try to negotiate a cease fire on the sundeck and pilothouse... so they don't get to you all.'

'What will we do till then? They've got RPG-7's too,' I said.

'Our heli-patrols can open up with Aden machineguns from the air... at one thousand eight hundred and fifty rounds a minute can strafe them till they cease firing onto you.' Kohli's curt manner relieved us considerably. 'We sign-off now till ten thirty IST.'

Just then Jeet and Napoleon shouted out together. And Jeet alone said. 'Naval and Coastguard ships are coming from the Mumbai side.'

All of us stuck in the pilothouse peered intently northwards at the approaching Indian Naval squadron.

Part 3

The Naval Finale

A Techno-Thriller

I

The six of us, trapped in the pilothouse of the Malabar Star, turned and looked towards the north. Through the shattered glass of the front of the pilothouse. The five clear-cut silhouettes that bore down onto the Malabar Star slowly clarified into clearly defined surface combatants. Pillars of dark smoke rose upwards from their boilers as they steadily steamed towards us.

I could identify the menacing-looking gun turrets and the deadly missile canisters visible on the decks of the Indian warships. Their masts were bristling with aerials of sophisticated electromagnetic systems. Even the two Coastguard vessels accompanying them had weapons on their prows.

The sight of the warships and offshore patrol boats immensely bolstered our psychological capacity to endure a prolonged battle of attrition with the AJTF. Now everyone stared fixatedly at the approaching armada. And attempted to draw in as much psychic vigor and energy as possible into ourselves.

Two Indian Naval ships and one Coastguard vessel veered eastwards towards the shore. Then in formation, turned and continued towards us at an angle. They stopped north of us, about five hundred meters away from the prow of the Malabar Star. Slowly they executed quarter turns. The sea gurgled and churned from the propeller wake under their stern's, till the vessels prow's faced the Malabar Star.

Jeet peered intently at the vessel north-east of us and said, 'the Coastguard ship Vajra. It's Forty Millimeter Swedish Bofors mounting is trained on our ship.'

He then focused on the next in line Naval vessel. I recognized it as a Leander class frigate.

Jeet informed us. 'Vindhyagiri, a British designed, Mazagon Dock's manufactured anti-submarine warfare frigate. Because of its Vickers Armstrong twin Four Point Five Inch gun, can be used for surface action too.'

The squat warship next to it reverse-thrusted its propellers about five hundred meters away from us. It stopped almost dead north to the Malabar Star. I recognized the Russian ordnance on its deck. Four closed barrel-like missile canisters in addition to a twin barreled gun turret on its prow as well as immense radar arrays, exuded a deadly lethality.

'Godavari... here Contractor's flagship,' Jeet disclosed.

D'Costa, Perez, Napoleon, Columbus and I watched the Naval deployment fascinated.

Jeet turned to the third Naval vessel, a heavily armed guided missile destroyer which swung out towards the west followed by another Coastguard ship. They sliced southwards, past us and turned.

The lean, long, low warship distinguished by a white guardrail running from jack staff to the stern was easily identifiable by me. Clearly visible were a twin barreled gun turret, anti-aircraft missiles, anti-shipping missiles in canisters and four multi-barreled Air- Defense Guns in mini-turrets.

'Russian Kashin II destroyer of the Indian Navy. Its twin barreled Three Inch gun is bearing on us,' I said.

'Right,' Jeet assented. 'The Ranvijay.'

The longish Coastguard vessel with the Ranvijay sailed along a wider curving path to a point almost exactly south-east of us. There it slowly spun on its axis, till its prow pointed directly at the Malabar Star.

'Another Three Inch gun, the Italian Otto Melara is aimed at us,' Jeet revealed. 'That's from the Coastguard offshore patrol boat the Sangram.'

The Ranvijay meanwhile slewed eastwards, turned completely and advanced from the south side towards us. The destroyer slowed down and stopped five hundred meters away from us. The stationary combatant circled gradually till its prow faced us. The Ranvijay was now to the south of us.

Five combatants now were around the Malabar Star. Three to the north and two to the south of us. To our east was the island Janjira fortress and the Indian mainland beyond it. To our west was the open sea.

***

Then, the two Sea King commando version helicopter's flew to the Coastguard vessels and hovered over their helipads. And gently landed.

The Russian Helix loitered over the Ranvijay for a few minutes, then landed on its helipad.

Simultaneously to the landing of the three helicopter's onto their mother ships. Two Sea Kings took-off from the helipads of the Godavari and the Vindhyagiri. They were Sea King's too, but another version. I recognized stubby British Sea Eagle air-surface missiles on hard points on the choppers in the air now.

D'Costa sighed and vocalized the sense of release he felt, 'at long last our Navy and Coastguard have come.'

'To finish these Al Jahiz bastards once in for all,' Napoleon added.

'Provided we don't get finished too,' Perez gravely said.

A perplexed-looking Jeet murmured, 'odd they're not covering the west side open sea?'

'There's a large gap to the west. They can get into their dhows and escape,' I said.

Jeet thoughtfully regarded the warships and patrol vessels. 'Yes can escape westwards. Maybe left the gap on purpose?'

'Radar guided guns and rockets covering the gap, I think,' said a supercharged Napoleon. 'If escape in their dhows, will blast the bastards and bloody finish them in one minute.' His dramatic statement instantly pumped him up stupendously. He literally glowed with pleasure at hearing himself speak.

'Purposely left the gap. Speed and endurance of our ships much more than their dhows. Hundreds of miles of open Arabian Sea to catch up and destroy them,' Jeet agreed.

Columbus suddenly yelled. 'They're coming close slowly.'

Outside the squadron began closing in. The half-a-kilometer or so gap between the Malabar Star and the Naval and Coastguard vessels began to lessen. While in the air the two anti-shipping missile laden Sea King's flew sorties over the Malabar Star.

Hooters blasted from all the approaching vessels. As they neared, a vague and persistent electromagnetic hum began enveloping the Malabar Star. It was like being in a microwave oven, being however blasted by vibrating low frequency audio waves only. Gun turrets on the advancing ships came alive. Slowly, the activated heavy guns twisted and turned. Their long twin barrels began to rise and lower. A barely audible, but distinct sound of alarm-like sirens came over.

'Contractor's closing in,' Jeet said nervously. 'They'll start killing hostages.'

'Not using the right tactics.' Perez added.

Thoughts regarding the impossibility of effecting an attack or boarding without consulting us formed in my mind. Before I could say anything a crackling burst of static jarred my ears.

'It's ten-thirty,' informed Napoleon as he switched on the ship's main radio and enhanced the volume slightly.

Outside the Naval and Coastguard vessels were about a hundred meters away.

***

The six of us focused all our attention upon the radio. We began to listen in to the communications.

Zwankwid's hysterical voice raged on in a desperate ireful frenzy. 'Western Command Center... Naval Communications Center... Western Command Center...'

'Receiving you loud and clear,' Commodore Kohli responded.

'Move your ships away... move those Navy ships away,' screamed Zwankwid. 'At least a kilometer away... or I'll start killing the hostages in two's!'

Sounds of a click came over. The low electronic humming enveloping us enhanced considerably when the same sounds came in through the radio.

A razor sharp, biting voice spoke. 'This is from the Bridge of the INS Godavari. Repeat, I'm speaking from the Bridge of the INS Godavari.' The delivery and tone of the voice was remarkably effective. It sounded coercive and threatening enough to scare the wits-off any ordinary listener. 'I Darius Hormusjee Contractor, Rear Admiral, Flag Officer Commanding Western Fleet, direct you to leave the Malabar Star. Repeat, clear-off the Malabar Star... I can blast you into pieces within a fraction of a second, with highly effective ordnance designed to smash you into unrecognizable fragments!'

We tensely remained as quiet as possible in the pilothouse of the Malabar Star as we listened to the exchange going on, on the radio.

Jeet surveyed the Godavari too, peeping over our pilothouse instrument panel. He exuded an all attention focused onto a single point like feeling. He muttered almost to himself. 'Get them to flee on their dhows... to chase them and destroy them one by one.'

Through the open line we could clearly discern Zwankwid's fiery breath wheezing in and out of his nostrils. 'All hostages will be finished.' Then he stunned us with an exceptionally loud blazing roar. 'Finished... completely finished. And you will be held responsible.'

A series of clicks came over the radio. The roar of clattering rotors swamped us through the set. The operations room of the Godavari had connected the channel to the radio's from the overflying helicopters.

A tense, crisp sounding staccato voice interrupted. 'Echo 003... echo 003... Sea King one in strike position, aligned Sea Eagles... request permission to open fire... aligned Sea Eagles, request permission to fire.'

A second voice tersely asked. 'Victor 002... victor 002... am tracking target from above the Janjira fortress... awaiting firing orders.'

All six of us watched the two Naval Sea King's hovering over the fortress. The British Sea Eagles were just in front and above the rear wheels, just below the fuselage doors. We were focused fully onto the drama being played out. There was no rational way of determining the AJTF's reaction.

Then the continuous whirring of helicopter blades emanating from the radio ceased abruptly. The operations room of the Godavari had terminated the link.

Contractor returned. 'You leave me with no option but to do the worst.' He barked out the statement in a tough, loud and fast manner. He expressed his determination to use brute force if necessary.

He paused, altered his voice considerably and suggested as gently and persuasively as he could, 'your only chance is to get into your dhows quickly and sail away as fast as possible.'

We heard murmured consultations going on among the terrorists for about half a minute.

Then Zwankwid came in on the line. 'Watch the forecastle deck'. His insecure loud manner had an ominous, menacing ring. 'Keep your scopes trained onto the forecastle deck... the forecastle deck.'

***

Now the six of us clustered around the wheel. We grimly looked downwards over the unpowered consoles of the Malabar Star's navigation pilothouse, onto the now dismal, gloomy and empty forecastle deck.

An aged tourist with tousled gray hair confusedly strolled out. The plump matronly appearance of the woman clutching his left arm gave the impression it was his wife. They looked like American tourists. The panic stricken couple dizzy with dread and bewilderment, shuffled unsteadily towards the jack staff of the Malabar Star.

An unseen terrorist gruffly bellowed, 'keep walking forward to the end.'

The benumbed work ravaged man who looked like a skilled worker of some sort, shivered and shuddered as if in deep shock. He semi-dragged his trembling wife who was petrified with sheer fright. They reached the stem of the Malabar Star. The doomed man glanced downwards at the sea below. Contemplating whether to make a break for it. His sorrowful wife tugged at his arm, and he gave up the idea.

Instantaneously a firing squad-type of volley of AK-74 shots rang out from somewhere within the ship. Multiple lead projectiles thudded and slammed into the couple, tumbling and spinning inside their torsos, creating severe bleeding. This manifested itself in large crimson, red patches of blood on their clothes. Agonized screams of mortal torment half left their lips. And cut-off as both toppled over and fell with a loud splash into the water.

A despairing D'Costa shook his head regretfully and wailed sorrowfully. 'Oh my God.' He made the sign of the cross. 'May Jesus have mercy on these damn bloody fools.'

Contractor had gone too far. The plan to entice the terrorists away from the Malabar Star had failed. It had provoked the AJTF into killing two tourists.

Kohli called over the radio in a grim manner that reflected the extreme urgency of the situation. 'To the Al Jahiz Tiger Force... calling the Al Jahiz Tiger Force...'

Zwankwid responded immediately. 'Aha five more minutes, five minutes more and another two accursed Americans go down.' He delivered his warning with a hefty dose of a kind of a forced frenzied enthusiasm in his voice. He tried to show he actually enjoyed the execution; and he craved to continue the killings.

Kohli cryptically announced, 'the Flag Officer Commanding in Chief of the entire Western Navy, Vice Admiral Konda Venu Rao will talk to you.'

***

Within a few seconds the top boss of India's Western Navy came on the line. 'This is Vice Admiral KV Rao, F-O-C in C Western Naval

Command.' The succinct, authoritative manner indicated that the speaker was an individual used to command. 'I'm directing my fleet commander to stay away till further orders... he'll move his Task Force half a kilometer away from the Malabar Star... in order to negotiate further regarding the release of the passengers and crew.'

Ecstatic whoops of delight and satisfactorily sated apprehension came over the radio. The terrorists were besides themselves with elation. They'd achieved a temporary victory over the mighty Indian Navy.

Hooters blared on the ships. Sea water churned from under their sterns as powerful propellers reverse thrusted. To the north of us the Godavari, Vindhyagiri and the Vajra began to move backwards. To the south of us the Sangram reversed. But the Ranvijay turned a complete circle to return to its previous position. Within a few minutes three of the Western Fleet's capital ships and the two Coastguard vessels stopped about half-a- kilometer away from the Malabar Star.

Scarcely had the vessels stopped when Zwankwid's now lower decibel guttural voice came through. 'Regarding our demands...'

'We need time... we need time,' Preston broke in from the shore based WNCCC. 'Indian authorities, government of the United States and UK are working on your demands.'

In the pilothouse D'Costa muttered under his breath. 'Release those damn prisoners, and let them leave my ship.'

'Waiting for the pre-positioned Amphibious Task Group to arrive,' Jeet whispered.

On the radio Zwankwid tried to sound smooth and equable as though conversing with close friends. 'We shall resume killing the hostages in two's if our demands are not met.'

Preston calmly requested. 'We need time. We also request a ceasefire on the pilothouse. You must leave the individuals there alone. Then till seven tomorrow morning?'

'Agreed,' Zwankwid abruptly assented. 'We'll contact you at seven-oclock Indian Standard Time tomorrow morning.'

Kohli immediately said, 'we resume contact at zero seven hundred hours... repeat zero seven hundred hours... our response should be ready by then.'

We heard a flick of a switch. The terrorists had switched-off their radio.

II

Perez promptly activated his "secure against eavesdropping" radio.

Napoleon hurriedly switched-off the ship's main radio in a smooth and swift manner.

'Perez reporting… Perez reporting… from the pilothouse of the Malabar Star.'

Preston's brisk voice came on the secure line. 'Reading you loud and clear… Rear Admiral Contractor will speak to you all from the Godavari.'

'Contractor speaking.' The clipped officer-like voice somehow exuded the F-O-C Western Fleet's authority and control. 'I presume you've heard the exchange on the open line and seen its consequences?'

'Right, sir, we're in a siege situation in the pilothouse,' Perez gravely answered.

'Let me speak with the Captain.' Contractor's request was like an order. Yet he sounded cordial and friendly. 'I want to know more about your situation.'

D'Costa placed himself near Perez and spoke into the radio. 'Jesus Antonio D'Costa, Master of the Malabar Star speaking.'

'Captain D'Costa I want you to know we're determined to rescue you and your passengers and crew.' Contractor's sharp, biting voice pierced through the sounds of whirring helicopter rotors which were returning to their parent ship's – the Godavari and the Vindhyagiri.

Contractor continued, after the choppers had landed, using the right combination of authority and restraint; nevertheless he still managed to be more than a trifle reassuring. 'It will be a difficult job, but we'll succeed.'

'Right.' D'Costa exhaled a long breath of slow release. 'I've got to save my passengers and crew and the ship anyhow.'

'A report about the six of you in the pilothouse is with me,' Contractor said earnestly; then he snapped. 'But I need details.' He paused and emphasized. 'Details about the precise location of the rest.'

'No idea about their exact location.' D'Costa gazed speculatively at us. 'Except they're somewhere in the lower deck cabins below.'

Jeet leaned towards the radio. 'I'm Jeet speaking, sir, some of the terrorists are positioned on the sundeck behind the funnel and the lifeboats.'

D'Costa quickly added, 'on the open deck to the rear of the pilothouse.'

'My staff reported spotting them from the helicopter's with high powered binoculars and telescopes,' Contractor agreed.

I spoke out aloud. 'I'm David Adams. They haven't fired at us since the arrival of your squadron.'

'I saved you then?'

Jeet quickly explained, 'assaulted us with AK-74's. But before could use their RPG-7, the choppers arrived and they disappeared from view.'

'Like they used weapons meant for the Afghan good guys,' I added.

'That's really our problem,' a laconic Contractor disclosed. 'They have more weapons of the good guys.'

***

'According to the briefing I had with the F-O-C in C, West, earlier,' Contractor's terse, anxious manner indicated he spoke about a crucial problem of significant consequence. 'Their dhow's have been modified to carry French anti-shipping missiles!'

Jeet and Napoleon gasped with shock almost in tandem.

D'Costa numbly scanned the open Arabian Sea as if for succor.

'We didn't know that.' A worried Perez said finally. He sounded curt yet full of concern.

'A top secret CIA report via Interpol to Naval intelligence,' Contractor informed us. 'Says they cannibalized French Aerospatiale surface to surface or SS-12M missile canisters-off obsolete Libyan Susa class missile boats.'

'British manufactured, I mean the boats', I said. 'We'd better look and check.'

'Right, the Susa boats were built by Vosper Limited, Portsmouth,' Contractor remarked briskly. He paused and suggested, 'you better visually check them out.'

Jeet bent low and scuttled to the shattered glass of the pilothouse windshield, where it curved towards the side. He made a deep, long inspection of some of the dhows which were visible.

Perez followed him and peered outside too.

D'Costa, Napoleon, Columbus and I adjusted our position. The modified station enabled us to view a couple of boats too. They'd come slightly forward of the stern area. Now moored alongside the starboard side of the Malabar Star, they could also be directly viewed by Contractor's fleet.

Jeet leaned close to the radio. 'There's a canvas covered large cigarette canister-like shape... in front of each dhow's wheelhouse cabin.'

'That's it, the French Aerospatiale anti-shipping SS-12M launchers,' a deadly serious Contractor grimly told us.

A stern, severe Napoleon stared so hard at the dhows, that his eyes were in danger of popping out. 'Lateen type bent masts for sails show they're dhows. But are fake because I can make out powerful diesel engines.'

Contractor immediately proceeded to familiarize us with more intelligence from the top secret CIA report. 'Those dhows went to Poti, a Caucasusian town on the Black Sea. Got powerful diesel engines secretly installed there at the Ordzhonikidze shipyard along with extra fuel tanks. The missiles were mounted at an undisclosed Naval base in Libya itself.'

Perez bent over his radio and quickly queried, 'Libyan's don't have the capability?'

'CIA tracked down a French ordnance engineer,' Contractor revealed.'Had been paid heavily along with others to do the installation.'

I stared at the dhows outside. Preparations to hijack the Malabar Star had encompassed three continents – Africa, Europe and Asia.

'Means they can hit back at your ships,' D'Costa lamented half to himself.

'Not to worry. My Operations Room has factored in the threats.' Contractor inoculated his strong, powerfully delivered statement with a generous dose of optimism and confidence. 'Especially if my squadron has to launch an assault.'

***

D'Costa looked downwards with a blank, vacuous expression on his face. His mind was clueless and empty regarding the subject of rescuers attacking the hijackers on his ship.

Perez crinkled his blue eyes and tried to think.

Jeet was comfortable despite the situation. 'I'm Jeet, sir, I estimate they're about twenty of them spread out inside the ship... and around the funnel and lifeboats.'

'What is your estimation of the modified dhows?' Contractor asked thoughtfully.

'Separate crew permanently on the dhows, sir.' Jeet tried to utilize his mind which wasn't stumped by the situation. 'Have moved from the stern to the starboard without anyone getting on or leaving the boats. Crew of the boats are a separate entity. Means the teeth, or fighting component, is separate and thereby fully focused on its mission. So an assault will be highly expensive.'

A burst of static filled the air. Preston who'd been listening in from the WNCCC interrupted. 'I've just received a communiqué which informs us that the US Marine Amphibious Task Group... the USS Saipan escorted by the USS Arleigh Burke and accompanied by the UK's HMS Cornwall... will arrive at around sunrise.'

'We're to hold-off the AJTF till the American's and British are in position,' Kohli added.

Then Contractor signed-off. 'That's good news. I'll defer from any action till the arrival of the Task Group... enforce a stay on all active measures till tomorrow morning.'

Preston gave "to the point" directions. 'WNCCC to pilot-house party, we're closing transmission, terminating the secure link. Keep the line powered till tomorrow morning, over and out.'

III

A sharp roar jerked me into an instant wakefulness the next morning. The din rose steadily to a crescendo and abated in commensurate increments within a few seconds. I blinked once or twice then opened my bleary eyes.

As I stiffly sat up and yawned, the roars came on again. I identified the source of the sounds. Fighter aircraft.

Jeet as fresh and energized as ever enthusiastically said to me, 'the US and UK amphibious unit has arrived.'

A wide awake D'Costa, Perez, Napoleon and Columbus were exuberant, especially Napoleon. He was slightly out of breath with excitement.

Two Navy blue aircraft zoomed over us. Their low level sortie took them directly over the pilothouse. Their narrow nose's; relatively bulbous plexiglas canopy's over their cockpits; and just behind the cockpits the two large jet inlets flush with the fuselage gave the aircraft an angry bumble bee type of look. Their wings angled slightly downwards from the top of the fuselage, accentuated the angry bee-like effect. Two wheels, black tires clearly visible, were swept back, flat against the middle of the wings.

I recognized the McDonnell Douglass manufactured aircraft from the original British Aerospace design. 'Harrier's of the US Marine Corps.'

'Vertical short take-off landing aircraft,' Jeet said.

Under the fuselage was a General Electric Twenty-Five Millimeter five barreled machinegun on the left side. On the right side was a three hundred round gun magazine pod. I recognized air to surface anti-shipping Harpoon missiles on inner under wing pylons. The outer hard points had air to air Sidewinder missiles.

The Harrier's returned to the USS Saipan. The VSTOL aircraft hovered over the sea, near the edge of the flight deck. Then they kind of drifted or slipped inwards. And dropped straight down onto the deck, bouncing almost indiscernibly, before remaining motionless.

All our attention now focused onto the Saipan.

***

The vaguely menacing yet immensely reassuring aircraft carrier-like combatant was about half a kilometer away, directly to the west of us. On its flight deck helicopters were being raised from internal hangars by elevators on the stern and port deck edges. Crew in purple shirts attended to the whirly-birds. Red shirted men loaded ordnance onto hard points on the short winglets of two attack helicopters.

The flat-top Saipan had the standard US Naval gun, the FMC Corporation,USA, manufactured Five Inch gun, on two recesses on its prow under the flight deck. This was its offensive armament to hit the enemy.

A Vulcan Phalanx Close In Weapons System or CIWS gun and a General Dynamics Corporation's Rolling Airframe Missile or GDC RAM installation were in the remainder two stern niches. On the island superstructure extension on the prow side was another Vulcan Phalanx; and on a deck above it was another GDC RAM. Also three manually operated Twenty-Five Millimeter cannon were on the starboard and port side. This defensive armament covered all threat angles from any incoming aircraft or missiles.

Saipan was the Naval Commander Amphibious Task Group or CATG's flagship. It also carried a little more than a battalion of US Marines along with their air transport (helicopters), sea transport (landing craft), armor and heavy weapons. The CATG Rear Admiral Daniel Alexander was overall in charge; and the Marine Amphibious Unit Commander operated under him.

Napoleon's raged-looking face was lit up like an exceptionally bright Christmas bunting. The expectation of the coming confrontation pepped him up considerably. He cast his arm southwards. Due west of the Ranvijay. 'There's another American ship.'

All our eyes turned to view the warship.

***

The sleek hydrodynamic lines of the US guided missile destroyer the Arleigh Burke didn't exactly seem to be an exceedingly effective weapons platform. This especially when compared to the Ranvijay just next to it. But I knew this was highly misleading.

Napoleon and Columbus stared at the Arleigh Burke with a kind of a "we've been terribly let down" expression on their faces. This was an effect caused by the lack of visible weaponry on the destroyer. Save the Five Inch gun on its prow, its anti-shipping Harpoon missile launchers, torpedo tubes and two Vulcan Phalanx's nothing else was visible from outside.

The Ranvijay by its side was bristling with missile canisters, guns and electromagnetic weapon control systems on its masts and upper decks.

'Use Vertical Launch Systems or VLS. The twenty-nine pods are behind the Five Inch and in the stern area there's a sixty-one pod VLS above the helicopter landing pad,' I said.

All eyes on the pilothouse gazed at the VLS pods which were not fully flush with the flat deck.

I continued, 'the complex Aegis System used for missile fire-control is in planar panels on the deck superstructure.'

Jeet caught on. 'So the mast looks empty when compared to the Ranvijay.'

'Yes,' I added. 'The VLS is a smaller adapted version of the launch systems used for years before, in submarines carrying intercontinental ballistic missiles.'

Also noticeable on the Arleigh Burke's heli-pad was a Sikorsky Sea Hawk helicopter.

A highly relieved and lightened Napoleon and Columbus turned away and began viewing the British frigate west of the Godavari.

***

D'Costa, Perez, Napoleon and Columbus looked at the Royal Navy Type Twenty-Two Frigate which was configured conventionally like any other warship. All its weaponry was visible from the outside.

Jeet and I took in the weapons systems.

The first batch of the Broadsword Type Twenty-Two class of frigates was primarily for an anti-submarine warfare or ASW role. However, due to the lessons learnt at the 1982 Falklands war its armaments were enhanced. The second and third batch manufactured had their hulls lengthened and new armaments incorporated. The third batch vessel here the HMS Cornwall, was not only a deadly ASW frigate but an highly potent anti-air platform with its tried and tested two into six cell Sea Wolf missile launchers and the Dutch Thirty Millimeter Air Defense Gun the Goalkeeper. It also carried manually operated Thirty Millimeter Rarden cannon on its starboard and port side.

Its Mark Eight single barreled Vickers Armstrong Four Point Five Inch gun and the addition of two into four US Harpoon surface to surface missiles made it a deadly sea to sea combatant too.

Napoleon alerted us. 'There's a different type of helicopter on it.'

I revealed, 'Westland Lynx. I can see British Sea Skua anti-shipping missiles and an Oerlikon machinegun on its weapon winglets.'

All of us focused our attention onto the frigate and its air component.

Captain Rodney Le Harrington from his enlarged Action Information Organization within his ship, would be able to hit back with great effectiveness at anything thrown against him.

Options to deal with the AJTF began to fill my mind. We knew that the Cornwall also carried a SAS Boat Troop contingent. Men especially trained to execute hostage rescue mission from the sea were onboard.

Then Napoleon warned us.

'It's seven-o-clock.' He switched on the Malabar Star's main radio.

***

Zwankwid's low decibel guttural voice came in on the air. 'Al Jahiz Tiger Force... this is the Al Jahiz Tiger Force... calling the Communications Center...'

'Western Naval Command Communications Center receiving you loud and clear,' Kohli acknowledged him on behalf of the team of negotiators at the shore based center.

Each and everyone in the pilothouse centered their attention onto the radio.

'We note the presence of the ships of the Yankee imperialist American dogs and British scum.'

I quickly glanced at the armada surrounding the Malabar Star. The Vajra, Vindhyagiri, Godavari and the Cornwall were to the north. The Sangram, Ranvijay and the Arleigh Burke were to the south. The Saipan lay to the west. All the vessels wallowing in the grayish-blue waters greatly enhanced my self-confidence.

'Any attempt to come closer and we'll execute everyone onboard. Besides we'll engineer a severe retribution elsewhere.' Zwankwid voiced a warning that sounded threatening. He waited a moment then enquired critically, 'the release of Amjad Mubarak and ten members of the Al Jahiz Commando Force and the Al Jahiz Killer Army has not been carried out.'

'We need more time.' Kohli's conciliatory tone wasn't too convincing. One could detect a clear hint of coercive menace in his voice. 'We are waiting for a cabinet decision regarding the matter... the Union Cabinet meeting is still going on.' We heard a sharp inhalation and he continued, 'however, I have information that officials of the Union Home Ministry have worked out a detailed plan to release your list of prisoners.'

'By air... by air... fly them to Maqdisho.' Zwankwid calmly explained how to effect the release of his compatriots from Indian jails. 'Our contact there will signal us on their arrival.'

We heard a slight swishing sound. Then Preston elaborated on the American angle. 'Modalities of Amjad Mubarak's release are being worked out right now in Washington.'

'Place him on a flight to Maqdisho and leave him,' demanded Zwankwid. 'No modalities or confusing language. Your English has many tricks to fool us... we are not interested in them... we only need Amjad Mubarak's release as fast as possible.'

'The United States' government is examining just that possibility.' Preston's clipped, official-like enunciation gave the impression of an extremely professional and able negotiator. He stalled for more time using some more English language tricks. 'His possible release might be plausibly realizable in the near future.'

'Aha, I did a MBA a long time ago,' Zwankwid said. 'I used to use English words "possible" and "plausibly" pretty often then. Now I would much prefer you used appropriately helpful words like "definitely" and "certainly"... the words you use can by synonymous with phrases like "killing of hostages" or a word like "executions"!'

'Oh no, his release is definitely a possibility.' A confused Preston appeared bewildered by the educated "class" displayed by Zwankwid. He proceeded to announce with considerable concern. 'An emergency meeting by the Director of National Intelligence with the President of the United States and UK's PM is taking place right now. All other heads of agencies concerned are also attending the meeting. They are discussing the Amjad Mubarak matter.'

'A Jimmy Clarke and his wife Sylvia of Fredrickton, Texas, paid with their lives for the proximity of the Indian ships. They joined two

Indian crew, Gonzalo Tavares and Sean Mendes.' Zwankwid paused to let the import of his statement sink in, and added, 'names have been chosen at random from the passports. Anytime we can begin to eliminate the passengers.'

In the pilothouse D'Costa involuntarily shivered.

Perez bit his lip but stayed still.

Hot breath wheezed in and out of Napoleon's mouth. But he remained quiet.

Columbus didn't show any emotion on his face.

Jeet appeared deeply in thought.

I gazed at the squadron of helicopters on the flight deck of the Saipan. The crews had completed their jobs. I could make out four distinctively different types of choppers. They were ready for possible combat missions. The sight of them enabled me to draw in enough psychic inspiration to remain calm and cool.

Over the ships main radio Kohli eased the tension somewhat. He reiterated, 'the Indian government views your threat with great seriousness. We do not underestimate the gravity of your words.'

Preston sounding every inch a negotiator that he was, added, 'we need time… a new deadline. Maybe till seventeen hundred hours Indian Standard Time?'

Muted sounds of a frenzied discussion taking place among the terrorists came in on the air. The seconds ticked by. Our mood in the pilothouse began to chill considerably with suspense as time passed by.

'Right, seventeen hundred hours would be perfect.' Kohli's terse voice broke the short silence. 'The Indian government decision should be ready by then… a flash has just come to my table. The Director General of prisons has just been informed of the possible releases. He has started making the necessary arrangements.'

'By the grace of almighty God we have decided to hold-off the execution schedule till seventeen hundred hours IST… no Indian and American and British ship's may come closer to the Malabar Star. They may remain where they are only. Otherwise we'll begin mass executions.'

An ominous tension which fraught the air earlier eased somewhat. Still the faint click of the terrorists switching-off their transmission almost made me jump with nervousness.

Then the "secure against eavesdropping" line on Perez's radio crackled to life.

IV

Almost simultaneously Perez adjusted the volume of his portable set.

Kohli made a call. 'Pilothouse party on the Malabar Star... the Malabar Star... do you read me over.'

'Pilothouse party from the Malabar Star,' Perez acknowledged on the secure line. 'Receiving you loud and clear.'

Kohli solemnly informed us, 'the F-O-C Western Fleet from the Godavari and the US Commander Amphibious Task Group or CATG from the Saipan will confer. Le Harrington will also be on the air. We at the WNCCC and you all on the pilothouse have to listen in and answer when spoken too.'

We glanced at the Godavari, then the Cornwall and thence onto the Saipan.

Helicopters on its flight deck were being readied for a mission. Distinctly visible were queues of armed fritz helmeted figures in combat fatigues, weighed down by heavy equipment. One by one US Marines stepped into two Super Stallions and two Sea Knights.

This inspiring sight bolstered our nerves and immeasurably enhanced our will to resist and fight on.

All of us moved closer to Perez's radio and began to listen.

Contractor put out a call. 'CATG USS Saipan... come in...'

A young American voice made a curt announcement. 'CATG coming in on the line, sir.'

'Well?' said an affable sounding gentleman. His amiability was very much in contrast to the tight rank voice of his Indian counterpart. 'Daniel Alexander speaking.'

'Le Harrington on the line also, from the Cornwall.'

Alexander inquired politely, 'we're covering the north, south and the west. What about the large bay a little to the south-east. It curves inwards?'

'I notice a patrol boat and the Kashin II covering that angle.' Le Harington's remark had a professional air.

'Yes the Ranvijay and the Sangram will spot them,' answered Contractor confidently. 'The Sangram's Three Inch Italian Otto Melara and two Seven-Point-Six-Two machineguns will destroy their modified dhow's within seconds. Over and above the Ranvijay being there also'.

I turned and looked at the Sangram and the Ranvijay. The guided missile destroyer the Ranvijay looked far more menacing. Besides its Russian Three Inch gun, it had four Air Defense Guns or ADG, AK-630's covering the threat angles. They could be used to engage a sea level target too with devastating effect.

'What if they slip ashore during the night?' Le Harrington asked.

'We've cordoned-off the mainland.' Contractor succinctly made us aware of another aspect to the problem.

Kohli from the WNCCC proceeded to clarify. 'Army's Southern Command has rushed a regiment to nearby Murud and Danda Rajapur which is opposite the fort.'

All of us, stuck in the pilothouse, gazed eastwards. Nothing was visible amongst the ancient ruins and the houses of Danda Rajapur. But outside the precincts of the village, one third of the way up a bare hill, were a row of olive green trucks and a couple of land rover-type vehicles parked.

'A couple of one tonners and jonga's can be seen,' Jeet muttered.

'Your army has secured the shoreline?' Alexander tried to verify Kohli's intelligence.

'Right,' confirmed Contractor from the Godavari. 'General Officer Commanding or G-O-C Maharashtra, Gujarat and Goa sub area, Major General Jasbir Singh Oberoi is tactical commander in the field. He's in constant touch with my operations room.'

Kohli further disclosed, 'additionally four companies of the Maharashtra State Reserve Police have sealed-off every road, street, bylane, *kucchha* pathway or country tracks. It's next to impossible to get away through the mainland.'

'Darius,' Alexander said. His hearty and jovial manner didn't fully conceal his determination to succeed in his mission. 'We've got the blighters trapped all right. We can now focus on extricating the hostages.'

'Right Daniel. But there's a lot of tricky hard work ahead for us.'

'I propose we send a helo attack squadron for a recce over the Malabar Star.'

***

On the Saipan's flight deck seven helicopters were readied for an immediate combat mission. I identified a command and control Huey and two Super Cobra heli-gunships. And two Super Stallions and two Sea Knights which were full of troops.

D'Costa, so far calm and composed, suddenly was besides himself with worry. 'Killed two hostages last time when the Indian Navy and Coastguard ships neared us.'

'That was D'Costa,' Perez divulged over the secure line. 'Master of the Malabar Star.'

'You don't know of the exact location of the hostages,' Alexander said. 'We have technology that can possibly identify spots where they are.'

'Sir, we have to take care.' An apprehensive D'Costa advised caution. 'I can't lose more passengers.'

'I'm all for holding-off till the Cabinet decision is communicated to us,' Contractor assented.

A disturbed, uneasy D'Costa visibly fretted with concern. He made a few discouraging noises. However he didn't say anything further.

'Our current exigency demands a spot photo and infrared imaging... reconnaissance of the Malabar Star and its environs. Mandatory to familiarize my staff and Marines with the locale.' A cordial Alexander gently persisted. 'We'll back-off if needed. But a recce is a vital and imperative and necessary action.'

'If have to assault them,' Le Harrington added. 'Must gather intelligence first. My SAS Boat Troop needs inputs in case have to launch a rescue attempt.'

Alexander confidently assured us. 'Our pilots have been appropriately cautioned in their pre-mission briefing.' He paused and continued. 'The officer overall in command of the Marines is a veteran of Grenada, Panama and the Gulf war.'

'Experienced combat veterans usually can be trusted to stay within mission parameters,' Contractor agreed. 'Which means we can risk a reconnaissance.'

'The heli-recce mission is a go then,' Alexander said. He spoke louder than usual. As if the statement into the radio was also an order to others listening in with him.

We could detect the CATG signaling the start of the operation.

***

On the flight deck of the Saipan the two blade rotors on the command and control Huey and the two Super Cobra gunships began to turn. Within moments the seven bladed rotors on the troop carrying Super Stallions began to revolve faster and faster. Finally the troop transport Sea Knights came to life. Two sets of three blade rotors, one over the pilot's cockpit and the other over the large aircraft rudder-like rear rotor pylon, began to spin. The helicopter mission was underway.

The general mood in the pilothouse lightened considerably.

The two Super Cobra's lifted-off and hovered at various points over the Saipan. The attack helicopter's covered the airspace for the remainder whirlybirds. The Huey ascended next. It rose to a higher altitude than the heli-gunships. Then the squat, boat hull nosed Super Stallion's and the Sea Knights, heavy troop transports, large rotor blades whirring around furiously, shuddered and strained their way upwards.

'Carrying their full complement of Marines and heavy equipment,' Jeet whispered.

The helicopter formation remained stationary high in the air for some time. Then four different types of rotors tilted appropriately and the squadron turned and flew northwards.

Jeet scanned the Naval ship's helipads. 'The Navy and Coastguard choppers are onboard still.'

'Not participating in the Marine helicopter prowess show,' I said.

The Naval helicopter's were on their respective vessels. The Sea Hawk was on the Arleigh Burke. The Lynx was still on the Cornwall. The two Sea King's with the Sea Eagles were on the Godavari and Vindhyagiri. The commando version of the Sea King's with their Aden Cannon were securely stationed on the Sangram and the Vajra. The Helix also was on the helipad of the Ranvijay.

The Huey, similar to the old Vietnam favorite Utility Helicopter or UH which became known as Huey, here clearly controlled the show. It swept around the Vajra. Then cruised parallel to the shoreline. At a point between the mainland and the Janjira fortress, the pilot pulled back the helicopter. And hovered about while adjusting his altitude.

Two sleek and narrow Super Cobra's banked and slowed down. They drifted into a kind of airborne defensive position. Sophisticated sensors were on their noses. A three barreled M-197 cannon poked menacingly out from under their cockpits. It could fire twenty-millimeter bullets at seven hundred and twenty rounds a minute. Hard points on each winglet had nineteen tube two-point-seven-five inch Folding Fin Aircraft Rockets or FFAR's for air to surface interdiction. Complex avionics and powerful twin General Electric engines atop the fuselage enabled them to alter their bearings with lightning rapidity. The deadly killer machines made a complete three-hundred and sixty degree sweep then faced the Malabar Star again. Anytime they could swoop down and strike, annihilate any threat within seconds.

The Huey skimmed over us covered from above by the heli-gunships. The helmeted pilots momentarily glanced down at us. Helmeted Marine Corps officer's in orange lifejackets cast long searing looks at us. The chopper flew over us followed by the troop transports.

Two lumbering Super Stallions and two ungainly Sea Knights, laden with combat ready marines over flew us. The combined roar of main rotors powered by sophisticated Sikorsky and Boeing engines, heaved at least a ton of humans and their combat gear.

The Super Stallions veered leftwards while flying straight ahead. It carried three engines atop. Two to the left of the centerline and one to the right. On its rudder-like tail was a single elevator or fin-like extension. To the left was a single tail rotor. The unsymmetrical engine alignment and dorsals tend to veer the tail booms leftwards as they flew.

The decibel level enhanced to the point of deafening us. The Malabar Star began to vibrate and shake. The ship's deck rattled and quaked. The chopper's surged past pitching and heaving due to natural air turbulence. The powerful wash of their main rotors considerably enhanced the atmospheric disturbance around us. Then the machines shuddered and thundered past.

When the deafening sounds abated considerably, Jeet quietly observed, 'wearing out the AJTF. Stressing them to create a fear psychosis.'

D'Costa became a trifle reverent. 'Pray to almighty God that those damned terrorist bastards don't start killing my passenger's again.'

***

The Huey turned and lost altitude. Then it flew straight towards the Malabar Star's port freeboard.

Stress levels among us began to rise. The atmosphere rife with tension, became as brittle as a sheet of frozen ice. Nerves on edge we waited for the expected lethal reaction from the AJTF.

'Careful, they can fire RPG-7's at it,' I quickly observed.

'Super Cobra's watching the sundeck from high above,' Jeet said. 'Can spot them and strafe them with devastating efficiency.'

'Still it's a risky maneuver,' I retorted. 'Why risk it?'

Jeet side glanced at me and pointed at the Huey that had over flown the Malabar Star and had turned to fly another sortie, over the vessel's starboard freeboard. 'Taking photographs, electro-optical and infrared.'

'Got an infrared Linescan device onboard,' Perez added.

So they were getting a heat signature profile of the Malabar Star from all angles I thought. Possibly detect and map the location of the hostages down below.

Jeet justified their patrolling moves. 'Checking all angles of attack, probable landing spots, all aspects needed to launch a successful assault.'

The seven helicopter squadron formed up into a tight formation again and over flew the Malabar Star once more. Soon the vessel shuddered and vibrated as if about to burst at its rivets as the entire air armada resoundingly rumbled past on a low level over flight.

We caught a brief glimpse of the pilots in their cockpits. Their sweaty hands were glued to their collectives and cyclics as their helicopter's trembled and reverberated under their large rotors.

D'Costa, Perez, Napoleon, Jeet and I continued watching the air show.

The normally unimpressed Columbus was awe struck. But I noticed he studiously avoided looking upwards after a while. He determinedly kept his eyes away from the skies.

The squadron suddenly climbed dramatically and broke formation. Now seven helicopters began to overfly the Malabar Star at various altitudes. They zigzagged about and flew pre-planned cris-crossing patterns. We could see various pilots, crew, officers and men minutely scanning the Malabar Star.

'I inhaled and exhaled quite audibly. It took me quite an effort to remark, 'some display?'

'Must return to the Saipan soon.' The creased brow of Perez furrowed deeply with contemplative speculation. 'They're guzzling plenty of fuel.'

Scarcely did he make the observation that the Marine Corps chopper's changed the direction of their sorties and began to fly towards the Saipan.

V

A desultory hour passed since the US Marine Corps helicopter pilots touched down on the flight deck of the Saipan when Perez's radio crackled to life.

A terse, no nonsense American voice briskly directed. 'Keep the line open… this channel going. CATG is to shortly discuss an urgent matter with the F-O-C Western Fleet… the Captain of the Cornwall… the WNCCC and the pilothouse party is requested to listen in to the discussion. You may let out information if asked.'

Almost immediately a genial sounding call came through. 'CATG to F-O-C Western Fleet…'

'Contractor speaking, receiving you loud and clear.'

D'Costa, Napoleon, Perez, Columbus, Jeet and I remained still, eyeing the radio.

Alexander proceeded to inform Contractor. 'Intelligence from the helicopter recce inputted real-time into our Integrated Tactical Amphibious Warfare Data System, or ITAWDS computer's, has struck pay dirt.'

'Your ITAWDS should pass on some information to us too.' The normally severe Contractor cracked an uncharacteristic joke. I perceived a vague, almost imperceptible trace of envy in his statement. Probably at the sophisticated hardware at the disposal of Alexander.

'Right,' Alexander continued in an easy detached manner. 'We have a complete thermal signature profile of the Malabar Star.'

'Has it revealed anything significant?' Contractor asked.

I knew that in multi-colored heat signature photographs, points occupied by humans have a distinct color. Will be in various shades of green to orange-red. Experts with specially programmed computerized equipment can figure out plenty of details.

'Luckily the Malabar Star is thin skinned below the pilot-house. Not armor plated or anything,' Alexander clarified. 'Specialist photo-interpreters at our ITAWDS have identified the probable location of the hostages.'

Le Harrington came in for the first time. 'Good news, we can get to them.'

Alexander continued, 'they're in what appears to be a large dining room.'

D'Costa heaved a sigh of relief.

'Only two individual cabins are occupied,' Alexander said. 'We think Zwankwid, Zohran and Wassif are in one of these cabins.'

'Means options other than just negotiations are viable,' Le Harrington remarked.

'Some of the options may be dangerous to the hostages,' Contractor added.

'I don't think it's too risky.' Alexander injected a note of enthusiasm into his voice. 'So I intend inviting your staff and Le Harrington's staff over to the Saipan to plan our next move.'

'Yes that will be necessary.'

Alexander emphasized. 'We've reviewed the intelligence. We've analyzed computerized versions of every hypothetical scenario we'd face. And have decided upon the only option favorable to us.'

'And we at the Cornwall agree with the CATG's decision.'

The deadly silence on the pilothouse of the Malabar Star suddenly enhanced in intensity. This exacerbated our anxiety levels considerably.

Chock-full of suspenseful apprehension we listened to the two commander's of two formidable Naval armada's discussing our fate.

'After reviewing the intelligence gathered by us, we've come to a final decision.' A calm and composed sounding Alexander paused, and proceeded to crisply convey the option he'd decided. 'We intend launching a rescue mission before the five-o-clock deadline!'

***

Contractor immediately retorted sharply, 'at this juncture it will be an extremely risky operation.'

The ridges on D'Costa's furrowed brow deepened enough to crinkle his eyes. He jerked towards the radio and said, 'this is D'Costa Master of the Malabar Star. I don't think you should attack now. These AJTF bastards are sure to mow down too many of my passengers and crew.'

'We think we can minimize hostage losses, although they'll be an element of risk,' insisted an icy cool Alexander.

'It might just be worth it. Expensive but we'll eliminate those damn fools.' The tone used by Contractor revealed his bloodthirsty instincts. 'However we've got to get clearance from our higher authorities.'

'As I'm awaiting a sure green signal from London and Washington through our Secretary of the Navy to the Chief of Naval Operations... to my overall Fleet Commander... to me,' a cordial and expansive sounding Alexander said. 'I think in the interim you ought to send your staff over to the Saipan with the commander of your Marine Commando Force. Le Harrington's staff will come over too with the in charge of the SAS Boat Troop.'

'I'll send a select staff over,' Contractor agreed. 'But the Master of the Malabar Star should have a say in the matter.'

Alexander attempted to sound placatory. 'Our plans are fail-safe. We're certain we can infiltrate the SAS commando's from the port side undetected. All their dhows are anchored at the starboard side.'

'As long as the Indian Navy and Coastguard is in it, from the planning stage to the actual operation, it's okay with me,' Contractor forcefully pronounced. 'Especially as the operation will be conducted in Indian territorial waters.'

An adamant D'Costa nudged me as he moved closer to the radio. 'No, no, no... I am absolutely not convinced.' He shook his head insistently. 'There can be no attack on my ship.'

A sharp crackle of an electrostatic charge suddenly sputtered momentarily through the set. When the disturbance died down a sharp voice broke through. 'Kohli speaking from the WNCCC... F-O-C in C, West, coming in...'

***

Barely a second later a commanding voice came through. 'Vice Admiral Konda Venu Rao speaking.'

'Sir.' We detected Contractor's manner stiffening instantly although he wasn't visible to us.

'Gentlemen,' the top boss of India's Western Navy said. 'Please hold on for about a minute. I'm receiving a top secret communiqué. The text of the Union Cabinet decision conveyed through the Ministry of Defense to Naval Headquarters is coming through... regarding our future course of action.'

This brought us some respite on the beleaguered pilothouse. Our fate and that of the other passengers had already been decided by the higher Indian authorities. I tried to guess what would be in the classified message being transmitted to the overall Western Naval Commander's office, then gave up. My mind was too dense with disquiet.

Then the secure line buzzed again. 'Vice Admiral Konda Venu Rao here... I am afraid our higher authorities veto any attempt to board the Malabar Star... no rescue mission is sanctioned... repeat... no rescue operation is permitted in Indian territorial waters as of now!'

***

A sharp click came over the radio. The F-O-C in C, West, had gone-off the air.

On the Malabar Star D'Costa, visibly buoyed up with the greatest of relief, turned and regarded us. He even managed a wan smile. 'Thank God negotiations must be continued.'

'They've killed two US citizens already.' Alexander's laconic remark sounded a trifle intimidating as it knifed through the air from the radio.

A deep intense and fervid hush ensued. It aggravated the apprehensive feeling the CATG's remark brought on.

Within a few seconds Alexander broke the daunting silence of an uncertain, doubtful future expectancy that had overcome us. 'There's no other alternative other than launching a strike.' We heard a sharp intake of breath and he continued in a sharp incisive manner. 'In spite of the Master's objections and your government prohibiting an assault,' the US Rear Admiral paused and injected an unalterable, irrevocability into his manner. 'We intend going ahead with the rescue mission!'

'In that case,' parried an irrepressible Contractor. 'Regrettably offcourse, I'll have to stop you by force.'

***

The temperature in the pilothouse dropped by more than a few degrees. The six of us involuntarily trembled and shivered internally with the effect of Alexander's and Contractor's words. This in spite of us hearing the exchange only on the radio.

A tired D'Costa haggardly regarded the radio with narrowed eyes of fury. The situation had extracted a terrible toll on him. Besides he seemed to have lost the capacity to vent out his indignation.

Almost immediately a low frequency disturbance filled the air and enveloped the pilothouse via the radio. Although I didn't hear anything from outside, the Indian and US and UK warship's being too distant; a vague electromagnetic type of buzzing from the wireless now added an air of alarming distress to the ambience of grim foreboding already permeating in the pilothouse.

Jeet turned to me with a half apologetically expression on his face. 'Switched on all their radar systems.'

In addition to their navigation radar systems; and powerful air and surface search mast mounted radar – the surface combatants had switched on all their missile and gunnery fire control systems. This caused a humming sound that the radio was inadvertently transmitting.

All six of us turned and focused on Contractor's squadron. The vessels had begun to maneuver in short sharp movements.

I observed with a sinking heart. 'Contractor has to deflect two American warships, the Royal Navy frigate and their helicopter's as well as the aircraft on the Saipan.'

To the north and south of us Contractor in the Bridge and his tactical team in the Operations Room of the Godavari began taking immediate offensive measures. Smoke began belching out of the funnel's of the warships. The respective Captains of the Vajra and Sangram as well as those of the Godavari, Ranvijay and the Vindhyagiri began to alter their vessel's bearings. Now at battle stations they steamed into tactical positions to menace their former allies with their surface ordnance.

VI

To the north of us the Godavari changed its bearings. Its prow pointed directly at the Saipan. Aiming towards the American amphibious assault ship were four deadly looking anti-shipping missiles. Covers of the four elongated bins had been removed. The surface to surface Styx's could be triggered-off anytime. The targeted Saipan was only about a kilometer distant; only a fraction of the heat seeking Styx's maximum eighty-three kilometer range.

'The bins are angled. Looks like they'll skim over the Saipan?' Jeet said.

'Infrared sensors in its nosecones seek heat radiating-off the hull and superstructure of the target. It will blast five hundred and thirteen kilograms of explosives right into the vessel,' I replied.

Perez distraughtly added, 'one missile can cause serious harm. Four missiles at virtually point blank range means end of the Saipan.'

Napoleon pointed to the Russian Fifty-Seven Millimeter gun. 'Its gun is aiming at the Saipan also.'

'Relatively point blank range also,' I answered. 'It doesn't need to use its Muff Cobb gun director radar.'

Godavari's gunnery gunner could hammer out a devastating two point eight kilogram shell at one hundred and twenty rounds a minute right into the Saipan.

Jeet then focused on the retractable surface to air missile launchers.

'Their anti-aircraft missiles have been powered too.'

Two wicked-looking surface to air missiles code named Gecko could be seen ready for action. I detected its Pop Group missile guidance system, a small barrel-like mounting on the bridge, had acquired a radar 'lock on' onto the Saipan. The Gecko's had been brought to bear upon the target.

Two into fifty kilograms of high explosives could rocket-off at two and a half times the speed of sound, right into Alexander's flagship.

***

The Vindhyagiri altered its bearings too. Unlike the Godavari, it remained on the same spot but turned on its own axis. And stopped when it faced the Cornwall which was less than a kilometer away.

Its Vickers Armstrong, Mark Six, Four Point Five Inch gun had been activated. The entire twin barreled turret moved slowly on its axis, from side to side. I could imagine the gleaming brass shells in the rotary feed magazine and feeder hoist. Ratings would lift up and ram replacements into the breech the moment the firing began.

'It's Dutch gun fire control radar is energized,' Jeet said.

Normally the Director steers radar beams onto the target. The radar reflection duly processed assists in track aligning the Four Point Five Inch. It slews on rotary traverse rails and it elevates or ranges on signals from the Director.

Now at virtually point blank range hitting the target required the gun to be just pointing at it.

***

The other vessel to the north of us was the Coastguard offshore patrol vessel the Vajra. It reversed rapidly for about a furlong. Frothy white sea water churned under the spotless white stern as the patrol boat altered its bearings and stopped. It starboard side faced the Cornwall's relatively long hull.

Barely visible on its prow were a couple of Coastguard gunners. They were manually traversing and elevating the Forty Millimeter Bofor's mounting to aim at the Cornwall. The moment Contractor signaled the go ahead it could rake the decks of the Cornwall with murderous fire.

***

To the south of us the Ranvijay now also pointed directly at the Saipan.

'Uses the same anti-shipping missiles that the Godavari has,' Jeet said.

This meant that five hundred and thirteen kilograms of high explosives from each of the Ranvijay's four infra-red homing Styx's capable of raining rack and ruin, added to the mortal danger Alexander's flagship already faced from the Godavari.

I scanned about the Ranvijay and commented. 'Its twin Russian Three Inch is aiming at the Arleigh Burke.'

The Owl Screech Fire Control System was powered. It emitted and received return signals and converted them into empirical computer data for the gunnery officer to utilize; to track align the Three Inch onto its target.

Here despite the close range, Owl Screech was being utilized. It moved slowly from side to side. The gun turret slewed on its traverse rails, moving in synch with its Director. Its twin dark barrels depressed appropriately to zero onto its target. At ninety rounds a minute it could hurl a six point eight kilogram explosive into the Arleigh Burke. Enough to seriously endanger or sink the US guided missile destroyer.

'Their SAM's are aiming at the Arleigh Burke also.' Napoleon pointed at a large mounting above the three inch. It had two angled, hand-like attachments with clearly recognizable missiles under each one.

The anti-aircraft guided missiles code named Goa had to be guided by a controller even after it fires-off. Two large mountings of what appeared to be a confusing tangle of sensors and radar antennae were the Peel Group fire controllers utilized to hit air targets up to thirty-one kilometers away. Here however the pointed noses of two long missiles aimed directly at the Arleigh Burke.

At close range the two Goa's blasting-off at two times the speed of sound would knife through the superstructure of the Arleigh Burke and actually ignite parts of the vessel. It would cause disabling meltdowns near its impact and penetration points due to its combustible velocity over and above the blast effect of its sixty kilogram warheads.

***

From near the Ranvijay the Coastguard offshore patrol vessel the Sangram also faced the Arleigh Burke.

Jeet regarded the vessel. 'It's Italian Otto Melara Three Inch is aiming at the Arleigh Burke too.'

The live Otto Melara traversed slowly on its axis. Then remained stationary. A single long barrel pointed directly at the American guided missile destroyer.

If the situation blew up the Otto Melara could blast a six-kilogram projectile at the rate of eighty-five rounds a minute into the Arleigh Burke.

***

The sunny sky was virtually cloudless. Because of this visibility over the panoramic scene unfolding in front of us in the calm Arabian Sea was exceptional. Silently we watched the scene outside. The Indian warship's ordnance could cause a terminal catastrophe to the American's and the British.

D'Costa and a not unworried Perez speechlessly watched the show.

A restless and edgy Napoleon was deeply participating in the activity outside. Varied expressions formed on his ragged-looking facial features every time an Indian vessel moved.

'Indian squadron at battle stations', Jeet muttered tensely.

Not a little concerned and beginning to feel apprehensive at the ultimate outcome of the situation that had developed, I said, 'Contractor's solved his immediate tactical problem.'

A troubled Jeet nodded anxiously. 'They'll react. I mean the American's and the British.'

Now each one of us remained hushed and silent. We inarticulately watched the portentous scene outside with bleak, pessimistic expressions of grim foreboding on our visages.

The Captains of the respective Indian combatants would be receiving constant inputs from their technicians manning the various types of sensors – gunnery, missile and tactical monitors. Threat priorities would be worked out against any American and British moves and weapons activated accordingly; when and if they received firing orders. Contractor's squadron was exceedingly menacing indeed. Smoke emanating from the funnels indicated their engines were idling at full tilt; ready to execute maneuvers anytime.

Then the US and UK Navy ship's began to move. Exhaust steam fumed out of the multiple funnels in seething puffs. The cumulative efforts of thousands of American and Britons unskilled and skilled, besides engineers and technical specialists suddenly burst into life. The Saipan, Arleigh Burke and the Cornwall began to slice through the waters of the Arabian Sea in various directions.

VII

The Arleigh Burke's forward Five Inch mounting slewed around in an arc. Its barrel depressed to cover the low strung, port side superstructure of the Ranvijay. Normally the Engagement Controller will use classified software in his gun fire control system console to process information, select correctly fused ammunition and alter the degree of traverse and the angle of the barrel's elevation, even the deflection in aim required – till the Five Inch shell zeroes into the target. Now at close quarters, much less than its twenty-three kilometer effective range, he just pointed the weapon at the Indian guided missile destroyer.

The Five Inch has a six man crew, none inside the twenty-five ton automatic gun. They man software that automatically checks whether right ammunition is being used from the ready service loader; that the round is in the breech; that the breech is shut properly and that other turret mechanisms are all right.

'At close range will cripple the Ranvijay,' Jeet said.

'Yes,' I replied. 'The thirty-two kilogram shell exploding through the muzzle at twenty rounds a minute can cause havoc and ruination to the Ranvijay.'

Napoleon queried, 'I can see two quadruple Harpoon launchers above the heli-hangar.'

'Too close range,' I disclosed. 'They'll streak over the Ranvijay.'

'Think will hit the mast and shred to pieces the Russian Big Net A air search radar and the Head Net C air/surface search radar,' Jeet added.

'If use an impact fuse,' I let out. 'If so Ranvijay's weapon system's will be blinded.'

'What about the Vertical Launch Systems?' Napoleon asked.

'Unusable too', I revealed. 'Too close range for their Tomahawk Cruise's. Don't have any other short range surface to surface weapon in the VLS pods.'

D'Costa, Perez and Columbus gazed at the offensive installations.

Jeet blithely observed, 'too close range for them to be fully effective, except for the gun. It's what's giving Contractor a chance!'

***

Earlier the Saipan riding high above the surface of the sea had pointed southwards. We on the Malabar Star could observe its port freeboard. Now it had changed its bearings. The flat prow with two Five Inch mountings recessed into the port and starboard corners aimed at the Indian warships.

Observable through the shimmering heat haze was the starboard Five Inch. Its long barrel was aligned towards the general area of the Ranvijay and the Sangram.

From the port side niche the other Five Inch swung across. Its long barrel was pointing to the general direction of the Godavari, Vindhyagiri and the Vajra.

The Saipan's offensive armament was live and a real threat to Contractor's squadron.

***

To the north of us was the Cornwall. Le Harrington had maneuvered his vessel so that he faced the Godavari, Vindhyagiri and the Vajra at an angle. This enabled him to bring his Vickers Mark Eight, single barreled Four Point Five Inch to bear upon the Godavari.

The Mark Eight single barreled mounting was a more advanced version of the Mark Six twin barreled gun that was on the Vindhyagiri. Electrical training and elevating mechanisms done by drive motors depressed the barrel ten degrees from horizontal to enable it to hit the nearby low level targets.

The Gun Controller supervised the loading and firing operations from a primary control position. He trained and elevated or depressed the gun on instructions from the radar Director or as here the visual aiming sight operator.

In case the situation warranted it, a High Effect shell or a Multi Role Fused shell which had four choices of settings could hit the Indian combatants. The Post Impact Delay shell would be most effective here.

It would be able to penetrate the Godavari, Vindhyagiri and the Vajra's outer steel plating and explode within the ship where it could cause more damage.

'They've got Harpoon's too,' Jeet said. 'But can't hit our nearby ships?'

'Yes,' I retorted. 'Le Harrington is too close to the Indian warships. Doesn't have enough range to launch the Harpoon's successfully.'

All six of us in the pilothouse of the Malabar Star then remained mute, although being highly interested spectators.

***

Alexander had effectively retaliated. He had got the Captains of the Cornwall, Arleigh Burke and the Saipan into taking defensive measures and into focusing ordnance onto Contractor's fleet.

Anytime Alexander or Contractor so desired, highly sophisticated ordnance could slam into each other. High explosives designed by the best brains from many nations now readied to hurtle across narrow patches of sea. Anything targeted would be smashed into smithereens, literally pulverized into unrecognizable fragments.

As time passed Jeet began to restlessly turn and glance at each one of us in turn. Then he remarked dryly, 'stalemate... both sides can hit each other and...'

The ever observant Napoleon suddenly cried out a warning.

D'Costa, Perez, Columbus, Jeet and I instantly focused our gaze on the chief engineer.

Napoleon excitedly pointed at the helipads of the Godavari and Vindhyagiri.

VIII

A missile laden Westland Sea King lifted-off urgently from the Godavari's helipad. Swiftly it gained in altitude then banked northwards and hovered its way onwards.

Then another Sea King, rotors whirring, soared-off the Vindhyagiri's helipad. Its complement of two air to surface anti-shipping missiles would add to the firepower of the Godavari's helicopter. Speedily it altered course and trailed the first chopper flying full tilt northwards.

'British Sea Eagles,' Jeet revealed.

One missile each with a kind of a colored band across its rocket fuselage was affixed on hard points a little behind the fairings of both the British manufactured helicopters.

From our south the Helix from the Ranvijay rose from its helipad, wheeled away and hurtled on northwards. It proceeded to accelerate towards the two Sea King's. Visible on the Russian manufactured Indian helicopter was two advanced type of anti-shipping missiles.

'Their NATO codename is Sapless. But we call it Uran,' Jeet divulged.

The Helix with the Sapless missiles joined the two Sea King's. The three chopper formation clattered onwards and slowed down at a point about a kilometer away. Then they broke formation and began to fly random S turns. Then reverse S turns. They kept up long lazy, two ovaltype figure of eight patterns continuously in the air.

The Indian Navy pilots varied their cruising altitude. Sometimes they skimmed across at nearly wave top height; then rose expeditiously to disparate altitudes. This complex maneuvering required a high level of flying proficiency. And the three choppers fluttering and flitting about could execute anytime their anti-shipping combat missions against the American and British warships.

***

Alexander established he was a clear-headed and quick thinking foe. He reacted swiftly to the Indian helicopter threats.

The four blade rotors on the US Navy Sea Hawk on the helipad of the Arleigh Burke began to whirr. With neutral cyclics the pilot wristed his throttle outwards to increase engine RPM's considerably. Consequently through a series of transmission gears increased the rotor RPM's.

Outside we observed the four main blades gyrate faster and faster.

A four bladed tail rotor countered the sideways thrust by rotating with appropriate power.

The collective was raised to the required degree and left pedals applied.

The shuddering Navy blue chopper surged upwards. It hovered for a few seconds above its helipad. The Light Airborne Multi-Purpose System or LAMPS III helicopter carried two stubby missiles with fins just behind its nose and with larger than normal fin stabilizers folded around its rocket fuselage.

The pedal was applied in the direction of the turn while maintaining position with their cyclics; altitude with their collectives and rotor RPM with their throttles.

A little shakily as though weighed down by its ordnance, the helicopter turned and faced the Janjira fortress.

The cyclic was pushed downwards. Through a series of mechanical linkages swash plates tilted the rotor disc forward. Immediately a considerable proportion of the powerful rotor downwash rushed backwards, thereby propelling the Sea Hawk forward. Simultaneously, outward throttle was applied to "open up" fuel lines into the steaming General Electric power plants.

'It's carrying infra-red homing Norwegian, Penguin air to surface antishipping missiles,' I said.

The Sea Hawk accelerated forcefully towards the fortress and rounded it. From the other side it executed low flying patterns. Using the medieval fortress as a cover it popped up now and then. As if to look at the Indian warships and hide. It kept repeating a "pop up and peep" maneuver.

I knew that the infrared or homing to heat emissions Penguin could go around an obstruction – fly around the fortress – then its nosecone heat seeker will angle it onto the Indian surface combatants with devastating consequences.

Then Napoleon alerted us. 'Another helicopter is taking-off from the Cornwall!'

***

The Westland Lynx hurtled-off the Cornwall's helipad. It carried a complement of four British Aerospace Sea Skua anti-shipping missiles. About a kilometer away, high in the sky, it slowed down and settled into flying long circular patterns.

The Sea Skua's threatened the Indian surface combatants from far less than its sixteen kilometer maximum range. The Lynx had to "illuminate" the targeted ship with an onboard radar. Then the Sea Skua loosed-off would home onto the radar reflections and follow it till it hit the "lit up" vessel. The semi-active radar homing guidance system made the missile a deadly threat to Contractor's squadron.

The atmosphere inside the pilothouse had become brittle like ice, threatening to crack anytime.

D'Costa, terribly affected, remarked, 'I can't believe this is happening.'

Perez remained speechless and still as he watched the helicopter show outside.

Columbus kept his eyes down and away from the action.

Only Jeet, Napoleon and I gravely yet actively participated mentally in the proceedings going on.

Jeet turned to the Saipan and suddenly cried, 'scrambling their Harriers.'

Despite the distance and the relative humidity due to the heated air passing over the calm seas, we had no difficulty in picking out details on the American amphibious assault ship.

***

All six pairs of eyes in the pilothouse of the Malabar Star turned and viewed the Saipan.

On Alexander's flagship a VSTOL Harrier rolled-off the flight deck. It appeared as if it was weightless, trembling unbalanced, then ascended rapidly almost vertically. Powerful Rolls Royce Pegasus Vectored Thrust turbofans powered the jet fighter.

One by one three more Harrier's shuddered-off upwards. They altered the thrust angles of their turbofans to join the first aircraft and banked sharply above the Saipan's island superstructure and slipped towards the western horizon.

Clearly visible on hard points under the Harrier's as they veered-off were their complement of missiles besides its General Electric Equalizer which was a five barreled heavy machinegun.

'Carrying two air launched versions of the Harpoon anti-shipping missile each,' Jeet said.

'Yes,' I answered, eyes having taken in also the long narrow white painted projectile with smaller fins behind its nose and relatively large tail fins which were on inner wing pylons. I recognized the air to air Sidewinder's too. 'Besides hitting Contractor's vessels with the Harpoon's; can shoot down his helicopters in the air too.'

'Deadly threat to us, men,' Napoleon interestedly observed.

D'Costa, Perez and Columbus remained silent.

Outside conditions were ideal for air to surface interdiction missions as well as for air to air operations. The blue sky was clear with only a few scraggly cirrus clouds around.

The formation of four US Marine Corps Harrier's flew far to the west, almost over the horizon. They began flying in distinct although overlapping, long, large elliptical patterns. One Harrier always pointed "head on" towards Contractor's warships at any given time. Ready to loose-off its radar homing, highly effective explosive hardware.

'Are flying at optimal distance away for the airborne Harpoon's to strike,' I revealed. 'Unlike the ship borne one's that are too close to their targets.'

Jeet took his eyes-off the aircraft and focused on the US, UK and Indian surface combatants one by one. And yelled out almost instantly. 'They're powering their anti-incoming missile systems... Air Defense Guns or ADG guns and missiles!'

IX

I immediately peered at the warships outside. The Godavari carried four ADG Assault Kalashnikov or AK-230 turrets to give it a three-hundred and sixty degree defensive cover. One twin barreled gun was positioned just in front of the main mast, the other was situated on the base of the second mast on the port side. Correspondingly there were two more AK-230's on the starboard side.

The ADG operator 's are assisted by a Drum Tilt Guidance System. The white colored upended whisky keg-like sensor and guidance package broadcasts radar beams onto the target. Signals reflecting back are processed and converted into electronic directions to the AK-230 Gatling's. At longer ranges there would be time to compute data regarding the trajectory of the target. Here at relatively close range there would be more of a manual element from the Godavari's ADG operator's.

Two forward AK-230's turned and twisted as though awakening from a long sleep. Their long dark twin barrel's elevated and slewed along an arc while pointing in the general direction of the far-off Harriers. The five kilometer range AK-230 could hose the aircraft or any incoming Harpoon with thirty millimeter shells weighing about half a kilogram at the rate of five hundred rounds a minute.

The rear, starboard side AK-230 with the assistance of Drum Tilt "locked on" to the Lynx with the four Sea Skua's.

The rear port side AK-230 moved from side to side, barrel elevated to aim eastwards at the Sea Hawk with the Penguin's which was taking cover behind the Janjira fortress.

***

The northwards bearing Vindhyagiri carried a single AK-230 on the roof of its helicopter hangar. It elevated and slewed, aiming towards the general direction of the jinking Sea Hawk. It's ADG operator aided by Drum Tilt was tracking the elusive US Navy helicopter with its deadly infrared seeking Penguin's.

The weapon was pretty effective and lethal looking. The wall of lead blasting-off from the twin barrel mountings would certainly destroy the targeted aircraft. In fact the slugs slamming out of it appeared like it could obstruct and terminate anything in its way; including an incoming projectile. It was an anti-incoming missile gun too.

***

I turned my attention southwards. Jeet and Napoleon did so too. D'Costa, Perez and Columbus didn't alter their focus.

The Ranvijay faced the gradually reversing Saipan. The Kashin II carried four AK-630 Gatling guns which were a more advanced version than the Godavari's and Vindhyagiri's AK-230's. It utilized a Bass Tilt Guidance System which radar was mounted separately in a small gray upended whisky keg-like shaped installation. Its sensor package acquires the target. Beams bouncing back are speedily analyzed and processed in the computation package. And lightning directions can be electronically communicated to the weapons package; slewing the AK-630 mounting and elevating or ranging or aligning its barrels onto the "locked on" target.

'Its barrels are much smaller when compared to the AK-230?' Napoleon interestedly noted aloud.

'It has a range of only two kilometers, so has a shorter barrel,' I replied.

'But each turret has six barrels which spew out thirty millimeter projectiles at three thousand rounds a minute… the gun part matches the American Vulcan Phalanx.'

The two forward AK-630's now were being steered onto the distant Harriers which carried the deadly Harpoons. The AK-630's could effectively close the airspace between the aircraft and itself with great efficiency.

The two rear AK-630's traversed in an arc, pointing at the Sea Hawk when it showed itself from behind the Janjira fortress. Here there would be an enhanced human element to the targeting due to the close range.

Should the operators aided by Bass Tilt perceive any potential danger an instant electronic signal would trigger-off the powered AK-630 turrets into action. Switch on an overwhelming current-like, daunting shield of lead similar to a wall right in the way of the incoming missiles. This besides being able to shoot down the enemy aircraft and the helicopters.

***

Jeet pointed to the Sangram and the Vajra and said, 'their main guns haven't altered their bearings. But they've brought out two Seven Point Six Two Light Machine Guns'.

I could clearly discern the Coastguard sailors manning two British Enfield or Bren gun-like weapons on both the vessels respectively. The machine guns had a distinctive thick magazine over their barrels. Resting their bipods on the deck they aimed their guns at the Sea Hawk.

Now the five Indian vessels were more than adequately armed to counter an air threat. Contractor definitely had the ability to cope with anything thrown against him from the air.

***

Then Jeet, Napoleon and I next observed the Arleigh Burke.

The Close In Weapons Systems or CIWS Vulcan Phalanx had been energized. Six short, dark barrels peeped out from under a stubby white colored, large missile nosecone shaped mounting.

The sensor package, the Vulcan, was in the top white radar transparent housing. From here pulse doppler radar tracks the incoming aircraft or projectile. From below the gun was another radar that tracks the outgoing lead. The lower part of the white housing has a super efficient com puter that processes both the signals bouncing back – from the incoming threat and the outgoing lead. It eliminates the difference by electrically slewing the entire integrated unit and hydraulically tilts the single unit of the white housing, drum magazine and the cannon between them. Till bullets from the General Electric six barreled Gatling known as Phalanx, strike the target. A burst mode of two hundred rounds can be set too.

On the Arleigh Burke the CIWS positioned below the bridge covered the angle of threat from the three Indian helicopters.

The Vulcan Phalanx situated on the aft superstructure, above the Harpoon canisters, were slewed and tilted appropriately to cover all possible angles of approach of the Indian helicopters.

It looked like the Sea Eagles' or Sapless' blasting-off from the helicopter's would meet a deadly reception of depleted uranium slugs. Deadly enough to shred the air to surface ordnance into harmless fragments before they threatened the American destroyer.

The distance between the helicopters and the Arleigh Burke meant that the entire automated system would be viable. The Vulcan Phalanx's complex sensors and super efficient microprocessors dual radar reflection "split eliminating" would ensure that its stream of slugs homed suitably onto any incoming threat. The streaking twenty millimeter curtain might also "kill" the choppers.

***

The battleship gray, looming island-like American amphibious assault vessel lay placidly in the waters of the Arabian Sea. Its prow pointed eastwards. On a forward extension on its island superstructure was a Vulcan Phalanx.

On a deck above it was an easily recognizable GDC RAM mounting.

On an EX-41 launcher were twenty-one Rolling Airframe Missiles. It tilted as a unit, and slewed in a module that was similar to that of the Vulcan Phalanx.

Both anti-air systems were energized. But they were not pointing at the Indian helicopters. Instead they traversed in an arc covering the incoming angle of the Styx's of the Godavari and the Ranvijay. Side to side they moved as if waiting for any movement to be discerned from the elongated bins, to open fire. They were on a systems "mod on" or automatic mode.

I said, 'A screen of bullets and small rockets will be guided onto the incoming Styx's by the most sophisticated anti-missile system that exists to date.'

Twenty millimeter rounds of depleted uranium at three thousand rounds a minute would be the Vulcan Phalanx's bestowal to the barrier. Nosecone heat seekers in twenty-one rockets homing nine point one kilograms of explosives, each into the incoming Styx's would be the GDC RAM's contribution to the barricade. Besides the Saipan had three manually operated twenty-five millimeter automatic cannon on its port and starboard side.

Napoleon nodded.

'Contractor's got eight Styx's on the Godavari and the Ranvijay. Besides his SAM's the Gecko's and Goa's. Can fire them one by one. What happens then to the Saipan?' Jeet queried.

'I prefer not to think about it,' I answered.

D'Costa, Perez, Jeet, Napoleon and Columbus laughed at my retort.

***

The long hulled Cornwall faced the Godavari, Vindhyagiri and the Vajra. It's anti-aircraft defenses' were switched on.

The super efficient six celled Sea Wolf canisters were open on the prow and the stern. It could "kill" aircraft and incoming missiles. In trials it has hit even incoming Naval shells. Now the entire six celled launcher slewed and elevated in tandem with its Director, aiming at the general direction of the Indian choppers.

On a platform behind, below the forward mast was the Hollandse Signaalapparaten's Goalkeeper CIWS. It's I band search radar was scanning the helicopters at sixty RPM. The Dutch weapon's surveillance and tracking radar were linked to a General Electric thirty millimeter Avenger gun. This weapons package had far more killing power than its American Vulcan Phalanx competitor. Firing milk bottle sized depleted uranium shells at four thousand two hundred rounds a minute from seven barrels, it could shred to pieces the helicopters within range; and even destroy any incoming Sea Eagles' or Sapless thrown against it.

On the deck below the forward mast, on the port and starboard side, were two manually operated thirty millimeter Rarden automatic cannon.

Gunner's manning these aimed their weapons at the trio of Indian helicopters also.

***

The sun shone down directly through patches of cirrus and brightly lit up everything below.

'The three Indian Navy chopper's have had it,' I said. 'All the US and UK weaponry are focused on them.'

Jeet thoughtfully replied, 'if the fight starts with the helicopters. I think those missiles the Styx's and their Harpoons will be let loose first.'

D'Costa stared unblinkingly at him. 'I think it's a waste of time and money. They have to concentrate on the AJTF till my passengers and crew are safe.'

Perez shook his head in agreement.

Napoleon suddenly blurted out, 'this Zwankwid, Zohran and Wassif must be rejoicing somewhere inside.'

'If they're aware of the full import of the warships movements,' I thankfully expressed my comprehension of the ticklish situation we faced. 'They'll just visually see some vessels moving with some movement of the weapon systems.'

'I think they'll be aware of the situation and might take advantage of it somehow,' Jeet offered.

Immediately in the pilothouse, the stress and strain of the oppressive, anticipatory tension we all felt, started becoming excruciatingly intolerable.

X

An alarmed D'Costa and Perez turned and regarded Jeet who silently began to look around outside.

Napoleon trembled and twitched with shock as though he'd just been electrocuted. 'Bastard... those dhows have French missiles.'

D'Costa rewarded him with a look of warning. 'Language, men.'

Then galvanized into immediate action, being nearest to the shattered starboard side window of the pilothouse, he leaned out and peered at the dhows. 'They're still there.' He sounded bitter, strained and full of despair.

A so far silent Perez asked, 'untenanted?'

'No, think crews are inside them,' Jeet answered.

Spittle in my mouth heated up with a bitter-tasting premonition of our imminent destruction. I hoarsely spat out, 'Are they ready to fire? They'd score a big victory if they damage the capital ships?'

An indestructible Jeet restrained himself. He remained extremely still and hushed, in a momentary trance of deep contemplation. Then his eyes focused on us. 'The French SS-12M's are wire guided. Their craft is modified to carry two missiles per canister and two canisters per dhow.'

Queasily, gut churning with nauseas panic, I enquired, 'what if the AJTF use them now?'

Five dhows wallowed lazily in the steaming, sunny and calm Arabian Sea on the starboard side of the Malabar Star. There were no signs of life on them. Whether the crews had come onboard along with the terrorists or were invisible in the interior of their vessels, we couldn't make out. But clearly visible on each dhow: the canvas covered cigarette box-like shape in front of the wheelhouse. The launchers of the highly effective at close ranges, wire guided Aerospatiale SS-12M's.

I heaved a sigh of relief. 'They're still covered by canvas sheets.'

Immediately a significant amount of weariness and unease seeped out of us.

Then Perez's "secure" radio suddenly squawked to life.

***

Contractor's sharp authoritative voice came in over the radio. He spoke to Alexander. He sounded exaggeratedly ruthless and severe, like hardened steel. 'You are given a warning!' He paused. This aggravated the tense, nervy, pulse pounding anxiety overcoming us. 'Any movement dangerous to my ships, including the launching of a rescue mission... and I'll open up with everything I have. Blast your entire squadron to kingdom come!'

Alexander quickly roared back from his tactical nerve center on the Saipan, 'you've put me in the lion's den. But like my namesake Daniel, I'll extricate myself and ultimately fix you.'

'Unlike Alexander the "great" versus Darius of Persia,' replied an equally sharp Contractor. 'This time I Darius have the absolute upper hand.'

'You've got to contend with my Harpoons and Penguins besides my Five Inch guns... looks like I'm going to send Darius's vessels to the Davy Jones locker soon!'

'I can hit your Saipan with eight Styx's and SAM Gecko's and Goa's above the waterline. And torpedo you from two angles at and below the waterline. That will end the effectiveness of your flagship first.'

There was a short silence.

Then Contractor emphasized, 'I repeat my Styx's, Gecko's, Goa's, Sea Eagles' and Sapless' as well as my British twin Four Point Five Inch... twin Russian Fifty-Seven Millimeter and twin Three Inch... and Italian Otto Melara Three Inch... will certainly punch holes through your Vulcan Phalanx, Goalkeeper and Rolling Airframe Missile defenses as well as through your heavy machineguns... sink your capital ships!'

'We can hit back,' insisted Alexander, sounding a trifle threatening. 'Our air launched Harpoons from the Harrier's will sink your five combatants maybe faster.'

Despite the somber, depressing gloom the situation evoked, Contractor altered the tone of his voice and continued pleasantly, 'if so it'll be my great pleasure to let my heavy ordnance ensure you accept my cordial invitation... to join me undersea at the bed of the ocean.' He sounded like he was announcing an invitation to a wedding reception.

No one laughed. All of us remained taut and tense in a disturbed daze of stunned restraint. The joke and the consequent lull in the atmosphere was too fragile; especially with all the sophisticated devastating weaponry activated on both sides.

Le Harrington came in. He cryptically warned, 'there'll be global ramifications and pressures against Indian's worldwide.'

'Why bother, by then the only ramification we'll face will be the massive ocean pressures undersea.'

Once again Contractor proved he had his wits about him.

Suddenly he signed-off.

Lazily I looked at Contractor's flagship, feeling the humor of his remark, ears still focused onto the radio. Then I literally convulsed, involuntarily, with overwhelming shock! A puff of smoke shot up high in the air from the Godavari and formed a screen over it.

All six of us looked around.

Another cloud rose over the Ranvijay.

Then the Saipan became invisible in a dense opaque cloud of dust.

From somewhere near the Arleigh Burke's Harpoon canister a cloud of smoke shot out and enveloped the ship.

The Cornwall too was engulfed in a haze of smoke.

XI

My heart stopped beating for a moment. Contractor had escalated force levels once more.

Napoleon very much in the confrontation trembled with nerves. He swore. 'That Baa-vaa bastard Contractor will finish us all with his stunts, men!'

D'Costa turned and glared at him. 'Becoming a junglee boam... shout-type of bugger again.'

A suitably reprimanded Napoleon remained quiet.

Jeet saw the look of confusion on my face and clarified. 'Parsi's affectionately called baa-vaa's in Mumbai. Have strong character and classic acts.'

'We're getting a birds eye view of the Parsi Contractor's strong character,' I remarked, at ease because I'd identified what was being utilized by the capital ships.

Perez looking outside, began breathing in short sharp breaths.

'Both sides have complex counter-measures and jamming systems.' I attempted to calm everyone down. 'Those are chaff rockets... firing-off radar blinding strips of metal, glass or plastic fibers coated with aluminium metal film... and infrared sensor distorting rockets!'

'Radar sets on both sides will go blank', Jeet added. 'Heat seeker heads of infrared homing weapons like the Styx's and RAM's will not function properly.'

For a moment my mind dwelt upon the Scottish physicist Sir Robert Watson Watt, for all practical purposes the inventor of radar. Today developmental upgrades of the same contraption that registered a radar reflection blip of overflying aircraft, were in use. His Radio

Aided Direction And Range finding apparatus or RADAR had evolved to a frightening degree.

Outside clouds of dense smoke-like radar blinding chaff almost obscured the surface combatants. Periodically dazzling shafts of infrared thwarting flame flared upwards, hung in the air, and descended slowly to a permanent extinguishment.

An involved and concerned Jeet glanced at the warships surrounding us. And abruptly wrenched his head back - as his eyes passed over the Janjira fortress.

'God! That's it,' he said out aloud. 'I've a brilliant idea. A perfect solution that should satisfy both sides.'

***

A flock of snowy white seagulls suddenly cawed and screeched shrilly as they ascended from somewhere at the stern of the Malabar Star. Possibly disturbed in some way while questing for edible refuse discarded from the galley.

But five pairs of eyes in the pilothouse of the Malabar Star ignored the cacophonous interruption. Instead we stared uncomprehendingly at the rock-like Jeet.

He ignored us and leaned towards Perez's radio. Perez switched on the line. And Jeet literally hollered at the top of his voice.

'Sir, I'm Jeet speaking to F-O-C Western Fleet... Jeet from the pilothouse of the Malabar Star...'

'Jeet... yes one of the group in the pilothouse.' Contractor's stiff-lipped voice indicated he'd give Jeet a fair hearing. Yet he gave the impression that he'd brook no nonsense from him or anyone else. 'What have you to say?'

'Sir, I've a solution to the emergency situation that's developed, sir.'

'Then shoot. Out with it.' Contractor put on a loud ebullient and hearty manner calculated to spur Jeet on.

Before Jeet could continue he was interrupted.

'We're nearing the deadline.' A combative yet composed and collected Alexander broke in. 'So mister Jeet you'd better tell us how to resolve the crisis.'

Jeet steadied himself. He unwaveringly focused onto the radio and suggested, 'somehow get the Al Jahiz Tiger Force to transfer the hostages to the Janjira fortress. Then launch a combined rescue attempt!'

***

'To the island fortress?' Alexander queried tightly.

'Right, sir,' Jeet assented. 'Tell Zwankwid we're favorably considering the release of the prisoners. So move all the hostages to the fortress.'

Alexander doubtfully remarked, 'easier to attack them in the fortress.'

'Yes we don't have to assault the Malabar Star,' Jeet said aloud into the "secure" channel, 'also we get the measure of them when they transfer the hostages into the fortress.'

'Aha... brilliant suggestion, provided we get them to transfer the hostages before it gets too dark.' Contractor's hearty approval revealed his receptiveness to Jeet's idea. Then he became serious. 'But we've got to get Zwankwid to agree.'

'Bluff them we're going to release their list of prisoners, sir,' Jeet insisted. 'It's our only hope.'

Sounds of whispered consultations somewhere in the background came over the "secure" line. I couldn't decipher them or identify the source. Whether they were American or Indian voices couldn't be ascertained.

Outside the Naval warships remained focused upon each other, instead of on the terrorists in the Malabar Star. Smoke belched out of their funnels. Shipboard turbines gulped in enormous quantities of fuel oil to power their systems. High in the air the Harrier's and helicopter's guzzled expensive aviation fuel as they flew combat air interdictor missions. Ready to strike anytime they received firing orders.

But after a few seconds I began to get a definite feeling that both sides favored rescuing the hostages from within the fortress; without having to step into the Malabar Star.

Then Contractor made an instant decision. 'Indian Fleet Commander to the US CATG...' he said cryptically. 'This is a good idea to buy time as we're nearing the seventeen hundred hours IST deadline.'

'It's okay by me.' Alexander unequivocally proceeded to make a decision. 'We agree to unilaterally suspend any action regarding the rescue mission... till we settle the matter of transferring the hostages into the fortress.'

***

A terse Contractor instantly conveyed a recommendation vital to the wellbeing of the Indian, US and UK combatants. 'Then I suggest an immediate reduction in our force levels.'

'We can't be on full combat readiness indefinitely,' Le Harrington opined from the Cornwall.

'Right I okay your proposal.' Alexander's voice became considerably stronger and significantly graver. 'Provided you comply with your suggestion, I'll reduce my combat readiness to previous levels.'

Each and every one of us in the pilothouse heaved a tremendous sigh of extraordinary relief.

D'Costa unable to restrain himself, literally shouted with delight into the radio. 'Good to see the end of us versus us. And the continuation of us versus them like before.'

Jeet ignored the Master of the Malabar Star and recommended.

'And, sir, if I've read the situation correctly, Zwankwid might have to be scared slightly somehow… get the helicopter-gunships to conduct a few strafing runs… then when they come on the radio, tell them to shift the hostages.'

XII

Within a few minutes from three separate directions the airborne helicopters turned towards their mother vessel's.

The US, UK and Indian warships who were moving slowly away from each other, stopped to let their chopper's return.

The US Navy Sea Hawk with its complement of two Penguin's abandoned its elusive patrolling behind the Janjira fortress. It flew to the Arleigh Burke and descended safely onto its helipad.

The Royal Navy Lynx with the four Sea Skua's, dropped slowly onto the Cornwall's stern helipad, and remained there. Its rotors slowed down considerably and stopped.

The two Sea King's with the Sea Eagle's, from the Godavari and the Vindhyagiri returned to their parent vessel's. The Godavari's helicopter made a singular and safe landing on the frigate. The Vindhyagiri's chopper landed and remained static on the Leander class frigate's helipad.

The Helix whirred away singly towards the Ranvijay and dropped gently onto its helipad.

Far-off we observed the Marine Harrier's with the air launched Harpoon's and Sidewinder's return to the Saipan. The jump-jets broke their elliptical patterns and flew to their mother ship. One by one they stopped mid-air at a point over the sea near the flight deck. Then slid sideways onto the flight deck and dropped slowly, thudding gently on the reinforced steel plating.

***

With their helicopter's safely onboard, the Indian warships began to move. Long low shapes bristling with ordnance and sophisticated sensor systems slid through the churning waters to their previous positions; facing the Malabar Star. Their Russian, British, Dutch and Italian hardware had been deactivated. I could sense Indian Naval officers and men heaving a sigh of relief that the situation hadn't exploded into a direct, bloodily expensive confrontation.

To the west the large rectangular shaped Saipan slowly altered her bearings. It came to a standstill when her long, broad prow pointed southwards once again. Its Harriers were being towed away on the flight deck. Its Five Inch's, RAM's and Vulcan Phalanx no longer menaced the Indian squadron. All weapons and sensor systems had been turned-off.

The Arleigh Burke to the south of us and the Cornwall to the north of us, steamed to their previous positions too. Their heavy ordnance – sensors, gunnery and missile systems had been de-energized.

The combat readiness levels on the US and UK ship's matched the force levels of the Indian vessel's. The respective Captains and their tactical teams, the gun crews, the radar and various systems operators would be at rest to ease their nerves and refresh themselves; yet they'd be alert in case the situation got out of hand in the near future.

***

Napoleon jerked upright abruptly. His sudden, hasty movement attracted our attention.

'The Coastguard helicopter's and the Marine helicopters are about to take-off.'

All of us turned and viewed the concerned vessel's.

On the Vajra the Sea King commando version with the Aden Cannon's rotor's began to rotate slowly. Men in blue uniforms were entering the helicopter lugging rifles and LMG's.

'MCF coming onboard,' Jeet said.

On the Sangram an identical situation was taking place. Armed MCF men were boarding the chopper with the Aden Cannon, which was ready to take-off.

On the Saipan the command and control Huey and two Super Cobra helicopter-gunships lifted-off. They made for the Janjira fortress.

The two Coastguard helicopter's large Westland rotors whirred faster and faster and the chopper's soared-off. They made for the area between the mainland and the fortress. Then they began to patrol in a steady, level and oval pattern, keeping all the while to a fixed altitude.

Jeet thoughtfully stared at the helicopters as they executed long, lazy cruising turns. 'Something to do with their cannons... as I'd suggested, a strafing mission to scare Zwankwid and company is coming soon.'

XIII

From high in the sky over the Janjira fortress the Marine Corps officers in the command and control Huey took charge. They began to vector the Super Cobra's and Sea King's on sorties over the Malabar Star.

The two US Marine helicopter gunships hovered alongside the fortress. Their noses were aligned towards the starboard side of the Malabar Star. Their three barreled M-197 gun's turned and twisted along a hundred and ten degree slewing arc, under their cockpits.

The comparatively larger Sea King's momentarily remained stationary, hovering on the other side of the fortress. Its Aden Cannon were clearly visible in their pods which added to the deterrent effect of the helicopter's.

Then the "secure" line came to life. Perez altered his attention focus and adjusted the radio.

'Lieutenant Colonel Wellington Praxedes Barros is commanding the combined helicopter squadron,' came a crisp sounding American voice. 'You are to switch on your ships main line and listen in to their cross-talk.' Then the channel closed down.

Napoleon quickly adjusted the main radio appropriately. And we began to hear radio chatter of the pilots on the open frequency that the terrorists were tuned onto.

D'Costa and Perez gravelly listened. Columbus also showed some interest in the matter.

Jeet, Napoleon and I alternated our sight from the radio to the choppers outside.

Jeet said, 'cross talk broadcast on the open line so the AJTF hear it and get stressed.'

***

'Tiger one, tiger one,' Barros called. 'Are you sighting the Al Jahiz bogey's?'

'Roger, roger red fox. Optically got a bead on those Al Jahiz sonofabitches.'

'Tiger two, tiger two... machineguns ready?'

'Roger, roger, M-197's heavy and loaded. Can't wait to slam high explosive incendiaries and armor pierce at seven hundred and fifty rounds a minute!'

The two Super Cobra's slowly advanced forward.

'Bravo seventeen and bravo eighteen,' Barros called from his vantage point in the Huey, high above the Janjira fortress. 'Are you ready... are you ready, over.'

'Roger, roger, red fox,' a heavily accented Indian voice replied. 'Ready to blast twenty-five millimeter Aden Cannon shells into the AJTF.'

'Bravo eighteen reporting, on full readiness to open fire with my Aden at one thousand eight hundred and fifty rounds a minute.'

'Okay tiger one and tiger two... and bravo seventeen and bravo eighteen,' Barros crisply directed. 'Time for a little action.'

'Tally ho, tally ho,' came a chorus of exultant yells.

***

The two Super Cobra's swooped down side by side and leveled-off a little away from the starboard freeboard of the Malabar Star. Power generated by their main General Electric turbo shafts energized their wicked-looking M-197's. They poked out from underneath their cockpits like the proboscis of an exotic flying insect. Two into three dark, long barrels turned and twisted over a comparatively large slewing limit, with great menace.

The comparatively less agile and heavier Sea King's hovered at a higher altitude, much higher than the US Marine helicopter-gunships.

'Tiger one and tiger two... proceed to execute a strafing run.'

From the airspace between the fortress and the Malabar Star, both Super Cobra's opened up. Shells blasted out of two M-197's with a deafening clatter. Tracers at intervals in the bullet feed lit the streams of lead as it hosed across the empty sundeck for approximately one point two eight seconds. A pre-set sixteen round burst limiter had been used.

'Bravo seventeen and bravo eighteen open up.'

From high above, the noses of the two Sea Kings tilted downwards as the helicopter's hovered in the air. The power fuller Aden's slammed twenty-five millimeter shells downwards onto the sundeck. Shells hit the Malabar Star at an angle at one thousand eight hundred and fifty rounds a minute. The lethal cacophony lasted only for around a second.

Then the two Super Cobra's climbed with a thunderous sound and swerved over the Malabar Star.

The Indian pilots above, opened up too; dousing their heavier Rolls Royce Gnome's with added fuel. The already thunderous roar enhanced in decibel level as rotor RPM's increased. Cyclics and collective sticks were adjusted and the appropriate pedal pressure applied. And the Sea King's ascended rapidly sideways and passed over the pilothouse.

Suddenly Zwankwid's voice came in over the main radio. The ploy had worked.

***

'Tiger one and two... and bravo seventeen and eighteen.' The terrorist leader's rough, guttural low decibel voice reeked with rancor and malice. 'I'll finish you all and all those with me.'

There was a moments silence, save for the helicopter sounds. They veered-off and flew back towards their mother ships.

Alexander's voice came over the open line. 'Calm down, calm down... just my pilots getting a little brash.'

'Maybe because we're close to resolving your problem,' Contractor added.

The line crackled for a moment. Kohli came in from the WNCCC. 'Right we're close to a solution.'

The American negotiator Preston also from the WNCCC spoke. 'Both US and Indian authorities may be favorable to the demand of releasing the prisoners.' He calmly and courteously mediated. 'But you have to satisfy certain conditions. Give some guarantees regarding the passengers and crew with you.'

The AJTF boss and his men were invisible to us. Yet I sensed Zwankwid's exultation. He smelt a certain victory.

'Very good indeed.' An euphoric Zwankwid made great attempts to hide his ecstatic exhilaration. But didn't succeed too well. 'We can negotiate the conditions and give the needed guarantees!'

XIV

'You have to be in a better situation than on the ship,' Preston said in an unhurried and deliberate manner.

'We're happy on this ship and can wait indefinitely,' Zwankwid insisted. 'Off-course the price will be paid by the hostages.'

'By better situation I meant for the passengers and crew to be released,' Preston imperturbably carried on. 'After we comply with your demands, we need to be clear about the manner in which they're going to be set free.'

'You have to give us certain guarantee's regarding their safety… if the imminent release of ten persons in Indian jails is to take place,' Kohli added.

'Fly them the Maqdisho and leave them alone there,' Zwankwid calmly explained. 'And Amjad Mubarak is to be flown to Maqdisho too… when our contact there signals us, we release the hostages.'

'According to a report with me the Union Home Ministry has tentatively cleared the list of ten prisoners!' Kohli let out the timely news. 'They've been moved to Indira Gandhi International Airport already.'

'Good. We're highly pleased that the Indian government has finally shown some sense.' For a moment Zwankwid let his delight show. Then he became serious. 'What about our brother Amjad Mubarak?'

Preston from the shore based WNCCC came in on the air. 'The US State Department…' his neutral voice sounded flat and impersonal. 'Has approved the release of Amjad Mubarak!'

Straightaway sounds of a raucous victory celebration came over the radio. Whoops of delight were interspersed with yells of glee. Zwankwid, Zohran and Wassif reveled in their unique accomplishment.

***

'But... but...' Preston attempted to interrupt the party. 'We're still working out the details of his flight to the destination you mentioned.'

An ominous hush rapidly descended on the open line.

'Your words mislead us in no way.' Zwankwid suddenly became grave. His voice carried more than a potent hint of extreme menace. 'All you have to do is place him on a flight.'

'That depends,' Preston replied keeping the right degree of tension in his voice. 'On how you vacate the Malabar Star and release the hostages.'

'Now when and how will you release the hostages?' Kohli quickly queried.

'We require safe conduct for my dhows,' Zwankwid declared. 'We'll keep some hostages till we reach international waters... then on to an undisclosed destination. There we'll release them.'

'Not enough of a guarantee,' Kohli said.

'I think... I think...' Preston sounding as casual and detached as ever to elicit confidence, suddenly slipped in an innocent sounding suggestion. 'Move the hostages to that nearby fortress. It's empty, isolated and surrounded by the sea.'

***

Zwankwid instantly responded, 'what if you have infiltrated the fortress?'

'Move in an advance party.' Kohli tried to allay his fears. 'We guarantee your safe passage to check out the fortress. Then return and take the rest of the hostages across.'

'Too risky,' Zwankwid insisted.

'It's a necessary condition,' stipulated a composed and self-possessed Preston. 'Otherwise I cannot convince my government that we've extracted a concession out of you... to give up Amjad Mubarak.'

He was hazy about what concessions the US government needed. But that was one of the secrets of the art of hostage negotiations.

The six of us in the pilothouse remained silent and still while listening in.

'I'd love to see the interior of the "Jazire Meharuba" or the "Moon Fortress"... where our glorious brothers once ruled over a part of Hindustan,' Zwankwid remarked wishfully; then he spat out vehemently. 'But not now. It's too dangerous.'

'Impossible, impossible,' Contractor snapped equally forcefully into the discussion. 'Not moving into the fortress means the siege continues.'

'Send a dhow across with some men,' Alexander amiably advised. 'To check out the interior.'

The various contrasting decibel levels and tones used while suggesting the next course of action to the terrorist's, did it. Sharp sounds of frenzied consultations in hoarse whispers could be heard for a few seconds over the open radio line.

'Is the move to the fortress acceptable?' A hard sharp Contractor interrupted their parleying.

'Right we agree,' Zwankwid's controlled voice said. 'I'll send a dhow with four hostages with my men to check out the interior. Any funny business and we'll kill the four first... besides taking severe retribution on the others.'

***

After a little while the engines on one of the dhows sputtered and coughed to life. Unshaven men in dirty vests and cut-off jeans, stained with oil, were visible in its wheelhouse cabin. The vessel sidled near and touched the freeboard of the Malabar Star.

With a kind of a vexed disquietude that tends to overcome one in situations like this, when any new development takes place; all of us in the pilothouse visually followed the course of action taken by the dhow.

A dark skinned crewman clambered atop the cabin. He laid a wooden plank from the dhow to the Malabar Star. Then signaled with a wave of his right hand.

Four armed terrorists came onto the dhow. Three bearded track suited men, AK-74's ready for instant action, waited on the open deck. One man pointed his weapon towards the Malabar Star and motioned across the plank.

A frightened gray haired American couple gingerly stepped on to the plank. They shuffled onto the top of the dhow's cabin profusely sweating with nervousness. Then they descended down a wooden ladder into the cabin.

Then another couple, far younger in age, followed the earlier two. They cautiously lowered themselves down the open hatchway, and disappeared in the cabin beneath. They appeared to be Britons.

Then the diesel engines powered and the dhow began to move gradually. It drifted clear of the Malabar Star. A short stocky seaman used all his strength to turn the wooden steering wheel. The boat drifted in a semi-circular arc, till the prow faced the fortress, then began chugging forward at a steady speed.

An entrance into the dark ominous fortress lay on the western side. An arched gate on the walls of the fortified enclosure led to an ancient Looking landing. Medieval boats might have moored here during the yester years.

The dhow closed in and stopped adjacent to the western side of the landing, bypassing the slippery stone steps that led down right to the sea.

A plank was laid from the boat to the landing. And two terrorists got onto the fortress entrance.

Both held AK-74's ready in one hand and held portable radio's in their left hands. They spoke continuously into the handsets while treading on with great deliberation and care into the aged stone archway. With maximum awareness and total restraint they carefully looked inside. When satisfied after a few seconds, they turned and signaled towards the dhow.

Immediately two other terrorists followed the two frightened couple's onto the landing. The hostages stood silently on the pavestones and hesitantly looked about. Uncertain expressions of suspicion and doubt manifest on their fearful faces revealed their feelings.

Then the first two motioned to the other two. They got the hostages moving. And within seconds the group of four terrorists and four hostages disappeared into the forbidding ramparts of the medieval fortification.

***

A full forty-five minutes later a terrorist came out of the arched rear entrance to the fortress. The expression on his face revealed that he was satisfied the fortress was empty. He glanced at the dhow. Then faced the Malabar Star and waved his right hand with his AK-74 about while speaking rapidly into his portable set with his left hand.

'Would have been in touch all the while,' observed a thoughtful Jeet. 'But they want to see him in person.'

'Ensure he wasn't coerced into signaling an all clear.' I added. 'Before taking the decision to send the rest of the hostages inside.'

Columbus suddenly cried out, 'other dhows are coming closer.'

The other boats closed in. Passenger after passenger along with the captive crew shuffled over a wide, wooden plank onto the top of the cabin's of the dhows. From there they gingerly clambered down. They lowered themselves through open hatches and disappeared into the cavernous interior of the three dhows.

Armed terrorists, positioned at various points, watched the prisoners with hawk eyes.

When fully loaded, the three boats edged away from the Malabar Star, turned slowly, and chugged forward. Their waterlines were considerably higher on their freeboards than previously, due to their loads. They took the same route as the earlier boat towards the landing of the fortress.

At the landing the terrorists disembarked and formed a semi-circle, AK-74's ready, and guardedly watched as the passengers stepped onto the landing.

The three boats emptied soon. The big group of hostages were on the large pavestones of the landing. The American's were mostly retired couples. The Briton's were a younger lot. A terrorist signaled them.

And the normally feisty, laughing passengers, now morose and cowed down, gloomily followed the armed terrorist's into the fortress. Soon they completely disappeared within its black stone portals.

'No Zwankwid, Zohran and Wassif with them,' I observed.

'Means they're still onboard,' D'Costa took in a deep worried, concerned breath and exhaled with a worried gasp. 'With God alone knows how many more terrorists.'

Jeet solemnly nodded. 'They might be hidden in the other dhows also, with their radio.'

Before we could do justice to his inference, the "secure" line crackled to life.

When appropriate adjustments were made to the radio, Kohli came in. 'Switch on your main radio and switch-off this channel. The AJTF is coming on the open line.'

XV

Zwankwid spoke through the open line. 'The hostages have been moved into the Jazire Meharuba.' He struggled to repress his glee; yet I detected he was a trifle nervous. 'Any attempt to rescue them will cause a bloodbath... we'll kill all thirty-six passengers and ten crew.'

The six of us in the pilothouse digested his threat. None of us made any attempt to react or did anything to reveal our inner feelings.

Kohli's voice came through from the shore based WNCCC. 'We're satisfied with the location of the hostages in the Janjira fortress.' The Indian Navy Commodore's calm and composed manner was calculated to bolster Zwankwid's confidence. 'The flight to Maqdisho is scheduled to leave tomorrow morning... hence we request a postponement of the deadline.'

Before Zwankwid could reply, Preston came in. 'We've just received a communication from the US State Department that Amjad Mubarak has been flown to Islamabad.' He sounded extremely official, but a trace of apology was clearly noticeable in his voice. 'Arrangements have to be still completed to connect him to Maqdisho... from where he'll be left alone to go wherever he wants... therefore we second the proposal to postpone the deadline to the coming morning. By which time he'll be en route to Maqdisho.'

The two negotiators implied the AJTF had secured a tremendous victory. This was enough for the terrorists to exult. For a few moments we heard intensive consultations in euphoric sounding whispers through the line.

Finally Zwankwid returned. 'The deadline is moved to eight-o-clock tomorrow morning.' He paused and emphasized. 'Zero eight hundred hours IST.' Then he attempted to ensure we took him seriously. He hissed out an ominous threat. 'After zero eight hundred hours we'll start killing the hostages in two's every two hours.'

***

We switched-off the set. Then the "secure" link came alive.

'Contractor speaking, we have seen them taking the hostages into the fortress. But we didn't observe Zwankwid, Zohran or Wassif outside?'

'The ringleaders and others may still be inside the Malabar Star,' I said with detached urgency.

'Or may be on one of their dhows,' Jeet interjected. 'To try to escape later.'

Alexander responded immediately from the Saipan, 'we can safely ignore them. We must concentrate on the hostages and their exact location. We're reorienting our rescue plans towards extracting them from inside the fortress. But need more intelligence.'

'I know the entire layout,' Jeet said. 'I can help.'

'How?' Alexander asked.

'Used to take an interest in the art of warfare. Read a lot on the subject and also visited old fortresses including this one, sir.'

'Interesting?' a neutral Alexander commented.

An unaffected and composed Jeet clinically analyzed his teens. 'Couldn't imagine anything other than warfare; and was out alone. Studied various fortification including this one, inch by inch.'

'Great, you can help us.' There was far more than a great deal of satisfaction in Alexander's statement.

***

'Inside to the main eastward facing gate is a white pained mosque called Panch Phir. Also around they're five white structures which are mosques which have space to hide hostages inside.'

Jeet continued, 'around a largish water tank is a bath-house which can hold some prisoners. Near the ruined siddi's palace is a school and remnants of a residential area.'

'No cover there to hide in?' Contractor gently refocused Jeet onto the immediate problem.

'Right. Under the north facing battlements are passages. Then come granaries. But rooms under watch towers and passages facing west are suitable to hiding hostages. Also facing the rear entrance, the one they took the hostages in from, is a soldiers barracks. Highly suitable to hide people in. Almost directly opposite, under the battlements are passageways leading to an ammunition dump in a watch tower. Besides under each tower are possible hiding places.'

D'Costa, Perez, Napoleon, Columbus and I breathlessly listened on.

'And there's a secret entrance on the eastern part of the north facing wall…'

A dead silence greeted Jeet's announcement.

'There's a small tunnel. It slopes from the inside of the rampart wall downwards all the way to the sea below, which touches the wall at a considerably lower level, sir.' Jeet let out his trump card.

Alexander said, 'good, Jeet, you've helped us a lot. Now we intend to send out a Pioneer Remotely Piloted Vehicle or RPV. But my staff feels it's too large and will enrage them enough to do something rash to the hostages.'

'What'll we do then?' Contractor forcefully questioned.

'We have a smaller Unmanned Aerial Vehicle or UAV called Dragon Eye. I feel its TV camera will be of great use to us in detailing the inside of the fortress.'

***

On the deck of the Saipan the UAV was readied. It was launched by throwing it into the air by a long elastic band. Then the airborne Dragon Eye was vectored through a hand held control box towards the northern side of the fortress.

From the pilothouse we saw the small hobbyist-like model aircraft fly on. It was propelled onwards by two small propellers, one on each wing. When it reached its pre-planned location, it veered rightwards and flew towards the fortress.

'Onboard TV camera's giving us a clear picture of the fortress walls,' Alexander said. 'Can see the head of a narrow square shaped tunnel at sea level.'

'One person at a time can crawl unobserved into the fortress, sir,' Jeet reported.

The video feed from the UAV was received on a small laptop-like console. Apparently Alexander and his staff were watching the pictures coming in while speaking to us on the "secure" line.

The Dragon Eye curved around the fortress and overflew it, camera's humming.

'Can see terrorists in groups near some of the hiding places.' Alexander laconically announced. 'Presume they're got the unseen by us hostages under cover nearby.'

'Pinpoint the locations on the video,' Contractor added. 'It's where they're hiding them. Close-by.'

The UAV photographed the entire inside of the fortification from about ninety meters high in the sky. As it reached the area around the rear entrance the terrorists opened fire.

Bursts of AK-74 bullets speeding upwards came from many directions. The fusillade hit the Dragon Eye. A wing sheared-off and the UAV nose dived into the sea.

'They've finished the blasted small airplane,' a horrified Napoleon said.

D'Costa gave him a warning look.

'No problem,' came in Alexander. 'We've recorded the video feed and have full scale images of the interior of the fortress.'

XVI

Jeet's incessant prods on my right shoulder shook me awake early the next morning. I half opened my sleepy eyes. Memories of the previous evening passed through my mind as I forced consciousness to overcome my sleepiness. Right from the time the sun had set, till my eyelids had shut, sounds of the helicopters shuttling between the Indian, American and British surface combatants had kept me alert. I also recalled boats from the various ships, full of personnel, making their way to the Saipan. A big operation was being planned.

I sat up and rubbed my eyes. My ears picked up the vague, muted and distant sounds of clattering helicopter rotors. They were airborne. But were somewhere far away.

Jeet charged with excitement whispered aloud to me, 'about to strike. Going to launch the rescue attempt.'

It was a little before six in the morning. Outside it was still dark save for the first vague incandescence in the east of the still invisible early morning sun. A large semi-circular halo of dim, murky luminescence glimmered upwards from behind the large hill that overlooked the town of Danda Rajapur. This and the little illumination afforded by the half moon and the twinkling stars high in the cloudless sky, bathed the fortress with a gloomy, eerie, sepulchral light; a funeral type of illumination that evoked bleak and melancholy feelings.

'Too late for an attack,' I said. 'Normally should have struck earlier in the morning'.

'Think chopper's not equipped for a night operation,' Jeet answered.

'Oh need visual references to fly effectively.' I understood why the assault was at first light.

Slight slivers of the early morning sunlight began to show in the eastern horizon. Enough for us to sight the dark shapes of the warships around us.

However, the hill behind Danda Rajapur would block the full effects of the emerging sun for some more time.

Then came the first inkling of the impending rescue mission.

***

The vague helicopter sounds slowly enhanced in decibel level to a thunderous clatter. A squadron was high in the air over the fortress. Clear cut silhouettes of two US Marine Sea Knights and one Super Stallion and an Indian Coastguard Sea King gradually lost altitude. Before they could descend further, the firing began.

Sporadic bursts of sub-machinegun chatter and the deeper single cracks of automatic rifle fire came through from all over the fortress.

The four helicopters were still in the air. Their rate of descent had slowed down considerably.

Waves of exhilaration tinged with flashes of nervousness passed through each one of us.

'So they've infiltrated in earlier,' Jeet said as calmly as he could.

'Unfortunately.' I looked hopelessly at the dark ramparts and bastions.'We can't see a damned thing.'

'Still.' Napoleon turned and eyed Jeet approvingly. 'They must have gone through that tunnel you showed them.'

Everyone favored Jeet with awed looks of a new respect.

Then, a visibly perturbed D'Costa joined his hands in fervent prayer. 'Hope none of our people get hurt.'

Perez and I waited tensely for the action to abate; and for the end results to become apparent.

The shouts and yells interspersed with the short sharp bursts of automatic fire that reverberated from various parts of the fortress suddenly stopped. A deadly, ominous silence followed, save for the helicopter sounds. The firing had lasted only about five seconds.

'The firing has stopped,' an icy cool Jeet noted. 'Means they've effected the rescue.'

***

While the Super Stallion flew patrols overhead, Marines in combat fatigues from the Sea Knight abseiled down ropes onto the fortress. From the Coastguard Sea King black clad MCF men slithered downwards, their compact MP-5's ready for action. Once on terra firma the "fast roped" Americans and Indians raced away to predetermined positions as rapidly as they could.

The sharp barks of non-commissioned ranks directing their assault teams came through the early morning air.

Then, the Sea Knight dropped gently onto the hill with a flagstaff on it, inside the fortress. US Marines quickly led groups of rescued hostages to the dual rotor chopper. Due to the rear rotor above the open ramp being at a far higher level on its pylon than the front rotor, the rotating blades didn't pose a threat to the emplaning passengers.

From our position in the pilothouse we could see only the top of the Flagstaff Hill inside the fortress. And the sea around the island fortification.

Lightweight glass fiber reinforced plastic Rigid Raider assault craft of the SAS Boat Troop floated near the entrance of the tunnel. Inflatable's of the MCF were also around. This confirmed that the SAS and MCF had got in undetected earlier. And the firing we heard was them executing their deadly dangerous, risky mission.

A tense portentous silence ensued. The big helicopter's had flown away. One of them carried a group of passengers to the Saipan. It left them on the amphibious assault carrier, and returned to carry another batch of passengers away.

Then the "secure" line screeched to life. Perez quickly adjusted the set.

'The good guys have won.' The elation in Alexander's voice was unmistakable. 'We've won round one'.

***

'Indian Naval Commando's, the MCF and a SAS Boat Troop unit infiltrated undetected through the secret passage. However, they had to silently knife two terrorists on guard at the head of the tunnel. Equipped with special night vision scopes they could crawl to certain pre-selected positions.' Kohli couldn't stop his delight from showing while making his cryptic sounding report from the WNCCC. 'When the sleepy terrorists focused upwards at the helicopters, they moved in and killed all the fourteen terrorists... without a single hostage getting hurt.'

'Been inside from zero five hundred hours,' an exultant Contractor added.

'Thanks to information from Jeet and the video feed from the Dragon Eye, we got in a good sized force inside,' Alexander continued. 'Our tactical planners selected the right spots for the infiltrating force to secure.'

Le Harrington commander of the SAS Boat Troop, said, 'my report confirms fourteen terrorists killed… all thirty-six passengers and ten crew are safe and sound.'

The mood lifted instantly in the pilothouse.

Jeet said thoughtfully, 'have to confirm Zwankwid, Zohran and Wassif's deaths.'

'Are they dead or still in the Malabar Star or in those dhows which are manned by separate crews?' I added.

'Moving everyone to the Saipan for due processing and debriefing.' Alexander's curt signal came in. 'I intend vacating the fort of all living beings as soon as possible.'

'Police authorities will takeover, including of the bodies, soon,' Contractor informed.

Just then Kohli from the WNCCC directed us, 'switch on the main line.'

Napoleon did so and the large radio burst into life.

A hysterical Zwankwid's maniacal scream of intense rage scorched through the line.

XVII

Outside a large flaming orb, the sun, had risen far above the Rajapur hill. The consequent luminosity heralded a bright new morning. Because of the early morning sunlight the forbidding black stone fortress and the sea around were fully visible.

Closer, five mechanized dhows lay in the calm waters between the fortress and the Malabar Star.

Then I noticed something new. The two lifeboats of the Malabar Star had been lowered from their davits by the terrorists. Possibly in the night. Now they wallowed lightly in the gentle swells near the westward facing landing to the fortress.

Zwankwid raved and ranted uncontrollably. 'Sons of pigs, filthy dogs that live in gutters. Servants worse than cockroaches and worms, you have betrayed me… you have betrayed me… I shall kill everyone of you, and blow apart the Malabar Star.'

We heard a scraping sound. 'The treacherous act of killing our brothers…' He controlled his voice till he had no emotion showing. This enhanced our anxiety levels to a higher degree. He now exuded a clear-headed clearance above everything around, that was exceedingly aggravating. 'Will prove one of the costliest blunders you have made.'

Jeet shook his head as he turned and gazed at each one of us in turn. 'Means we're going to pay! We're the only ones left, still stuck to the AJTF.'

'Where are you? Tell us your location,' Preston no more behaving like a negotiator, asked forcefully with not a little venom in his voice.

The very next moment the angry click of the terrorist's switching-off the line came through.

***

The ever vigilant Napoleon suddenly alerted us. 'A US Marine Huey has taken-off from the Saipan.' He made a long searching three hundred and sixty degree visual sweep of the sea around, and added. 'A US Navy Sea Hawk is in the air from the Arleigh Burke.'

This caused us a welcome mental respite. Within less than a minute a Huey from the Saipan, with a familiar red cross painted on its side, hovered over the fortress. Shortly afterwards it landed on the Flagstaff Hill. A couple of Marines, red crosses on vests over their combat fatigues identifying them as a casualty evacuation team, disembarked. With cell phones in their hands they made their way down the hill.

The Sea Hawk touched down near the casevac Huey. A US Navy officer accompanied by a petty officer and two armed men stepped out. It looked like they'd mount guard over the medics; who probably had come to check the fourteen dead bodies.

Jeet soberly regarded them. 'Time has come to all out attack this ship and rescue us.'

Contractor came in on the "secure" line. 'Are determining the location of Zwankwid, Zohran and Wassif.'

'Are they still in the Malabar Star? Or are they, which is more likely, in their dhows?' Alexander queried.

Six pairs of eyes in the pilothouse simultaneously turned towards the dhows. And the collective gasp that ensued indicated the degree of the unexpected bombshell that had shocked us!

Napoleon cried out first, 'bastards have removed the canvas covering their missiles...'

'Readying to launch their Aerospatiale SS-12M's,' Jeet immediately interrupted him. He hollered urgently into the radio. 'Going to fire their antishipping French missiles anytime... can fire their SS-12M's anytime!'

XVIII

In the narrow waters between the Malabar Star and the fortress, the five dhows had maneuvered into seemingly random positions. Their idling engines and tiny streams of froth bubbling from under their sterns, indicated their propellers were threshing about. They could move immediately. Two large cigarette box-like canisters mounted side by side were distinctly visible on each dhow. Steel plating fixed behind the missile boxes on the front of the wheelhouse's were to deflect the missile back blast. Now their crews or whoever were in the boats could fire their ordnance at the US, UK and Indian combatants anytime.

Then a dhow made a break for it. Its engines roared as it increased its speed. The modified boat raced southwards, its prow pointing almost directly at the Ranvijay.

The instantaneous reaction on the Ranvijay encompassed its Three Inch gun and ADG AK-630's. The Skipper and his tactical team in its Operation Room were ready to counter the threat from the dhow. Now the Kashin II focused its ordnance on the specific threat.

The Three Inch slewed on its traverse mounting. Its twin dark barrels ranged, depressed, following the movement of the dhow.

The ADG operator's had activated their starboard and port side "Bass Tilt" guidance systems. The computation package gave processed return H and I band signals to assist the operator in electronically guiding the weapons package. The short, dark, multiple barrels of the AK-630's depressed downwards. The entire mini turret-like mountings also slewed appropriately, track aligning the advancing dhow.

The dhow veered towards a point on the forward part of the freeboard of the Ranvijay. Suddenly a piercing tongue of orange-blue flame followed by a puff of thick white smoke enveloped its missile canister. Two SS-12M's rocketed-off at the head of a wispy white vapor trail towards the Ranvijay. And immediately the dhow dodged towards the west and made a run for the open sea.

Both Ranvijay's portside AK-630's promptly opened up. The two six-barreled muzzles flared flame. A stream of smoke extending outwards marked the pathway of the slugs. A shapeless ball of crimson flame floated along the track. A muted, eerie sound like that of onrushing wind filled the air. The two mini turrets had erupted, discharging a streaming barrier of thirty millimeter shells at three thousand rounds a minute, towards the incoming SS-12M's.

"Bass Tilt" proved its efficacy immediately. The explosive obstacle of lead hit home over a patch of the empty sea, about halfway to the Ranvijay. The first SS-12M thundered into the AK-630 barricade to its destruction, with a mighty explosion of flame, sound and debris. The second Aerospatiale missile blasted into nothingness within a fraction of a second. A pillar of frothing seawater fountain headed upwards and rained downwards along with fragments of rocket fuselage, oxidized metal and spent thirty millimeter bullets. These scattered over a portion of the grayish sea.

'Must've fired their wire guided missiles blind,' I said. 'Because they turned away too sharply.'

The rest nodded in acknowledgement; but continued raptly watching the spectacle unfolding outside.

The same dhow suddenly altered its bearings and turned and faced the Arleigh Burke's portside freeboard.

***

The Arleigh Burke's Combat Information Center was on full alert. Technicians and specialists were at their displays and consoles. The outcome of their vigilance was plainly visible.

Two Vulcan Phalanx's on automatic mode covered the threat angle. Their slewing module's and cannon tilt readiness was 'locked on' to the stationary dhow. Preset burst's would have been programmed in. The CIWS operator's had readied their anti-missile defenses.

Two entire mountings on relatively thick bases slewed around slowly, keeping the General Electric Gatling guns in their tilt modules aiming at the dhow.

Then a pair of SS-12M's were loosed-off from the dhow. The short sharp tongues of flame and back blast as well as the puff of white smoke enveloping the box, signaled that the rocket fuel of the two missiles had ignited. Two Aerospatiale projectiles shot-off at the head of a steamy, smoky trail en route to executing their lethal mission.

Instantly the six barrels of the forward Vulcan Phalanx and six barrels of the aft mounting opened up. They hurled a stream of explosive depleted uranium slugs at the incoming targets.

The disparity in the radar signals from the incoming and outgoing projectiles were eliminated almost instantly by a super efficient computer in the computation package inside the lower part of the white housing, over the cannon. Electrical connections hydraulically slewed the entire mounting; and depressed the white housing, cannon, outgoing tracker radar and magazine as an integrated module. Till the deadly curtains of twenty millimeter bullets, in preset bursts of two hundred rounds each, firing at fifty rounds a second, closed in towards the incoming missiles.

There was a crimson flare at the muzzle's of both CIWS cannons. A shapeless cloud of orange flame floated along a thin wispy, smoky track on which two streams of bullets slammed outwards. Within a fraction of a second the deadly crossfire hit the French SS-12M's.

A searing ball of flame preceded two stunning blasts which took place within a microsecond. Continuous explosions midair shred the incoming missiles into smithereens. Wreckage spattered away horizontally and peppered the hull of the Arleigh Burke harmlessly. A cloud of semi-burnt fuel, oxidized explosive dust and pulverized wreckage remained in the sky for some time in the clear blue sunny morning air, before dissipating away.

The dhow turned westwards and surged outwards for the open sea, through the large gap between the Arleigh Burke and the Saipan.

The Skipper of the guided missile destroyer turned his vessel slightly.

His forward Five Inch gun barrel followed the movement of the fleeing dhow.

D'Costa, Perez, Columbus, Jeet and I silently watched the dhow racing away.

Napoleon heatedly remarked, 'the Arleigh Burke has to fire back to take revenge against those AJTF bastards.'

***

The Arleigh Burke's slewing gun mounting, and depressing barrel was track aligning or electronically following the path of the escaping dhow.

Jeet pointed to the gun. All our eyes moved from the dhow to the Five Inch.

Suddenly the moving turret stopped. An orange white flame flared at the muzzle of the gun, and a clap of thunder rent the air. Simultaneously a shell rocketed out of the barrel, through the ensuing cloud of smoke, towards its target.

The first shell landed a little ahead, a few degrees to the port side of the now fairly fast moving dhow.

From the Combat Information Center the Engagement Controller had cleared the shot. He went through a checklist including ensuring the correctly fused ammunition from the ready service loader was in the breech. Then the gunner had triggered-off the round.

Now software automatically incorporated the speed of the moving target; rate of change of range; speed of the shell and the time it took to reach the target in its calculations. It worked out deflection. How far away or near it had to aim to register a hit.

Visible to us was the entire Five Inch mounting slewing around slightly. The long single barrel ranged, depressed appropriately to the electrically transmitted corrections.

Inside the turret live ammunition was raised by a hoist and automatically placed in the breech and the breech ramed shut. The below deck gunner received a clearance. He then fired-off the thirty-two kilogram, one hundred and twenty-seven millimeter round.

A little less than three seconds later, the gun stopped moving. Instantly came a large flaring orange-white flash and a cloud of smoke at the muzzle of the long barrel. The thunder clap-like sound a fraction of a second later heralded the next shot zooming away.

It landed slightly short. A little before the stern of the rapidly departing dhow. But the resultant massive splash raised at least a ton of water. The seawater cascaded onto the dhow. The shivering, shuddering vessel pitched and rolled momentarily as though hit by a massive wave in a severe mid-ocean thunderstorm.

'Like in older Naval gun battles. Got a small spread of salvo. A straddle. A splash over and a splash short of the target... to aim for in between,' Jeet said.

'It's far more complex than that today,' I answered. 'They're using radar to guide the gunner in his aiming.'

The gun mounting traversed to a minute degree. The barrel elevated ever so slightly. Again a series of electronic corrections had been transmitted to the gun train and elevation motors.

Within three seconds another flash of flame flared around the end of the muzzle. A muted clap of thunder rent the clear blue and still although humid air. Another flaming Five Inch projectile lanced-off, angling straight at the dhow.

The top secret data integrating gunnery software finally delivered its explosive payload with a deadly accuracy, slamming it right into the cabin of the dhow.

With a thunderous roar a white hot explosive wall of flame with an orange core enveloped the dhow, blasting it into fragments. Pieces of dhow debris along with a few tons of water rose a couple of stories high before falling into the sea. A fraction of a second ago a dhow had raced away in the relatively calm waters; now a small oil slick and a couple of burnt, blackened wooden beams floated around the same spot, under a hazy spell of cordite smoke.

XIX

Three dhows of the remaining four hugged the freeboard of the Malabar Star. A single dhow edged away from the other three but stopped in the waters clear away from the Malabar Star, between the other dhows and the Janjira fortress. Its prow faced a gap somewhere between the Godavari and the Vindhyagiri.

Both the frigates reverse thrusted. Smoke belched out of their Babcock and Wilcox boilers as they moved backwards. They carried the same propulsion system. But the Godavari displaced more tonnage than the Vindhyagiri and so moved a wee bit slower. Then the Vindhyagiri stopped first. And the Godavari halted nearby a little later. Space had been created between them and the dhow menacing them.

The Vindhyagiri's Four Point Five Inch was readied for a low target engagement. Its turret slewed on its traverse rails. Its twin barrels depressed, aligning onto the stationary dhow.

The Godavari's Fifty-Seven Millimeter was also electrically traversed and twin barrels depressed to bring it to bear upon the dhow. Besides its AK-230's were drawing a bead onto the targeted boat too.

Seconds ticking away became minutes, and nothing happened.

'Bugger's aren't going on and firing their bloody missiles?' a fidgety, impatient Napoleon observed.

'Contractor can act anytime.' I didn't take my fascinated eyes off the dhow. 'They've already signaled their hostile intent by firing their SS-12M's from the other boat.'

***

Then Contractor opened up. The Godavari's two port side ADG AK-230 operator's hosed a long burst onto the dhow. A "micro sonic boom-like" cacophony rent the air. Bright orange flashes of flame flared at the muzzles of the Russian Gatling's. The long, dark, twin barrels slammed shells weighing about half a kilogram, at the rate of five hundred rounds a minute, at the dhow.

The crew of the boat hid in the interior of the vessel as they took a severe beating. Chunks of wood flew into the air, but before any further damage was done the AK-230's stopped firing.

Then the surface heavy ordnance of both the frigates opened up.

A momentary eruption of belching crimson flame followed by a large puff of smoke enveloped one of the muzzles of the twin Four Point Five Inch. Then came a loud thunder-clap-like boom. Concurrently the fiery discharge of a "High Effect, Direct Action" fused shell, designed to explode on impact, lanced at the virtually point blank range right into the unprotected dhow.

Simultaneously a series of six precisely spaced (time wise) dhum... dhum... dhum... dhum... dhum... dhum – signaled a three second burst from the Godavari's Fifty-Seven Millimeter which bludgeoned onto the defenseless dhow.

No deflection was needed at what was a fraction of the full range of the nineteen kilometer capable Four Point Five Inch. Or the eight kilometer range of the Fifty-Seven Millimeter.

A tremendous gout of flaring flame enveloped the dhow. The massive, fiery ear shattering detonation of the twenty-five kilogram Four Point Five Inch shell fragmented the targeted boat. The synchronous series of devastating Fifty-Seven Millimeter, two point eight kilogram shells blasting away, further shred the fragments into pieces.

We suffered a fleeting microsecond of intense earache; aggravated by the horror of detecting muffled screams that died out immediately as the modified dhow blew up.

The dhow had shattered and disintegrated. Wreckage slammed around in all directions, including upwards along with a massive volume of sea water. Smoking fragments of shattered, distorted wooden beams and overheated pieces of bent, warped and twisted steel scattered all over.

Also dropping, seemingly from the sky, were a gruesome assortment of bloody, burning heads, torsos, arms and legs.

Soon all that was left was a few floating wooden beams, most of them near cinders, some of them still flickering with red hot flame. Also visible was the grisly, hideous spectacle of parts of charred human bodies floating about in a rapidly expanding, and still hissing and bubbling, overheated oil slick.

Contractor had taken pre-emptive action. He revealed that he'd strike first if he perceived any threat to his vessels.

XX

Of the three dhows hugging the freeboard of the Malabar Star, one chugged around it and turned and faced the Saipan. Then it sped up, engines racing and accelerated through the clear blue waters straight towards the Saipan.

It reminded me of the July 7/8 night of 1944. Second World War Japanese forces erupted into a sudden, maniacal Banzai or suicide charge on the island of Saipan. The battle is part of US Marine Corps history. The Americans had repulsed the enemy successfully. Now the amphibious assault carrier named Saipan faced another Banzai-like charge. The small, insignificant, puny-looking dhow, with its deadly ordnance, advanced towards the towering stern of the Saipan.

'They've turned and are sailing away,' Napoleon said, looking at the Saipan.

'Creating space for their weapons to be effective,' Jeet answered.

D'Costa, Perez, Columbus and I gazed at the amphibious assault ship.

It now faced the west and was moving away. Its Westinghouse steam turbines were generating thrust at full tilt. The docking-well in the stern was closed and water was being pumped out from inside.

Perez further alerted us, 'there's a Harrier ready to takeoff.'

Visible on the flight deck was a Harrier with ground crew around it. Alexander was escalating force levels by bringing his aircraft into the low intensity conflict. After a little while the ground crew moved away and the short takeoff Harrier slipped-off the deck and climbed into the sky.

It took a long curve in the sky northwards then banked and turned and over flew us. Besides its heavy five barreled machinegun and magazine under its fuselage and Sidewinders on its outer wing pylons – the inner wing pylons had two wicked-looking air launch Harpoons.

'Can't hit them with their Harpoons,' Jeet conjectured. 'They might hit our vessels?'

'Can wait till they move away, then strike them from the air,' I replied, watching the lone aircraft settle into flying patterns somewhere high in the sky to the south of us.

Meanwhile, the advancing dhow didn't close in. The Saipan was moving away faster. Clearly sighted by us was the Vulcan Phalanx and the GDC RAM's in stern recesses under its flight deck. Both "last ditch" defensive weapons were tilted and slewed to intercept any incoming threat from the sea level dhow.

Then the inevitable occurred. Four acute tongues of flame flared into a smoky cloud; through which four SS-12M's rocketed-off from their canisters. They zoomed towards the large, towering stern of the moving away Saipan.

***

From the Saipan Alexander assisted by the ITAWDS controlled the entire task group. Within the Saipan, defensive armament was managed by the Captain, Executive Officer and his tactical team. They had allocated their ordnance to face the incoming threat.

Simultaneous to the SS-12M's approaching, sharp tongues of flame and a large cloud of smoke enveloped the EX-41, GDC RAM canister on the starboard niche of the Saipan. Electrically activated mechanical linkage had pumped hydraulic fluid around, to transmit its traverse and tilt movement. Now an indeterminate number of RAM's from among the twenty-one loaded in, weighing nine point one kilogram each, flared out towards the incoming French missiles.

The volley of RAM's spun directly into the flight path of the threat. Its nosecones had locked onto the radar signature of the SS-12M's. Fins opened out as its radar antennae picked up refracting radar echoes and guided the RAM's to near the incoming projectiles. Then they wriggled somewhat and partially altered their bearings as their infrared seekers homed onto the glowing heat emanating from the SS-12M's. The impenetrable barrage of RAM's, contrails tracing a wispy, smoky pathway, began to accelerate to twice the speed of sound.

Not even a fraction of a millisecond passed before the white hot, supersonic anti-missile RAM's established their effectiveness. Within an instant with a bright yellow flash and a series of booming, reverberating, rumbling explosions the four Aerospatiale missiles exploded midair.

Fragments of missile casings, aero fins, fuselage shoes and internal electronic hardware scattered all over in various directions; before spraying like dust over a large patch of the Arabian Sea.

The dhow veered into a long curve and made a break for it. It sped north westwards towards the largish gap of the open sea between the Saipan and the Cornwall.

***

The single Harrier aloft changed its bearing to enable it to execute an air interdictor mission. Now it flew southwards, then U turned and approached the northwards fleeing dhow from the south. Ready to "kill" the escaping vessel with a lethal Harpoon.

The Harpoon was a fire and forget weapon. Target radar signature data has to be fed into the missile through a command and guidance subsystem. Here the Texas Instruments frequency agile terminal guidance seeker would be set for a bearing only launch. The radar seeker would operate during the entire flight path to the target. Remain "locked on" to the dhow under terminal guidance.

High above the Harrier reached optimum range that would enable it to strike effectively. The aircraft dived, aiming its nose at the targeted dhow and loosed-off a Harpoon. The missile's jet propellant ignited as it streaked away at the head of a large, dense smoke contrail.

The crew of the targeted dhow spotted the incoming Harpoon. They took immediate evasive action. They twisted and turned their vessel desperately. One could sense their tension and nervousness.

The Harpoon's nosecone radar window scanned to forty-five degrees on either side of the missile's flight path. The active radar seeker transmitted return signals to a microprocessor. This altered them into electrical directions to the steering unit or servo controller, which moved actuators which directly made minor fin adjustments. Now this maneuvered the Harpoon into keeping the dot of the radar return reflection right into the center of its target acquisition window. As the dhow's movements didn't go outside the forty-five degree limit, the Harpoon was still right on target.

Pre-programmed computers communicated its final directions to the servo controller to the actuators to the tail fins. This means a final trajectory was programmed in from a bunch of selectable final trajectories. Like 'pop up and swoop down' or strike directly at the target.

The final move here was a direct hit. The dhow stopped suddenly. The McDonnell Douglas Astronautics developed Harpoon simply altered its final descent and dived steeper downwards right into the cabin of the dhow.

***

The kerosene jet propellant fuelled Teledyne turbojets rammed two hundred and twenty-seven kilograms of China Lake Naval Weapons Testing Center, California's "blast penetration explosive" at a little over three fourths the speed of sound, into the dhow's wheelhouse. And detonated right inside with a thunderous ear-splitting explosion.

It was probably the most destructive overkill in the history of past or present Naval engagements. An immense, blinding orange-white fireball flashed ferociously in the humid air, like a trembling miniature sun.

Pressure waves from the intense, deafening, pulverizing detonation flared outwards. It even affected us, relatively far away, in the pilothouse of the Malabar Star. We felt a blast of searing heat momentarily on our faces.

At ground zero the murderously effective super heat wave vaporized the dhow into disintegrating cinders. A dense enveloping cloud of smoke reaching all the way to the sky above, rendered the remnants of the dhow invisible. If there were any remnants left around to view. The shockwaves and the vacuum caused by the sudden explosive rushing away of the air, sucked up a massive mushroom of water.

It was like observing a smaller over ground nuclear test at Alamogordo, New Mexico or the Bikini Atoll or Siberia or some such place. Mild tremors from the invisible concentric rings of resultant shockwaves, continued to reach all the way to the Malabar Star for more than a few seconds.

Then, along with the plunging seawater miniscule fragments of incinerated dhow debris rained downwards like hailstones. Within a minute all that could be sighted from the pilothouse of the Malabar Star was a tiny spattering, bubbling patch on the sea. An overheated oil slick.No wreckage was visible under the thick writhing pall of smoke. This too gradually drifted away as the mild sea breeze prevailing dissipated it.

XXI

To the north we sighted the Cornwall. The Royal Navy frigate which earlier had been facing us had turned and was steaming away, northwards. It clearly was running on its power fuller Rolls Royce Spey turbines than its Rolls Royce Tyne's in its Combination Of Gas And Gas turbines or COGAG system. These gas turbines couldn't reverse. This would need a too large to be practicable gearbox. So to increase range between it and the low level sea targets here, the Cornwall had to turn and speed away. This looked like it was fleeing the scene of the action.

In the pilothouse of the Malabar Star all six of us grimly watched the British Skipper using tactics to enable his warship to become a potent factor in the surface engagement taking place.

Le Harrington took his combatant to a pre-determined point away from the dhows threatening his vessel. Then he stopped and slewed the Cornwall on its axis so as to have its port broadside facing the terrorist's boats. He had created the minimum range required to ensure the effectiveness of his heavy ordnance from his Action Information Organization against the low level targets.

Aiming over the Cornwall's bows at the two remaining dhows was a Mark Eight advanced version single barreled Four Point Five Inch. Also a six celled Sea Wolf anti-missile canister on the forecastle deck was angling towards the dhows. The Dutch Goalkeeper CIWS's heavy machinegun was bearing onto the two threats that were hugging the freeboard of the Malabar Star. A manually operated Rarden cannon also added to the firepower of the Type 22 Frigate. Le Harrington's impeccable seamanship enabled him to bring his sophisticated weapons into action anytime to defend his ship or to strike at the terrorist's boats.

'The Lynx is taking-off.' Napoleon pointed at the now distant frigate's helipad.

We gazed at the helicopter hovering upwards and away from the Cornwall. It carried a full payload of four Sea Skua air to surface antishipping missiles.

The chopper flew southwards, over us, and then steadily flew patterns in the air that it could break away from when it needed to strike. Le Harrington was now fully prepared to take on anything thrown against his ship.

***

Two modified dhows emerged from the protection afforded by the freeboard of the Malabar Star. Their engines roared noisily and smoke poured out of their exhaust funnels as they ploughed side by side through the placid waters. A little ahead they separated and increased the gap between them. Then from two angles they advanced upon the now distant Cornwall.

On the deck above the bridge of the Cornwall the Type Nine One One radar/optical Sea Wolf Director was slewed and depressed, aiming at the advancing threats. The forward Sea Wolf canister moved in tandem and pointed at the target as guided by its Director.

As soon as the crew of the two dhows aimed their vessels onto the relatively large freeboard of the Cornwall, that they fired their SS-12M's.

Eight missiles, four from each angle sped away through the ensuing fire and smoke towards the intended target.

Instantly two computer controlled Sea Wolf missiles responded. They shot out of the forward six celled canister and zoomed separately, accelerating to two times the speed of sound at the two different incoming salvos. The operator due to the targets being at a fraction of Sea Wolf's five kilometer range as well as being at a relatively low altitude, used a TV tracking system within the radar Director. He visually acquired the target.

In the command and guidance system used both missile's were directed simultaneously through coded corrections through a microwave link. The system can automatically home the missile onto anything on a high speed collision course. And to do so the operator simply commanded a "dip" at the appropriate point.

Both Sea Wolf missiles dived and exploded within the proximity of the SS-12M's. A searing orb of flame preceded two stunning blasts. They hit a couple of the incoming missiles and destroyed them. The consequent blast effect deflected the remaining SS-12M's and they splashed harmlessly into the sea.

***

Both the dhows, now defenseless, sped away in different directions. One chugged westwards. The other sped northwards. Le Harrington slewed his frigate on its axis and enabled his Goalkeeper to draw a bead on one of the approaching dhows.

The self-contained I band search/surveillance and tracking radar of the integrated with the gun Goalkeeper's sensor and computation system was next to the Vulcan Phalanx. But its thirty millimeter cannon had far more hitting power.

Now the Naval version of the General Electric GAU-8A elevated to about minus thirty degrees or depressed to track align the moving dhow. The Avenger as the gun was called, also slowly slewed on its traverse rails. Then opened fire.

It angled a supersonic stream of bullets from its seven revolving barrels at the helpless advancing dhow. An eerie sound like that of a number of oversized pneumatic drills simultaneously drilling away at a particularly rocky surface rent the air. A crimson flare at the gun's muzzle headed a dense, dark smoky trail that followed the path of the slugs.

Four thousand two hundred rounds a minute of armor piercing incendiary slammed into the boat at one thousand and sixty-six meters per second. The sheer velocity sheared chunks of dhow away like a giant meat cleaver in action. The pyrophoric effect of the Staballoy sub-caliber high density depleted uranium slugs ignited parts of the boat that it struck.

The dhow caught fire as it was being shred to pieces. Then the fuel tank blew up with a large fiery eruption of flame and a dull thump. The dhow shattered into large splinters and disappeared into the sea with its crew who didn't survive the assault.

Silently we watched the spectacle from the pilothouse of the Malabar Star.

'Now will strike the other dhow with a Sea Skua from the Lynx,' Jeet said.

Then the six of us focused our gaze at the helicopter and the remaining dhow.

***

From high above, the two Rolls Royce Gem turbo shafts powered Lynx tracked the westwards fleeing dhow. It flew a distance away, keeping optimal range to be able to execute its anti-shipping interdictor mission.

The four semi-active radar homing guidance British Aerospace's Sea Skua's on its winglets exuded a deadly lethality.

The Lynx descended away from the moving dhow, flying from east to west. Then it switched on its Ferranti Seaspray surveillance and target illuminating radar. The Seaspray's beams flowed through the Lynx's radar transparent nose. Crew in the chopper selected a missile using a Control Indicator. And maneuvered the helicopter to keep the target "illuminated".

The unit indicated that the missile was armed and its radar homing head was "locked on" to radar reflections from the dhow. Then a Sea Skua was released.

The Lynx pulled away to a position that kept the target "illuminated" for its Sea Skua to home onto.

The anti-shipping missile dropped for a short distance under auto-pilot control. Its boost motor ignited and it accelerated away to a fixed cruise speed. Then a sustainer motor (different rocket propellant ignited and generated thrust) descended the Sea Skua to an intermediate height.

The crew of the dhow spotted the missile. Instead of taking a sharp turn to evade the Sea Skua, they tried to race their boat. Then attempted to turn. The speed of their forward movement made the turn a shallow, long curve. The incoming Sea Skua's fins altered slightly to simply adjust its bearing to keep the dhow in its nosecone homing window.

As it approached the dhow it dropped further to sea skimming height and plunged with a deadly accuracy into the stern area of the racing away boat.

An orange flare flashed momentarily followed by a blast. The dhow shattered into large pieces and the hull turned turtle and caught fire. The battered, flaming wreck floated a little under the water. And there was no sign of any of its crew who presumably met with a certain death.

After a while, left behind in the oil darkened patch of sea, under a pall of smoke, were burning embers and the floating wreckage. These remnants would probably be destined to end up as flotsam and jetsam at some unknown beach.

***

Scarcely had our acutely thrashed and flagellated psyche's recovered from the shocking, violent spectacle of the terminal hammering of the five dhows when D'Costa brought us back to our immediate problem.

'If Zwankwid, Zohran and Wassif were killed in the dhows, we won't know?'

But there was a feeling of relief in the pilothouse as we digested D'Costa's remark.

Jeet was deeply in thought. 'I can't understand them. They used faulty tactics. Attacked the warships one at a time; except the last attack in which two boats went for the Cornwall.'

I added, 'ought to have all rushed together and fired their SS-12M's. That way they'd damage or cripple the capital ships, instead of challenging them one by one...'

'And committing suicide,' Perez interrupted.

'Or hug the freeboard of the Malabar Star and fire... Alexander and Contractor wouldn't have been able to hit back for fear of hitting us.' Jeet added to my speculative thoughts, paused and continued. 'Like it may have been a prolonged diversionary?'

A sudden familiar clamor assailed out auditory sensibilities and disrupted Jeet's statement.

The six of us quickly looked out at the source of the sounds over the Janjira fortress.

An instantly hyperactive Napoleon immediately struck his head out of the pilothouse. He peered at the origin of the discordant-sounding whirring rotors. Then he twisted and turned his head and then pointed excitedly at the airborne US Navy Sea Hawk over the fortress.

XXII

Something was terribly wrong with the Sea Hawk tottering over the Janjira fortress. The pilot seemed to be racing his engines. Consequently, the rotors gyrating at various RPM's, clattered with a loud sound. But the chopper didn't lift-off further or execute any maneuver. As though the pilot had engine trouble and couldn't get his controls to work.

'The casevac Huey is flying away and turning back,' Napoleon said.

We looked where he pointed. Far away almost over the southern horizon we spotted a rapidly disappearing speck. The dark green shape of the low flying Huey swept along at treetop height over the sea and curved towards the Saipan.

Not just a little puzzled we turned and watched the casevac helicopter.

Jeet's face screwed up in deep contemplation. 'Somehow they've got into the Sea Hawk helicopter and are trying to escape!'

'Can't fire their rockets and missiles at it?' D'Costa glanced at the Arleigh Burke, Ranvijay and Sangram.

Perez, Napoleon and Columbus regarded Jeet and me.

'The Huey pilot is returning the long way because of the surface engagement that has taken place,' Jeet quickly verbalized a possibility. 'And they've to confirm the terrorists have commandeered the Sea Hawk.'

I continued, 'Air Engagement Controller of the Arleigh Burke's Aegis Air Combat System will threat prioritize the blip on their consoles. Will allocate a reaction or weapon to bring down the chopper if certain the terrorists are in it'.

Napoleon added, 'if so, also means bastards have killed Americans in the fort!'

***

The "secure" line crackled. Perez switched on the set.

A desperate call came in on the line. 'ITAWDS to group in the pilothouse, the Sea Hawk isn't responding to our signals. Have you seen anything?'

'During the Naval fireworks,' Jeet responded quickly. 'Zwankwid, Zohran and Wassif and whoever was with them were hiding in the fortress and have seized the helicopter.'

'Are you sure?'

'Dead certain,' Jeet answered. 'They've killed the American pilots and their guards and are trying to fly away.'

Meanwhile outside the sounds of the Sea Hawk's rotors enhanced considerably. It ascended slightly. The powder blue LAMPS III reluctantly tottered and wobbled upwards.

A collective exclamation of overwhelming confusion left our lips.

'What's wrong with the Sea Hawk?'

Jeet stared hard at the helicopter. 'The lot in the Sea Hawk cannot fly it properly.'

'Not wristing the throttle with the correct amount of collective and cyclic stick. And wrongly applying the pedals,' I offered thoughtfully. 'The throttle, collective and cyclic stick as well as the pedals are common to all helicopters. The rotor brakes, transmission gear and clutch assembly vary. Requires a different touch in different types of choppers.'

'Incredible but true,' Jeet asserted. 'Because of the noise of the Naval guns and missiles, we somehow didn't hear the shooting inside the fortress.'

'If terrorists are in the Sea Hawk we'll have to shoot it down,' Contractor sharp decisive voice dealt with how to solve the immediate problem.

A calm and composed Alexander from the Saipan said, 'I'm clearing a Standard Surface to Air Missile strike against the Sea Hawk.'

***

The smoke steaming out of the Arleigh Burke's boilers enhanced in density and volume. The warship adjusted its position slightly on its own axis. It had brought the airborne target within the kill zone of its Standard SAM's which were in their VLS pods. The guided missile destroyer moved a bit and suddenly stopped.

'They're going to shoot down the helicopter,' Jeet said.

'Means convinced the terrorists are in it.' I enhanced the intensity of my gaze at the Arleigh Burke. 'Won't destroy an astronomically expensive helicopter just like that.'

'Pray they're no US Navy personnel prisoner onboard,' Perez added.

'Think they've killed them all first and then left in the chopper,' Napoleon gravelly surmised.

Then the six of us watched the spectacle unfolding outside.

From the Arleigh Burke one of its dish shaped Raytheon SPG-62 "microwave illuminator" slewed in a small arc. Its reflector pointed directly at the low altitude Sea Hawk. It followed the erratic movement of the rogue helicopter.

From SPY-1D phased array radar beams reflecting-off the chopper, the UYK-7 computers gleaned information regarding altitude, range and armed the selected Standard Missile. The Weapons Coordinator, responsible for Standard Missiles supervised the monitoring of the pip on an air intercept console in the anti-air section.

Outside there was an ominous emptiness and stillness. The Arleigh Burke's Aegis System's hexagonal planar panels from which thousands of narrow beams were being broadcast outwards, and echoes duly received appeared curiously benign and innocuous.

Then a massive flaring explosion of orange-white flame blazed over the area of the forward VLS. A cloud of glowing white hot smoke obscured the entire bridge superstructure. A single Standard missile lifted-off slowly, gradually accelerating upwards at the head of a thick, dense, white smoke contrail. The Air Engagement Controller had ignited the Aerojet/Hercules solid fuelled missile to "toss" it upwards.

***

'It's a MR or Medium Range version,' I said. 'Its short length gives it out.'

'Let's see it "kill" the helicopter,' Jeet motioned with his head at the rapidly vertically climbing missile which soon became a minute speck in the sky.

We remained engrossed at the scene outside.

Using the Mark-99 Missile Fire Control System software, the Controller sent guidance signals by radio to an onboard digital computer. Before the missile reached the limit of its ascent a two-way telemetry link commanded a "tilt" downwards at the Mark-99 MFCS software assisted, calculated point.

From the Arleigh Burke the SPG-62 "locked on" to the helicopter. Its I and J band beams refracted-off it creating a wide angle "homing basket" of radar reflections bouncing-off the target.

Meanwhile, the speck with its tell tale smoke contrail tilted. It writhed and wriggled as its radar transparent nose wobbled. For a fraction of a second the plunging missile trembled, then steadied as though it had eased itself onto a super fast lane of a motorway. Now it dived downwards, accelerating towards the Sea Hawk.

The Standard Missile had tilted almost vertically downwards. Its semiactive radar seeker micro-processor electrically directed its steering unit or servo controller into activating the actuators to directly adjust its tail fins to alter its flight path. Till it had "locked on" to a particular reflecting-off SPG-62 beam in the "homing basket".

We watched the radar beam riding, plunging missile.

An air crackling sonic boom became louder and louder. Rocket thrust and gravitational force increased the speed of the missile to above its usual Mach two point five limit.

Suddenly the terrorists at the controls of the Sea Hawk managed to get the helicopter to move erratically. The nose jerkily rose a little.

The diving missile moved too fast for its terminal guidance to initiate a correction. For a microsecond it appeared as though it would plummet past the tail of the Sea Hawk. Then a brilliant, blinding flash enveloped the General Dynamic's missile and the helicopter.

***

A laser emitted a beam at the same angle as the 'locked on' seeker head. The intensity of the return signal enabled a digital processor to work out the proximity of the missile to the Sea Hawk. At the preset, right distance from the helicopter it detonated the high velocity blast fragmentation warhead.

Within the blink of an eye the dazzling crimson flare was followed by a tremendously intense, thunderous bang. About six thousand fragments designed to tear into pieces aircraft fuselage slammed into the Sea Hawk's tail boom. The shrapnel shred the tail stabilizers and tail rotor and the blast effect vaporized them. The fused up remains of the rear of the helicopter plunged downwards and crashed into the sea.

The Sea Hawk's damaged fuselage from the rear wheel to the nose hurled forward. As it lurched ahead it tilted downwards and accelerated onwards. The still rotating four bladed main rotor imparted a powerful forward thrust to the flaming wreck. But the anti-clockwise gyration of the rotor began to be counter-balanced by the clockwise rotation of the tail rotor-less fuselage.

The body of the mortally damaged Sea Hawk whirled around as it advanced. It also descended erratically as it lost power. The motion along with leaking fuel lines enhanced the volume of smoke billowing from the blazing onboard fire. Crackling, spattering electric sparks flared out of the severed electrical connections.

The whirling rotor fanned the blazing fire and the streaming currents of electrical sparks. The doomed overheated wreck with its broiling simmering occupants hurtled on. The cockpit and cabin doors suddenly flew open. A centrifuge-like effect came into play. One by one scorched figures shot out of the whirling chopper with considerable force. After a long momentum aided flight in the air, three bodies toppled into the sea.

'Terrorists... they are terrorists,' Napoleon bellowed. 'Wearing blue tracksuits.'

Then the fiery, ruined wreck struck the water. Smoke belching upwards turned black. The rotary action of the whirling underbelly splashed water upwards. Then seawater flooded the compartments. The main rotors stopped rotating. And the remains of the Sea Hawk vanished into the murky depths of the sea. A bubbly slick of oil darkened water under a pall of dark smoke of unburnt hydrocarbons drifting into nothingness, marked the spot where it had sunk.

The "secure" line crackled. Perez switched his radio on.

'They have been terminated,' Alexander cryptically announced over the air. 'But be prepared...'

'We're about to launch a combined assault. Board the Malabar Star.' Contractor tersely interrupted from the Godavari.

All six pairs of eyes in the pilothouse of the Malabar Star turned to the Godavari, then to the Saipan.

XXIII

From the flight deck of the Saipan the command and control Huey, used for tactical air control, lifted-off. Two Super Cobra heli-gunships were in close attendance. Two troop carrying Sea Knights ascended immediately afterwards.

Napoleon, ever watchful and wary, alerted us. 'Great... boats with US Marine buggers coming also.'

A couple of vessels had emerged from the Saipan's docking well at its stern. A battleship gray motorboat followed by two Landing Craft Utility's or LCU's approached the Malabar Star from the west. A couple of armed Marines were onboard the motorboat besides its crew. While the LCU's were crammed with combat ready Marines in full battle gear. The three vessel squadron curved southwards and turned towards us, advancing slowly.

Meanwhile, the sounds of the helicopter rotors enhanced. The green camouflaged colored Huey flew over, performed a sharp turn and proceeded to hover high up in the air. Clearly visible to us were helmeted figures, one of whom would be Barros the officer in charge. The other troop carrying Sea Knights vectored into positions then flew patterns over the waters between the Janjira fortress and the mainland.

Two Super Cobra's flit about nearer. From under their noses their proboscis-like three barreled M-197 machineguns were aligned onto the sundeck of the Malabar Star. The lethal M-197 had a large slewing limit. This enabled them to be centered onto its target ship as the heli-gunships raced up and down. Both choppers could fire twenty-millimeter slugs at twelve rounds at second anytime; as they flew on courses parallel to the stationary Malabar Star.

The motor boat and the LCU's began to move towards us slowly and cautiously.

Then I heard sounds from within the Malabar Star. Like the kicking open of doors from somewhere below. However, all our attention was focused on the helicopters and the slowly advancing boats.

Suddenly, a loud hurrah came from the upwards leading companionway.

In the pilothouse the six of us froze momentarily.

A squad of SAS Boat Troopers and MCF men swiftly raced up the port side companionway and got onto the sundeck. The group of heavily armed men took up positions. An assortment of M-16's from the SAS Boat Troop men and Hecklar and Koch Machine Pistol 5 and AK-47's with the MCF were trained at the door of the pilothouse. I noted some of the MCF men had crossbows. Probably to kill terrorists silently when entering the Malabar Star.

The chill that passed over us subsided immediately. Waves of exhilaration tinged with a sense of absolute relief coursed through our bodies.

'Buggers are wet,' Napoleon excitedly informed us.

The disrupted pattern muted brown and green in the SAS Boat Troop uniforms and the sleevless black vests worn by the MCF were dripping wet.

'Boats and helicopters were a diversionary,' an elated Jeet said. 'The SAS Boat Troop and MCF have swum here and infiltrated this ship earlier.'

Outside, the motorboat and LCU's accelerated around in a wide arc and neared and stopped alongside.

Then a loud hammering sound interrupted our observations. Someone knocked repeatedly on the still closed armored door of the pilothouse.

***

'All friends,' a tremulous Perez shouted at the top of his voice.

A thrilled D'Costa hollered, 'Master of the ship with some passengers and crew.'

Both Napoleon and Columbus went to the armored door. They twisted the circular steel handle and pushed it open.

Outside, a SAS Boat Troop non-commissioned officer stood with a group of armed men. On seeing us they relaxed slightly.

D'Costa stepped forward. A MCF Lieutenant came in and regarded him. 'So you're all rescued.'

XXIV

Outside, the sea suddenly filled up with various types of boats. Two motor launches surfaced from the Murud jetty and chugged towards us. For an instant a shaft of nervousness coursed through my body. The boats resembled the terrorist's dhows. Then, the sight of khaki uniformed Maharashtra policemen onboard reassured me completely. Elsewhere in the waters police speedboats moved about. Officers and men in them checked the patches of oil and wreckages of the destroyed terrorist dhows. They paid particular attention to the pieces of human bodies floating around. For police investigation purposes they'd have to collect them later.

Then the "secure" line crackled to life. Perez refocused his attention to his set. A signal came in from the Saipan.

'Parties from our small boats upturned the bloated face down bodies of those that fell from the downed Sea Hawk. That they're terrorists is confirmed. We've made positive identifications of Zohran, Wassif and Zwankwid. Repeat Zwankwid al-Jahiz is dead. The deadliest terrorist in the world today has been eliminated from the face of the earth. Great day for us!'

Napoleon and Columbus whooped in ecstatic joy. D'Costa and Perez were too drained of energy and kept quiet. However their eyes twinkled with ocular versions of smiles of satisfaction.

Awaiting the coming alongside of the launches to take us away, I'd started feeling normal again. Thoughts usual to my psyche started filling my mind along with urges and needs. I craved for a cigarette.

I also felt like just after the climax of a hostage thriller movie – I'd never felt more at ease with myself.

Jeet, although equally delighted, watched the scene around with hawk's eyes. Then he turned to me and said not a little wearily, 'so our trials and tribulations end finally. And we're safe and sound.'